KNIGHT

ON

EDGE

A JORJA KNIGHT MYSTERY

KNIGHT
ON
EDGE

ALICE BIENIA

Issued in print and electronic formats.
ISBN 978-1-990193-19-4 (Paperback)
ISBN 978-1-990193-18-7 (EPUB)
Editing by: T. Morgan Editing Services
Cover Design by: 100Covers.com
Published by: Cairn Press | Calgary AB Canada

For Malcolm, Paige, and Hannah
You light up my world.

ONE

One thing I've learned as a private investigator is that all narratives are possible until they aren't. A good investigator assumes nothing, develops a skeptical mindset, and doesn't take anything for granted or at face value. It's harder to do than one might think. But in this case, I was certain. Sherrie's husband, Ben Langcaster, was cheating on her.

"Are you sure, Ms. Knight?" Sherrie's tear-filled eyes pleaded as she lifted her gaze from the photos spread out on the battered desktop that separated us.

I slid the box of tissues closer to her. "Yes, I'm certain."

Of all the services I provide through my company, Knight Investigations, infidelity cases are my least favourite. Sure, they help to pay the bills, but the hours of mind-numbing surveillance, days of eating fast food in my car, and the reaction I get from the client when I deliver the news is hardly compensated for by the fee I charge. Case in point.

Sherrie pulled a handful of tissues from the box and held them against her mouth to muffle her sobs. Her shoulders caved in on themselves, making her look even smaller than her five-foot two-inch frame allowed. As much as we all had a deep-seated need for closure, I suspected Sherrie Langcaster now regretted her decision to hire me.

Sherrie came to see me nine days ago. My first impression of her was that of a woman who had lost herself in the process of taking on the role of wife and mother. She was petite, soft spoken, wore her mousy-brown hair in a short bob with feathered bangs, and avoided making eye contact, which contributed to the impression. I could tell from the moment she arrived for our first meeting that she was still questioning her decision to open up an investigation.

I had met women like Sherrie before. Women who wanted to know if their husbands were cheating on them, yet what they really wanted was another explanation for their husband's lack of interest in them—the increased late nights at the office, weekend trips out of town, phone calls taken in another room, the brushed-off and vague responses to questions asked. Unfortunately, most of the cases I took on ended like Sherrie's.

Sherrie's thin shoulders shook as she continued to sob, and there was little I could say that would make her feel better. She was still young, relatively speaking. She could live a whole new life if she chose to move on. But I knew it would be hard for her to do.

I had asked Sherrie to tell me a bit about herself. She described a life that revolved around her son, now seventeen and a year away from college. It's partially what brought her to my door. Soon it would just be her and her husband. But they had grown apart, and there were more troubling signs. They hadn't been intimate in over a year. Ben started buying new clothes and working out. He bought new cologne and no longer used the brand she had been buying him for Christmas for years.

Sherrie told me she thought it might be the impending empty nest that was making her feel this way, but she couldn't shake the feeling that Ben was seeing someone. She worried he might be biding his time, waiting until their son left for college, to ask for a divorce. She thought it would be best to find out the truth now, that somehow it would help her prepare for what was to come.

I pushed back the sleeves of my burgundy sweater and surreptitiously noted the time on my watch. She'd been crying for three minutes, but it felt like thirty. I reminded myself that a good detective also shows empathy and stays patient. I cleared my throat. "Can I get you some water...or anything?"

Sherrie continued to dab at the tears still slipping from her eyes. "Who is she? I want to know."

"I'm sorry, I can't tell you that." I had to protect the woman's identity. If her husband wanted to tell her, fine, but she wasn't going to hear his mistress' name from me. I had no desire to become party to a future harassment charge filed by the other woman, or worse.

The few photos I presented to Sherrie showed her husband kissing a dark-haired woman. In each of the photos, the woman either had her back to the camera or her features were obscured by Ben Langcaster's frame. They had met three times in the eight days that I had Ben under surveillance, each time at a different motel on Calgary's outskirts. I had paid the motel cleaning staff to gain entry to the room after they left. The rumpled bedsheets and used condoms made any other plausible reason for Ben to be meeting the woman at a motel unlikely.

It had been easy to discover the woman's identity. I followed her home after she left the motel to what can only be called a mansion, set back on an acreage along Highway 8. She had driven her car straight into one of the four-car garage bays and didn't leave until morning. The next day I followed her from the house to the Pine Valley Spa and Golf Club, a private club located halfway between Calgary and Bragg Creek. Once there, it took no time at all to confirm that the lady in question was Mrs. Kate Barrett, current wife of Cole Barrett, president and COO of Encore, a private equity firm.

The other thing I've learned in the last three years as an investigator and my previous fifteen years as a forensic analyst is that developing critical thinking skills, keeping an open mind, and applying a certain level of skepticism to the data and evidence gathered didn't always guarantee a clear-cut answer. There are always things you don't or won't ever know, and circumstances you can't control as an investigator. And that's why just when I thought I had closed another successful infidelity investigation, I found myself in the middle of the most convoluted murder case I had ever undertaken.

TWO

I turned toward Macleod Trail and groaned when I realized I had mindlessly followed the route I take to work instead of going to Luis' place. I shifted lanes and looped around until I was heading back downtown. Raising my hand apologetically to the driver behind me, I wormed my way across three lanes of rush-hour traffic and entered the liquor store parking lot. Luis Azagora is an Inspector with the Calgary Police Service and he and I were seeing each other regularly now. We had even expressed rapturous feelings for each other by saying the L word.

With the wine firmly planted on the passenger seat, I continued down to Fourth Avenue and headed west. A few minutes later, I shoehorned Gab's Mustang into an almost too small parking space in front of Luis' condo building.

I still referred to the car as Gab's Mustang, but technically it was mine, since I had bought it off of her. Three months ago, my best friend Gab Rizzo got engaged, and she was now living in France with her fiancé. I was happy for Gab, of course, and we talked every few days, but it was hard not seeing her. I thought the Mustang would ease the separation, but instead, it stirred up nostalgia, evoking memories of the road trips Gab and I had taken over the years.

I dashed across the street and Luis buzzed me into the building. A waiting elevator took me up to the tenth floor. I made my way down the hall to my right until I reached the last door. Luis had left it unlocked for me.

"Hey Luis, I'm home," I called out as I stepped inside. Although we spent three or four nights together each week, we were a long way away from sharing a residence. We did, however, keep an overnight bag at each other's place.

I headed for the kitchen, which was down a short hall from the entrance.

Luis came around the kitchen counter. His chestnut-brown eyes lit up. My breath caught in my throat. How could this man have this effect on me after all this time. A little bit of me melted inside.

"I've been thinking about you all day." He wrapped his arms around me, bent his head, and his lips met mine.

This was our third attempt at a relationship. Maybe the first attempt didn't count as Luis hadn't committed to being exclusive, and I had foolishly thought I'd be okay with that. Our second attempt also failed. Luis had acted as if my job as private investigator and sole proprietor of Knight Investigations would somehow tarnish his reputation as top cop and head of Calgary's Special Crimes unit. It left me questioning whether I wanted a relationship with him—or any man, for that matter. But events that led us to believe we had lost each other for good drove some clarity into our respective thoughts about what was important in life, and career choice dropped a notch on the list. At least for now. Perhaps the saying 'third time's a charm' would hold up for us.

"All day?" I asked jokingly, as we pulled apart. "Didn't that make it hard to concentrate, Inspector Azagora?"

His fingers brushed back a strand of dark hair that had fallen across my cheek. "You have no idea, babe."

My breath quickened at his soft touch. "Well, I've been thinking about you all day too." I tucked the errant hair behind my ear and sniffed appreciatively. "Wow, it smells amazing. What are you making?"

He took the bottle of wine from my hand and pulled me into the kitchen. "Chicken parmigiana, quinoa, and tomato salad."

"Mumm." I ran my hand along his strong forearm up to his shoulder and around to the back of his neck. I leaned into his six-foot-two-inch frame, and he bent his head and kissed me again. His hand on the small of my back pulled me in closer. A faint trace of warm, woodsy aftershave enveloped me. I pulled back slightly and looked into his deep-brown eyes. I raised an eyebrow. "How long until dinner?"

A tiny muscle jumped in his strong, chiselled cheek. "Fifteen minutes. Or we can warm it up later."

His mouth found mine. I undid the buttons on his shirt as we staggered against the counter.

"I've been thinking about all the things I'm going to do to you tonight," Luis murmured against my ear.

"Then you better get started, Inspector," I panted.

· · · · ·●· ●· · · ·

IT WAS WELL AFTER nine in the morning by the time I left Luis'
condo. Luckily, my car hadn't been ticketed or towed overnight. I
hugged myself against the still cool morning air as I waited for the
light to change, then ran across the street and slid into Gab's car.
No, my car. As I navigated out of the downtown area, I was rerouted
twice as several streets were barricaded. I wondered if it had anything
to do with the phone call Luis got this morning. Or was 3:42 a.m.
still the middle of the night?

Luis hadn't said much after the call, except that he was needed at
work. He was showered, dressed, strapped, and out the door by 3:52
a.m. How was it possible that he looked even hotter in a suit than in
in his usual home attire of jeans and a Henley shirt? After he left, I
lay awake until the morning light crept into the room. It had taken
a while for me to get to know the real Luis, the Luis who just left,
the one he rarely let anyone see. In that respect, we were both alike. I
didn't often let my guard down or let people in, and neither did he.
Besides Luis, the other people I had opened up to were Gab and my
friend Mike Saunders.

I had told Luis about my past in our second attempt at a relationship. I wondered if the news that my father had killed my mother
and then himself had something to do with him pushing me away.
He knew that my brother blamed me somehow for their deaths and
cut me from his life, leaving me adrift in a sea of strangers.

Luis didn't have family in his life either. His history was complex—he was born in Puerto Rico, his mother hailed from Brazil,
and his father, whom he had never met, was American. At least that's
what his mother had told him. To his knowledge, each of his three

siblings had a different father. Tragically, his mother struggled with drug addiction all her life and had passed away years ago.

When Luis was ten, his older brother, who was thirteen at the time, was killed by members of a drug gang. By then, Luis' two older sisters, already in their twenties and each with a child of their own, were grappling with their own addictions, making it impossible for them to care for him. After his brother was killed, his mother moved to Florida with the latest man to enter her life, but they didn't want Luis tagging along. Luis was sent to live with a great-aunt in Chicago, who it turned out, didn't want him either. But it was the move that saved his life. He had worked hard to get to where he was today, but his past, like mine, left lingering scars.

THREE

I was late getting to the Salty Dog where I was meeting Mike for coffee this morning. Mike Saunders was the other man in my life, the one I wasn't sleeping with. I had been tempted from time to time over the years, but we were good friends, and I didn't want to risk screwing that up.

I opened the door and ducked inside, grateful for the interior's warm air. Mike was taking off his jacket at a table near the window. I pointed to him as the host approached and made my way to where he stood.

"Hey, Mike. Sorry I'm late."

His broad face broke into a grin, and he gave me a bear hug. "Just got here myself." He pulled out a chair for me and I sat. "So, how's my favourite private eye?"

"Wow. I'm your favourite now." I laughed. "What happened to the other two private eyes you know?"

"You've always been my favourite. But I'll admit, it's a big fish small pond situation."

A server appeared and we ordered coffee. She recognized Mike as one of the regulars and they exchanged some light banter. I hadn't seen much of Mike over the last six months. He had taken on a consulting job that sent him across the country to meet with policing units from coast to coast. He had been part of a seven-person taskforce charged with bringing back data on the current state of policing in Canada and making suggestions for change.

He looked tired, the lines around his eyes deeper than when I last saw him. His grey hair, which he often wore in a ponytail, had been cut short and was just now starting to curl against his shirt collar in the back. A flash of melancholy ran through me, its weight pressing down on my chest. Time marched on, and neither of us was immune to its effects.

The server left to get us coffee. Mike turned back to me. "That was quite the trip down here this morning. I got routed over to Blackfoot and had to come in the back way. Lots of police officers around. Any idea what's going on?"

"No. Azagora got called out in the middle of the night. He was showered, dressed and out the door in ten minutes. I knew it was serious when I went into the washroom this morning and found a damp towel on the floor."

Mike laughed. Mike and Luis knew each other professionally, but Mike knew more about Luis' personal life than he should, because of me. Trivial things like that Luis was a bit of a neat freak, or that he got up at 5:00 a.m. every morning to work out, even on weekends, and bought his clothes in triplicate so he didn't have to shop as often.

Mike had been a police officer before he retired from the Toronto police force and started working as a consultant to Global Analytix, the lab I used to work at before becoming a private investigator. He also provided training to Calgary Police Services from time to time.

Mike and Luis had a lot of respect for each other. I cringed inwardly as I remembered the times I had slagged Azagora to Mike during the off portions of our on-and-off relationship.

"So how are things going with you two? Think you'll make it work this time?"

"That's the plan. But then again, it's early days. How about you. Are you back for good now?"

"That's the plan," he echoed, laughing. "That was the longest six months of my life. The travel and being in a new city every two days was exhausting enough, but the constant meetings...all day, every evening." Mike shook his head.

"Yeah, that couldn't have been much fun." Mike was an introvert like me, so I knew the lack of downtime to recharge would have left him feeling drained. "But it went well?"

"In one sense, yeah. The taskforce heard the same thing over and over, in almost every jurisdiction. Everyone's short-staffed. The new recruits, when they can find them, aren't getting enough of the right kind of training. Where adequate and well-trained officers are available, an enormous chunk of their time goes to addressing calls about suspicious persons or doing welfare checks. Not to mention the paperwork that follows." Mike paused as the server returned with our coffee, then picked up where he left off.

"We analyzed data from the last two years, and fewer than ten percent of the calls they took resulted in criminal charges. Most of those ended up going nowhere. When I was a cop back in Toronto, we put a lot of focus on organized crime. It's gotten ten times worse now that the criminals are using technology to get what they want. Not to mention that the number of home-grown dissidents has tripled in the last five years. Our police officers are struggling to keep up. We can't fight this kind of crime with manpower alone."

"So, what's the answer?"

"A massive overhaul of the way we police. It has to start with a different philosophy, a different focus on how we hire and train. We need a different structure, and a lot more technology. It's not going to happen overnight, but the longer we wait, the worse it's going to get."

"Yikes. So, what happens next?"

"We presented our findings last week. We have a few more follow-up sessions booked, but other than that, we're done."

"And you? What are you going to tackle next?"

Mike sat back as the server returned and poured our coffee. After she left, he continued. "For starters, I'm going to take a couple of weeks off. I have some thinking to do. With all the changes that are being considered, there'll be some opportunities coming up too."

"Anything you care to share?"

"I'm looking at a new opportunity that sounds pretty exciting. Remember Willie at Global Analytix?"

"You mean, William Carlton Smith, head of the security and threat management division at Global?" Mike always referred to him as Willie, but I had never heard anyone call him anything other than William when he was working at Global.

"That's him. You knew he left Global last year, right? He's partnered up with a guy who ran a cybersecurity firm, and they're setting up a new company, the CanNet Security Agency."

"Interesting."

"Willie contacted me while I was on the road. They want to expand their company into a full blown, all-encompassing investigative agency. He wants to include a private investigation arm that handles high-profile or intricate cases. You know, fraud, embezzlement, corporate espionage—that sort of thing." Mike took a sip of his coffee. "You and I have joked around about working together someday, right? You've got real-world experience, and your former forensic lab expertise gives you a unique set of skills that I'm sure Willie will be interested in. We could work together. What do you think?"

I swallowed. I had worked hard to set up Knight Investigations and get to the point where I was making a living at it. But I'd be lying if I didn't admit the 'what's next' question hadn't entered my mind. I had managed to take on some interesting and challenging cases, but a good part of my revenue still came from cornflake cases. That's what I called the infidelity investigations, skip traces, and the personal insurance fraud cases. Cornflakes. But if I poured enough cornflakes into a bowl, it kept me fed until a meatier case came along. Lately the cornflakes were losing their appeal. Would I still want to be doing this ten years from now? I had thought about expanding Knight Investigations and taking on another one or two investigators. But that came with its own challenges.

"I don't know, Mike. You know I don't do well with bosses and authority and..."

Mike cut me off. "I know, I know. I have no desire to be a flunky in somebody's organization and I know you wouldn't want that either. It has to be the right position at the right level. I suspect some hard negotiating would be needed to get us what we both wanted. I'm meeting Willie next week. I'll know more by then. At least think about it."

Mike and I continued to chat over coffee and through lunch. By the time we parted ways, Mike had extracted a promise from me that I would give some serious consideration to the possibility of working with Willie's new company. I had argued that it didn't need serious consideration as we were at the idea stage not an actual job opportunity stage, but Mike said he wanted me to be ready, because things could move quickly. And that was part of the problem, because I was already feeling the effects of the recent changes in my life—Gab moving across the planet, and Azagora and I committing to either making our relationship work or ending it once and for all. It seemed like a lot, but in hindsight, it was a mere ripple before the tsunami hit.

FOUR

I STEPPED AROUND A homeless man huddled next to the door and entered the building that housed my office. I popped into the small café on the main floor, picked up a large coffee and took the stairs up to the second floor.

I had texted Luis when I got home after my meeting with Mike yesterday, and later that evening, but I didn't expect a reply. Something was happening downtown, and police had restricted access into the core while they dealt with the situation. Great timing for the chief of police—he was away on vacation with his family. Not so great timing for Luis, who was filling in for the chief. As the situation downtown was still ongoing this morning, I suspected Luis never made it home last night.

I made my way down the gloomy corridor to my office at the end of the hall and unlocked the door. A distinct musty odour comingled with what smelled like left-over Chinese food assaulted me. Gab and I had tried everything to get rid of the odour over the years, but nothing worked.

Gab had owned the original lease on the office, and we had shared the space until she moved to France to attend a ten-month culinary course at the Cordon Bleu. I had taken over the lease at that point, but now that Gab wasn't coming back, I'd have to give it more thought when the lease came up for renewal in November.

I closed my office door, squeezed past the front desk, and entered the main office. It was as dark and gloomy as the rest of the building, although it did have a small window, which offered an unobstructed view of the alley and the brick wall of the building next door.

I sat at the ancient wooden desk, booted up my computer and took a sip of my cooling coffee. As soon as my computer was up, I checked the latest news on the situation downtown. A video clip from Global News had been posted thirty-four minutes ago. I opened it and listened to the reporter, who was positioned near the cordoned-off area downtown.

"Officers were called to the downtown early yesterday morning and have been here ever since. As you can see behind me, barricades have been erected and traffic has been redirected from the area. Several buildings were evacuated over the course of the day and night and the investigation is ongoing.

"The K-9 team has been called in, but the buildings in question remain closed. Officials have not confirmed the nature of the threat at this time but say the downtown business community has been put on high alert. Police are asking citizens to watch for suspicious activity, strange packages, or anything that appears out of the ordinary. Businesses in the area who can work remotely have asked employees to work from home until the investigation is concluded. We'll have more for you on this as the situation unfolds."

It sounded tense. Calgary, like any city of its size, received bomb and other threats on a regular basis. Most turned out to be just that—threats, or the culprits were found and arrested in a matter of hours. This was different. I hoped Luis and everyone working on resolving the situation would stay safe.

I massaged the growing pressure in my temples. Although there was no urgency, I needed to give some thought to what Mike and I had discussed yesterday. Although Mike didn't have details about the so-called opportunities that might be coming up at CanNet, the question facing me needed to be addressed. Did I want to mothball Knight Investigations and work for someone else? Something I swore I'd never do. Then again, never was an unreasonably long time.

I opened a Word doc and started listing the pros and cons. The pay would likely be better, or at least more predictable. The type of work might be more challenging, or at least more of it. Fewer cornflakes. Mike made it sound as if CanNet employees would have access to state-of-the-art tools and databases. There would undoubtedly be more opportunity for learning and growth.

My thoughts were interrupted by my phone buzzing on the desktop. I glanced at the screen and picked up.

"Jorja? It's Sherrie Langcaster. I'm sorry, but I didn't know who else to call."

Sherrie was no longer my client. Our contract ended five days ago, when I presented her with my final report and an invoice. But she sounded scared, so I asked, "Is everything okay?"

"No."

"What's going on?"

She didn't reply, but I could hear her ragged breathing.

"Sherrie? Are you okay?"

"It's...Ben. I'm worried."

Here's another reason I disliked infidelity cases: It often didn't stop once the contract ended. There was the aftermath. Sometimes clients called back wanting to make sure that the information I gave them was correct or to ask for details not in the report. Sometimes they said I was dead wrong, because their spouse denied cheating when confronted. Some even claimed that I hadn't done a proper job and wanted their money back.

"Okay. Take a few deep breaths. Tell me what happened."

"Ben and I had an...argument. Two nights ago. He stormed off and he hasn't been back since. He won't answer my calls. I'm worried."

"Did you confront him about the information I gave you? Is that what the argument was about?"

"Yes."

"Maybe he's gone off for a day or two to think things over."

"I think...I think my husband might do something."

A shiver shot down my back. "Take a deep breath, Sherrie. Something? Like what kind of something?"

"I think he might...hurt...someone."

"Why would you think that, Sherrie?"

"Because my gun is missing."

FIVE

I found Sherrie sitting at the very back of the café, a glass of water on the table in front of her. Oversized, black-framed sunglasses dwarfed her face. I stopped to pick up a coffee and continued back to where she sat. Sherrie took off the sunglasses as I sat across from her. I could see that she'd been crying.

"Thank you for coming." Her voice was just a notch above a whisper.

While I drove here, I questioned my decision to meet with her. She had sounded scared and somewhat desperate when she called, but I still had no idea what she wanted from me. Maybe the real reason I had come here was because I couldn't ignore the fact that her gun was missing, and she thought her husband might harm someone.

"What's going on, Sherrie?"

Her throat bobbed and she swallowed a half-dozen times. I hoped she wasn't going to be sick.

Sherrie's eyes darted to the left then right, although there was no one sitting anywhere near us. She leaned forward, her fingers shaking as she brought them up to her lips. "I think he…I think he's planning to kill someone."

Her voice was so quiet, so whispery, I almost had to ask her to repeat herself.

"Someone? You mean himself?"

Sherrie pulled a tissue out of her purse and dabbed at her eyes. "No. I think he's going to kill her." Sherrie hiccupped into her tissue.

"Ah…Sherrie? Who are you referring to?"

"You know." She leaned over the table so her voice wouldn't carry. "That whore."

Wishful thinking. "Okay, let's see. Your gun is missing, and you think your husband might kill someone. The someone being the woman he's been seeing. Why would you think that?"

She gulped a mouthful of air, then shuddered. Her hand shook as she picked up her glass and took a sip, spilling some as she put it back down.

"Is the gun registered?"

She shook her head. "It belonged to my brother. He passed away in 2021, complications from Covid. He had other health issues. My sister-in-law said I could have it. She knows I'm nervous whenever Ben is away on business."

The perfect reason to arm someone with a gun. "When did you last see the gun?'

"Two weeks ago. I was getting some notepaper out of my night-stand, and it was there."

"Okay—but just because the gun is missing doesn't mean your husband took it. Or that he's planning to kill someone. I don't think you should be telling me this, Sherrie. If you believe he's going to hurt someone, you should be talking to the police."

Her eyes widened and she shrank back, shaking her head. "I can't. I can't. What if I'm wrong? It could ruin everything."

"Ruin everything? What do you mean?"

"His job. Ben's a lawyer. He's been working on a big acquisition deal. If they thought..." Her voice faded away.

Last week, I informed her that her husband was cheating on her. Now she's telling me she thinks he's going to kill someone, but she won't go to the police because it might tarnish his reputation. This was a first.

I don't know if she realized I wasn't working for her, and the way things stood right now, I was glad I didn't have a contract with her that would require me to hold what she told me in confidence. Why was she telling me this? Did she want me to find her missing husband?

"Take a deep breath. Why don't you start at the beginning and tell me what happened."

She twisted her hands together, rubbing one with the other, and nodded. "Okay. Thursday, after I left your office, I went home. I cried all afternoon. How could Ben do this! I mean, I suspected, but not really. It's just that once the thought went through my mind, I started obsessing and I couldn't let it go. That's why I came to you. But I never thought he'd actually do this to me." She pulled another tissue from her purse and blew her nose.

"Ben was working late that night. He's been working on a big acquisition for one of their clients. But all night, I kept thinking he was with that woman." She took a huge breath. "The next day, I was a wreck."

"Your husband wasn't home when you got up the next morning?"

She pressed her lips together and shook her head. "He sometimes works all night. There's a couch in his office," her voice broke.

"Take your time. What happened next?"

"I drove Matt to school and then went out for groceries. I didn't know what else to do. I wanted to confront Ben, you know, about the affair...but I couldn't. I called his cell, but he didn't pick up. I was furious. What if Matt had been hurt? What if it was an emergency?"

"Matt's your son, right?"

"Yes."

"Okay. Go on."

"Matt had a soccer game after school that day. I picked him up afterwards and we ate late. Matt asked where Ben was. I said he was working on a big merger or acquisition, but it felt like I was lying for him. I didn't want to upset my son, but I knew what he was doing. Had been doing.

"I had a splitting headache, so I took some pain killers. I went to get a sleeping pill from my nightstand, since I didn't sleep at all the previous night. That's when I noticed my gun wasn't where it should be."

"Where is that?"

"In my nightstand. Beside the bed. When I got the gun from my sister-in-law last year, I put it in my nightstand. I've never taken it out."

"So, that was Friday night?"

"Yes. Friday night. I checked the other nightstand and the dresser. The gun wasn't there. I knew I hadn't moved the gun. I searched everywhere, but I couldn't find it.

"Ben showed up sometime during the night. At least, he was there Saturday morning when I got up. I asked where he'd been, and he looked at me like I was crazy. He said something nasty like, *Working. How do you think we pay for all of this?*

"Matt went out with his friends, and Ben went out to play golf. We didn't talk at all that day. I made dinner and left the food in the fridge and went up to bed early. I'd been thinking about Ben all day. How he was cheating on me and acting like nothing was wrong. I called his cell, but Ben wouldn't call me back. I texted him at least five times that evening. He couldn't even spare ten seconds to text back." Sherrie's head jerked as a man walked past us to the washroom. She breathed out noisily.

"Sunday, he tells me he has to go to work. I don't know what came over me, but I snapped. I started yelling at him. I've never yelled at Ben in the whole time we've been married. I just kept screaming. I called him a dirty lying bastard. I don't even remember what happened next. You know...all I could think of was him...and that whore.

"The next thing I remember is I'm sitting at our kitchen counter. Matt is there and Ben tells him to go back upstairs. Ben keeps saying calm down, and every time he says it...I just hate him more and more. And more." The last few words come out through clenched teeth.

Sherrie's chest heaved, her throat tightening as she swallowed over and over. Suddenly I was afraid that she's the one who's done something crazy.

SIX

It took me a few minutes to calm Sherrie down. She was ripping her tissue to shreds, a small pile of white pieces already stacked in front of her.

"So, you confronted your husband about the affair."

She nodded. "I wanted to know who it was—how long it had been going on." She looked up, her eyes wide, her lips twisted in disbelief. "He lied to me, Jorja. He said I was imagining things. There was no affair."

"Typical," I muttered under my breath. "So, what happened?"

"I screamed that I had proof. I got the photos you gave me from my purse. I threw the photos at him and ran upstairs and bolted the bedroom door. I just sat on the floor crying, but he didn't come upstairs and try to console me or talk or apologize or anything. I've never felt that angry in my entire life. I've never understood hate until now."

"Did you see him after that?"

"No. I finally took some sleeping pills and by the time I woke up the next morning, Matt had already taken himself off to school. Ben's car was gone. I don't know when he left. For a minute, I thought I imagined the whole thing. But I hadn't imagined that my gun was gone. It wasn't there.

"Later that morning, I called Ben's office, but the receptionist said he was in a meeting. I asked her to tell him to call me, that it was an emergency. He never did." Sherrie's chin trembled. "He didn't come home that night, either."

"Listen, Sherrie. It's too soon to panic. You said you're worried about Ben, that he might hurt someone. Why? Is Ben a violent man?"

"No. I've never seen him raise a hand to anyone."

"Then why would you think that he could hurt someone, or what...kill his mistress? Even if he decided to end the affair after you confronted him, why not just break up with her?"

Sherrie shook her head. "I don't know. I just know something terrible has happened."

"Have you tried contacting your husband today?"

"He's not at the office. They said he didn't come in to work today. I think Ben took the gun and now...now he's missing."

I didn't think Ben Langcaster was missing. By Sherrie's own admission, he was often away overnight.

"Wait a minute. You just told me that he's often away from home a day or two at a time. I'm not sure if there is enough here to declare him missing. And I'm not sure I'm following your logic. You said you noticed your gun missing last Friday but you didn't confront your husband about the affair until Sunday, right? So, if he took your gun, it means he did it before he even knew that you had found out about the affair. In that case, it seems unlikely that he took it to kill his mistress."

"I guess." She rubbed her forehead. "I don't know."

"Have you reported him or your missing gun to the police?"

"No. I can't. Like I said, it isn't registered. They'll start asking questions. Ben must have taken it. He's the only one who could have."

"So, you want me to…what? Find out where Ben is? I'm not sure if I can do any more than that."

"I don't know. What you said…I guess…no. I just didn't know what to do, and I'm so upset."

"That's okay, Sherrie. You've suffered a big shock. Do you have someone you can talk to? Sometimes it helps to talk things through with a friend."

"I feel better after talking to you." Her still moist eyes met mine. "I'm sorry. I shouldn't have called you. You can send me a bill for your time if you like."

"No, that's fine, Sherrie. Do you want my advice?"

"Yes." Her voice wavered. "What should I do?"

"I've dealt with a lot of infidelity cases. Most of them end up like yours. Each person is different, so I can't tell you what you should do. But I can tell you what not to do. Don't let this fester. It'll never go away until you deal with it. If you decide, in your mind and your heart, that you can forgive him, then you can try to make a go of your marriage, or if you think you'll never be able to forgive him, then it might be best to move on. Either of those options is going to require you to talk to your husband."

My sage advice was met with the sound of Sherrie blowing her nose. She was crying again. The man who had passed us on the way to the washroom came back out. He glanced at Sherrie as he slid past our table.

Another thought occurred to me. "Sherrie, are you afraid of Ben? Are you worried that he'll hurt you?"

"No. I mean, not really. I just don't know him anymore. I thought I could trust him...and now I can't."

"I'm sorry you're going through this difficult time. I still think it would be a good idea to let the police know your gun is missing."

"No. I won't go to the police. At least, not yet."

I left Sherrie at the coffee shop, still worried but a tad calmer.

With more than half of the day gone, I debated whether to head home or back to the office. I checked my phone messages. Nothing from Luis. I turned the car back in the direction of the office.

On the drive back to the office, I couldn't help but worry about Sherrie's mental state. Her description of the rage she felt when Ben denied the affair made the hair on the back of my neck stand up. And it sounded like she had blacked out or something—as the next thing she remembered was being in the kitchen. How often did that happen?

As I mulled over what Sherrie told me, I couldn't help but notice the great leaps in faulty logic. It didn't make sense that Ben would want to kill his mistress the day after his wife confronted him about it. Possible, yes, but highly improbable. Sherrie was adamant Ben had taken her gun. But what about the son? He had access to it as well.

Perhaps Ben had some other reason to take the gun. Could he have noticed Sherrie's anxiety or strange behaviour and figured it was because she did know about the affair even before she confronted him? Maybe he removed the gun because he was worried that she might harm herself if the affair came to light.

I stroked my eyebrow to lighten the pain that suddenly appeared above my right eye. Was I reading Sherrie all wrong? Her concern over her philandering husband. Ben not showing up for work. Had something happened to Ben? Maybe she thought being left a widow was better than being left for another woman. Could Sherrie have killed Ben for ruining the life she was so desperately clinging to, and she was now spinning lies to cover it up?

SEVEN

THIS TIME, I BYPASSED the café on the ground floor and headed straight upstairs. As I neared the end of the hallway, I saw that an envelope had been half-slid under my office door. My mouth went dry. My experiences with random stuff getting shoved under my door weren't good ones. Before I could pick it up, Florence came out of the English Language School across the hall from my office.

"Jorja." She waved the piece of paper in her hand. "We have been evicted."

"Evicted. Why? What happened?"

"Look." She pointed at the envelope that had been left under my door. "You have one too."

I retrieved the envelope and unlocked the door. She followed me into the small reception area, which was barely large enough to hold a desk, chair, and two filing cabinets.

I opened the envelope while words poured out of Florence's mouth. "What am I going to do, Jorja? How can I find another space so quickly? It costs too much to move. I need to change every-thing—the website, the business cards, the brochures. Who will pay for that?" She switched into Filipino, her native language, and her pace of speech accelerated.

I scanned the letter. It was a formal notice of lease termination. According to the contract terms, I had sixty days to vacate the premises.

"What can we do now?" Florence's nostrils flared as she tossed her paper onto the reception desk. She turned to me, the unanswered question still visible on her face.

The building owner had made no effort to maintain the ugly cinderblock structure that housed our offices, inside or out, in the three years I'd been here. The rumour on the street was that he was waiting for someone to make him an offer on the land, which was worth a lot more than the rental income the space generated. Looks like that offer finally materialized.

"I'm afraid there isn't much we can do, Florence. He's following the terms of the contract and has given us the full notice required."

Florence buried her face in her hands. I gave her shoulders a gentle side hug. I understood the significance of location for her clientele, composed of new immigrants who relied heavily on central and accessible public transit. While updating an address on a website might be trivial, Florence faced having to update printed materials, workbooks, and other physical resources. Her office was also larger than mine, featuring two expansive meeting rooms that she had repurposed into classrooms.

"I'm sorry, Florence, but it looks like we'll have to move. If I can help you pack up or anything like that, let me know. I'd be happy to."

Even though we didn't work together, I thought of Florence as my co-worker. We saw each other almost every day, even if it was only to exchange a few words in the hallway or the shared washroom. I borrowed office supplies from her and in return helped her troubleshoot computer issues. I realized I'd miss her.

She lifted a tear-stained face to mine. "Thank you, Jorja. You are a good friend." She wiped the tears from her face, picked up her notice and, shaking her head, left.

I rubbed my temples to try to ease the pressure. I didn't need to deal with a move right now. On the other hand, this might go on the pro side of the list I had been building when Sherrie's call interrupted me. If I packed in Knight Investigations and went to work for CanNet with Mike, I wouldn't need to worry about an office.

With my computer finally awake, I checked email and then scrolled for updates on the crisis unfolding downtown. The city was on high alert for a terrorist attack and the situation had garnered national news attention.

Business owners, doctors, and politicians were all weighing in on the situation. City Hall had deployed their Emergency Management Plans, and workers had been instructed to head home. All seven of the downtown daycares were closed, leaving hundreds of parents unable to work. The Minister of Safety had requested additional help from federal agencies.

Images of the 9-11 attack in New York flashed through my mind. *Is it happening here*? I broke out in a cold sweat as my mind churned through a whirlwind of terrifying possibilities. I heard a door slam, then another. People were heading home. I needed to leave too. I sent

Luis a text message—a simple 'I love you' and prayed it wouldn't be for the last time.

It didn't take me long to get home. The streets were eerily empty. I unlocked the door to my condo, kicked off my shoes, and headed to the bedroom. *What a day.* I changed into jogger sweatpants and pulled on a Bruce Springsteen T-shirt from a concert Gab and I attended, poured myself a scotch, and turned on the TV. Channel upon channel carried news about the situation unfolding downtown. Although there were no new developments, reporters near the barricaded areas were running through the timeline of events that had occurred since yesterday morning.

The thought of what might happen, the thought of losing Luis, gripped me in the same fear I had felt when my brother called me to tell me that our mother had been shot. It would be hours before I got news that she hadn't survived.

I took a sip of scotch and felt its warmth as it slipped across my tongue and down my throat. After watching the same news over and over for an hour, I pried myself off the couch. Holding the glass against my chest, I wandered around the room.

My condo felt cold, sterile. There were no plants, family photos, or pictures on the walls. Other than a small bookcase, its shelves crammed with self-help and psychology books, and a vision board pinned to the hallway wall, there was little else to offer insight into the person who lived here. If I didn't know any better, I'd say a university student lived here, one who furnished the place with pieces lifted from their parents' house. Except I was a smart, forty-one-year-old, grown-ass woman who ran her own business.

I cringed when I realized this was the sight that greeted Luis when he first met me, and on every visit to my condo since. I had half-heartedly joked I was going for the minimalist look. To his credit, he never said a word. At least the place was clean.

I could see how glaringly different our two places were. I mean, the man had a baby grand piano tucked into the corner of his living room, a nice large dark-grey sectional with blue and orange accent pillows. Actual accent pillows. He had artwork on the walls. All the tables sported vases or interesting art objects, and plants occupied the occasional nook or corner. Live plants. I turned and gazed around the room. The space that once felt cozy and secure now left me with an ache in my soul, a longing for something elusive and intangible.

EIGHT

Despite the three glasses of scotch I'd drunk, or maybe because of them, I hadn't slept well. My night was plagued by disturbing dreams, none of which I could now recall. I had sent Luis another text last night to let him know I was thinking of him, but I hadn't heard anything back. Not surprising, given the situation.

I had gone for a quick run to clear my head, showered, and then watched the news for a few hours. It was already afternoon when I headed back down to the office. I needed to get my mind off the constant catastrophizing, and sitting at home all day glued to the television wasn't going to do it.

Traffic was sparse, and it was only when I got close to the railway tracks that I saw the roadblocks that had been set up to keep nonessential people from entering the downtown area. For the first time in a long time, I managed to park right in front of my office building. Two minutes later I was upstairs.

The silence was stifling. Most of the tenants had chosen to stay home. I swivelled my chair around, my eyes taking in the room's dingy, patched walls and water-stained ceiling. It was a crap office, and I wouldn't miss the musty smell or the way the cold air seeped in right through the walls in winter, but my throat closed in, anyway.

A noise from behind startled me. I swung back around.

"Ryker." I stood up to shake his hand. "Hi. Long time no see. What brings you to my neck of the woods?" My heart thundered unreasonably against my chest. Detective Ryker Cain worked homicide, so this couldn't be about Luis, but the hours of news I had watched took my thoughts in that direction anyway.

I waved at one of the beat-up chairs in front of my desk and Ryker lowered his five-foot ten-inch frame into it. He looked good; well fed, fit, no sign of grey in his light-brown hair.

"Married life seems to agree with you. But I gather this isn't a social visit."

I had met Ryker through Mike, and we had gone out a few times. This was before I met Luis. But Ryker had been looking for the right woman to settle down with, and I was still debating if I ever wanted to let another man into my life, after recently dumping my narcissistic boyfriend, so it never went anywhere. Now, he was happily married with two kids.

"No," he sighed, "unfortunately not. I came to ask you some questions about a murder I'm investigating."

I stiffened. Had Sherrie Langcaster's husband been found?

"Any chance you can tell me who's been murdered?"

"We're waiting until next of kin is notified."

I nodded. "How do you think I can help you?"

"Your car was seen parked on the northside of Range Road 40, near Highway 8 last week. Want to tell me what that was about?"

I made a conscious effort to not let the surprise show on my face.

I shook my head. "Why, is that a crime?"

"You drove past the intersection three times in one hour, two Mondays ago, and your car returned the next day and parked on the side of the road for four hours."

Was this about Kate Barrett? I shrugged. "I was tired. Best to pull over, right?" This had to be about Kate Barrett. Had she been murdered? What if Sherrie was right and Ben had killed her? But I wasn't about to spew any such theories without knowing more.

"Our guys picked up your plate from one of the traffic cameras out there. Most of the side roads are being monitored where they intersect a highway. There've been too many accidents out there. You know anyone living out that way? Say, in Elbow Valley Estates?"

Damn. The intersection he mentioned was two kilometres from the Barrett place. But Kate Barrett would have to drive right by it if she was going into town, which is why I chose the location. I shook my head. "Nope. All my friends live in the city."

"Come on, Jorja. Don't do this."

"Do what? No, seriously, I have no idea what you want." I unfurled my fingers and rubbed my hand down my thigh, glad the desk hid the move. "I don't know anyone who has been murdered. At least not recently."

"Maybe not, but it sure looks like you were surveilling someone."

I picked up my coffee, now cold, and swallowed a mouthful. I didn't like where this was heading.

"Jorja, I'm asking as a friend. Did you have someone who lives out in Elbow Valley under surveillance?"

I remained silent. If I admitted to having followed Kate Barrett, it would lead to more questions, maybe justifiable in this case. But clients expected a certain level of confidentiality from me, and I wasn't about to give up Sherrie Langcaster's name.

"I'll take that as a yes. Don't suppose you want to tell me who hired you."

"You know I can't tell you." That was as close to an admission I had been doing surveillance as he was going to get. I felt bad. Ryker had put his neck on the line for me more than once, but respecting my client's right to privacy was essential to both my reputation and building my business.

"I guess we're going to have to do this the long way. Thought you might be willing to help us save some taxpayer dollars." He shook his head. "I don't have to remind you this is a murder investigation. If you know anything, it's best you share that sooner rather than later."

"Sorry that I can't help you with whatever it is you're working on."

Ryker stood. "Okay, have it your way, Jorja. I'm sure I'll be talking to you again soon."

I cursed under my breath. This is the other reason I hated these infidelity cases. One could never know what hidden agenda the client had in mind when they hired me.

NINE

I THOUGHT ABOUT RYKER'S visit all the way home. Kate Barrett must have been murdered. Why else were they interested in who had been parked down the road from her property? If Kate Barrett was dead, the investigation into her murder would inevitably unearth her affair with Langcaster. But I refused to be that private investigator who rolled over on her client at the drop of a hat.

I debated whether to give Sherrie a heads-up, but I decided it was a bad idea.

Luis called me as I walked in the door. "Hey, babe. Glad I caught you. I can't talk long. Just wanted you to know that it's over. And that I love you."

"Oh, thank god." Just hearing his voice brought tears to my eyes.

"What—that it's over or that I love you?"

"Both. Was anyone hurt? Have you had any sleep these last two days?"

"No casualties. Caught two hours yesterday. I'm heading home to shower and change, but I have to head right back out. Can't wait to see you, babe. I'll call you tomorrow."

After, I poured myself a celebratory scotch and curled up with it on the couch. An all-too-familiar worry returned. I was drawn to have a drink no matter what the occasion or mood—happy, sad, tense, or relaxed. I had an addictive bent, which is why I've been known to eat an entire box of cheerios while on stakeout or why my collection of self-help books far exceeded what any normal person would read in a lifetime.

My worry was justified. My father had been an alcoholic—the very worst kind. When he was drinking, which was almost every night, he would get angry, and when he got angry, he would take it out on my mother—or me, if I got in the way. Now that I was older, I knew something had started him down the path to his final annihilation. Was it just beer with friends until it got away on him? Or had there been some dark, unchecked, and unfettered beast living in his mind? I guess I'd never know.

I turned on the TV. The ticker tape at the bottom of the screen read, "Three men who kept the city on edge for fifty-six hours have been arrested and are in police custody. The city has lowered its high-alert status to moderate. Police remain in the downtown area, the airport, the water treatment plant, and at other major infrastructure across the city."

As I waited for a live newscast, my thoughts turned back to Ryker's visit this afternoon. Could Sherrie have wheedled Kate Barrett's name from her husband and killed her? Or could she have searched through her husband's phone records, discovered an unfamiliar number, and found her that way? Or was the homicide victim Ben Langcaster?

I swallowed back the rest of my scotch, flipped the TV channel to the news and turned up the volume. The reporter, a woman about my age but with short blonde hair, was speaking to a police spokesperson. The terrorist threat had been resolved and three men arrested. The camera then turned to Acting Chief of Police Luis Azagora.

My breath caught in my throat. That man was seriously hot. He looked tired, but his voice was strong, energetic. He had managed to change into a clean crisp pale-green shirt that highlighted his light-brown skin. The checkered suit jacket and brown dress pants fit him to a T. I silently cursed the reporter. Luis' presence on TV was broadcasting waves out to all the single, eligible woman out there.

Luis thanked Calgarians and downtown business owners for their swift and organized response to the situation and expressed his gratitude to the Mayor, city councillors, and other officials for their efforts in keeping Calgarians informed on progress. He concluded by extending his thanks to all the officers, firefighters, and emergency personnel, both local and provincial, for their help in bringing the situation to a successful close.

When asked by the reporter if any destructive devices were found, Luis affirmed that police had deactivated two such devices, but refused to reveal where these devices had been discovered. He ended by saying the police would not be providing any further information about the three arrested individuals. Their focus would shift toward finding if the men acted alone or in collaboration with others.

Next up was the Minister of Public Security who praised CPS for their handling of the situation. "Faced with one of the worst threats we've ever experienced, Inspector Azagora's team stepped up to the challenge. It's moments like these that shape officers like Acting Chief Azagora into brave leaders."

As pleased as I was to hear these words of praise being heaped on my man, I never expected that it would trigger more changes in my life.

TEN

The next morning, the foiled terrorist attack still dominated the news. I was about to head off to work when something on the TV caught my ear. I rushed out of the bathroom and turned up the volume.

"While the city was gripped in the throes of a terrorist attack, Calgary police were called out to the city's thirteenth homicide of the year. A passerby noticed the body in the early-morning hours on Tuesday near Shaw Millenium Park and called 911. The woman has been identified as Kate Barrett, a well-known philanthropist and wife of financier Cole Barrett. The Calgary homicide unit is investigating, and they are asking anyone who may have heard or seen anything near the vicinity of Shaw Millenium Park late Monday night or early Tuesday morning to contact them or Crime Stoppers."

My stomach sank. How could Kate Barrett be dead? My mind immediately went to Sherrie and her missing gun. Ryker's visit came back to me. Did I know anything that could help police with their investigation? My phone vibrated on the coffee table. I didn't need to see the name on the screen to know it was going to be Sherrie Langcaster.

"Hi Sherrie."

"Did you see the news this morning?" Sherrie's voice was muffled. It sounded like she was calling me from inside a broom closet.

"Yes, I did. Sherrie, I can barely hear you. Where are you?"

"Just a minute," she huffed. I heard someone call out and then Sherrie's muffled reply followed by a door closing. Sherrie was out of breath when she came back on the line.

"Did you see the news about Kate Barrett? She's dead."

"Yes, I just saw the news. Did you know Kate Barrett?" I never gave Sherrie Kate Barrett's name. Could she have somehow figured out that she was the woman her husband was cheating with?

"What if...is she the woman? The woman my husband was seeing?"

She's still fishing for information. I didn't want a phone call from Sherrie every time a woman was found dead. "Why would you think she's the woman your husband was seeing?"

My question was met with a long silence.

"Sherrie?" I had a bad feeling about what was coming next.

"My husband works for Cole Barrett. He...he's met Kate Barrett. So have I...twice."

I didn't like the fact that she had met Kate Barrett. Maybe she knew more than she let on. "I thought your husband worked for Finchman Law?"

"He did. He does. He's been assigned to be Cole Barrett's legal counsel on some big merger deal or acquisition. I can't believe he'd do this."

Did she just say she thought her husband killed Kate Barrett? "Aren't you jumping to conclusions, Sherrie? You can't assume every woman your husband has ever met is the one he's cheating with. If you think Kate Barrett was your husband's mistress, you should be talking to him not me."

My palms grew sweaty. Why was I trying to convince Sherrie that she was wrong? Was it because I didn't want to think about how my role as investigator might have led to her death? If Ben had lied to Sherrie about the affair, I doubted he'd come clean now. On the other hand, I wasn't about to confirm Sherrie's suspicion that Ben had been screwing his client's wife. "Has he showed up, by the way?"

"Yes. He came home sometime last night. He was here this morning, like nothing's happened. I've hardly spoken to him."

"Sherrie, I don't know how you think I can help you. If you have any reason to think your husband had anything to do with Kate Barrett's murder, you need to tell the police."

I knew she wouldn't go to the police. And now that her husband was back, she had even less reason to. She was oscillating between hating Ben and trying to protect him at the same time. Or maybe it was her and her son's lifestyle that she was trying to protect.

Although I had refused to acknowledge the connection between Ben and Kate Barrett when Sherrie suggested there might be one, I suspected that Sherrie knew Kate was her husband's mistress. A tightness formed in my chest. The fact that Kate had been murdered mere days after my surveillance on her ended was troubling. Despite Sherrie's somewhat chaotic state of mind, the fact remained that Ben Langcaster had disappeared for two days, Sherrie's gun was missing, and the woman he had been cheating with had been found dead.

After my call with Sherrie ended, I finished packing up and headed down to the underground garage where my car was parked. But the sickening feeling that I may have played a part in Kate Barrett's murder wouldn't leave me. Should I be the one going to the police?

I mentally rehashed what I knew about the situation. Sherrie's husband had been having an affair with Kate Barrett, but that didn't make him a murderer. He might have even been relieved to find out that Sherrie knew about the affair. If he wanted to save his marriage, he could have simply ended his relationship with Barrett. Killing her seemed...well, extreme. Unless Sherrie was stringing me along. Maybe she had known that Kate Barrett was her husband's mistress all along. Could she be that conniving?

The tightness in my chest grew. I knew my role in Kate Barrett's murder was innocent enough. I was just doing my job. Still, I couldn't get the Barrett murder out of my mind.

ELEVEN

THE OFFICE WAS EERILY quiet today, not unusual for a Saturday. Luis was still caught up in the aftermath of the failed terrorist attack, and he wasn't sure when he'd get back to any sort of normal schedule. We made plans to get together later in the week, although I wished it could be sooner.

The news was full of emerging details about the men who had been arrested and speculation as to the origin of their planned attack. There had been no more details about Kate Barrett's murder other than confirmation that the police were treating it as a homicide. It had been two whole days since I had heard from Sherrie, and hopefully she had moved on.

My thoughts turned to Mike and his excitement at exploring possible opportunities at Willie's—or William Carlton Smith's—new company. I opened the list of pros and cons I had created two days ago. The list was looking pretty balanced, at least in terms of number of items listed for each side.

I laced my fingers together behind my neck and stared at the ceiling for inspiration. After a while, I found myself counting the number of divots in the ceiling tiles. I needed to talk this over with someone, but it couldn't be Mike. I knew where he stood on the situation. Which left Luis or Gab.

I checked my watch. It was already going on midnight in France, so calling Gab was out of the question right now. Luis was at work and wouldn't have time for a chat until much later tonight.

When I set up my private investigation business it had been the quickest and most direct path to a new career that would suit me, allow me to earn a decent amount of money, and let me be my own boss. The licencing requirements had taken virtually no time to complete, and my problem solving and analytical skills were well developed from my years as a forensic lab analyst. Skills that I now applied to different problems.

Marketing gave me the most grief. Now that I had been in business for three years, some of my clients found me through referrals, but my income was erratic. Speaking of which, if I didn't drum up some more business soon, I'd be eating cheerios again for breakfast and dinner.

I sat up and stared at my computer screen. Maybe it was time to touch base with Tom Rannelli, my contact at Heritage Insurance, to see if they had any work for me. Heritage Insurance didn't have an internal fraud investigation unit, so they outsourced their suspected fraud cases to investigators like me. Tom had told me, on more than one occasion, that he could give me as much or as little work as I wanted. But instead of sending him an email I found myself typing Kate Barrett's name into the browser.

Although I had conducted preliminary research on Kate Barrett when I had Ben Langcaster under surveillance, there had been no reason to dig much further than to learn the basics about her since

Ben was my focus. My initial research revealed she was married to Cole Barrett, she belonged to the exclusive and very posh Pine Valley Spa and Golf Club, owned an art gallery, and appeared to be very well off.

Cole Barrett was listed as a financier, but most people knew him as the president of Encore, a private equity firm that had more than once been in the news regarding their controversial business tactics. I wasn't sure what all he financed, but an article in the Canadian Business magazine quoted him saying that the next best thing to being filthy rich is knowing how to access other filthy rich people's money. It appeared the Barretts were well known in certain circles, but I didn't run in those circles.

It was easy to get lost in Kate's online presence. But then again, I've also been known to peruse funny cat videos and to read those terrible dating tips people have gotten from others, like *true love is unconditional*. Unconditional love was what got my mother killed. I could be as forgiving as the next person, but I'd seen too many relationships continue despite the abuse, cheating, lying, or gaslighting, only to end in disaster, to believe that love will conquer all.

The next two hours of my life flew by in a flash. By the end of it, I knew that Kate Barrett had, at age thirty-one, been named one of Calgary's Top 40 Under 40. She earned a BA in Fine Arts from the University of Calgary and then moved to Florence, Italy, and obtained a Liberal Arts degree from one of Italy's top art and design schools—Santa RISA or the Santa Reparata International School of Art.

She was twenty-four when she met Cole Barrett. He was nineteen years her senior and married at the time. Cole's marital status didn't stop him from divorcing his second wife three months after meeting Kate and making her lucky Mrs. Barrett number three. Or maybe not so lucky, given the current circumstances.

After her marriage to Cole Barrett, Kate opened the Nuwest Art Gallery and set up the Rising Star Art Foundation, which offered annual scholarships to deserving students enrolled in accredited art programs in Alberta.

Kate Barrett wasn't your typical starving-artist type. She came from a wealthy family. Her grandfather made his money in the oil industry. Kate's father, Francis Gallagher, had invested in diamond exploration in northern Canada, just when international attention had turned to the great white north as a potential alternative to the blood diamonds being mined in Africa and South America. His hard work paid off when his company's discovery in Northern Saskatchewan was bought out by Ekati Diamonds for thirty-two million dollars. Raised to be a risk-taker, Kate's father took the money he got from Ekati Diamonds and invested heavily in lithium exploration—which was now in high demand the world over.

Sad that with all the money Kate Barrett had access to, she wasn't going to be able to enjoy any of it. Had Cole Barrett discovered that his wife was cheating on him and decided to end things his way instead of exposing himself to yet another costly divorce? Could she have been killed as a way to access her money through an inheritance? Or had she been killed by a jealous wife executing her revenge?

Why was I left feeling that Sherrie Langcaster had known something was going to happen to Kate Barrett when she called me last week? Something about the way she acted didn't sit right with me. Was she always as nervous and scatterbrained as she had been with me that day? Or could her decision to hire me have been a calculated move? Had she already known what I would uncover? And the meeting four days ago—had she set it up to pre-emptively divert suspicion from herself and make me a witness to her fears that her husband intended to hurt someone, even before Kate's body was found? Was Sherrie Langcaster trying to set her husband up for the murder?

My phone cut the silence and I jumped. For one brief second, I thought it might be Detective Ryker Cain, following up on his promise to discuss my presence near the Barretts' house last week. But it wasn't Ryker. Sherrie's name was on the screen.

I hesitated. If I didn't answer, it would go to voice mail, but she'd likely keep calling. I needed to politely but firmly tell her I was no longer working on the case. I took a deep breath and hit the accept button.

"Hi Sherrie. Look, I'm sorry..."

"Jorja, I'm in trouble. You have to help me. Please. *Please*. I don't know what to do. I've been arrested."

TWELVE

Monday morning found me sitting in Neil Trent's home office. The office was located at the front of his 1920s Craftsman-style house and faced Elbow Drive. The glimpse I caught of the interior of the home from the front door told me the place had been remodelled in recent years. White-oak, hand-scraped hardwood floors led from the entrance into the office and the rest of the main floor. The walls were painted a soft ivory, which complemented the warmth of the hardwood. Modern gold coloured light fixtures adorned the ceilings, casting a soft glow throughout the spacious rooms.

I sat in front of a massive walnut desk. Behind it, wall-to-wall, built-in bookcases held just the right mix of leather-bound books and interesting art objects. Neil stood at the sideboard across the room and called over his shoulder, "Sugar? Cream?"

"Thank you, but I take mine black."

Neil turned, two steaming mugs of coffee in his hands. He was wiry and fit but a slight stoop to his shoulders betrayed his age, which I guessed to be early seventies. His blue eyes sparkled below a shock of white hair and his thin, craggy face held a network of wrinkles, demarcating the years gone by. He wore a plaid shirt and jeans, and his cowboy boots clacked as he crossed the floor and set one of the mugs in front of me.

"Black it is."

"First of all, thanks for looking into this on such short notice."

Neil chuckled. "All my clients give me short notice. People rarely want to talk to a criminal lawyer unless they have to."

After Sherrie's desperate call, pleading for help, I had reached out to Mike, who in turn gave me Neil's name. Neil was semi-retired, but Mike said he was one of the best criminal defence lawyers he had ever run into.

"Have you been able to speak with Sherrie Langcaster?"

"I spoke to her Saturday evening and in more length yesterday. I was there when she was officially charged with Kate Barrett's murder."

I grimaced. "That's fast. Do you know what they have on her? Tell me she didn't confess."

"No, she claims she's innocent. Problem is, they have the murder weapon."

"Let me guess. A gun?"

"Bingo. You know anything about that?"

"Sherrie called me in a panic a few days after I gave her a final report, confirming that her husband was having an affair. She told me her gun was missing and that she was worried her husband would use it to hurt or kill someone."

Neil raised his eyebrows. "Interesting. Someone. Not himself?"

"That's what she said. I had a similar reaction"

"Run through the timeline for me if you don't mind."

"Thursday before last, I told Sherrie that her husband was cheating on her. She called me the following Tuesday and told me that the day after I confirmed that Ben was cheating on her she discovered her gun was missing. She apparently confronted her husband about the affair two days later. He denied it. They had a big row. When she called me on that Tuesday, she said she hadn't seen or heard from him since their big argument on Sunday."

"Interesting. So, she discovered her gun missing *before* she confronted him."

"That's what she told me."

Neil tapped his fingers on the desk and leaned forward slightly. "If that's true, we might be able to use it. What's the deal with the sports bag and bloody T-shirt?" Neil asked.

"Bloody T-shirt? She never said anything to me about a bloody T-shirt."

Neil grunted. "You think she knew it was Barrett her husband was cheating with? I don't expect you mentioned her name in your report."

"I didn't. I did give Sherrie two photos. Ben Langcaster is facing the camera, but Kate's face is obscured. I have other photos that show both clearly, but I didn't give those to Sherrie."

Neil took a slurp of coffee and set his mug down. "Hmm. It's possible the husband broke down and gave her Barrett's name during the fight. But when I talked to her, she insisted she didn't know who her husband's mistress was until they arrested her for Kate's murder."

"Well, she called me right after Kate Barrett's murder made the news. I mean, like, seconds later. She was worried Ben had killed her.

I asked her why she would think that. She said because her husband was on special assignment and working for Cole Barrett and he would have known or at least met his wife. I told her she should talk to her husband, otherwise she was going to keep assuming every murdered woman was her husband's mistress. I hate to say it, but at the time I wondered if she could have killed Kate Barrett and was trying to set her husband up to take the fall. But when I suggested she call the police, she seemed horrified by the idea. And she refused to report her gun missing. If she were trying to set him up, she missed a good opportunity to throw suspicion his way."

Neil nodded. "And now that Sherrie has been arrested?"

I pushed a strand of hair behind my ear and pursed my lips as I considered Neil's question. Initially my gut had told me that Sherrie had a hand in Kate Barrett's murder. I took a deep breath and reminded myself that a good detective doesn't jump to conclusions or voice opinions based on nothing but gut feel. They stay calm, they ask questions, they keep on digging. Forcing my mind to take a step back wasn't easy.

"I really don't know. I don't have details around Kate Barrett's murder in what I am sure is a still-evolving investigation. It's not like someone killed her at home or her club. What was she doing downtown in the middle of the night? Sherrie's nervous and jumpy. It took me three tries to get a semi-rational answer out of her when we talked last week. She's scared, of course, but is it because she's worried that her husband did kill Kate Barrett and will be accused of her murder or because she herself is guilty?" Neil's eyes never left my face as I spoke.

I squared my shoulders. "I know. I'm ducking your question. But for good reason. The stakes are high, the situation is ugly, and I really don't have enough information to offer up a solid opinion."

"Good answer." Neil sat up and slapped his palms on the table. "I'd like you to work on this with me, if you're interested. Do some of the legwork to help me build her defence. What do you say, Jorja?"

I hadn't seen this coming. It was one thing to stay open minded long enough to ferret out facts that would allow me to provide an informed opinion, but Neil was asking me to help him to defend Sherrie regardless of if she was guilty or not.

"I...uh...I am interested. I'll be honest though. I think I'd have a hard time working to defend someone who was guilty.

Neil sat back. "It's my job to defend my clients whether I think they're guilty or not. It can be tough. When I get a client that I suspect is guilty, I focus on challenging legal guilt rather than tying myself in knots to try and counter the prosecutor's accusations of factual guilt. Of course, I prefer to work with clients I believe are innocent."

"Does that mean you believe Sherrie is innocent?"

"At this point, I'm choosing to assume she is telling me the truth. Or at least her version of it."

I nodded. "Okay. Then you can count on me to help you build your case. What about my earlier engagement with Sherrie? Will that be a problem?"

"Shouldn't be. You weren't on contract with her when she called you two days ago or the few times in the days leading up to her arrest, were you?"

"No. My contract with her specified that all services rendered would end when the report and final invoice was delivered to the client and paid. Sherrie paid her invoice the day I gave her the report. She signed off on both the report and the amount owing and I have a timestamp for both."

"Good. The prosecutor might whine about you working both cases, but the law is clear. As long as that contract ended before this one is undertaken, they can't stop you from making a living."

"Okay, great. One more thing—the detective investigating Kate Barrett's murder, Sergeant Ryker Cain, paid me a visit. A traffic cam near the Barretts' house picked up my car going past their property and later parked a few kilometres down the road from their place. I shrugged it off. Besides my confidentiality agreement with Sherrie Langcaster prevents me from volunteering case information. On the other hand, Ryker didn't mention the Barretts, nor whose murder he was investigating. If they believe I know anything, they'll subpoena me. Just thought you should know."

Neil nodded. "Thanks for mentioning it. I hate surprises, especially the further down the road we go. We're going to have to be on our toes on this one. Kate's family wields a lot of influence, and Cole Barrett is demanding, aggressive, and outspoken. They'll be putting a lot of pressure on the Crown Prosecutor to see this case resolved as soon as possible."

"What happens next?" I swallowed the rest of my coffee and set the cup down. "You mentioned something about a bloody sports bag? Do you need me to look into that?"

"Not yet. When I first met with Sherrie, she mentioned that she had found a sports bag with a bloody T-shirt in it. She was distraught and wasn't making a whole lot of sense at the time. I'll get more details from her on that. Maybe chat with Ben Langcaster, see what he has to say. Even though they have the murder weapon and traced it to Sherrie, they'll be looking for motive. It won't be long before they start pursuing the possibility that Ben Langcaster was having an affair with Barrett. Especially when they discover that he works for Cole Barrett and would have known the missus."

"I agree. Even if Ben Langcaster lies through his teeth and denies any involvement with Kate Barrett, they'll uncover the truth. Somebody is sure to have known about the affair. Unfortunately, that's going to make things look even worse for Sherrie."

"This isn't going to be easy. We're going to have to move fast. The prosecutor will claim that Sherrie found out who her husband's mistress was and then killed her. They'll remember your vehicle in the vicinity of the Barretts' place and obtain your case files by issuing a court order. That will confirm Ben Langcaster's affair and provide them the motive they're looking for. We're going to have to throw enough doubt into the equation to show the jury that none of what the prosecution has definitively proves that Sherrie killed Barrett."

"Or we need to find enough evidence to persuade them that someone else did it."

"Right." Neil grinned and rubbed his hands together. "Then we'd better get started."

Neil and I spent another hour getting all the paperwork in place and discussed next steps. I left Neil's office knowing that we were going to work well together. He was forthright, knew his stuff, and was as keen and focused as a pointer dog on a hunt. I just hoped Sherrie was telling the truth.

THIRTEEN

The Helix Tower, a sixty-two-floor steel-and-glass skyscraper, was one of Calgary's newest, and the first twisted building in the city. Each floor of the tower was rotated incrementally during construction to give the building its unique twisted shape. The bottom forty floors held shops and offices and the top twenty-two, condominiums. Several minutes before eight o'clock, I turned off the car engine and got out. I crossed the street and joined the stream of people funnelling through the tower's revolving doors.

A lot had happened since I met with Neil Trent. News had leaked that Sherrie Langcaster had been charged with Kate Barrett's murder. Given Kate's birth family's high profile in the community and her husband Cole's reputation for being a business bulldog, the media were of course clamouring for more information, particularly around Sherrie's connection to the Barretts and possible motive, but the police were keeping mum on the subject.

Cole Barrett had issued a statement to the press about the devastation his wife's death was having on him, her family, and the art community. Reporters had pressed him on whether he or his wife knew Sherrie Langcaster, but their questions were fielded by his spokesperson, Edna Moss, who asked that the Barrett family be allowed privacy and time to come to terms with what had happened.

After signing in at security, I took the elevator up to the thirty-ninth floor. Cole Barrett's company, Encore, was to the left. I stepped through the double glass doors and my feet sank into thick navy carpet. A large floral display partially hid the young woman seated behind the reception desk. I gave her my name and told her I was here to see Ben Langcaster. She asked if I had an appointment.

"I called him yesterday. I know he's a very busy man, but I told him I only needed a few minutes. I'm working with his wife's lawyer, on the Kate Barrett murder."

Mentioning Kate Barrett had the effect I wanted.

She asked me to take a seat. It's true that I had called him yesterday—three times, to be precise. I left a message each time. The third message said if he didn't call me back, I'd drop by his office in the morning and if he didn't want me to create a ruckus it would be best to see me.

Part of me was surprised to find Ben at work, carrying on as normal. Surely, he knew that all eyes would be on him. Even if his co-workers didn't know about his affair with Cole's wife, they would certainly be speculating about the possibility at the water cooler. How else would one explain why their wife killed the bosses' wife?

Twenty minutes later, a tall, slender woman with angular features entered the reception area. Her light-brown hair was pulled back into a low bun and her brown eyes were magnified by her teal framed glasses. I recognized her as the spokesperson with Cole Barrett when he gave his statement to the press. Her midi-length navy skirt swished as she made her way across the thick carpet.

"Ms. Knight?"

"Yes." I stood up and held out my hand.

"Edna Moss, VP of Communications." Her fingers barely brushed my hand. She turned abruptly. "This way, please."

I followed her down another hall, this one lined with oil paintings of the Rocky Mountains, and into a smaller reception area. This space offered a deep-charcoal sofa and two black leather armchairs separated by a stunning marbled green coffee table made of malachite. Several teak cabinets displaying Indigenous artifacts were arranged artfully around the room.

I cleared my throat. "It's so tragic what happened to Mrs. Barrett. Did you know Mrs. Barrett very well?"

Edna Moss didn't bother to look at me when she replied. "Of course, I knew her."

Wow. Just a tad rude. "I...I'm sorry for your loss. I'm sure she'll be missed by the whole community."

Edna marched me past Cole Barrett's office, which occupied the corner of the floor. Floor-to-ceiling windows offered a spectacular view of both the downtown high rises and the Rocky Mountains to the west. Cole Barrett was not inside.

Half a dozen other offices opened onto the reception area. I assumed they belonged to Barrett's inner advisors. Edna Moss made a beeline for the office furthest from Barrett's. She paused at the door and stood aside.

I stepped into a decent-sized office filled with teak furniture. Ben Langcaster jumped up from his chair, looking like a schoolboy who had been caught rifling the teacher's desk. The sleeves of his white shirt were rolled up, his suit jacket was slung over the back of his chair. He was a few inches taller than me, and lean, like a runner. Wavy brown hair, long on top and short on the sides, topped his diamond-shaped face. He reminded me a bit of the American actor, Jake Gyllenhaal, but clean shaven.

"You have a meeting with Mr. Barrett in fifteen minutes," Edna announced before she walked away.

Ben scratched the back of his neck and blew out his breath. "You shouldn't have come here."

"Yes, but since you didn't answer any of my calls, you left me no choice." I had introduced myself on the phone as the investigator working with Neil Trent, Sherrie's defence lawyer.

"Yes, yes. I should have called back," he said, shaking his head. "But this isn't a good time."

"Is it ever a good time when one's wife gets charged with murder?"

"I only have a minute." He pulled out one of the padded chairs from a round teak table that stood near the window and waved me toward it. I knew he was seven years older than Sherrie, but he looked younger. Cheating agreed with him.

Ben glanced over his shoulder, sat, and leaned across the table toward me. "I can't discuss this here."

"I'm surprised to find you at work. I would have thought you'd be taking a few days off—given the circumstances."

The muscles in his neck tightened. "We've been working on this acquisition for months. The competition doesn't care if my wife has been arrested." His eyes darted to the door and then back to me. I glanced at his clasped hands, the knuckles white with tension.

The circumstance I had in mind was the whole messed up situation where his mistress had been murdered, possibly by his wife, while he sat in the dead woman's husband's office and acted like he had the man's best business interests at heart.

"Look, I'm glad Sherrie's got herself a lawyer. I'll pay her legal bills of course. But other than that, there's not much else I can do for her. She hasn't been herself lately."

Yeah, I bet. What a jerk. This guy wasn't even considering what impact his adultery and lack of attention to his marriage might have had on his wife. "Oh? What do you mean, not herself?"

"She's been jumpy, irritated. She gets angry at every little thing. I told her to make an appointment with Dr. Kapolka, but she wouldn't."

"Dr. Kapolka?"

"Her psychiatrist."

My stomach dropped a notch. I was glad she was seeking help for whatever troubled her, but this was the sort of thing that could end up working against her case. "She was seeing a psychiatrist?"

"Yes. On and off for the last ten years. She has RSD."

"RSD?" I'd never heard of it. "What is RSD, if you don't mind my asking?"

"Rejection Sensitive Dysphoria. She has a deep-seated, intense fear of rejection. People with RSD tend to interpret ordinary social interactions that you or I would think nothing of as rejection. It's why she avoids social situations. People with RSD typically have low self-esteem and struggle to control their emotions."

So, this is how it's going to go. This guy really is an ass. "Are you telling me that you believe your wife is capable of murder?"

"I don't know. But when she gets angry, she becomes this whole other person."

I felt the gut punch on Sherrie's behalf. Ben wasn't the caring, loving husband she thought him to be. If I were to guess, I'd say Sherrie's marriage was over.

"We're going to do everything we can do to build a credible defence case for your wife. That means you're going to come under fire."

He rubbed the back of his neck. "What do you mean?"

Did this guy really think he could keep his affair hidden? "The police are looking for a motive. The first obvious possibility is that you gave your wife the motive she needed to kill Kate Barrett."

His eyes jumped from me to the door then back again. He rubbed his forehead. "What the hell are you talking about?"

I kept my voice low. "I know. And soon, the cops will know, if they don't already, about your relationship with Kate."

"What relationship? There was nothing going on," he hissed, keeping his eyes on the door.

I didn't expect an admission from him. But I wondered if the denial was his way of dealing with the stress or the emotions he was feeling, or if he was trying to buy himself more time. "Oh, come on. There are photos that say otherwise."

"How do you know about those?" His eyes widened and his lips twisted in anger. "You. You're the one who blew up my marriage."

"No, Mr. Langcaster. You did that yourself."

Ben's fist tightened on the table. "You must have a confidentiality agreement with my wife. I'll sue you if those photos come out."

"Come on, Mr. Langcaster. I don't have to tell you that I can be subpoenaed in a case like this. I'll have no choice but to turn over the files."

Ben rubbed his hand over his mouth. His hand was shaking. His eyes shifted from me to the door and back again.

"Sherrie said you stormed out of the house when she confronted you. Where were you from Sunday before last until Thursday night?"

"I don't have to answer you."

"True. But we're working on establishing Sherrie's innocence. If she didn't kill Kate, then who did? Someone took Sherrie's gun from your house. I'm sure the prosecutor has proof that it's the same gun that killed Kate Barrett, otherwise they wouldn't have charged her. There are two other people in the house who had access to it. You and your son."

Ben shifted closer. The muscles in the arm he rested on the table between us stood out like sinewy ropes. "You leave my son out of this. He had nothing to do with any of this."

"I'd like to. So, if your wife's innocent, and your son is innocent, that leaves us with..." I raised an eyebrow.

"Are you crazy! Why would I kill her?" He leaned toward me, his face ashen as he checked over one shoulder then the next. "If this gets out, I'm finished," he spit out through clenched teeth. His voice dropped another notch. "Do you understand what it's going to do to me?"

How did this guy not believe that he was already finished. News of the affair would come out. "I do understand. And it will get out. So, let's for a minute assume you and Sherrie are both innocent. Who wanted Kate dead? If you want to avoid being the defence team's scapegoat, you need to help me find another candidate."

"Look, I told you..." His head snapped up.

Edna Moss stood at the door. "Mr. Barrett is ready for you."

Edna waited while I stood and then walked me back to the reception area. As we passed the corner office, I heard laughter. Cole Barrett was standing with his beefy hand clamped onto the shoulder of the man standing next to him. Both men were laughing, in that hearty 'we're all good buddies here' way. I recognized the man with him—The Minister of Innovation and Technology, although I couldn't remember his name.

Edna walked me out to the main hallway and waited until the elevator came. Cole Barrett didn't seem to be as devastated by his wife's death as he would like the public to believe. Ben Langcaster was definitely scared, but he seemed more afraid that his role as an adulterer would be exposed than the possibility that he could be accused of murder.

How could he look Cole Barrett in the eye everyday knowing that it was likely his affair with Kate that got her killed? And how could he be so seemingly accepting of his own wife's guilt? Or did he believe another motive would magically materialize which would absolve both him and Sherrie of Kate's murder?

Edna Moss waited until I stepped into the elevator. Ben seemed nervous around her. Was she always this standoffish or had Kate Barrett's murder made her wary of everyone? The doors closed as another thought crossed my mind. Had Edna Moss been standing outside of Ben's office the whole time we had talked?

FOURTEEN

I EXITED THE BUILDING and debated whether to move my car or leave it parked and walk to the crime scene. Since the air had warmed up considerably while I was meeting with Ben, I decided a walk would do me good. Besides, I still had over an hour left on the parking metre.

The Helix Tower was located two blocks south of the Bow River. A pathway ran parallel to the river along the entire northern edge of the downtown core. At noon it would be packed with people taking a walk or jogging over their lunch break.

I headed west along the river path and mulled over my conversation with Ben. It was obvious that Ben had been rattled by my visit to his office. He seemed certain that if Cole Barrett found out that he'd been screwing his wife, he'd more than fire him. Men as power hungry as Barrett had long reach. As long as rumours and speculation about his affair with Kate remained unconfirmed, Ben might be able to proclaim his innocence...but only for so long.

What was disturbing to me was how little Ben seemed to care that his wife was sitting in jail. Did he really think she killed his mistress? He certainly wasted no time throwing her under the bus. Surely, he didn't think she'd keep his affair a secret out of some misplaced sense of loyalty to him. Of course, once Sherrie admitted that she knew he was cheating on her, it would give her the motive the prosecutor's office was looking for. And in all fairness, she had tried to throw suspicion Ben's way when she told me that her gun was missing and that she thought Ben might use to kill his mistress.

I stepped past a small group of toddlers, their hands clutching the colorful handles of the safety walking rope strung out between them. The movement momentarily jarred me out of my head. The trees lining the river path had recently leafed out, their bright green leaves a feast for my eyes. I wasn't a fan of Calgary's long winters, but the cold didn't bother me as much as the lack of greenery.

I continued west. The entire south bank of the Bow River had recently seen a massive upgrade. Flood mitigation structures had been added and the river pathway system widened and made more visually appealing. Although construction along the main walkway was complete, several connectors linking the river path to the adjacent downtown streets were still waiting to be completed. I found the small dirt path I was looking for.

According to the information Neil Trent had shared with me, Kate Barrett's body had been found less than a block off the pathway, between Eighth and Tenth Street. The path I'd been looking for was little more than a track carved out by cyclists and pedestrians cutting across a grassy knoll which separated the river pathway and Third Avenue. Following the track as it veered away from the main path, I continued until I came to the spot where Kate's body had been found.

Pieces of crime scene tape still flapped in the breeze. Bundles of flowers lay on the ground. A small inner-city playground occupied the green space to my left. A large utility box stood next to the right of the track. A mural depicting a bright-blue sky over a skateboarding park had been painted over the pale-green metal. The painting showed kids skateboarding through half-pipes, jumping off the banks, and sliding down handrails. I stopped and surveyed the area.

Beyond the utility box there was a parking lot and beyond that, high-rises. There were no streetlights nearby and the utility box would have helped hide the spot from any passersby who could have been out at that time of night. There was no vehicle access to the spot, so Kate had to have either taken the river pathway like I did or walked in from the avenue.

I continued past the bundles of flowers lying on the ground and followed the track to where it intersected Third Avenue. I looked back. The track had a curve in it, making it difficult to get an unobstructed view at the area near the utility box.

I gazed at the buildings lining Third Avenue. A tiny historic church stood on the corner, surrounded by luxurious condo buildings. Unlikely someone would have been looking out their window at precisely the time Kate was murdered. If any of the buildings had security cameras, they would likely be aimed at the building entrances not toward a playground or the parking lot beyond.

I turned back. What brought Kate down here in the middle of the night? Her body had been found at 5:08 a.m. by someone out for an early-morning run. Neil told me the coroner's report showed that she had been killed sometime between midnight and three a.m. Robbery had been ruled out as Kate was found wearing a gold-and-silver Cartier watch and her ten-carat diamond wedding ring. She had been wearing slim-fitting camel-coloured pants, black two-inch heeled boots, and a black leather jacket over a cream-coloured cashmere sweater. Clothing that told us she hadn't been out for a morning jog or run.

Although Neil said he would send me a copy of the police report, I took some photos to help me remember the area or spot anything out of the ordinary that might pop out at me later. Highly unlikely, of course, as I didn't have anything specific that I was looking for and the police would have combed the area thoroughly.

Kate had to have come down here to meet someone. Was it Ben? But why pick downtown, just blocks from her husband's office. *Ben's office, too.* Had Ben called her after his fight with Sherrie? Did he meet her here to warn her that his wife knew? Or had he met with her to tell her he had to break it off with her for the sake of his marriage? Then how did Kate end up dead?

I wondered where the gun had been found. If Ben used Sherrie's gun to kill her, why hadn't he taken more care to dispose of it where it wouldn't be found. Then I thought back to the conversation I had just had with the man. He had wasted no time in making it sound like Sherrie might be unstable. Had he intended to frame her? But why? Doing so could backfire and end up exposing him as Kate's lover, a secret he was trying to conceal.

I turned around and headed back to my car and as I walked, another niggling worry entered my mind. If Sherrie was the one who had killed Kate, I could imagine her panicking and throwing the gun away as soon as she could. I pushed aside the thought. If I was going to be of any use to Neil, I couldn't allow myself the lazy luxury of jumping to conclusions. Sure, the police had the murder weapon, a gun registered to Sherrie's brother and last seen in her possession. And Sherrie had known about Ben's affair. Despite my not revealing Kate Barrett's name to Sherrie in my report, she could have found out who it was by digging deeper into Ben's phone records or credit card statements. But there could be other explanations. As unlikely as it seemed, maybe Ben had killed his mistress. I didn't see a grieving man when I talked to him this morning. I saw a man afraid that his career and reputation would be destroyed if Cole Barrett found out about him and his wife.

The legal system presumes a defendant is innocent until proven guilty. As defense attorney, Neil was responsible for upholding this fundamental principle. I forced my mind to take a step back from my earlier observations and opinions of Sherrie. Not accepting how obvious things looked would be the best thing I could do at this point. It wasn't going to be easy.

FIFTEEN

THREE O'CLOCK FOUND ME sipping tea with Chelsea Meier, on the patio of the Britannia Club, a private sports and social club where the Langcasters and Meiers were members. Chelsea Meier was the mother of Sherrie's son's best friend.

Part of Neil Trent's defence strategy required that we come up with a few character witnesses to help solidify Sherrie's image as a kind, giving woman, who only wanted what was best for her family. I was hoping Chelsea Meier would be one of those witnesses.

Chelsea was Sherrie's polar opposite. For starters, she was tall and confident in her bearing, while Sherrie came across as timid, uncertain of herself. I could tell from the way she spoke to the staff, waved at fellow guests, and kept up a running commentary about the club as she led me out to the patio that she was an extrovert.

Chelsea put her cup down and threw a lock of long black hair back over her shoulder. "We couldn't believe it when we heard. I tried calling Matt's father, but he's not answering, poor man. My son, Conner, said Matt hasn't been at school. I can't even imagine what he's going through right now."

"Do you know the Langcasters well?"

"I know Sherrie better than Ben. And of course, Matt. He and our son have been friends since primary school. Matt's a real sweetheart. He's been a good influence on Conner, helping him keep his grades up. I keep telling Conner, no matter how good you are at sports, no sport agent is going to look at a dropout."

I nodded. "You're lucky your son is into sports. So many kids get into trouble because they don't know what to do with themselves. So, you've known Sherrie's family for a long time. What can you tell me about Sherrie? What is she like?"

"Sherrie's really quiet...nice. Just a typical mom. I can't believe she could have done this."

"Was anything bothering Sherrie lately?"

"I know she's going to miss Matt when he goes away to college. It's come up in conversation more than a few times, and Sherrie doesn't usually talk much. It's going to be hard on her. I have two more to keep me hopping after Conner leaves home."

"Sherrie's pretty involved with her son's activities, is she?"

"I'll say." Chelsea chuckled appreciatively. "She's always bringing snacks for the team and is the first one to volunteer to help out with fundraisers or year-end award ceremonies. She likes doing the boring behind-the-scenes stuff. Thank goodness for that. I call her mighty mouse. She may be little and unassuming; but she's got a lot of energy in that little body of hers. I worry about her sometimes. She puts all her energy into making Matt and Ben's lives run smoothly and she doesn't do anything for herself. It's not healthy. I tried to get her to join my walking group. We walk every Tuesday and Thursday, rain or shine, but she declined."

"But the Langcasters are members at this club. That must give Sherrie an opportunity to do something outside of the home or Matt's school and sports events."

"You'd think." Chelsea laughed. "Sherrie doesn't use the club much. I think they got a family membership because the cost is the same as for two individuals. When I first met Sherrie, I tried to get her to join me and my friends for tennis, or to have lunch, or a spa date, but she always declined. After a while, I stopped asking."

I was starting to see how Sherrie's RSD might be affecting her life. "And Ben? What's he like."

"I don't know him as well. He works a lot. I mean *a lot*. Late evenings, weekends. He usually makes it to year-end celebrations at Matt's school and the occasional big game they have. We don't see him very often. I know he jogs in the morning. Sherrie thinks the world of him. She's always going on about Ben did this or Ben did that. Whenever I ask her what she thinks of, say, the city's new rules around planting trees, or the efforts to revitalize the downtown, she tells me what Ben thinks about it. It's hard to get her to express her own opinion."

"Sherrie never complained about her husband's long work hours?"

"No...not really." Chelsea's eyes clouded over, as her fingers inched her teacup around and around.

"I get the feeling there's something else you're reluctant to tell me."

Chelsea shook herself back to the present from wherever she had momentarily disappeared to. "Oh," she startled. "Sorry." She inhaled loudly, pursed her lips, and slowly exhaled. She tilted her head to one side and stared at the table for a minute, then looked up. "I know it's probably nothing, but I saw Sherrie at the club about a month ago. In the parking lot. She almost ran Ben down."

"Ran him down?"

"Yeah." She nodded, then glanced over her shoulder furtively. Her voice dropped a notch. "I had dinner with some friends of mine, here at the club. It was already dark when I left. I saw Sherrie sitting in her car in the parking lot. I was surprised to see her there. I started to walk over to say hi. Then I saw Ben come out of the club. I thought Sherrie might be waiting for him, so I just climbed into my car. But Ben didn't go over to Sherrie's car. He was walking across the parking lot, when I heard this revving noise and Sherrie's car shot out of the parking stall. She drove straight at him. At the last minute, Ben jumped out of the way." Chelsea's eyes widened. "She didn't even slow down."

"You're sure it was Sherrie?"

"Yes. She drove right past me. I've never seen her look like that. She was angry. I'd say more than angry. Enraged. There were maybe a dozen cars in the parking lot, but I don't think she spotted me. She was looking straight ahead at Ben."

I rubbed my eyebrow as a sudden pain pierced my eye. "Is it possible she didn't see him? You said it was dark."

"It was dark, but the club keeps the parking lot pretty well lit."

"Did you mention this to anyone?"

"I told my husband." She winced. "And the gals in my walking group." Chelsea leaned forward. "I asked her about it. The next time I saw Sherrie, I mentioned I thought I had seen her in the club parking lot that night. She just laughed it off and said something like, 'four-dozen brownies didn't bake themselves.' It was after that when I told my friends. They thought it was odd too."

"And this happened a month ago?"

"That's right. It was my friend Devi's birthday that night. April nineteenth."

I left my meeting with Chelsea feeling perturbed. Chelsea had described Sherrie as a quiet, nice woman who was perhaps overly focused on her son and husband, but all that went to pieces when she described the incident with the car. Sounded like Sherrie had anger-management issues. Sherrie herself had described how she had gotten so angry at Ben the night she confronted him about his affair that she didn't remember part of the evening.

Neil Trent had been right when he said we had our work cut out for us. Chelsea Meier would make a good character witness—for the prosecution. If Chelsea was right about the date, and it sounded like she was, Sherrie had tried running her husband down, before she hired me. Did that mean she had known about Ben's affair back then? Worse yet, Chelsea had shared her story with several other people, which probably meant everyone who knew Sherrie had heard the story by now. It didn't even matter if Sherrie truly hadn't seen Ben on the night she narrowly missed hitting him with her car. Perception is reality. And the current perception of Sherrie by those who knew her, was that she was a quiet, mousy woman, who had finally snapped.

We needed to find something that would raise doubt in the jurors' minds about Sherrie's murder charge. This was the first time I had worked with a defence lawyer, and the idea that we could be helping Sherrie duck a murder charge didn't sit well with me. Her history of emotional outbursts, her recent blackout after her fight with Ben, and an eyewitness who swore she had tried to run her husband down was making our job harder than it should be.

SIXTEEN

Today Neil Trent had shed the jeans and plaid shirt and was wearing a suit with his cowboy boots. He was chatting with someone just inside the doors of the courthouse when I arrived. He gave a small wave when he saw me. I waited while he finished talking with the man and then shook hands. His face broke into a grin as he crossed the marble-tiled lobby and joined me. "Okay if we grab a coffee?"

"Of course." I followed Neil into a small café just off the main lobby. It was buzzing with conversations, the clientele a mixture of people in suits and those wearing their daily best. Neil nodded at several people as we made our way up to the counter. He chatted with the young woman behind the counter while she poured our drinks. Searching for somewhere to sit, we spotted two women leaving and snagged their table.

"Thanks for meeting me down here. It's court day. At least it's not like when I was working full time. I'd be running from one court room to another without a minute to spare. So, tell me, what have you found?"

"I've been trying to run down a couple of character witnesses for Sherrie, but it's not looking good. Sherrie's a homebody and ninety percent of her social life seems to revolve around her son and his activities. I asked around at the Britannia Club, where the Langcasters are members, but no one there knows her very well. I talked to a few of the moms who she would know, but they also claimed they really don't know her. I mean other than who she is.

"Seems the person who knows her best is Chelsea Meier, the mother of her son's best friend. She painted a very consistent picture of what we already knew. Sherrie seems nice, doesn't socialize much, other than to support her son's school and sports activities, and her husband Ben is a workaholic."

Neil took the lid off his coffee and stirred in two packs of sugar. "That's a good start."

"It went downhill from there. Chelsea went on to tell me how a month ago, she saw Sherrie trying to run her husband over outside the Britannia Club."

"What? Sherrie?"

"Yeah. Says she's positive it was her. Pointed her car right at Ben, who was walking to his vehicle in the parking lot and gunned it. Worse yet, Chelsea shared the story with her husband and several of her friends."

Neil's forehead creased. "Damn."

"I also spoke to Sherrie's husband, for a few minutes. Ben Langcaster was quick to tell me that Sherrie has been seeing a psychiatrist and has been diagnosed with RSD. Rejection Sensitive Dysphoria, intense fear of rejection. He claims his wife keeps her feelings hidden until something tips the pent-up fear or anxiety and then she flies into a rage. Afterwards, she doesn't remember all that she said or did. Unfortunately, I heard something similar from Sherrie the day she called me after her big blowout with Ben. She said she had never felt that much rage and hate before and didn't quite remember what all happened after their fight."

"That's not what I was hoping to hear." Neil shook his head. "No point talking to the psychiatrist, we won't get anything from him...or her. Knowing Bree Jager, she'll be doing everything she can to show the jury Sherrie isn't the meek, mild-mannered woman she appears to be."

Bree Jager was the lawyer for the prosecution. Neil had a great record as defence lawyer, but the three times in his career that he lost a trial, it had been to Bree Jager.

Neil took a few gulps of coffee, set the cup down, and checked his cell phone. "What's your impression of Langcaster?"

"I only caught a few minutes with him at his office. He's been ignoring my calls. I'll keep pressing him for answers. Right now, he's waiting for the other shoe to drop. He knows if or when news of his affair comes out, he's finished working for Cole Barrett. I let him know that as far as we're concerned, he's not off the hook. He claims he's innocent, but he refused to say where he went when he disappeared for four days or how he thinks the gun might have gone missing. I think he's hiding something."

Neil gave me a curt nod. "Well, keep on him. I spoke to Sherrie about the gun. She says she saw it two weeks prior to discovering it missing. Unfortunately, she also claims no one but her, Ben, and their son had been in the house over that two-week interval."

I didn't want to go there, but I might as well see what Neil thought. "What about the son? Could he have heard his parents arguing and decided to end what he thought was the root cause?"

"It's a possibility. I hate bringing kids into a parent's defence, let alone using them as a scapegoat."

"Can he provide Sherrie with an alibi? She told me Matt was home the night she and Ben fought, and that he was at home with her the nights Ben was missing."

"It seems Sherrie wasn't home all those evenings that her husband was away either."

I rubbed the back of my neck. "Seriously?"

"She told me the day after she called you about Ben's absence and the missing gun, she couldn't sleep so she went out. Drove around for a few hours to try and clear her head. The day after her big fight with Ben, she says she drove down to the Britannia Club to see if Ben's car was there, and when she didn't see it, she drove to his office."

I let out an audible sigh. "Great. So, the traffic cameras probably picked up her vehicle driving by Ben's office the night Kate was murdered."

Neil nodded. "Which puts her just blocks from where the body was found." His brows knitted together in a tight furrow; his lips pressed into a thin line.

"Do we know when she got back?"

"She says around midnight but doesn't think her son heard her since he was asleep."

"What about the bloody T-shirt? Did Sherrie say anything more about that?

"Sherrie says that the day before she got arrested, she found her husband's sports bag with his T-shirt, covered in blood, stuffed behind the garbage bin at the side of the garage."

"So last Friday then. She was arrested on Saturday."

"That sounds right. When I asked her to tell me about it, she said, when she went back to look for it the next day, the bag and T-shirt were gone."

"Did anyone else see this sports bag and bloody T-shirt?"

"She said she asked her husband about it, which led to another argument. She thinks he got rid of it after she confronted him."

How convenient that the bloody T-shirt has disappeared. I took a sip of coffee and bit back a snide comment. "Is she saying her husband killed Kate Barrett?"

"Not in so many words."

"Do you think this bloody sports bag and T-shirt are worth pursuing? It won't hold much weight one way or another unless we can find someone or someway to corroborate her story."

Neil didn't answer right away. He was probably weighing the implications if we did find it. Might not prove to be the smoking gun we hoped for. On the other hand, if it incriminated Sherrie in any way, would she have brought it up?

"I'd hate to go in a direction that could ultimately backfire. If you get a chance, see what her husband says about it. Maybe it has nothing to do with the murder. Just as likely he got hit in the face with a tennis ball and bled all over himself."

"Right." I drained the rest of my coffee and set the cup down. "Where do we go from here?" It was still early days in our investigation, but we didn't have a firm lead on which we could build Sherrie's defence case.

Neil stretched and sat back. "It's up to the prosecutor to prove Sherrie's guilt, beyond a reasonable doubt. Let's take a different approach. All we need to do is introduce that doubt. Maybe Barrett's death had nothing to do with the affair. There's a lot of money in the Barrett and Gallagher families. Not everyone gets that rich by being a nice guy."

"Do you want me to dig into her life, see what I can find?"

Neil grunted. "Can't hurt. But what I really need is for you to find a way for that damn gun to have gotten into the killer's hands...not Sherrie's." Neil pushed his shoulders back, picked up his coffee, and stood. "Gotta run. Sherrie's bail hearing is up in ten minutes. Keep at it, Jorja. Something tells me there's more going on here than meets the eye." He gave me a smile and strode off, his cowboy boots clacking on the tile. Neil had years of practice exuding a calm and confident exterior, but for one brief second, I had seen the worry in his eyes.

SEVENTEEN

"Jorja, have you found a new office space yet?"

"Hi Florence. No. I haven't even started to look. How about you?"

"Everything is so expensive. I don't know what to do." Her forehead furrowed as she clutched her coffee cup with both hands.

We exited the small café on the main floor of our building and headed toward the staircase. "What about places like community centres, private schools, or churches. A lot of them are struggling to pay their bills. Maybe they'd be willing to rent out some of their space to you. It might mean offering your classes at different times and in different locations if you can't get dedicated space at one place, though."

Florence came to an abrupt stop and the lady behind us ran into her. "Jorja." Her mouth hung open. "You're a genius. Why did I not think of that?" She covered her mouth with her hand, and we continued up the stairs. "I will look for churches near downtown or the C-Train line."

"It's just an idea, but you never know if you don't investigate."

"So smart." Florence laughed. "That is why you are an investigator." We reached the second floor and Florence sped up. She got to her door ten steps ahead of me. "Thank you, Jorja. I go investigate now," she called out over her shoulder and disappeared inside.

I unlocked the door to my office, slipped past the front desk Gab had occupied when we shared the space, and stepped into the back office. Neil Trent had sent over the first tranche of information he had received from the prosecutor's office, which included the police report, coroner report, and witness statements. It wasn't good news. Ballistics on the gun they had found near the scene matched the bullet they retrieved from Kate Barrett's body.

I took a sip of coffee, slipped off my shoes, and booted up my computer. If Neil was going to win this case, we were going to have to build a different scenario than the one that was unfolding. The one thing I learned in my time as a forensic lab analyst is that my little cavewoman brain will invariably try to convince me that my first impression, or what I think is correct, is actually correct. Nobel Prize-winning psychologist, Daniel Kahneman dubbed this as 'what you see is all there is' thinking. He was able to show that we typically make our decisions and judgments based on the information we have—no matter how incomplete it is.

Good investigators, and good analysts, have to train themselves to appreciate that there may still be many things they don't know and make a conscious effort to keep digging. If Sherrie Langcaster stood any chance of escaping a hefty jail sentence, I was going to have to assume nothing, believe nothing, challenge and check everything.

I unzipped the digital file Neil sent me. I opened the police report and the crime scene photos. Kate Barrett lay on her back in a pool of blood. She had been shot twice with a 9mm Luger. Robbery wasn't likely the motive as whoever killed Kate hadn't bothered to take her watch or ten-carat diamond wedding ring. The value of the ring alone was close to sixty thousand dollars. There were no signs of an assault or a struggle. The first bullet had punctured her heart, and the second bullet severed her Carotid artery. Exsanguination time was estimated at less than three minutes.

I stared at the photo and asked myself if there could be any circumstance under which this could have been a robbery. The photos showed what jewellery was not taken. Could Kate have been wearing a pendant or necklace worth much more? Could she have been carrying a purse or briefcase? Was there a purse?

I searched through the remaining reports and photos. Kate Barrett's BMW was parked a block away on Third Avenue. Her driver's licence and registration were in the car. When the police located it, the passenger door had been standing open. Had someone been with Kate that night? Or had a passerby noticed the car, checked for valuables inside, and then walked off without shutting the door?

The ballistic report confirmed that the Glock 19 Gen 4, found roughly two hundred metres from the body, in the grass-and-shrub-covered slope leading down to the river was the one used to kill Kate. Why would the killer leave the gun in a place so likely to be discovered by police? Or had they aimed for the river and undershot, then failed to locate it in the dark?

The police traced the gun registration to Sherrie's brother and discovered that he had passed away. They spoke to his wife who told them that Sherrie now had the gun. Which explained why the police showed up so quickly to arrest Sherrie.

I shifted through the rest of the evidence from at the scene. Two faint footprints were found leading away from the body and toward the riverbank, then disappeared. One of the footprints appeared to have left a smudge of blood.

I stared at a close-up photo of one of the footprints. It was made by a boot, size ten and a half. I perked up. Sherrie was a petite woman. Those prints couldn't be hers. My excitement faded as quickly as it appeared. They could have been left by whoever found the body, moving in for a closer look to see if she was alive.

Zahir Singh was the early-morning jogger who noticed the body and called it in. I read his witness statement. Not much there that I didn't already know. He had noticed two homeless people sleeping in the small playground when he ran past it but no one else. Police had eliminated his runners as the possible source of the footprints found near the body. I scrolled through the remaining pages of data, but there was no further mention of the footprints.

Police canvassed the area for witnesses and spoke to another homeless individual who provided the police with his first name—Butch. He told police he saw a shapeshifter, or shadow ghost, in the form of a faceless humanoid, standing near the body. Police noted that he was severely intoxicated at the time.

After going through the report a second time, I sat back and thought about what the evidence might be telling us. Kate was found in a part of town she wouldn't typically frequent and certainly not at one or two o'clock in the morning. She hadn't been dressed like she was out for a jog. Had she come alone? Had she been meeting someone? Kate had been shot with a gun that was last seen in Sherrie Langcaster's possession. The killer did not stop to take some very valuable jewellery, which strongly suggested a motive other than robbery. But maybe something had been taken. There was no mention of a purse or briefcase near the body or in Kate's car. Could the killer have taken it?

The angle of the two footprints, which ended abruptly, pointed toward the small park. Had the killer walked or ran across the park and then to the riverbank, and tossed away the gun, which landed short of the water? I could almost hear the prosecutor's stance on this playing in my head. *Sherrie shot Kate, panicked and, instead of taking the gun away with her, tried throwing it into the river but missed her mark.* And when they found proof that her husband was having an affair with Kate Barrett, it would only improve her ranking as possible killer. Not to mention Sherrie's lack of alibi on the night Kate was murdered. The evidence was pretty damning. But nothing should be taken at face value.

EIGHTEEN

Kate Barrett's funeral was being held at Saint Mary's Cathedral. I joined the other hundred people filing solemnly into the church. I was wearing my very best funeral attire—a black pencil skirt and matching suit jacket over a dark-burgundy sleeveless blouse. A pair of sensible black pumps completed my ensemble.

The cloying fragrance of lilies hit me even before I got inside. When my mother died, some women she knew had arranged for two bouquets of lilies to be delivered to the community hall where the memorial had been held. The community hall had been packed that night, though most of the people weren't there for my mother or her loved ones but came out of morbid curiosity. I closed my eyes against the memories that flooded back.

One of the young women standing just inside the doors handed me a prayer card. The church was already filled to capacity. Tall floor vases overflowing with white flowers of every kind imaginable stood next to every second pew all the way up to the altar.

My eyes travelled up the aisle to where a gleaming white-and-gold coffin rested on a raised platform, its base encircled with white linen. The altar held at least a dozen massive floral arrangements, even more elaborate than those in the aisle. A large, framed photo of Kate Barrett stood to the right of the coffin.

I crept up the aisle looking for a vacant spot. Had all these people known Kate Barrett, or were they here out of curiosity too? A woman sitting with a man I assumed was her husband and two young girls pulled the youngest onto her lap, scootched over, and patted the space next to her. I thanked her and lowered myself onto the wooden pew. Craning my neck, I noticed the sorrowful music playing came from the far left of the church, where a man and two women played violins.

The ceremony was late starting, and my back was already feeling the effects of the wooden pew when Kate's family entered the church. Cole Barrett led the small group up the aisle. Today his demeanour was sombre. He held the arm of an older woman, who I guessed might be his mother.

Several feet behind Cole came a distinguished-looking man, whom I presumed to be Kate's father, and following him a man and woman with two teenage boys. Next came a couple with a young girl of about ten or twelve, and lastly a heavier-set man with an unsteady gate. I knew Kate Barrett had three brothers and figured these must be them and their families.

After the immediate family were seated, another cluster of people headed up the aisle to the pews reserved for friends and dignitaries. I saw Edna Moss, today wearing a black knit dress and a look every bit as sour as the day she led me into Ben Langcaster's office. I spotted the Mayor, former Mayor, and the Lieutenant Governor of Alberta.

The man with the woman and two teenage boys turned out to be Sebastian Gallagher, Kate's oldest brother. He spoke about his little sister being a spark of joy and about her having to learn to stand her ground while growing up with three older brothers. He talked about her determination, her good and kind nature, and her desire to help others. Their mother passed away when Kate was eight, and he referred to another tragic event which took Kate years to recover from, and how art had played a major factor in that recovery.

The ceremony took almost an hour. Afterward, the family and close friends gathered at the foot of the cathedral steps where four chauffeured limousines stood ready to transport them to Queen's Park Cemetery where Kate would be interred. Edna Moss was one of those friends. I had to find a way to talk to her. Her presence with the family told me she was more than just Cole Barrett's VP of Communications.

The heavier-set man whom I had seen trailing the rest of the Barretts, staggered and almost fell as he came out of the church. The man I assumed was Kate's father grabbed him by the arm. A woman behind me muttered, "Drunker than a skunk at his own sister's funeral." I turned, but the woman was already gone.

I gave wide berth to the reporters in front of the church who were trying to get comments from those who had been inside. That's when I saw Ben Langcaster slinking away on the far side of the church steps, his face turned from the reporters. *Bold move Benny.* I had wondered if he'd have the chutzpah to show up. I'm sure more than a few people would be distancing themselves from him, given that his wife had been charged with Kate's murder.

I hurried to catch up and once within hearing distance called out his name. He turned around, his face twisting in anger as soon as he saw me. I rushed to catch up as he turned on his heel and continued down the street.

"Leave me alone," he muttered as I reached his side.

"Mr. Langcaster—Ben, just a quick question. Please."

He kept walking. "You have one minute. That's my car ahead." I recognized it, the same black Cadillac he had been driving when he met Kate at their rendezvous spots.

"What traumatic incident was Kate's brother talking about in his eulogy?"

He looked at me like I was insane. "Why do you care?"

"I just want to know."

"She was kidnapped when she was seven. Her father paid the ransom, but Kate wasn't returned until a month later. Here's my car," he said, getting in.

I watched Ben drive away. The kidnapping had happened over two decades ago. It did, however, remind me that Kate Barrett came from a very wealthy family and married a man who was also wealthy, and that sometimes wealth attracted unwanted attention from those who craved it.

NINETEEN

After leaving the church, I swung by my condo for a quick change of clothing and then headed to the office. It was clear Kate Barrett's life, however short, had affected many, especially those in the art community. I tried not to think about my own funeral. By the time I reached the office, my mood had lightened. I was alive and vowed to make every single day count.

My phone rang as I unlocked my office door. "Hey Mike."

"Jorja. Where are you?"

"At the office."

"Got any plans for dinner? I met with Willie this morning and have more details about CanNet. Gotta say, it sounds interesting."

Damn. My stomach dropped. I realized I had been hoping the whole possible work opportunity with Willie's new company would vaporize. At least where I was concerned. Maybe that told me more than my meagre list of pros and cons.

"No plans for dinner." Luis was still mired in meetings and reviews in the aftermath of the most serious terrorist attempt Calgary had ever received. We did, however, find time to chat briefly almost every night.

"That's great. For me, that is. Salty Dog? Say sixish?"

I checked the time. It would give me three hours to find out more about Kate Barrett and who in her life might have had an issue with her. Nowhere close to the amount of time I needed, but it would be a start. "Okay. See you there."

Mike sounded excited. If I had to guess, I'd say he'd soon be working for CanNet. Did that mean he would no longer be able to provide training to Calgary Police Services? *Not my problem.* I sat at my computer and waited for the browser to open.

An hour later, I had nothing. There were dozens of news articles about the various acquisitions Cole Barrett's company had made over the last few years, along with articles slamming his business practices, which the articles referred to as buy, strip, and flip tactics. Encore, and other small private equity firms, bought undervalued assets, extracted what they could from them, then sold them off quickly in an IPO. Having been stripped of key holdings needed to generate the longer-term capital required to grow, companies subjected to the buy, strip, and flip process often went bankrupt a few years down the road.

But this wasn't the kind of information I was looking for. I dug deeper on Kate Barrett and excluded Cole Barrett and Encore from my search terms. My screen filled with references to the Nuwest Art Gallery on Twelfth Avenue, which Kate Barrett owned. I had already checked out the art gallery's website, but other than the basics, there wasn't much there of interest to me.

I shifted my attention to platforms that promote creatives. Nothing on Dribble and TikTok or Art Station, which to me, resembled Pinterest but for artists. Six pages down in the search results

I came across a blog post that referred to the art foundation that Kate Barrett had set up. The title read, 'Can art be separated from the misdeeds of its creator?' The article went on to say that if art couldn't be separated from the artist, then works of art produced by the morally indefensible needed to be excised. *Interesting.* The article made an obscure reference to a dilemma facing Kate Barrett's Rising Star Art Foundation.

Maybe it was nothing, but now that it caught my attention, I couldn't let it go. I started searching local newspapers and social media about the Rising Star Art Foundation in the months prior to the date of the article. I finally found a short congratulatory note on the Canada Council For The Arts website, which listed this year's scholarship recipients. Someone named Todd Paquet had taken this year's top prize—a two-year scholarship worth thirty-thousand dollars. Another post a week later said the top scholarship had been rescinded. I sat up.

I couldn't find any further reference to Todd Paquet or to what happened to cause the scholarship committee to withdraw the scholarship. Not surprising, since social media posts have a relatively short lifespan. If any mention of this had ever been made on Twitter or Facebook, it would be long buried under hundreds of thousands of posts.

Googling Todd Paquet's name brought up pages of Paquets but not a one named Todd. I did however find a Wolfgang Paquet, an artist who lived in Bragg Creek. He sold his artwork online through his company, WolfInk.

I checked my watch. I'd have to get moving if I didn't want to be late for my meeting with Mike. It was a stretch to think that a scholarship winner could have had anything to do with Kate Barrett's murder, but my job was to eliminate possibilities through investigation, not on gut feeling. It wouldn't be the first time someone felt wronged and allowed their resentment to fester until the lingering bitterness grew into a desire for revenge.

I was almost at my car when my phone rang. I dug my cell out of my pocket. My heart fluttered. "Hi Luis. How are you doing?"

"Hey babe. Okay. Looking forward to getting my life back to normal."

"You and me both. I miss you. You sound tired."

"Yeah. I'll sleep better when I have you in my arms."

A spike of giddiness shot through me.

"When will that be?"

"Tonight? One of our meetings got cancelled. If you're not busy, come over—I'll make you dinner."

Never fails. "Damn. I'm on my way to meet Mike. He wants to talk to me about a job opportunity."

Luis didn't reply.

After a few seconds, I added, "I can come later. Maybe bring dessert?"

"Deal, babe. But you'd better be prepared to be the dessert."

I was still grinning when I reached the car. I'd give Mike two hours; I owed him at least that. I could already feel the tension returning to my body at the thought of giving up Knight Investigations. But I promised myself to never say never.

TWENTY

The Salty Dog was packed. Even the outside patio was full, despite the cool wind that had kicked up as the day wore on. I was happy to find Mike nursing a beer at a table inside. I slid into the chair opposite from him.

I glanced at the beer in front of him. "I'm not late, am I?"

"I got here early."

A server materialized beside us, and I ordered a glass of Shiraz. "Oh, and can we please see the menu?" I had eaten here so many times I almost didn't need a menu, but it did change with the seasons.

"You must be hungry." Mike laughed after the server left to get my wine and the menus.

I felt my face grow hot. "I'm starving. I hope you don't mind."

"I love a gal with an appetite. So, what are you working on these days?"

"Remember when I called to get a name of a lawyer for a former client who had been arrested for murder?"

"The infidelity case, right?"

"Right. Well, Neil Trent hired me to help him build his defence case."

"Kudos to you." Mike raised his glass.

"Thanks, but I owe it to you. My former client got a good lawyer, and I'm getting a good chunk of work out of it." I did owe Mike a lot. He always had my best interests at heart. I told myself I wouldn't rush this dinner despite the promise of the hot molten dessert waiting for me.

"How'd your meeting with William go?"

The server returned with wine and menus and Mike launched into a recap of his meeting. His face grew animated as he leaned forward, the excitement in his eyes obvious.

"Man, Jorja, I wish I'd been born thirty years later. You know Willie has spent the last decade or so providing investigative services to the business community. Workplace fraud, cyberthreat prevention, workplace harassment and physical threats, labour unrest, that sort of thing. Well, he's teamed up with another guy who comes from the PIA side, and they have some serious investors behind them. This new company of theirs is going to provide top-notch twenty-first-century investigative services."

"Okay, hold on. First up, what's PIA?"

"Private Intelligence Agency. Private agencies that make their services available to governments, large corporations, or to individuals who have an interest in stopping crime, corruption, or perceived threats to these organizations. They gather and analyze open-source information to get the best intel they can on whatever is being investigated."

"So, a spy agency?"

Mike wagged his head back and forth. "Well, yes and no. PIAs aren't exactly new. Seventy percent of the national budget of the United States is earmarked for the private sector. That's roughly sixty billion dollars. Some of the functions that used to be performed by the CIA or NSA are being outsourced to private intelligence companies."

"I didn't know that."

"I knew, but I never would have guessed it was that much. What is new though, is throwing AI into the mix. Artificial Intelligence is going to change everything."

"So I've heard. Information is king. Always has been."

"Law enforcement agencies, intelligence agencies, and private investigators get most of their information from publicly available sources. I mean, how do you typically start a case?"

"Usually by doing an online search for any background or relevant information on the client and the target company or object of the investigation."

"Right. Now imagine if that could be automated. Instead of searching through hundreds of sources to find what you're looking for—all the information is analyzed and compiled into a concise bundle for you. Better yet, AI tools will access and integrate data from diverse sources, video doorbell cameras, CCTV footage, social media, licence plate and DNA databases, and so on. Accurate, up-to-date data. Investigations that take weeks or months could be wrapped up in days."

I thought back to the hours I had spent this afternoon searching for information on Kate Barrett and Todd Paquet with little to show for my time. "Are we really getting close to that way of operating?

I know we've been developing and using AI technologies for years. Facial recognition software, visual forensics, licence plate readers, and so on. Baby steps. But is the integration of all of this actually possible?"

"Baby is a teenager now. One of the things I heard over and over in my cross-country assignment was that police officers can't keep up. As the infosphere expands with the ever-increasing usage of computers for...well, everything, they can't deal with it all. It's frustrating for our officers to know that there's data out there that would help them solve or even prevent a crime from happening, but that they can't access it. The time to manually search, compile, and analyze all the data is prohibitive."

"Luis told me some of the police departments are now using AI algorithms to analyze historical crime data to predict potential criminal activity."

"The future is here, Jorja. It's going to be a whole new world."

Our food arrived and I took a bite of my potato-encrusted cod and felt my toes curl. Maybe I should learn to cook one of these days. That would be a good step into a whole new world.

Mike continued to talk about Willie's new company while we ate. CanNet was being structured to provide investigation services in four divisions: the Corporate Intel Division, Homefront Investigations, Blue Line Investigations, and the Public Integrity Assurance Division."

"Willie wants you in his Homefront Investigations Division."

"Homefront Investigations. What's all in Homefront Investigations? Sounds like it might deal with domestic violence."

"Yes, domestic violence, but also missing persons, and threats and crimes against vulnerable populations."

"So, women and children, LGBTQ, Indigenous peoples, and those with mental illness?"

"That's part of it, but don't forget seniors, racial or ethnic minorities, and threats against immigrants, refugees, or the homeless. You'd be dealing with threats of physical violence as well as harassment, stalking, extortion, sextortion, sexual exploitation, and blackmail. The list is long."

"What role is he offering you?"

"He wants me to help him finish setting up the divisions, finalize operational practices, and work out how the divisions will work together. Might take the better part of a year. Once everything's in place, he sees me as a great fit for heading up the Blue Line Investigations Division. It would handle everything that police services contracted out to us."

The fact that Mike referred to his future position in terms of 'us' told me his mind was already made up. I didn't know what to think—there was a lot to consider.

I stayed longer than I planned, and it was well after nine o'clock by the time Mike and I parted ways. To be honest, part of me was intrigued. The larger private investigation companies were already focusing on cybercrime. The old-fashioned gumshoe was going the way of the encyclopedia salesman.

It was time to put serious effort into figuring out what I wanted my life to look like five or ten years from now. I easily had twenty-five or thirty years of work ahead of me. A lot of professionals no longer retired at sixty-five. I wasn't the sort of person who would take up crocheting when I hit retirement age—if there even was a retirement age anymore. Mike was right, it was a whole new world.

My brain continued to spin, until I suddenly found myself parking in front of Luis' building. As I reached the front entrance, an older gentleman held the door open for me. I had a key to Luis' condo but didn't have a keycard to get into the building. Luis had given me the key so that I could lock up whenever I stayed over, since he was often out the door an hour or more before I was.

I got off on the tenth floor and made my way down the hall to Luis' condo. I opened the door, shrugged off my jacket, and stepped out of my shoes. Soothing music emanated from the in-ceiling speakers.

Luis was lying on the couch, his head resting on one of the accent cushions. The steady, rhythmic rise and fall of his abdomen, told me he was asleep. His hands were curled around an empty rocks glass which rested on his chest. The tension lines in his face were gone. I felt the familiar flutter in my stomach and fought back the desire to touch him.

I made my way past the couch and to the small portable bar. As I poured myself a scotch, I heard a low groan behind me as Azagora shifted, then sat up. I heard him set his glass down on the coffee table, and I turned. He looked over his shoulder and ran a hand over his still sleepy-looking brown eyes. "Babe, you're here. There're leftovers in the fridge if you're still hungry."

"Thank you, darling. What I mostly need is a stiff drink." I finished pouring and put the stopper back into the decanter.

"Good day, huh?"

I took a sip of scotch, walked over to Luis, and straddled him as he sat on the couch. "Better now."

He took the glass from me, sipped, and handed it back. I leaned forward and kissed him, the smooth, sweet, oakwood taste still on his tongue.

"Want to finish this in the bedroom?" he murmured.

I didn't know if he meant the scotch or me kissing him—but the answer to both was yes.

TWENTY-ONE

The Nuwest Art Gallery was located on Twelfth Avenue and close to my office. I decided to walk over. The door opened into a well-lit space. Every wall was covered with artwork, some five feet in height and other paintings no larger than a cell phone.

A woman with bright-red hair cut in a spikey shag was helping a customer. I wandered around the gallery. I could use some artwork in my condo. It would liven up the place and make it feel homier. And there was the rub. Although I felt comfortable and safe in my little condo, it didn't exactly feel like home. For me, home had connotations that couldn't be filled by nice furniture and pictures on the wall.

"Hi, can I help you?" A voice cut into my thoughts. My eyes came to focus on the large abstract painting I was standing in front of, slashes of blue against a yellow background. The redhead was standing next to it, her head tilted slightly to one side, a welcoming smile on her face.

"Oh, hi. I'm actually not here about the art. My name is Jorja Knight, and I am investigating the murder of Kate Barrett." I pulled out a business card and handed it to her, hoping she wouldn't ask me which side I was working for. "Do you have a minute for some questions?"

She gazed around the space, but we were now the only ones here. "Of course. We were all shocked when we heard. I still can't believe she was murdered."

"Did you know Kate Barrett? Did she spend much time here at the gallery?"

"I knew her, yeah, but not well. She dropped in from time to time. We could call her, of course, if we needed to. She organizes all the art showings and commissions the paintings." She swallowed, and her face flushed. "I mean, she used to organize the art showings."

"I understand she also ran the Rising Star Foundation. Do you know anything about the foundation?"

Her lips curled momentarily into a smile. "I actually got a scholarship from the foundation two years ago. And this year I was lucky enough to get work here as part of a work experience program. It's just for the summer but it helps to pay the bills, and I get to meet so many talented artists."

"Well, congratulations. It's obvious that you love art."

"Kate—I mean, Mrs. Barrett—said the hints of both surrealism and realism in my paintings reminded her of Toller Cranston's paintings. Maybe someday people will recognize what a great artist he was."

"That's quite a compliment...coming from someone like Kate Barrett. Can you tell me how the foundation is run?"

"I don't really know much about what happens behind the scenes. The foundation holds an annual gala, which is their main fundraiser. We also host evening events at the gallery, where one of the gallery artists is featured. The proceeds help support the gallery and the rest goes to the foundation. And the artist gets to sell their work, so it helps them too."

"How does one go about getting a scholarship?"

"You have to apply and there's this whole process you go through where Mrs. Barrett and the selection committee chooses that year's recipients. You have to be a Canadian citizen and enrolled in an accredited art program. You submit two pieces of your work and write an essay on what art means to you."

"What about this year's winners? I heard there was some sort of controversy."

Her eyes widened as she glanced over her shoulder. "I'll say. I mean who's to say where artists and creatives get their inspiration from, but that was just sick."

"Are we talking about Todd Paquet?"

"Yeah. I get it that there are as many different sources of inspiration as there are creatives—personal experiences, emotions, music, nature, objects, and everything and anything in the world around us. Or even beyond this world. But then there's the weird. I know weird, I dabble with surrealism." She laughed. "I like to think I'm open-minded, but in my opinion some works are more about the artist's ego than the art itself."

"You mean like the flesh dress that was displayed at the National Gallery of Canada in the late eighties?"

"Yeah, although the artist who created it said her intention was to illustrate the contrast between our inevitable bodily decomposition and human vanity. I'm more of the mind that people should be able to experience something personal through the art the artist has created, not be hit in the face with a statement that the artist is making, although others argue that's precisely what art is about."

I nodded. I was feeling pretty good right now about my choice to study science at university. "What did Paquet do that caused the committee to rescind his scholarship?"

"I heard this second hand, so don't quote me on this. In the essay he submitted he said he's inspired by death. After the committee chose him for one of this year's scholarships, they learned that he paints with real blood. Don't ask me where he gets it from. They dug further and discovered that he had a record. He stole a cadaver from the med school two years earlier. A neighbour reported a godawful smell coming from his apartment, is how they found it." Her nose wrinkled. "They also found some animals, I guess...in his apartment. None of them alive."

"Okay then. I can see why the committee might have wanted to rethink their choice. It seems they managed to quell any fallout after they rescinded his scholarship. At least I couldn't find much about it on the internet."

"He really trash talked Kate on social media. He showed up at the gallery about two weeks after it happened. Smeared a message in blood on the front window. Something about killing creativity. He also broke a window in Mrs. Barrett's car and threw a dead magpie onto the front seat."

"Were the police called?"

"Yeah. They made him take down his vile social media comments. He got a suspended sentence. Had to do forty hours of community service. I think he would have served the community best by leaving town."

"Have you heard where he is now, or know where I could find him?"

She pulled at the sleeve of her green smock. "I don't know where he lives. I saw him last week though."

"Where?"

She pointed out the front window with her chin. "Right there, across the street. He was just standing there staring at the gallery. It creeped me out."

"Did you call the police?"

"We were going to call them, but he left after about an hour. I haven't seen him since."

The day had warmed up significantly by the time I left the gallery, so I peeled off my hoodie and tied the arms around my waist. Not very likely that Todd Paquet killed Kate five months after his scholarship was rescinded. Then again, I knew from personal experience that revenge has a long shelf life.

TWENTY-TWO

It had taken three phone calls to get Ben Langcaster to agree to let me look at his home security camera video feed. Sherrie insisted that no one had been in the house between the time she last saw her gun and when she discovered it missing. So, either someone entered the house undetected or she, Ben, and their son were about to come under a lot more scrutiny.

It was early evening when I got to the Langcaster house. A curved driveway led to a three-car garage, which jutted out to the right of the main house. I pulled into the drive, got out, and surveyed the area. I caught a glimpse of a blue recycling bin tucked back against the edge of the garage. Not sure Sherrie would have seen anything crammed in behind a bin in that location unless she had walked over to it. I tested my theory. To have noticed the sports bag with the bloody T-shirt she claimed to have seen, she would have had to be standing almost directly in front of the three bins parked there. Odd that it had gone missing after Sherrie confronted her husband about it. Or had it simply been picked up on trash day?

The sandstone façade of the two-storey house was made to look statelier by large windows inset with black metal window grilles.

The house wasn't super modern, but it had been updated once or twice since the eighties. I peered down the treelined street. Most of the houses in the Langcaster's neighbourhood would sell for over a million dollars. I turned back and loped up the three brick steps to the oversized wooden door. A security camera was mounted five feet above my head.

Ben answered the door in a dress shirt and pants, his tie loosened at his neck.

"Come in." He stood aside as I entered, deep furrows between his eyes.

"Nice neighbourhood. Have you lived here long?"

"Thanks. We bought the place about fifteen years ago. I have to head back to the office, so make this quick. In here." He turned and led me through a set of double doors to the right of the foyer and into an office. It reminded me of Neil's office but smaller. A sleek oak-topped desk with black metal legs took up most of the space in front of the built-in bookshelves. Two upholstered armchairs angled toward each other filled the space by the front window.

Ben led me around the desk and waved his hand at the chair. He leaned over, tapped a few keys on his computer, and the video feed from the home security system came up. I sat in front of the screen. Ben's phone rang and he stepped out into the foyer to take the call.

The camera was angled so as to show the last few feet of sidewalk leading up to the steps, the steps themselves, and the front door. After a few minutes, a figure appeared, rang the doorbell, and when no one answered hung a flyer onto the doorhandle and left. I sighed. I watched as several more people came to the door, but neither Sherrie, Ben, nor their son answered.

I kept watching. A young man came out, turned to say something to someone inside, then jumped the three steps to the ground and disappeared from view. Their son, Matt, I guessed.

I could still hear Ben talking out in the foyer. Sounded like business. I glanced at the bottom corner of the screen. I was more than halfway through the video feed. A figure carrying a clipboard arrived on the doorstep and rang the bell. The front door opened. I sat up. After about thirty seconds, the figure stepped through the doorway and went inside.

I stopped the video and scrolled back. Hard to say if it was a man or woman as a ballcap obscured most of their features. Whoever it was wore a short twill bomber jacket, dark-green pants, and boots. A lanyard with an ID card dangled from around their neck.

I zoomed in on the card until it became almost too grainy to see. If I crossed my eyes, I could make out some letters that, when put together, might say, Green Energy. The name on the ID card was impossible to discern, but the photo looked like it might be that of a woman. However, it was too pixilated for me to be absolutely certain.

I noted the time and date on the video and hit the play button. The same person came out of the house twenty-two minutes later. Sherrie said no one had been in the house, but maybe she had set up a service call.

Ben returned a few minutes later. "Did you or Sherrie set up a service call in the last few weeks, maybe from the gas company?"

Ben shrugged. "No."

I scrolled back to the video of the serviceperson entering the house. "Someone was at the house, on the twenty-fifth of April. Know anything about that?"

Ben peered at the screen and shrugged. "No."

"Sherrie never said anything to you about a service call?"

"Look, I work, and Sherrie looks after Matt and the house. You'll have to ask her. Are you almost done here?"

"I need five more minutes." Ben ducked out of the room again. A minute later, I heard him back on the phone.

The rest of the video was about as useful as the first half. Three more people came and went, but no one else went inside. I fast forwarded the video to the days right before and after Kate Barrett was killed. The son came through the front door once, carrying a bag of groceries. I'd have to check the date, but I was sure it was the same day Sherrie called me to say her gun was missing. Then the video stopped recording until three days ago.

Ben stepped back into the room just as I reached the end. "Do you know which gas company you're with, Mr. Langcaster?"

He frowned, his lips curving downward tightly. "Direct Energy...Green Energy? Something energy."

"It looks like your family doesn't use the front door very often."

"No, we usually come in through the garage. Matt uses the side door. We have a keypad there, so he doesn't have to worry about a key."

"The camera was turned off two days before Kate Barrett was murdered and then turned back last week."

"So?"

"Any reason why that might have been?"

Ben scratched the back of his neck and shrugged. "No idea. Maybe Sherrie turned it off and forgot to restart it. I noticed it was off a few days ago and turned it back on."

"Neil Trent told me that Sherrie found a sports bag with a bloody T-shirt in it wedged in by the garbage bins. Did she ask you about it?"

"Accused me is more like it. I have no idea what she was talking about. I had a look later, but there was nothing there."

"Hmm. You didn't see it?"

"No."

"Would it be okay if I downloaded a copy of your security video? It's going to start overwriting the data in five days, and I'd like to preserve a copy before it disappears."

"Sure, but I don't want any thumb drives corrupting the computer. I'll send you a copy."

"I'd appreciate it." I dug out a business card for him with my email address. "Have you been able to talk to your wife since her arrest?"

"No, and I don't intend to."

"Why? Do you think she's guilty?"

"It doesn't matter what I think, does it? You and her lawyer are going to have to convince twelve other people that she isn't."

"We're working on it. Please don't forget to send me the video. Goodnight, Mr. Langcaster."

If I were to guess, I would say the Langcasters' marriage was over. Sherrie had been so focused on trying to make a perfect home for Ben and her son, that she failed to build a network of supporting friends and family for herself. Without that network, Sherrie was a sitting duck.

TWENTY-THREE

Edna Moss was just as standoffish as last time I was here. She retrieved me from the outer reception area, and I followed her rigid back into the executive lounge off of Cole Barrett's inner sanctum. Today she wore her hair down, which softened her angular features. The well-cut navy-blue pantsuit and metallic silver shoes made her look less...well, like a woman who had given up on herself.

"That was such a beautiful service for Mrs. Barrett. It's obvious by how many attended that she was well thought of and loved."

My attempt to initiate small talk was met with silence.

"How long have you worked with Mr. Barrett?"

"Seventeen years."

I found it odd that the VP of Communications was also acting as if she was Cole Barrett's executive assistant. Then again, maybe the company didn't need a full-time VP of Communications under more typical circumstances.

"Your job must keep you busy with all that is happening. What with the rumours of another possible acquisition, and then Mrs. Barrett's murder."

"Yes, it does. Please wait here." She waved her hand toward the seats in the inner waiting room. "Mr. Barrett shouldn't be long."

She made her way back to the office next to Cole Barrett's. The woman was like a vault. And I clearly didn't have the right code to make her open up even a bit.

My ten o'clock meeting time came and went. Forty minutes later, Barrett's office door opened, and three men came out. One of the men was Ben Langcaster. He paled when he saw me but otherwise didn't acknowledge my presence. The other two men made their way to the main reception area unaccompanied by Edna. I guess I got special treatment.

Cole Barrett strode out of his office, held up a finger to me, and continued into Edna's office. He said something to her, and she stood up and smiled. Obviously, he had the code. Edna put her hand on his shoulder and said something that made him laugh. *Oh my god.* Was she flirting with this man just days after he buried his wife?

A minute later, Cole left Edna's office and rushed over to me, holding out his hand. "Sorry for the wait, Ms. Knight. Would you like something to drink? Coffee, water?"

His hand gripped mine, almost crushing my fingers. We were eye to eye in height and although his voice was welcoming, the friendliness didn't extend to his piercing gaze. "No, thank you, Mr. Barrett."

"Please, it's Cole."

"Thank you, and I'm Jorja." I followed him into his office. Although he wasn't a tall man, he had broad shoulders and a powerful frame, like maybe he played football in college. He closed the door behind us and ushered me over to a round table at the far end of the office.

Snow-covered mountains jutted majestically against the bright-blue sky to the west and gleaming office towers to the south. "I don't know how you get any work done in here, with those views."

"Spectacular, aren't they." His chest expanded as he turned toward the mountains, as if he had anything to do with their creation. Unlike Edna, Cole jumped right into the conversation.

"You said you're working with the defence team on Kate's murder case, correct?"

"That's right." I was about to launch into my spiel that our investigation was two pronged: help Sherrie Langcaster prove her innocence and find the real killer.

"Tell me how I can help you."

I breathed easier. "First of all, please accept my sincerest sympathies on your loss." At his nod of acknowledgement, I continued. "There are several things that I'd like to ask you about. First of all, the police have ruled out robbery, mainly because your wife was found still wearing her diamond wedding ring and an expensive watch. Although worth a considerable amount, is it possible she could have also been wearing a pendant or necklace of equal or more value?"

He leaned forward and rested his clasped hands on the table. "That never occurred to me."

"Is there any way you can check to see if any of your wife's jewellery is missing?"

"We had all of Kate's jewellery insured. I'll have someone verify that her collection is intact."

"The police report says that Kate's driver's licence was found in the car, but it doesn't mention a purse or wallet. Was your wife in the habit of going out without one?"

Cole exhaled loudly and shook his head. "Kate loved her damn purses. She had one for every outfit. The police never asked me about that either."

"Her car was found nearby. The report made no mention of anything inside other than the driver's licence. Have they returned the contents of the car to you?"

"No, not yet. Kate had her car detailed regularly. I'm not sure there'll be much to return."

"Do you have any idea why your wife was downtown near the river path the night she was killed?"

"No, I don't."

"Did she frequent the area? Maybe walked or jogged the river path? Was one of her favourite restaurants near there?"

"Kate didn't like coming downtown. If she was meeting one of her friends, it was usually at the club."

"The Pine Valley Spa and Golf Club?"

"That's correct."

"What about visits to your office? It's only seven or eight blocks from where Kate's body was found."

"Sure, she's been to my office a few times. Never at night. Why?"

"I'm just trying to eliminate the most rational possibilities for why she was there that night. If you had to come up with the most likely reason for why your wife was near the Louise Bridge at that time of night, what would it be?"

He shrugged. "I can't even begin to guess. Maybe she went there with someone else, who had a reason to want to go there."

"Do you know anyone she might have been with that night?"

"No." He shrugged.

"Your wife didn't do drugs, even if just recreationally?"

"Kate? No. She barely drank," he scoffed. "Except for water. Had to be at least a gallon a day."

"And if she didn't go there with someone else that night?"

"Then it's likely she went there to meet someone."

"Any idea who that might be?"

"If you're asking me if she was there to meet Ben Langcaster, I'd say no."

I swallowed my surprise at his forthrightness. Rumours had surfaced about the possibility of Kate being involved with Sherrie Langcaster's husband. Why else would the public think Sherrie killed her husband's boss' wife.

"Why is that?" I relaxed, suddenly aware that my feet had been pressing into the carpet this whole time.

"Ben and I go way back. We went to the same university but then lost track of each other. Then about eight years ago I ran into him again. We had lunch, got caught up. I got Ben moved up in the queue to join the Britannia Club—there's about a three-year wait. We play squash there a couple of times a week. He's a good opponent but I beat him every time." Cole laughed. "Ben's a good guy. Smart as a whip. No entrepreneurial spirit though. He's like an oak tree, deeply rooted and unyielding in a storm."

"Is it just chance that he's here, working for you?"

"I don't leave things to chance. After being assigned to work on one of my earlier acquisitions, I came to an agreement with Finchman Law, his employer. I told them I wanted Ben Langcaster to be assigned to me for as long as I need him. They had no problem agreeing to that."

I swallowed. Might as well get to the point. "So, you don't think Sherrie Langcaster killed your wife because her husband was having an affair with her?"

"No. She still might have killed Kate. I understand from Ben that she has some mental health issues. Maybe it's why Ben never took any risks or put himself out there. Getting ahead in business requires a strong partner. Someone who can shmooze with the other wives and face questions from the media, when they inevitably come up. You need a thick skin, because the people who lose in business can be petty, jealous, even vindictive."

So that's how Ben was playing this with his boss. I cleared my throat softly, wishing now that I had asked for a glass of water. "If not Ben Langcaster, could your wife have been meeting someone else, someone she was seeing outside of your marriage?"

Cole looked amused. "Here's the thing. I loved Kate, but Kate was my third wife. My record as a faithful husband isn't stellar, and Kate knows...knew it. It's hard to keep that initial excitement going in a marriage. Kate and I had an understanding. If we dallied once in a while, so be it. Strictly sex that is, not to stray from our relationship. The rule was that we had to be discreet and our availability to each other always came first."

Didn't Cole know that his wife had been killed with a gun that was last seen in Sherrie Langcaster's possession? If Kate had been stepping out with someone else's husband, not likely the jealous wife would have killed her with Sherrie's gun. One part of me wanted to mention it right now, but it wouldn't serve our client very well. He was going to be in for a surprise if we didn't clear Sherrie's name before her case went to trial. So that left me with Sherrie as the best candidate if infidelity was the motive behind the killing.

I left the office more puzzled than when I arrived. Cole Barrett could turn on the image of a grieving husband when the cameras were pointed at him, but his conversation with me could have been about anything mundane, like the weather or traffic. Maybe he and Kate did have an open marriage, but I still found it hard to believe that he'd be okay working side by side with the man screwing his wife. What if he had found out that Kate and Ben's relationship was more than just sex? Could he have had Kate killed? Why not go after Ben? Why did I get the feeling that he was protecting Ben?

TWENTY-FOUR

I HAD LEFT MY car parked near my office, hoping the twenty-minute walk downtown would help me prepare for my meeting with Cole Barrett. Now I hoped the walk back would help me come up with a plan. The river pathway was quiet this time of day. Several women were out with their strollers and the occasional jogger ran past me.

After several blocks, I left the pathway and turned south. My route back to the office would take me past Luis' condo building. I still hadn't told him about Mike's and my conversation about possibly joining Willie's new company, nor that I needed to find new office space. The little time we had together since the terrorist attack had been spent on better things than our business lives.

I shivered as thoughts of our last encounter resurfaced. Luis' wounds ran so deep I once questioned if he'd ever be able to open his heart to me, or anyone else for that matter. Although it had taken time, Luis was slowly letting his guard down. The night he shared his past with me and the hurt, abuse, and betrayal he suffered as a young boy, were still hard for him to speak about. By exposing his deepest pain, he showed me he didn't want that pain to block the growing feelings we were developing for each other. I knew receiving love was scary for him, as it was for me, but we each had moved past our ingrained walls, and I knew the love we had for each other was genuine.

I drew myself out of my head and concentrated on my surroundings, the streetside trees with their tender bright-green leaves, the tubs of flowering plants standing outside of the shops or hanging overhead. As I walked, my thoughts returned to this morning's meeting.

Cole's ready admission and acceptance that Kate could have stepped outside of her marriage surprised me. So why was Ben Langcaster so afraid it would cost him his job if Cole Barrett found out about the affair? Or was he concerned that his real employer, Finchman Law, would be the one to fire him if they found out? His law firm might consider his behaviour unethical or at least unprofessional. Any thoughts that I might have had that Cole killed or had his wife killed because he found out she was cheating on him, had just been dampened. Unless Cole was lying to save face.

Cole portrayed his and Ben's relationship as that of friends, but men like Cole didn't make friends with the people who worked for them. I was left with the impression that it amused Cole to treat Ben like a younger brother or mentee—even though they were roughly the same age and similarly educated. It fed Cole's ego and perpetuated Ben's image as that of underdog, someone who would never reach Cole's business acumen, wealth, or social standing.

I needed to go down a different path. One in which neither Sherrie nor Ben were the killer. But the gun was a problem. Someone knew that Sherrie had a gun and had somehow obtained it and used it to kill Kate. If it wasn't Sherrie or Ben, then it left me the son, someone who broke into the house undetected and took nothing of value except the gun, or someone who seemingly had no reason to take the gun, like a maid, or service personnel. Someone Sherrie didn't even remember coming into the house because their presence was expected or an ordinary occurrence.

Back at the office, I sent Neil a quick email to let him know that a service rep from a gas company had entered the Langcaster home during the interval between when Sherrie last saw her gun and when she noticed it missing. It was a long shot, but it made me wonder if there could have been other people in the house, perhaps a friend of her son's or someone who had been hired to do the yard work.

Then I called Green Energy and asked to speak to a supervisor in the residential services department. A few transfers later, I was speaking to Rashmi Gupta.

"No madam, I do not see a service order for your address."

"Maybe I have the date wrong. Can you check for the entire week of April twenty-fifth?" I had lied and told her that I was Sherrie Langcaster and that someone from their company had made a service call on the twenty-fifth, but ever since their visit the furnace was making a strange noise when it came on, infrequently now that the weather had warmed.

"Sorry. I have no workorder for your address for any date this year. Are you sure it was someone from our company?"

"I...well, yes. I mean, the lanyard they wore said they were from Green Energy." I tried my best to sound hesitant, confused, hard to do with my growing excitement.

"Did you see any other ID, madam?"

"No. But they had a clipboard and a small case or toolkit with them."

"What was the service call about?"

"I'm not sure. My husband arranged the appointment. The person who came to the house said they would do a full inspection, to see if everything was working as it should be."

"We do not send out service personnel to do regular inspections or inspections of any kind."

"Oh dear...I wonder who I let into my house."

"I hope nothing was taken. Our representatives all wear a Green Energy uniform, and they call before coming to the house, to confirm the appointment."

"Oh. I didn't get a call. And the person who came wasn't wearing a uniform. I am going to have another look through my house to make sure nothing is missing."

"Please be careful in the future, madam. Is there anything else I can help you with today?"

"Thank you, no. You've been very helpful. Have a great day."

Finally, a lead. Why would someone enter Sherrie's house under false pretenses if not to steal the gun? If it had been an attempt to rob the place it was unlikely that they pocketed the gun when they came across it but didn't take anything else. And for the gun to show up as the one that was used to murder Kate Barrett was beyond unlikely.

The killer could have easily obtained a gun on the street. One that was untraceable. So why steal this one? Whoever entered the house wanted this specific gun. I reminded myself that correlation does not imply causation. It was too soon to draw any conclusions. Sherrie insisted that she hadn't killed Kate. For the first time, I was starting to believe we might have something to help her prove her innocence.

After the call, I messed around with the security video Ben had sent me to see if I could decipher the letters in the name on the lanyard but gave up after a while. I copied a part of the video and sent it to my friend Lennie, who ran a private security company, to see if he had any way to enhance the image.

I rubbed the back of my neck and stared at the water-stained ceiling tiles in my office. The facts and solid evidence in this case were limited, as they often are. Unfortunately, they could be tied to the premise that Sherrie Langcaster killed Kate Barrett out of jealousy or revenge. But there were other possible explanations. Just this morning, Cole Barrett told me that people who lose in business can be jealous and vindictive. Could someone have caused Cole Barrett personal pain by killing his wife in retaliation for perceived or actual wrongdoings?

Neil Trent was right. This case wasn't going to be easy. I wasn't ready to drop Ben Langcaster off my suspect list, but he would have to have had one heck of a reason to kill his lover and put his career in jeopardy. The son seemed an unlikely suspect. Even if someone offered him a pile of money to pilfer the gun or he had taken it to sell to a friend or an acquaintance, how would it have ended up in the killer's hands?

Cole Barrett wasn't in the clear either. Rumour had it that he was entertaining a business deal that would triple Encore's worth, not to mention his personal wealth. If he suspected his wife was going to ask for a divorce, it would be best to get rid of her before his wealth tripled. Then again, maybe the motive behind Kate's murder was as simple as a young man's festering hatred for the woman he blamed for withdrawing his art scholarship. That and that death inspired him.

TWENTY-FIVE

WolfInk was located in a small outdoor mall in Bragg Creek, a hamlet situated twenty minutes west of Calgary. I didn't think Todd Paquet killed Kate over a lost scholarship, but getting Todd Paquet off my list of possible suspects would get me one step closer to finding the real killer.

I parked my car and stretched, the evening sun warm on my face. I was taking a chance coming out here without any confirmation that the owner of WolfInk, Wolfgang Paquet, was any relation to Todd Paquet, but getting out of the city left me relaxed.

The windows of WolfInk were filled with paintings of wolves, some resembling those found in nature, some from an otherworld. I entered the small shop. The walls were hung with paintings, many of which were mountain landscapes. An occasional prairie landscape had infiltrated the collection.

A middle-aged man, with a scruffy grey beard and thick wavy hair down to his shoulders, sat at a huge worktable that dominated the centre of the room. He wore a muscle shirt and a ball cap, the peak worn backwards. He was bent over a small sculpture on the table in front of him. The table was covered with pots of paints and brushes, and several canvases in various stages of completion. I had read a description of the gallery online and knew that Wolfgang Paquet offered art classes in his gallery.

The man at the table turned.

"Hello. Are you Wolfgang Paquet?"

"Yes." He stood and stepped toward me. "What can I do you for?"

"I'm looking for a young man, name of Todd Paquet, also a painter. You wouldn't happen to know him, would you?"

"Sure, I know him. He's my nephew. Who's asking?" He rammed his hands into the front pocket of his jeans. At six foot four and close to three hundred pounds, he was an imposing figure.

"My name's Jorja Knight. I'm a private investigator. I'm looking into the death of Kate Barrett. She owned the Nuwest Art Gallery in Calgary and also founded the Rising Star Art Foundation. Have you heard of her?"

"I heard. What's this got to do with my nephew?"

"I heard he was pretty upset when he lost his two-year art scholarship."

"Lost? It was stolen from him. Some bullshit about him lying or cheating on the application form."

"I was hoping he could tell me what happened."

"I'll tell you what happened. Somebody didn't like the looks of him. Half that foundation money comes from the big oil companies. They don't give a damn about art. They give money to foundations like Rising Star to whitewash their business, which is killing people. Killing our animals. Polluting our drinking water. Killing the whole damn planet."

I wasn't here to defend the energy industry or debate the pros and cons of the various types of energy we were using to heat our homes or deliver food, medicine, and supplies to our communities. "I don't have a list of donors, Mr. Paquet, so I don't know who contributes to the foundation. But your nephew took whatever happened out on Mrs. Barrett, not the foundation's donors. I understand he defaced her shop and deposited a dead bird in her car."

"As soon as they found out he had a record, their attitudes changed. So he took something when he was a kid. They shouldn't have charged him at all."

Took something when he was a kid? The kid stole a cadaver. Wolfgang was still giving me an earful.

"Suddenly he's responsible for all sorts of things, not just lying on his application form. People like them don't like people like us."

He hitched up his jeans and took a step toward me. Wolfgang was coming across as loud, mean, and hotheaded. I had no idea which *them* and *us* he was referring to. Maybe he self-identified as an asshole.

"Are you saying your nephew didn't omit mention of his previous police record from the application form or damage Kate Barrett's car?"

"The car thing was after they called him a liar and publicly humiliated him. Why are you here? What exactly are you accusing my nephew of?"

"I'm not accusing him of anything. I want to know if he could have possibly been the person Kate Barrett was meeting the night she was killed. Maybe he saw or heard something."

Wolfgang glared at me. "You think I'm stupid. I should just tell you to leave, but I want this to end now." He pulled his hands from his pockets and took another step toward me. I sized up his hands. He could use those fists to pound rock and steel into the sculptures lining the shelves in his shop. I took a step back and swallowed.

"My nephew had nothing to do with that bitch's murder." He used his forefinger to emphasize each point he made. "In fact, he's in Costa Rica. He's been there ever since his forty days of community service ended in March."

The scowl on his face deepened, and I took a few more steps away from him until I could feel the door handle in the small of my back. "This time we won't stay quiet. If my nephew is wrongly accused again, we're going to sue. Got it?"

"Got it."

I backed out through the door and blew out the lung full of air I had been holding. Not the result I'd been hoping for. I walked back to my car and climbed in. I sat for a minute while my brain processed what had just happened. Hearing that Todd Paquet was out of the country should have been music to my ears. But either his uncle was lying or the girl I had spoken to at the Nuwest Gallery was mistaken about seeing him across the street from the art gallery a week before Kate was murdered. Or had Kate Barrett's death drawn Todd Paquet to her shop like a hungry wolf is drawn to the remains of a deer carcass?

TWENTY-SIX

I PULLED OPEN THE door to Starbucks and was relieved to see that a few tables were still unoccupied. I grabbed a coffee and settled myself at a table near the door. Following three lines of thought simultaneously about who or why Kate Barrett had been murdered left me feeling discombobulated.

Ben Langcaster might have had the best means and opportunity to kill Kate, but I couldn't come up with a plausible motive. Did I believe him when he said he never saw the sports bag and bloody T-shirt Sherrie had claimed she saw? Or was Sherrie the one fabricating things? He had disappeared in the days after he and Sherrie fought. He told me it was none of my business when I brought it up, but surely the police would have asked him the same question.

My conversation with Todd Paquet's uncle yesterday hadn't turned out how I hoped. Todd Paquet may have resented losing his art scholarship, but I couldn't envision Kate agreeing to meet him in that part of town in the middle of the night, let alone come up with a way for him to have lured her there. Still, I couldn't in all good consciousness eliminate him from my suspect list, at least not yet. Which left me Cole Barrett and the money angle. *Or Sherrie.*

A man like Cole Barrett had to have enemies, but it was hard to find anyone who would talk. I'd love a heart to heart with Edna Moss, his VP of Communications. After working with him for seventeen years, she must know the man well. But Edna Moss had already shown me that all I was going to get out of her were yes or no answers or no answers at all. So, I poked around until I found someone who was willing to talk about Cole Barrett. Wife number two.

The door to the coffee shop opened and a woman wearing a lime-green, short-sleeved Lululemon shirt with a matching headband and black leggings entered. I caught her eye, and she walked over.

"Jorja Knight?"

I stood and reached out to shake her hand. "Yes. And you must be Oriana. Can I get you something to drink?"

She waved her water bottle at me. "I have my water, thank you." She slid into the chair across from me. "So, you're a private investigator." At my nod, she continued. "What a cool job. I never would have pegged you for a PI. Whenever someone says private eye an image of Phillip Marlowe, with that trench coat and fedora, pops into my mind. Or Jim Rockford from the Rockford Files. Now he was a cutie. Sorry. You said on the phone that you're investigating Kate Barrett's murder?"

"That's right. I'm working with the defence lawyer for Sherrie Langcaster, the woman who has been charged with Kate Barrett's murder."

"Well, she got the wrong person, honey. She should have killed Cole."

"She claims she's innocent, so we're trying to find another candidate for the Crown Attorney to prosecute. How long were you married to Cole?"

"Seven years. Can't believe I stuck it out that long."

"What can you tell me about him?"

"He's loud, obnoxious, and has a massive ego. He's got a temper too. If you dare to cross him, watch out."

"Is he a violent man?"

"He never hit me, if that's what you're getting at. But he'll find some way to get back at you if he thinks you've discredited him or broken his trust. And he won't forget."

"Is that why you left him?"

"I left him because I was tired of sitting at home alone while he screwed other women. Serves me right, I guess. What goes around comes around."

"He was married when he met you?"

"Oh yeah. I knew it too, but foolishly I believed him when he said he loved me. It turned out to be a temporary infatuation at best. Thank god we didn't have any kids."

"Was Kate Barrett the woman he cheated with?"

"There were several, but she was the one he divorced me for. You know, I actually went to talk to her before she married him."

"You did? What about?"

"To warn her. To let her know that it wouldn't be long before her shine started to fade, and he'd be looking for someone new. I felt I had to warn her. She was so young, like maybe twenty-three or twenty-four. She was naïve. Of course, she thought I was just trying to get him back." Oriana rolled her eyes.

"I met with Cole a few days ago. There have been rumours that Kate was cheating on him, but he said theirs was an open marriage."

"Ha! That's a good one. Cole's a jealous man. Or maybe I should say possessive. I'm sure it's driven by his overinflated image of himself. He might act like *he's* in an open marriage, but there's no way he'd let his woman sleep with anyone. Not the Cole I knew."

"If he's a serial cheater, why does he bother to get married at all?"

"Money is a big part of it. And power. He likes to control people. If you haven't noticed, Cole's been marrying up each time. His first wife was just an ordinary hard-working gal. He met her at university. She didn't have much in the way of money, but she did put him through college, bought them a house, and gave him a couple of kids to earn her keep." Oriana unscrewed her water bottle and took a long swallow, then put the lid back. "By the time I met him, he swore he didn't want any more kids. I already had a daughter from my first marriage, so it wasn't a big deal. I wasn't wealthy, but my divorce settlement left me a few million. I did invest some of that money in his company. I did okay. The shares I got in return doubled in value. But Kate—that's a different story. I think if the girl had one eye in the middle of her forehead and three legs, he still would have married her."

"You think he was after her money?"

"Of course. And the poor love-smitten thing, she just opened her wallet and let her big strong man help himself. I heard she was the money behind Encore's last three acquisitions. I just hope she actually got shares in the company. I guess it doesn't matter now."

"Any idea of how Cole might react if he thought Kate might be leaving him?"

"Oh, he'd do whatever it took to protect his assets. I wouldn't be surprised if he's been funnelling money into offshore accounts. He's learned from his divorces. Or he's structured their finances in a way that she held all the debt and he the assets. That's why he always has so many lawyers working for him."

Oriana's comment sent off another thought in my head. Could Ben Langcaster have been working on such a structure, and warned Kate about it? I shook my head. Oriana was still talking.

"The timing of her death, along with the rumoured acquisition, makes me wonder."

"You think he could have killed her, or hired someone to do it?"

"Nothing about Cole Barrett would surprise me anymore. He's a dirty player."

"As in...?"

Oriana shifted and leaned forward. "He wanted my money but didn't want me involved in his business deals. But I couldn't help hearing bits of conversations I wasn't supposed to hear. I once heard Cole threaten to leak some dirt he found on the president of All-pro—one of the companies he acquired for his buy, strip, and flip business—if he didn't accept his offer."

"Interesting. I've read there's some controversy around the buy, strip, and flip business."

"Private equity firms like Encore are viewed as looters by the more established equity firms. They pillage the assets of the companies they buy then restructure them claiming they are trimming the fat and making them more efficient. They spin a new image for what's left of the company, which isn't sustainable in the long run, then flip it, and move on to the next victim."

"Corporate raiders. I thought that kind of thing was outdated these days."

"I don't think the big equity firms use this type of strategy. It's the smaller firms like Encore who still use the tactic. Encore's main goal for existence is to line the pockets of its owners as quickly as possible. It's certainly controversial, but Cole doesn't care. He goes after private firms using his threat tactics and god knows what else, and when he's ready to sell, offers shares in the company to public investors. The companies he's bought and flipped usually go bankrupt in a few years."

"You're saying the business practice itself isn't illegal, but the way Cole carries out those practices may be straddling the line."

"Oh, he's not straddling, honey, he's jumped right over to the dark side. He hires private eyes to dig up dirt on the owners of his business targets. He calls it leverage. He expected me to pass on any dirt I heard from any of the wives or girlfriends of these guys. I finally got tired of being used."

It made me wonder if Kate Barrett had also been coerced into spying for her husband. Maybe she found out something about Cole's business or one he was targeting, that she wasn't supposed to, and it got her killed. "Do you know anyone else I could talk to about this? I mean, his lawyers certainly aren't going to spill the beans. What about Edna Moss? What do you know about her?"

Oriana threw back her head and laughed. "You know he was cheating on his first wife with her, before I even came along."

"What? But she's still working for him."

"Yeah. Poor Edna. She never got picked, so she had to go back and stand in line with all the other wallflowers. I hear he's danced with her a few times. Makes you wonder why she's still there, doesn't it?"

"It does. Why do you think she's stuck around?"

"She's got something on Cole. I mean, business wise."

"Blackmail?"

"Maybe, maybe not. I'm betting Cole is scared to let her go, knowing what she does know about his business affairs, or maybe Edna's waiting for the right moment to strike."

After Oriana left, I kept rolling her premise about Edna over and over in my mind. It was an interesting premise, although it would be devilishly hard to prove. But it didn't even come close to explaining how or why Kate Barrett had been shot to death with Sherrie Langcaster's gun.

TWENTY-SEVEN

I HAD TWO TEXT messages by the time I got home. The first was from Lennie, saying that he had enhanced the image I had sent him from the Langcasters' security camera and that it should be in my inbox, and the second from Mike saying that he had set up a meeting for us with Willie and his partner next Thursday.

I threw my car keys onto the kitchen counter and changed into leggings and a T-shirt Gab gave me on my fortieth birthday. The front displayed a quote from the song My Way and read, 'I faced it all,' and the back said, 'and did it my way.' It was true to some degree, but as I've grown older, I've come to realize that doing things my way, on my own, hasn't always been the wisest choice.

Opening my laptop, I found Lennie's email. The attached photo showed a crisper image of individual that I was interested in, and the lanyard around their neck. Definitely a Green Energy lanyard. The photo ID showed a woman with a thin, long face, framed by ash-blonde hair. The name next to the photo was Elaine Gray.

I peered at the image of the person wearing the lanyard. The ballcap obscured the face but I made out a strand of dark hair tucked behind the ear. I focused on the hands. Long, slender fingers held a clipboard, no rings or other adornments. Sherrie would have to confirm, but my guess was that the service rep with the ball cap was a woman. Her hair colour was different from the photo on the Green Energy ID card that dangled from her neck, but she could have coloured it. Although the supervisor at Green Energy had no record of a service call being made to the Langcaster residence, I now had a name. Perhaps this person was with a different department, maybe there to upsell the Langcasters or sell them on the idea of an annualized monthly plan. Finally. This might be the break we were looking for.

I got up, poured myself a scotch, and settled back down on the couch. I sat there for a long time, sipping scotch, and thinking about life. I congratulated myself on how far I had come, all on my own, despite some major hiccups along the way. Was I ready to let go of the fear and uncertainty that was standing in the way of living my best life, a large life. Is that what I wanted? Was working with Mike and Willie at CanNet the right path to that life or just another diversion?

After a while, I got up and took down the vision board that hung in the small entryway and brought it back to the couch with me. I had put up my vision board when I was home healing from Jason Marr's knife attack. He had held me hostage after he killed three of my co-workers and injured dozens at my former place of business. The officers investigating the massacre at Global Analytix, had commended me on keeping a cool head. While I was held at knife point, I had begged the god I no longer believed in to save me. And when I was spared, I started to question everything. I questioned my beliefs, my childhood memories, my choice of profession, the dead-end relationship I was in at the time, and most importantly my purpose in life.

Like the art therapy that Kate's brother had mentioned at his sister's eulogy that helped Kate to recover from the trauma of being kidnapped, the vision board had been a way for me to express what I wanted without resorting to words. Whenever I found a photo or picture of something that depicted what I wanted in my life, I added it to the board. It sat empty for the first two months, and then I pinned a picture of a fluffy grey kitten and a red Ferrari 488 GTB. After a while, I added more pictures; most were of luxurious condos with outdoor patios surrounded by green foliage, and exotic locales to visit.

I unpinned the pictures one by one. I stopped at a photo of a confident-looking woman, sitting on a wooden stool, staring at the camera. I took a huge breath. She exuded peace, a certain happiness that crossed the space between her and the camera lens. I wanted that feeling. All the other photos and pictures were of physical objects. But who was I kidding. They wouldn't bring me that feeling. I knew I had to find that peace and happiness within myself, and everything else would materialize...or not.

I woke up at 1:58 a.m., my neck stiff from the awkward way I lay on the couch. I stared at the pictures all around me. I'd had no epiphany while I slept. I gathered up the pictures and the corkboard, carried everything into the bedroom, and stuck it all into the closet. I wasn't ready to toss everything out, but I had moved past wishful thinking. Taking down the vision board was the first step toward whatever lay ahead.

TWENTY-EIGHT

Green Energy was housed in its own four-storey building off of Crowchild Trail. Visitor parking was full, so I circled the building and parked on the street. The Green Energy campus was nicely landscaped, with outdoor seating areas for visitors and employees. I entered the building through the revolving glass doors and walked over to the security desk. I asked to see the head of HR and explained that I was part of an investigation team working on a murder case.

I was ushered to a set of chairs next to the security desk and told to wait. While I waited, I sent Mike a text saying I had made note of the meeting he set up for us next week with Willie and his partner regarding CanNet. I got A thumbs-up emoji back.

A woman got off the elevator and made a beeline for me. She was dressed in what I assumed passed for business casual these days—slim blue jeans, ballet flats, and a black jacket over a white T-shirt. She stopped in front of me. "Are you Ms. Knight?"

I stood. "Yes, I am. Jorja Knight."

"I'm Antonia Santiago." We shook hands. "Why don't we head upstairs."

I followed her onto the elevator. "You want a coffee or anything?" she asked as we got off on the fourth floor.

"Thank you, I'm fine."

She led me to her office, and I slid into one of the bright-green chairs in front of her glass-topped desk. She settled into her desk chair, crossed one leg over the other, and folded her arms over her stomach. "My understanding is that you're investigating a murder. How do you think we can help you with that?"

"I'm trying to find a woman by the name of Elaine Gray. We believe she may have information relevant to our investigation of the Kate Barrett murder. I pulled the enhanced photo Lennie had sent me from the Langcasters' security camera from my purse and slid it across to her. This woman visited our client's home on April twenty-fifth. We believe she may have taken something from the house that is pertinent to our investigation. As you can see, she is carrying a Green Energy photo ID. I need to speak with her."

Antonia sat up and stared at the photo. "That's one of our ID cards, but it's an old one. Our current ID cards have a different logo. See." She picked up her own photo ID card off her desk and handed it to me. "We rebranded last year."

The vertical line in the letter E on her ID had been shaped into a bolt of energy. I handed the card back to her. "When exactly did you rebrand?"

"Last spring. All the employee and contractor ID cards were re-done in May. So, it's been a year now."

"Nevertheless, I'd still like to speak with Ms. Gray."

Antonia tilted her computer screen, and her fingers flew over the thin keyboard lying on her desk. Her forehead furrowed. She typed some more, then scrolled. She shook her head. "Is that Gray with an a or an e?"

"Gray with an a."

After a few minutes, she lifted her head. "It looks like Ms. Gray is no longer employed by us."

"As in she was employed at Green Energy, but no longer is?"

"Correct. Her last day of employment is listed as March thirty-first, of last year."

"Is there a forwarding address for her?"

"I'm afraid I can't give you that."

"I know, I know, Privacy of Personal Information Act. What about her direct supervisor. Can I talk to them?"

"I don't know how that will help, but I can get her for you." She picked up her phone. "Margo, can you please come up to my office?"

A minute later a stout, dark-haired woman wearing purple framed glasses entered the room. "You wanted to see me?"

"Come in, Margo. This is Detective Knight. She has some questions for you about one of our former employees, Elaine Gray."

I stood to shake her hand but didn't explain that I was a private detective. "I understand Elaine Gray was part of your team?"

"That's right. We handle payables and receivables."

"Has Ms. Gray been back to visit since leaving? Have you heard from her, or do you know where I can find her?"

"No. I haven't talked to her or seen her since she left."

"Do you know if she stayed in touch with any of the other team members?"

"I don't think so. She kept pretty much to herself."

"If you had to find her, and it was urgent, who would you talk to or where would you look?"

"I don't know. She usually brought a lunch from home, but she always took it downstairs with her and ate it at one of the tables outside the coffee shop. You know—the Grind and Shine. She always had a coffee on her desk when she was working. Maybe someone down there?"

"Thank you." I handed her one of my business cards. "If you run into anyone who knows where I can find her, please let me know."

"I'll ask my team this afternoon, at our weekly meeting."

After leaving Antonia's office, I headed to the Grind and Shine in the lobby of the Green Energy building. I bought a coffee and chatted with the woman at the till, and the young man who was working behind the deli counter. He remembered Elaine Gray but said he hadn't seen her in a long while.

Finding Elaine Gray was even more critical than it had been before I entered the building. What viable reason could a former employee have for representing themselves as a service rep from a company they no longer worked for to gain access to someone's house? Especially the house of a woman who later claimed her gun had been stolen—the very same gun that was used to murder her husband's lover. Had we just found our smoking gun?

TWENTY-NINE

I was on my second coffee by the time Sal arrived. Her leg must be bothering her today, her limp more noticeable than the last time I saw her. She swore it was just a touch of arthritis, but I wouldn't be surprised if she was heading for a hip replacement. She noticed me in the far corner and limped over.

"Hi Sal. Glad you could make it."

"Sorry I'm late, doll. Damn C-Train wasn't running between Heritage and Erlton, had to use one of the commuter workaround buses."

"Well, you're here now. Can I get you something to eat or drink?"

Sal eyed my coffee then peered at the blackboard menu over the counter. "Since you're offering. How about one of them sausage-and-spinach breakfast bowls...and a latte."

I got up and grabbed my purse off the back of the chair.

"Maybe a muffin too. Nothing with nuts in it. Oh, and some fruit. A gal needs her vitamins. See if they have an apple or something like that."

I smiled and headed to the counter. I'd known Sal for close to two years now. She had attended one of my courses, back when I used to run weekend classes on how to become a private eye, which I did to supplement my income from Knight Investigations the first year I was in business. The fact that she was around sixty, and dressed like a bag lady most days, gave her an edge up in certain surveillance situations. I had used Sal several times over the years, and she always came through for me. More than that, she had my back. She'd walk across hot coals for me if I needed her help.

I ordered Sal's food and brought it back to the table on a tray. She had taken off her shabby, tan trench coat but still wore her woollen bucket hat. I unloaded the food and returned the tray to the counter. Sal was inhaling her breakfast bowl by the time I returned.

"How have you been, Sal?"

"Still here, ain't I? I take it this isn't a social visit."

"You're right. But I do enjoy seeing you." Sal wasn't big on emoting feelings, but over the years I had developed a soft spot for her. A horrible string of bad luck had led to her homelessness at one point. But in true Sal spirit she had fought her way back. She supplemented her meagre CPP cheque by bottle picking. The jobs she did for me kept her and her cats fed and helped to pay the rent on a small room in someone's basement.

"Yeah, yeah." She waved her hand across herself. "So whatcha got for me?"

"I'm working with the defence lawyer for Sherrie Langcaster."

"She's the one that offed that rich chick, Barrett. Right?"

"Allegedly. She claims she's innocent. We're hoping to prove her innocence, or at least find enough evidence to throw some doubt onto the situation."

"Gotcha." Sal pushed aside her empty bowl and started in on the blueberry muffin.

"Kate Barrett's body was found by a morning jogger just off the river path between Tenth and Eighth Street, morning of May ninth. Coroner figures she was killed between midnight and three a.m. She was shot twice."

"Twice, huh. Killer wanted to make sure she was dead." Sal took a large swallow of her latte, leaving a thin mustache of foam above her upper lip.

"The jogger didn't hear or see anything, but he noticed two homeless people sleeping in the playground near where the body was found. They were gone by the time the police arrived."

"You want me to find them, right, doll?"

"If you can. Or anyone else who might frequent the area at night. The police spoke to another man who goes by the name of Butch. He was intoxicated at the time, so they didn't give much credence to what he said. It didn't help that he claimed he saw an otherworld figure standing by the body. See if you can run him down too."

"Piece of cake."

"Be careful. Make sure you have your phone with you. And don't take any unnecessary risks."

"Don't worry about me, doll. I can hold my own. Standard rate?" Sal peeled her banana and took a huge bite, leaving a bit on the tip of her nose.

"Sal, here." I handed her a napkin and motioned toward my nose. She managed to smear the foam on her upper lip across her cheek. "Still there. Give it another shot."

She wiped her nose again and tucked the napkin into her coat pocket.

"Yeah, standard rate." I slid an envelope with five twenties across the table to her. "Here's a few bills in case you need to loosen somebody's memory. I'll send you an email with the exact location Barrett's body was discovered and the description of her car, which was found parked on Third Avenue."

"You lookin' for the gun?"

"No. Cops already have the gun. Barrett was still wearing her jewellery when she was found, all sixty-thousand-dollars' worth, but no sign of a purse or wallet."

Sal whistled. "That says something, don't it."

"It sure does."

I left Sal at the café working on a second muffin and latte. I worried that she sometimes took better care of her cats than herself. The likelihood that any of the homeless individuals who had been in the vicinity of the murder had seen anything useful was slim. Sal had a better chance of finding them than just about anyone else. Her side hustle picking bottles made her a familiar face to those who lived on the streets. My eyes suddenly prickled with tears. Who'd keep an eye on Sal if I moved on?

THIRTY

IF ALL WENT WELL today, Sherrie would be out on bail by this evening, but she wouldn't be heading home. Neil told me Ben Langcaster didn't want her home, as her presence would draw reporters to their house, and he was worried their son would get caught in the ruckus. Sherrie's sister-in-law had stepped up to say Sherrie could stay with her.

With Sal trying to hunt down possible witnesses to Kate's murder, I turned my attention back to the Langcasters' security video of a woman entering their house under the guise of being a Green Energy rep. I climbed into my car and headed back to Sherrie and Ben's neighbourhood.

A quick survey of the neighbourhood confirmed what I suspected. Although only six homeowners of the twelve houses on Sherrie Langcaster's block were home this morning, the ones I spoke with hadn't been visited by a Green Energy rep.

An older woman who lived across the street from the Langcasters did tell me that she had noticed a black SUV with tinted windows driving around in the weeks before Sherrie's arrest. She said she almost called the police one time when she came home and found it idling in front of the Langcasters' house. But when she went across the street to ask them what they were doing in the area, the car took off. Unfortunately, she didn't catch a plate or recognize the make of the car.

My head was spinning by the time I reached the office. I ducked into the small café and bought a coffee and a spinach, feta, and chicken panini. No telling how long I'd be at the office. Upstairs, I managed to keep my coffee upright while I unlocked the door. I could hear voices across the hall. Florence must be running a class today.

I made my way into the back office and set my coffee and sandwich down on the desk. I now had less than six weeks to vacate the premises, but it would take me less than an hour to pack up my computer and belongings. All the furniture, except for the round table and chairs, had come with the place. I'd probably just leave it behind, unless Florence could make use of it.

I retrieved my flip chart paper from where I stored it behind the filing cabinet and a roll of masking tape from what had been Gab's desk and got to work.

Two hours later I sat down at my desk and unwrapped the panini. I took a bite and stared at the wall, now covered with flip chart paper.

Across the top of each sheet, I had written what I considered to be the most promising premises or explanations for Kate's murder. They included robbery gone bad, financial gain through inheritance, life insurance, or business, and blackmail. Next to them, I had written love and lust. This not only covered the idea that Kate might have been murdered by Ben's wife but also the possibility that Kate's husband had a change of heart about sharing his wife with others. Or perhaps there was already someone new in Cole's life who wanted him for herself.

Next up was hatred or revenge, payback for perceived wrongs, or even the result of a psychosis—drug-induced or otherwise. I had also considered the possibility that Kate had been an unintended victim—simply a case of wrong place, right time, but I scrubbed the idea as the evidence we had, however meagre, didn't fit that scenario.

I listed everything we knew about Kate's murder down the left side of my chart and then added a plus sign or a negative sign under each of the premises at the top. A plus sign if the item or information could support the theory and negative if it opposed the hypothesis. The chart had a lot of blanks, which showed me where I needed to dig deeper to either confirm or eliminate one or more of these theories.

Even though I had yet to follow up on Todd's uncle's statement that his nephew had been out of town when Kate was killed, I put Todd Paquet on the bottom of my list of suspects. Sure, he could have killed Kate in anger over rescinding his art scholarship, but nothing concrete supported that theory. The item that really negated his involvement was the use of Sherrie's gun.

Every time I studied the chart, I kept coming back around to one sticking point—Sherrie's gun. The prosecutor would argue that the simplest answer was the best answer, and that the simplest answer was that Sherrie had used her gun to kill her husband's lover.

The gun was found a short distance from Kate's body. If Sherrie didn't kill Kate, someone had taken a lot of trouble to make it look like she did. Which meant they also would have had to have known her husband was cheating on her with Kate. Otherwise, what would Sherrie's motive have been?

The bigger question was why anyone would want to frame Sherrie. There's the obvious reason, of course—killers don't want to get caught. But most focus on establishing a watertight alibi and take great care not to leave any evidence behind. Framing someone takes added effort and didn't make much sense. Unless whoever murdered Kate was trying to kill two birds with one stone.

The minute that thought entered my head my mind raced with questions. Who would be the other intended victim? Ben lost his lover, and now his wife was charged with her murder. Could Kate's murder be a form of revenge against Ben? Or Cole?

Cole's ex-wife told me he was the kind of man who got whatever he went after, no matter what it took. Maybe Cole had known his old buddy was sleeping with his wife. Despite his claims of an open marriage, he might have seen it as an act of betrayal. Kate's murder could have been a way to keep his future finances intact, and framing Sherrie for the murder payback for Ben's lack of loyalty.

Neil was right. It always came back to the gun, and we had to show how it could have gotten into the killer's hands. Perhaps Elaine Gray had been hired to steal Sherrie's gun. Which raised the next question—who knew Sherrie had a gun?

Then there was Sherrie's claim that she found Ben's T-shirt, covered in blood, tucked away in a sports bag behind their garbage bin. Odd that she would bring it up, knowing that attention would turn to Ben. Was she trying to make it look like Ben killed Kate? It wouldn't be the first time I wondered if her call to me, saying that she was worried Ben would hurt someone with her missing gun, was part of her plan to set me up to bear witness to her lies after her own attempt to run him down failed. Assuming her reason for trying to run him down was linked to her suspicions of infidelity. Which also meant that she would have known about his affair before she hired me. Could she have done so in hopes that I would reveal his mistress' name?

I opened my desk drawer and rummaged until I found a half bottle of Advil. I took two tablets, hoping to dull my throbbing headache. I realized how little we had in the way of evidence to substantiate any of these theories.

If we were going to counter the prosecution's assertion that Sherrie Langcaster killed Kate Barrett, there were three pieces of information I needed to follow up on. Why had a woman entered Sherrie's house posing as a rep from Green Energy and was it indeed someone named Elaine Gray? Next, who else knew about Ben's affair with Kate Barrett? And lastly, who benefited from Kate Barrett's death?

THIRTY-ONE

I PULLED OVER TO the curb just as my car shuddered and died. I checked the gas gauge and tried to restart it but was met with a clicking noise. Sounded like the battery was dead, or maybe it was just a poor connection. Gab had warned me when I bought it off her that the Mustang was on its last legs. She had wanted to send it to the scrap yard, but I convinced her to sell it to me for the equivalent amount the scrap dealer would have paid her.

I climbed out of the Mustang and walked up the sidewalk to the modern three-storey townhouse. I had called ahead to say I would be stopping by. An East Asian woman with short grey hair answered the door. As soon as I told her my name, she pulled me inside, and peered up and down the street before shutting the door.

"I've already had reporters calling the house, looking for Sherrie, but I told them I don't know where she is. We don't need the media parked outside, watching our every move."

"No one does." I followed her past an office at the front of the house and down a short hallway into the main living space which combined kitchen, dining, and family rooms. Sherrie was sitting at the kitchen table drinking tea.

"Oh my gosh, Jorja." She jumped up and gave me a hug. "I haven't had a chance to thank you yet so thank you." She turned to her sister-in-law, whose name was Soo Jin. "I don't know what I would have done if Jorja hadn't been there for me. She's the reason I have the best lawyer in town."

"I'm sure you would have made out all right, but I'm glad I could help."

"Would you like some tea, Jorja? I have green tea, black, and Chinese oolong."

"Thank you, Soo Jin, but I've been in meetings and drinking coffee all day. I'm afraid I couldn't drink another drop."

"I'll take Koji Lee for a walk and leave you ladies to talk." At the sound of her name, a cream-and-brown Shih Tzu waddled into the room. Soo Jin scooped up the dog, making kissing noises, and carried her off.

"Your sister-in-law seems nice."

"She's more like a sister to me than sister-in-law. My brother was so lucky to have her in his life. You'd never guess that she has a PhD in biomedical research and a doctorate in cellular medicine. She's on sabbatical this year."

"Wow. Smart lady. And how are you doing?"

"I'm happy to be out of that place even though I have to wear this thing." She lifted a foot so I could see the ankle monitor. "I can't believe this is happening to me. It's like I'm in a nightmare, but I can't wake up."

"Well, hang in there. Neil has a great reputation."

"He's been so kind. I mean it. I can't thank you enough for finding him for me."

"I'd like to ask you some questions, if you don't mind."

"Not at all. Shoot." She grimaced as she said the word.

I pulled out my phone and brought up the picture Lennie had sent me. "You said no one had been in your home between the time you last saw your gun and then noticed it missing. But later I discovered someone did enter your house. This person." I turned the phone so she could see. "Looks like someone from the gas company, Green Energy."

"Oh wow. I guess I forgot about her."

"What did she want? You didn't book a service call, did you?"

"No. She said they were offering their customers a free safety check. To make sure there were no gas leaks or potential for leaks in any of our gas appliances. You know, like the furnace, and water heaters, and all the things using gas in the house."

"So, you let her in. What did she do inside? Did she go upstairs?"

"Yes. I was in the middle of baking a cake for the soccer team's annual outdoor dinner, so I told her to go ahead. She went into the basement first. Then later she came up and asked if there were any fireplaces upstairs and I told her there was one in the primary bedroom." Sherrie's eyes widened and she leaned forward. "You think she could have taken my gun?"

"It's a possibility."

"Why would someone from the gas company take my gun?"

"She no longer works for the gas company, hasn't worked for Green Energy in over a year. You don't recognize her, do you? Did she look familiar at all?"

"No. I didn't get a good look at her though. She was wearing a ballcap and didn't take it off when she came into the house." Sherrie stared at the photo again.

"But it was a woman?"

"I...I'm pretty sure. Her ID photo was of a woman."

"Is there any possibility it was a man?"

She lifted her hand to her mouth. "Gosh, maybe. I normally wouldn't have let her in...it's just that the cake was almost ready to come out of the oven." Her words tapered off.

"That's okay. But you saw this person up close. How tall were they? What about hair colour, distinguishing marks?"

"She or he was tall, maybe even taller than you by a few inches. I didn't notice anything else. She had short hair, but I suppose it could have been long but pulled back into a ponytail." Sherrie's eyebrows squished together as she tapped her index finger to her lips. "The more I think about it, it was a woman. She had brown hair. The eyebrows were brown. And she had grey eyes."

"Grey eyes?"

"Yes. At first, I thought they were blue. But when she was leaving, I saw that they were grey."

That might help. Grey eye colour was pretty rare. "Anything else."

"No. Like I said, I went back into the kitchen. When she was done, she called out from the front door. I went to let her out, but she already had the door open when I got there. That's when I noticed her eyes."

"Okay. Now, this is important, Sherrie. Could there have been anyone else in the house in the time between when you last saw your gun and when you discovered it missing? A housekeeper, a friend of your son's, your husband's co-worker, a neighbour. Anyone?"

"No. No one. I'm positive."

"Did you leave the house unattended? Say, to run across the street to get the mail, or to talk to a neighbour, or to speak to someone who was asking for directions?"

It took Sherrie longer to answer this time. "I did go get the mail a few times from our box down the street. I couldn't have been gone more than a minute or two. I didn't stop to talk to anyone. One time I saw a black car, idling just down the street from us. I couldn't see who was inside. The car had tinted windows."

"A car? What kind?"

"It was black. Some sort of SUV. Or maybe a crossover—I don't see much difference between those two."

"You saw this car once, or a bunch of times?"

"Just once."

Cars came and went all the time. At least in my neighbourhood. "What made you notice this particular car?"

"I don't know." Her forehead wrinkled, and she pulled at her bottom lip. She lifted her eyes to mine. "I...I guess I thought I recognized it."

"Whose car did you think it was?"

"I...I don't know." She shook her head. "I must have been mistaken."

This was classic Sherrie, doubting herself, questioning and second-guessing everything. "It doesn't matter if you think you're wrong. Let me check it out anyway."

"Now that I think about it, it doesn't make sense." She laughed nervously. "Silly, but when I saw the car, I thought it belonged to Cole Barrett. But that's ridiculous. I don't know if I've ever even seen him driving a car, so why would I think it was his?" Her gaze clouded as her eyes turned to her inward thoughts.

I left Sherrie feeling no more optimistic than I'd felt this morning. If her memory could be relied on, no one other than the people who lived there had been in the house except for this woman posing as a Green Energy safety inspector. I hoped Neil wasn't planning to put Sherrie on the stand at her trial. She became flustered whenever she was questioned or even when someone asked her to elaborate on something she said.

I climbed into my car and tried starting it but was met with the same clicking noise. I got out and googled reliable mechanics. An ad popped up for a garage in Marda Loop. It was a fair distance away, but their ad said it was run by two brothers who stood behind their work and offered a whopping six-month guarantee on any repairs, so I called the number

I thought about the SUV Sherrie had seen in the neighbourhood. A neighbour of hers also mentioned seeing an SUV idling in front of the Langcasters' house. Could it have belonged to Cole Barrett? I made a note to find out what kind of vehicle he drove. An hour later, my car had been towed to the shop and the tow truck driver had given me a lift to the nearest C-Train station.

The Advil I had taken earlier had long worn off by the time I got home. I dragged myself across the room and collapsed on the couch. It had been a long-assed day and I had little to show for it. So much so that feelings of ineptness were creeping in. I eyed the bottle of scotch sitting on the counter across the room. *Like that's going to help.* The voices in my head started their usual argument about my drinking, the louder one insisting I was stronger than this. After a few minutes, I got up and poured myself a glass. I took it with me into the bedroom, avoiding eye contact with the image in the mirror standing next to the dresser.

THIRTY-TWO

It was late afternoon by the time I arrived in the Langcasters' neighbourhood. My late-day start hadn't all been for naught though. My car was roadworthy again, and while I waited for it to be repaired, a man who had worked with Elaine Gray at Green Energy had contacted me. Although he hadn't seen Elaine since she left the company, he told me she was really into cosplay and suggested I check with some of the cosplay groups in Calgary. The other piece of information he offered up was that her favourite character was Katniss Everdeen from the Hunger Games. It wasn't much, but it might help me to find her.

I had spent an hour on the internet and found two local cosplay groups that sounded promising. One was located in town; the other had an Airdrie address. Neither of their websites listed member names.

I started with the Calgary Cosplay Society. Unlike the cosplay group in Airdrie, their website listed their Board of Directors. I contacted the Membership Director, Tula Thisbe. Although she couldn't give out member names, she had been very helpful once I explained why I was looking for Elaine Gray. She suggested that I might drop by the Pumphouse Theatre this evening, where a group of volunteers would be building stage props for their upcoming Who You Gonna Call: Ghostbusters charity event. Someone there might know Elaine or how I could find her.

Now, I realized my timing to the Langcasters' neighbourhood couldn't have turned out better. People were slowly returning home from school, work, or running errands. A woman six houses down from Sherrie and Ben's house pulled up to the curb just as I walked up to her door. I waited while she climbed out of the car and un-buckled her toddler from the car seat in back.

"Hi there. Can I help you?" she called out, as the small boy raced up the sidewalk.

"I hope so. My name is Jorja Knight, and I'm a private investi-gator. Two of your neighbours noticed a black SUV idling on the street. They're concerned someone could be watching the comings and goings in the neighbourhood, maybe planning a break-in. I'm canvassing the area to see if anyone else noticed the vehicle. It was here the week before last and noticed even prior to that."

"Golly. I don't recall seeing a vehicle like that. An SUV?"

"Yes. Newer model. Black, with tinted windows."

"No. Billie, stay there." She climbed the steps to the house and unlocked the door. As soon as it opened, the little boy ran inside. "He always runs in to see his hamster after daycare."

"Aww. That's so sweet."

She paused at the door and checked the street. "You said you're a private investigator?"

"Yes." I pulled out a card and handed it to her. "I couldn't help but notice when you pulled up that you have a dash cam. Any chance you could check it for me? I have the dates your neighbours noticed the vehicle. It should be quick to find the dates on your dash-cam video."

"Okay...well, come in."

She pulled her phone out and set her purse on the floor just inside the door. "I don't often look at the dash-cam video...right, here's the app." She opened the app for me and held out her phone.

It took me less than a minute to find the dates I was looking for. The first date didn't show anything on the street, but the second date showed a black Escalade. "There it is." I turned her phone so she could see what I was seeing.

"Oh my gosh."

"I'll just check the other dates, if you don't mind." I didn't have a third date, but I wanted to check the window of time that had been missing on the Langcasters' security video in case her dash cam had picked up anything useful. I slowed the frames as I got closer to the dates I was looking for. A young man appeared, carrying a sports bag. He crossed the street, glanced over his shoulder, and stuffed the bag into a garbage bin standing at the side of the road, ready to be picked up by the garbage truck. Then he crossed the street and disappeared from view. *Well, what do you know.*

"You find anything else?"

"Actually, yes." I noted the date at the bottom of the video, scrolled back, and pulled out my cell phone. "I'm just going to copy down the few licence plate digits I can make out." I didn't mention my interest in the young man stuffing a bag into a garbage bin.

"What are you going to do now? Has that car been back?"

"Not in the last ten days or so." I jotted down the four licence plate digits the dash cam managed to capture and noted the small scrape on the left side of the bumper. "There's only a partial plate but I'll try to run it. The fact that it's a big expensive Cadillac will help."

"Should we be worried?"

"Someone entered one of your neighbour's homes under false pretenses a couple weeks ago. Nothing was taken." A small lie, but I didn't want to rattle her further. It's probably nothing, but we'll check it out. Is there any way you can send me a copy of the video from April twenty-second to May fifteenth?" I handed her phone back.

"I'm sure there's a way, but I don't know how. I can ask my husband when he gets home."

"I'd appreciate it. You have my email address and phone number on my card. I can't thank you enough."

There was one other car within sight of the Langcaster house that was equipped with a dash cam, but the owner refused to share the video with me, saying if the police wanted to see it, he would be happy to share.

I walked back to my car and drove to the other end of the street, turned the corner, and parked. I would need to confirm that the young man I had seen on the video was Sherrie's son, but if it was it might explain what happened to the sports bag with the bloody shirt Sherrie claimed she found at the side of their garage. Maybe she wasn't as delusional as she sounded that day.

THIRTY-THREE

Parking was almost nonexistent at the Pumphouse Theatre, so I parked on Tenth Avenue and followed the walking path across the railway tracks. I crossed a small lot reserved for staff and people with limited mobility, noting several vehicles there.

The all-volunteer members of the Calgary Cosplay Society used their love of cosplay to raise funds for local charities through events, raffles, and the sale of promotional items. Last year they raised an impressive two hundred and sixty-two thousand dollars.

The main doors were open, so I let myself into the red-brick building. I paused at the small ticket booth and concession stand just inside the main doors and the woman working there directed me to the Victor Mitchell Theatre on the lower level.

I stopped at the entrance. Several people were chatting and laughing while they painted a huge sign depicting the Ghostbuster logo. A man came up behind me, carrying a paper tray and four coffees. "Can I help you?"

"I hope so. I'm looking for Elaine Gray. Would you happen to know if she's here tonight?"

"She's here. She's the one in the purple smock, there on the left."

"Thank you." I followed him as he continued toward the group, bearing coffee.

"Lani—someone to see you," he called out as we closed in on the group.

The blonde in the purple smock laughed at something one of her fellow workers said. She put down her paintbrush and stood. "Yes?" She looked at me quizzically.

"Hi, Elaine? My name is Jorja Knight. I'm a private detective. Do you have a minute to talk?"

Elaine hopped down from the low stage. "What's this about?"

I could see this wasn't the woman who had come to Sherrie Langcaster's house, but she definitely resembled the woman on the Green Energy photo ID she had been carrying. We moved off to one side.

"I'm investigating the murder of Kate Barrett. I'd like to ask you some questions."

"Kate Barrett? That's the woman who was found murdered downtown, right? Why do you want to talk to me?"

"You were employed at Green Energy, until last year, correct?"

"Yes, that's right." She glanced over her shoulder at her fellow cosplayers still laughing and talking as they worked. She turned back to me, her eyes wide with worry. "I left at the end of March, last year. What's this got to do with anything?"

"Did you turn in your ID card when you finished your employment at Green Energy?"

Her face went red, and she stiffened. "I called in sick my last three days. I got a letter the following week asking me to return the ID card, but my boyfriend and I were moving apartments, and everything was packed up. I figured I'd drop it off once I got everything unpacked. But I don't remember seeing it…and then I guess I just forgot about it. Don't tell me they've sent a private detective to retrieve their stupid ID card."

"No, I'm not working for Green Energy. So, you never gave or lent your photo ID card to anyone after you left?"

Her head reeled back. "No. Why would I do that?" Now that she knew I wasn't accusing her of anything serious, she was growing defensive.

"One more question, please." I pulled out my phone and located the photo of the woman who had gained access to Sherrie's house using Elaine's photo ID. "Do you recognize or know this woman?" I handed her my phone.

Elaine peered at the screen. "No. Hey, that's my ID. How'd she get it?"

"That's what I'm trying to find out." I took my phone back. "Looks like this woman used your ID to gain access to my client's house. I checked with Green Energy; they don't know who she is either or why she'd have your ID card."

"I swear, I don't know anything about this. Someone must have found my card and used it. Maybe I dropped it, or it got left behind at our last apartment."

I left with the address of Elaine's last apartment. On the off chance that the person now living there might have found the photo ID and could tell me what happened to it next, I went to the apartment. The woman who lived there now was Afro-Canadian and well into her sixties. She told me the previous owners had left behind some old plant pots on the balcony, an old pot lid, and a few bits of kitchenware, but a lanyard with a photo ID hadn't been among them.

I slid into my car, laid my head back, and closed my eyes. It had been a long day. My feet hurt, my head hurt, my bank account was five hundred and ninety-one dollars lighter, and I couldn't remember when I had last eaten. Worse yet, my attempt to find the woman who had entered Sherrie's house had just hit a roadblock. Not just any roadblock but one of those massive rockslides that take out a good chunk of highway and strand motorists for days. The Elaine Gray I had just found was three inches shorter than me and had bright blue eyes. She wasn't the woman who had entered Sherrie's house.

My phone buzzed. I turned my head and opened one eye. Sal's name and number were displayed on the screen.

THIRTY-FOUR

Sitting up took more energy than it should have. I picked my phone up off the car seat next to me.

"Hey, Sal."

"I got someone you'll want to talk to."

"Yeah?" I struggled to full upright position.

"I told her you might make it worth her while if she stuck around till you got here."

"Where are you?"

"The old Greyhound station."

"I'll be there in ten."

Why did I have to make it worth her while? What the hell had Sal done with the money I had given her? It was already growing dark, and my stomach rumbled. I took a deep breath. No point being peeved with Sal. She just might have found something to salvage the day.

Getting to the old bus station took me longer than ten, since Ninth Avenue was one way going in the wrong direction. I pulled into the parking lot keeping my eyes peeled for Sal.

The building housing the former Greyhound bus station was deserted. After Greyhound pulled their services out of western Canada, the building had been used for a variety of purposes, the most recent being a Covid-19 testing and vaccination centre. But now it stood empty waiting for the city to decide its fate.

I drove along the east side of the building and circled around to the back. Two figures sat on the single step in front of the boarded-up doors. I pulled up, killed the lights, and got out of the car. Sal stood up; the figure next to her remained sitting.

"Hey Sal."

"Took you long enough. This here is River."

"Hi River, I'm Jorja."

"Go ahead, girl, tell the boss lady what you told me."

River swung her body forward, creating the momentum she needed to stand. She was a big girl, shorter but heavier than me. She had that don't-mess-with-me look on her face, and I worried she might be holding a gun in her oversized pink bomber jacket.

"You bring the bacon?"

"How much bacon we talking?"

"A hundred."

I cursed silently, dug into my jean pockets, and pulled out all the cash I had on me. I peeled off two twenties and handed them to her. "I'll give you the rest once I hear what you've got."

Her eyes shifted to Sal and Sal nodded. "She'll pay. Tell her."

"I don't know nothing about no lady that got murdered. But last week, I was doing my rounds, you know, and I found a bag. Not one of them cheap vegan things...real leather."

"A purse?"

"Yeah. And not one of them bitty things. Bigger. Orange colour, Hermes."

"An Hermes bag. Any ID in it?"

Her eyes shifted to Sal, then back to me. "No. Just makeup, a mirror, and stuff like that."

Sal cleared her throat.

"Okay. A credit card. But I didn't use it."

"And the name on the credit card?"

She kicked at the pavement with the toe of her runner and stared at the ground. "Kate Barrett."

I took a sharp breath. "You still have the bag and credit card?"

"Nah. Pawned it. Bastard gave me two C notes. A bag like that's worth thousands."

"What about the credit card and the rest of the purse contents?"

River shrugged. "Sold the mirror for five bucks to a kid on the street. Tossed the card. It's no good without the pin."

"Where did you find this bag?"

"Back there." She nodded her head to the right. "Dumpster behind the Westin."

"When was this?"

"Last Thursday."

"Okay. Thursday." That was over a week after Kate's murder. "Was it near the top of the bin, or further down?"

"No, man, it was right on top. If I didn't take it, sure as hell someone would've." River shook her head and scowled.

If the bag belonged to Kate, why would it be at the top of the dumpster? But I couldn't ignore the details River was giving me.

"Where did you pawn it?"

"Pawn shop on seventh...by The Bay."

"You still got the ticket?"

Her eyebrows knit together. Her tone was still argumentative. "You kidding? I don't have the scratch to get it back. Besides, that asswad's probably sold it."

"You willing to talk to the police about this?"

"No cops. I told her." She jerked her head toward Sal. "The cops find me, I'm not saying a word."

"Okay, no cops." I peeled off a five-dollar bill and handed her the rest of my cash. "What if I want to talk to you again. Where do I find you?"

She stuffed the bills into the back pocket of her baggy, wide-legged jeans. "I'll be around."

"Okay. Thanks for the info, River. Stay safe."

She ambled off, hands in her jacket, the hems of her jeans dragging on the pavement.

"Watcha think?"

"Well, it would explain why the police didn't find a purse on the body or in the car. I'm puzzled by why it turned up so late. I suspect the dumpster behind the Westin gets filled up pretty quick."

"You think she's lyin', doll? Hope I didn't just waste your moolah."

"No, no, Sal. It's fine. I'll check out the pawn shop tomorrow."

I gave Sal a ride to her place and then headed home. I believed that River took the bag to a pawn shop, I just didn't believe her story about where she found it nor that there had been little of value inside.

THIRTY-FIVE

Urban Gems was wedged between a used furniture shop and a tiny no-name convenience store. Metal grates covered the front window and the door. Both were peppered with signs proclaiming the store was monitored by twenty-four-hour security. I opened the door and stepped inside, the air rank with stale cigarette smoke. A bald man with tattoo sleeves covering both arms sat behind one of the counters. "Can I help you?"

My eyes swept over the ancient Tiffany lamps, the shelves crammed with cameras, stereos, and electronic equipment, and settled on the glass counter in front of the man. I pulled my business card from my pocket and handed it to him.

"Name's Jorja Knight. I'm investigating a murder." My eyes flitted to the knives displayed next to rows of watches, rings, and gold chains. "I'm trying to track down a women's purse. Possibly an Hermes. Orange in colour. Girl says she brought one in here last week."

He rubbed the white whiskers sprouting from his chin and made a sucking noise through clenched teeth. "Don't recall no purse like that. She have her ticket?"

"She says she's lost it."

He shook his head, like he'd heard that story a few hundred times. "Can't help you. I take in electronics, gold, jewellery, swords, ornamental stuff like that. Purses, shoes, clothing—that stuff doesn't move."

"So, no purse?"

"Nope."

I took one last glance around the store and stepped back outside. One of them was lying, but given the contents of the pawn shop, my bet was on River. I called Sal on the off chance she was downtown. She answered on the fifth ring.

"Hi Sal. Where are you?"

"McDonald's on Eighth Street—near the train station."

"I'm east of The Bay. If you're going to be there a while, I'll come your way."

"See you when you get here."

I crossed the street and a minute later boarded a westbound C-Train. I knew the McDonald's location. It was a prime hangout for drug buyers and their pushers. There were always a handful of blitzed burnouts hanging outside. The cops showed up every so often and ran them off, but they inevitably returned, like homing pigeons.

I stepped past a young man sitting on the sidewalk, his back against the store wall, his legs sprawled out in front of him. His eyes were open, but he was somewhere else. Sal was sitting inside, nursing a coffee. I lowered myself into the chair across from her.

"Got anything new for me, Sal?"

"Maybe. I found the kid the cops talked to, the one who said he saw a figure from another world standing next to Barrett's body the night she was popped."

"You did? What did he have to say?"

"Not much. That's him, there." She pointed a thumb over her shoulder.

"The one lying comatose against the wall?"

"That's the one. Kid's a meth head, but he's been messing with some shit called White Lightning. It's a lot like meth, 'xcept it can cause paranoia and hallucinations."

"Great. I suppose that explains why he thought he saw an otherworldly creature. Did you manage to talk to him?"

"Nah. A couple guys told me he's been running around saying he saw a faceless creature and now it's coming after him."

My momentary elation turned to dust. "Great. He's not going to make a good witness."

"Yeah, but get this. Those two guys I was talking to said they were at some stash house last week and a guy was trying to trade an orange ladies' handbag for a bump."

I perked up. "Okay, you had me at orange handbag."

"They didn't know if there were any takers, but the guy's name is Josh."

"Josh. Does he have a last name?"

"My guys didn't know it. But seems our gal River was there as well."

"No kidding. I was at the pawnshop this morning. The one she mentioned—Urban Gems. The guy there said no one brought in a bag like that."

Sal shook her head. "There's no honour among thieves anymore. That skank took your money and lied to us."

"Looks like it."

"Maybe we should pay her another visit."

"You know where to find her?"

Sal squinted at the Ronald McDonald wall clock. "She works part time at the dry cleaners on Centre Street. Subs over the noon hour."

"Okay, let's go." Sal followed me outside.

I took a photo of the guy outside before we turned toward the C-Train station. I didn't think he'd be of any use to us, but it seemed like the prudent thing to do. Thirty minutes later, we were standing in front of the Laundry Palace in Chinatown. We didn't have to wait long.

Sal nudged me. "There she is."

I recognized the pink, satin bomber jacket, but today River had traded in the low-slung oversized jeans for a pair of black leggings and combat boots. A bright-yellow headband held back her mop of curly hair. She stopped in her tracks when she saw us, took a sharp look over her shoulder then back again. Several pedestrians pushed past her on the narrow sidewalk.

"Hi River." I closed the gap between us. "You want to talk to me, or the cops? Your choice."

River rolled her eyes. "You're going to make me late for work."

"Not if you talk fast. Now, about that orange Hermes bag you say you pawned. The guy at Urban Gems says he never took in a purse, not last week, not even last month."

"It wasn't Urban Gems...it was the other one."

"There is no other one downtown. Why'd you lie to us?"

We shifted closer until her back was up against the laundry's brick wall. "We're not leaving until we get some answers."

"Okay, okay. I didn't get the bag from the dumpster like I told you."

"No kidding. You got it from your buddy Josh, didn't you?"

Her eyes widened. "How'd ya know that?"

Sal cocked her head to one side. "What do you think detectives do, sweetheart?"

"I...okay, jeez."

"Okay jeez what?"

"I was at this party and my friend Josh was there. He had the bag. He was trying to flip it, but no one wanted it. The next morning, I went back. I gave him fifty bucks for it. I figured it was worth way more 'an that."

"Then what?"

"I took it home."

"What was in the bag?"

"Nothing."

"Come on, River, we're not stupid." Although I was feeling a bit stupid for believing her the first time.

"I told you. There was a credit card, some makeup, lipstick, a comb, shit like that."

"What else, River? What about the money, and the phone?"

"There was no money or phone. If there was, Josh probably kept it."

"How did he get the bag?"

"I dunno."

"Where is it now?"

She folded her arms across her chest. "I gave it to my roommate. She was going to throw me out. I owed her rent money."

"And the credit card, and all the other shit, as you call it?"

"I tossed the credit card. Sold everything else, fast. I don't need to be caught with some dead chick's bag."

"So, you knew whose bag it was."

"Josh did. He told me to get rid of it fast—that the cops would be looking for it."

"Who'd you sell the contents to?"

"I told you. Sold it to a kid for five bucks."

I groaned. "What kid?"

"I dunno. Just some kid. Now, come on—I'm going to get fired."

"We need your roommate's name and address and where this Josh lives, then you can go."

River's faced scrunched into a scowl. "I don't know where Josh lives. I only see him once in a while. I don't even know whose place we were at."

"Come on, River, it's us or the police. They don't need an address to find him."

River shook her head and mumbled her address and roommate's name. She swore she didn't know where Josh lived but she coughed up the address where the party had been held, the night she saw Josh trying to flip the bag.

We stepped aside as she shoved past us. "Hey, show some respect," Sal called after her.

Sal shifted her weight onto her good leg while I typed River's address into Google Maps. It was a kilometer north of where we were. I glanced over at Sal. "You up for a bus ride?"

THIRTY-SIX

RIVER'S ROOMMATE WAS A lot bigger than River, and meaner too. She and River occupied what appeared to be an illegal basement suite in a rundown fifties bungalow that hadn't seen maintenance in decades. I explained who we were and that we wanted to talk to her about the Hermes bag River had given her.

"She didn't *give* me no bag, you hear. She owes me three months rent. I took that bag off her and sold it on Marketplace. That bitch still owes me two and half months of rent."

"Who did you sell it to?"

"You never do a meetup on Marketplace? You post your shit and if someone wants it, they contact you and you make the exchange. Cash only. I don't want no bum cheques. There's too much of that floating around."

"Do you know where River got the bag?"

"She said she found it. That bitch better not be lying. I don't deal with no stolen shit."

"She told us she bought it off a guy named Josh at some party she went to last week. You wouldn't happen to know this guy, would you? We want to talk to him."

"Josh?" She rolled her eyes. "Dude's dead. OD'ed a few nights ago. That's why I don't do that shit."

Sal and I exchanged glances. *How convenient.* "Do you know Josh's last name, or where he lived?"

"Naw. I never caught a last name. There's a tripping tower on Seventeenth Ave. Someone there might know, but I don't go to them dope dens."

"Whereabouts on Seventeenth?"

"How would I know?" Her voice rose to a pitch.

"Did River happen to mention finding a phone or wallet?"

"Hell no. If she had, I'd have sold them with the damn bag."

"Okay, thanks." Sal and I turned and made our way up the rickety stairs to ground level. The roommate's voice followed us up the steps.

"You tell River I want my rent money, or she's gonna find her ass on the street."

Sal and I walked back to the bus stop. "What now, boss?"

"See if you can find anyone else who knew this Josh dude. I'll check with the DOAP team. Maybe they know something or heard about his death. How's your cash situation?"

"Down to forty."

Sal and I caught the bus back downtown. I stopped at an ATM and withdrew another hundred dollars for Sal and fifty for me. Drug users had a way of remembering things when you waved something green in front of their face.

After leaving Sal, I hiked back to the office. This case was in its second week, but we still didn't have anything that could keep Sherrie out of jail. Every time I grasped at a thread and pulled, it unravelled. All I had so far was a mystery woman who used a stolen photo ID card to enter Sherrie's house and possibly take her gun, an Hermes bag supposedly belonging to Kate Barrett, which surfaced momentarily before being snatched up by a faceless member of the general public, a dead drug user who could no longer tell us how the Hermes bag surfaced in the first place, and a meth head dabbling with a hallucinogenic called White Lightning who thought he was being chased by a faceless figure he saw the night of Kate Barrett's murder.

I updated the chart hanging on my wall and an hour later I was back in the Mustang heading home. My next step was to try to track down the black Escalade that neighbours had noticed on the Langcasters' street leading up to Kate's murder. Maybe it belonged to the woman who had entered the Langcasters' home using Elaine Gray's ID. With only four digits of an eight-digit licence plate visible on the dash-cam feed, I'd have a tough time locating it. If we could find someone who had known Josh, we might be able to learn where or how the Hermes bag ended up in his possession. But it was a long shot.

This case was driving me crazy. As Sherrie's defence lawyer, Neil didn't have to prove her innocence. The onus of proof lay with the prosecution. Too bad the prosecution had some pretty damning evidence.

THIRTY-SEVEN

After showering and catching five hours of shuteye, I was back at it. Remembering my lack of food consumption yesterday, I headed to my favourite breakfast place in Glenmore Landing. Ensconced in an armchair on the upper level of the café, with a breakfast burrito and a large coffee in front of me, I called Neil Trent.

He picked up on the second ring. "Can I call you back in twenty?"

"Absolutely."

The prosecutors' office seemed satisfied that they had Kate Barrett's killer. It wouldn't be long before they declared their investigation complete, which would shorten our time to build some sort of defence that wouldn't get blown out of the water on day one.

I wanted Sherrie to be innocent but pinning down someone else who could have wanted Kate Barrett dead was proving difficult. Maybe Cole had killed his wife to protect his future windfall. If he thought she might be gearing up to ask for a divorce or if he wanted one, he might have decided to get her out of the picture before his company's next acquisition. Husbands were always treated as potential suspects when their wives were murdered. So were boyfriends and secret lovers. We could speculate all we wanted, but evidence was sadly lacking. We couldn't even prove that the unidentified woman, posing as a Green Energy rep, had actually taken Sherrie's gun. I'd like to believe Sherrie when she said she had forgotten about the woman when I had asked earlier if anyone else but immediate family had been in the house between the time she last saw her gun and the shooting. But it's not something a normal person would forget, especially one facing a murder charge.

My phone rang just as I swallowed the last bite of my burrito.

"Hi Jorja. Sorry about that. How's it going?"

"It's going. Is this a good time to talk?"

"Good as any. What have you got?"

"It's been an interesting few days." I told Neil about the woman who had entered Sherrie's home and that I had traced the ID she used to a former Green Energy employee who lost her card over a year ago.

"Damn," Neil swore softly. "When are we going to catch a break."

"I haven't given up yet. I found some dash-cam footage showing an Escalade parked down the street from Sherrie's house and I have a partial plate. I'm hoping it belongs to the woman who entered Sherrie's house. The timing's about right."

"Hallelujah. Do you need help running down the plate? There can't be that many Escalades around with the digits you managed to catch."

"Thanks, Neil. If you can get me a list, I'll try tracking it down. One more thing. The dash-cam footage also shows a young man, whom I assume is Matt Langcaster, stuffing a sports bag into a neighbour's trash bin on May twelfth. I checked. The garbage was picked up later that same day."

It took Neil a moment to reply. "I'll talk to Sherrie and Ben again. Given what you've found, they might give me permission to talk to their son. Even if he confirms what Sherrie says she saw, we don't know whose blood it was. The husband can always claim that he got hit in the face playing squash and bled all over his shirt."

"Do you want me to do anything more about this sports bag?"

"Let's hold off on that for now. The garbage was picked up over two weeks ago. I'm not sure the police will want to send an army of officers in protective gear down to the landfill and spend thousands of dollars to search for something which may or may not be related to a murder."

"Yeah, I figured." Plus, it could backfire. For the defence to introduce evidence, the relevant material had to also be disclosed to the Crown. If we somehow managed to find the bag, and the blood proved to be Kate's, it could end up being the proverbial final nail in Sherrie's coffin.

"I'm also following up on an Hermes handbag that a girl says she bought off a friend, who has since died of a drug overdose. The bag supposedly had Kate Barrett's credit card in it but very little else. Some of her story doesn't quite add up though, so I'm still chasing it down. Might not lead anywhere."

"She still got the bag?"

"No. She gave it to her roommate in lieu of rent money she owes, and the roommate sold it through Facebook Marketplace. Cash. She says the credit card got tossed when they found they couldn't use it."

"Who found this bag and where?"

"That's not clear. The guy who overdosed told his friend that he found it. She originally told us that she found it in a dumpster about five blocks from where the body was discovered. I'll see if there are any CCTV cameras in the area that might have caught someone dumping or retrieving the bag."

"Might be the break we are looking for. If it's the vic's, why would the killer take the bag and then dump it? Or do you think a passerby noticed her, saw she was dead, and snatched the purse?"

"Maybe it had something in it that the killer wanted, and the bag was just a container that held it."

"Money?"

"Possibly. That or maybe information about something someone wanted. Maybe related to her husband's business dealings."

"I can't see Kate Barrett agreeing to meet someone she didn't know in a spot like that in the middle of the night."

I had already given this a lot of thought, so I didn't hesitate to share with Neil. "I agree. Either she knew whoever she went there to meet, or she was being blackmailed or otherwise threatened."

"Hmm. I like the threat angle. If she was bringing them information, they might have killed her once they had it. If she were being blackmailed, something must have gone wrong. Blackmailers don't usually kill their golden goose. Not unless they won't cooperate any longer. You said the guy who originally had or found the bag is dead?"

"Yeah. I'm not liking that he died from an overdose just days later."

"You think he knew something?"

"That or he was a loose end someone didn't want hanging around."

"You believe the girl who bought it off of him? That there was nothing inside?"

"She's already lied to my face twice, so no. If there was anything of interest inside, she'll be trying to figure out how to make a buck off it. Unless it was cash. But she still owes back rent and is facing eviction, so not sure. Of course, drug addicts don't always come up with the most rational of plans. I've got someone keeping an eye on her."

"Good work, Jorja."

"Thanks. Do we know what the prosecutor is chasing? Or have they stopped looking now that Sherrie's been charged?"

"I know they filed several ITOs, or Information To Obtain submissions, to obtain search warrants."

"Search warrants for what?"

"Kate Barrett's phone records and financial information, as well as her computers."

"Her personal finances and computers?"

"Yes. They've also asked for warrants to search records at her art gallery and finances related to the Rising Star Foundation."

"Wouldn't that imply that something has come up which makes them doubt how solid a case they have against Sherrie?"

"Maybe, maybe not. If they discover there's a large unexplained amount of money missing from her accounts, it might support the blackmail theory. If there is nothing there, it will solidify their assertion that Sherrie killed her husband's mistress out of jealousy. We'll eventually get the information through the disclosure process."

Neil and I disconnected after a few more minutes of conversation. I appreciated Neil's praise for the work I was doing but it didn't feel like I was making much progress at all.

As if I didn't already have enough swirling through my head, I got an email from Mike shortly after my call with Neil reminding me about our meeting with Willie tomorrow. It came with a twelve-page document outlining CanNet's future goals and plans.

I realized it wasn't just the case that was making me feel unsettled, off centre. My life was shifting. Part of me wanted to stand firm, stay the course. The other part was tentatively curious. The sensation brought back a memory from my childhood. A violent storm had approached our town, but instead of running inside as my mother urged, I had waited outside, a mixture of excitement and trepidation coursing through me. I watched and waited until the full fury of the tumult was upon me. Sometimes the rainstorms were welcome, but that particular storm ripped through the community, changing its shape forever. Another storm was brewing, but this time I had nowhere to hide.

THIRTY-EIGHT

Sebastian Gallagher was tall and fit, with dark, piercing blue eyes and a killer smile. He had the kind of good looks that make women like me wary, but he turned out to be as charming as he was handsome.

We were sitting in a small meeting room that faced out onto the parking lot of the building that housed his office. With all the niceties and banal chit chat out of the way, I got into the main reason for my visit.

"Your sister's murder wasn't the result of a random opportunistic shooting. Someone convinced her to go down to the Bow River, late at night. Someone went to a lot of trouble to obtain the murder weapon and then tossed it where it could be easily discovered. Your sister was still wearing expensive jewellery when she was found, which doesn't make it sound like a robbery."

Sebastian's brow furrowed and his eyes stared unseeingly out the window. He turned back to me. "But why? My sister never hurt or harmed anyone. She always gave more than she received back. Why would someone *plan* her murder?"

"I don't know, but I want to find out. Everybody I have talked to echoes your sentiments about Kate. She was kind, caring. Which is why I am starting to think it might be related to either her husband's business dealings or to something from her past."

"Cole Barrett has a way of rubbing people the wrong way. I think if someone wanted to get back at him for something he did, they would have targeted him. Hit him where it would hurt the most—his finances. Why kill Kate?"

"Can I ask you about your sister's finances? I assume she had a will. Do you know if she made any changes to it recently?"

"Kate's first will left all her assets to my father. When Kate got married, she changed her will and left everything to Cole. She updated her will again about a year ago. I know because I'm the executor."

"Was there anything driving her to change it?"

Sebastian tilted his head to one side. "I'd say no. Both her and Cole's financial situation had changed since they got married. It's good practice to keep these things current."

"Makes sense. Can you tell me who her beneficiaries are?"

"She left a third of her assets to her art foundation, a third to Cole, and a third to my two sons and our niece."

"Would you mind telling me what her assets were worth?"

"The lawyers and accountants are still working through all of her finances. She was well off but not extravagantly so. Our grandmother set up a trust fund for Kate and me and my brothers when she died. Kate used her money from the trust fund to back some of her husband's acquisitions. In turn she earned shares in those companies, which is why it's hard to give you a specific number.

There's a caveat in the will regarding those shares. They can't be sold without company approval. They're locked up until Encore grants permission to Kate's estate, or Encore becomes insolvent."

"Insolvent? As in bankrupt?"

"Yes. There's always a risk when one invests."

I remembered what Cole's ex-wife Oriana had told me. Had Cole Barrett found a way to line his pockets while leaving Kate holding interest in companies that were slated for demise in the longer term?

"I see. But if you had to come up with a rough figure for her assets outside her business investments?"

"I'd say with some stocks, hard assets like the building which houses her art gallery, her own investments, and personal items like jewellery, her car, and so forth...around eight or nine million."

I swallowed my surprise. It was a lot of money, but less than I had been expecting. "So, about three million to each of her three main beneficiaries."

"Yes—give or take."

"What about her house?"

"The house stays with Cole. He put a hefty down payment on it when they bought the place, but with the downturn in the real estate market, the remaining mortgage is almost as much as the current value of the property. The art foundation's third includes the art gallery. With proper management it'll keep generating the revenue it needs to pay for itself and fund the annual art scholarships. My niece and our sons won't have to worry about university tuition, when the time comes."

It was a lot of money to me, but it didn't change any of the beneficiaries lives significantly enough for them to have wished her dead. In fact, they might have gained more financially if she had been allowed to live a long, fruitful life.

"I can see why it'll take the accountants and lawyers time to sort it all out. Who knew the contents of her will?"

Sebastian shrugged. "I knew because she gave us an updated copy. Her lawyer, of course, and probably Cole. Beyond that, I'm not sure anyone else did. It's not a topic you get into over a lunch or afterwork drinks."

I sat back, disappointed. "You were close with your sister. Did she tell you anything? Was she worried about anything?"

Sebastian took a deep breath and blew it out noisily, then shook his head as if he couldn't believe what he was about to say himself.

"I can't help thinking that her death is related to her past."

"Her past? I don't understand."

"Katie was kidnapped when she was a child. My father paid the ransom, but she wasn't returned right away. The perpetrators were never caught."

The muscles in my entire body tensed. My brain went into overdrive.

Sebastian took a sharp breath and his eyes widened. "What if she saw one of her kidnappers—recognized him? It's possible, isn't it?"

I tried to process what he was saying. "I suppose. The police are looking for the most likely motives for her murder. But sometimes what's not so obvious ends up being the answer."

"Exactly. It's like that in mineral exploration. You gather what data you can, but then you have to go looking for more information, and usually that's not going to be found where everyone else is looking."

It took me a minute to digest this new scenario. "But the way she was killed, and how. The killer would have had to have known a fair bit about Kate, details of her life now." I was thinking about Kate's affair with Ben Langcaster, Sherrie's gun, and how all of it could fit in.

Sebastian clasped his hands together and rested them on the table between us. He leaned forward, and his eyes met mine. "I've always thought that the kidnappers knew Kate, knew our family. We just couldn't prove it."

THIRTY-NINE

I DIDN'T NEED TO coax the story out of Sebastian. The details were clearly etched in his mind and fell from his lips like a waterfall.

"I wasn't there when she was taken. I was away at university, McGill, working on my PhD, but I'll tell you what I know. It was a school day, a Thursday. Katie was in grade one and her class was preparing for their spring pageant, so Katie had been going to school early so that they could practice their songs. My mother dropped Katie off at Elbow Valley Elementary that morning, like she did most mornings. After dropping Katie off, my mother met some friends for breakfast, ran a few errands, and got home close to noon. She unpacked the groceries and went upstairs to take a nap. She was having a lot of headaches back then.

"By the time my mother woke up, it was already close to when she should be going to pick Katie up from school. When she went downstairs, she noticed there was a phone message on the answering machine. The message was from the school, wondering why Katie was absent."

I felt myself flinch. "Oh no. What did she do?"

"She jumped in her vehicle and drove to the school. The admin people told her Katie hadn't shown up for class that day. My mother was frantic. They called the police. My mother never forgave herself. She had been out with friends and then home napping while her baby was being terrorized somewhere."

"Your poor mother. Guilt is one of those emotions that can be all consuming." I knew guilt. Like a virus, it can lie in the body undetected for periods of time and erupt with a vengeance when we least expect.

Sebastian nodded. "It did consume my mother. I think it was the trigger that caused her health to deteriorate." He paused for a minute, deep in thought.

"I can see that it's left a lasting scar. It must be hard to talk about."

Sebastian swallowed and went on. "My father called me that evening to let me know Katie was missing. My parents got a phone call the next day. Just three words. Five million dollars. I arrived home later that evening. The police were at the house. They had set up equipment to record and trace the kidnapper's phone calls."

"What about your brothers. Were they home as well?"

Sebastian's jaw tensed and he shifted in his chair. "Rupert, my youngest brother, wasn't living at home at the time, but he was in Calgary. He was attending U of C. Michael, my other brother, was teaching English in Malaysia at the time."

I nodded. "Sorry. Please, go on."

"The second phone call didn't come in until three days later. We all thought something even worse had happened—that maybe Katie was dead. My father had started to get the money together. It's hard to come up with that kind of cash. The police were advising him to not pay the ransom. My mother insisted he pay. She was beside herself with grief and anger and guilt all rolled into one."

"I can't even imagine what your family must have been going through. And poor Kate. She must have been terrified."

His chest hitched as he took a breath. "On the second call, the kidnapper said, 'Get the money. You have five days.' That's all. The police had coached my dad, told him to try to keep them talking, but he never got that chance. It's like they knew the call was being traced. The police told my dad that the next time they called he should demand proof of life, and to repeat it, if necessary, even if it meant talking over them."

"So, by then, your sister had been gone over a week."

"Yes." Sebastian got up and walked over to the coffee station at the back of the room. "I need a coffee. Would you like one? Or a water?"

"Thank you, Sebastian, but I'm fine."

Sebastian returned with a mug of coffee, took a sip, and set it down. "My father convinced me to go back to university. My dissertation was coming up and he knew that I had to prepare. I didn't want to go but he said there was nothing I could do by staying. My mother was heavily sedated and kept to her room. My father was on his cell phone trying to get the cash together while keeping the landline clear at the same time. I did what I could. I made lunches and gallons of coffee, got groceries. But after a few more days, Dad convinced me to go back. I didn't want to go, but he said it was the best thing I could do."

"And all this time you didn't know if your sister was even alive."

He lifted his eyes. I could see how tight his throat was when he swallowed. "The waiting just about killed us."

"What about your younger brother Rupert. Wasn't he able to help out?"

"He swung by the house from time to time, but the cops made him nervous. I think my little brother was smoking a lot of marijuana in those days. Now he's progressed to more potent ways to ruin his life. From what I recall, he'd come home, fill his face in the kitchen, then leave again."

I didn't want to defend his behaviour, but we all dealt with stress differently.

"The next time the kidnappers called, Dad didn't need to demand proof of life." Sebastian pinched the bridge of his nose and closed his eyes. When he spoke again, I heard the emotion the memories were dredging up in his voice. "When he answered, Katie was on the line. My dad heard her crying. She kept repeating, 'Daddy, come get me, Daddy.'" Sebastian wiped away the tears in his eyes and ran his hand over his mouth.

I felt the pinprick of tears in my own eyes. "Oh god, Sebastian, I'm so sorry."

He wiped his eyes and gave me a weak smile. "It was hard to deal with at the time, but now that I have kids of my own, it breaks my heart."

I nodded, because nothing I could say would lessen the emotions my questions had dredged up.

"Anyway, after that, my father finished getting the money together. There were three more phone calls, each two days apart. The first was just the date for the drop, April twelfth. That's all they said. The next call demanded he give them his cell phone number. That kind of shook the police. Although not everyone carried a cell phone back then, they were in use. Maybe they just figured my dad would have one, given he was a successful businessman.

"The next call came in on his cell, the morning of the twelfth. They told my dad to get into his car at four p.m. and to drive west on Highway 8. Once the kidnappers had my dad's cell phone number, the detectives knew the kidnappers would be watching to make sure my father wasn't being followed by the police. They arranged for my father to wear a wire."

I rubbed my hands down the front of my pants and flexed my fingers to release some of the tension.

"Dad did what they asked. About ten minutes out of town, he got a call. They told him to pull over to the side of the road, get out, and remove the wire."

"What? They knew he was wearing a wire?"

"Either that or it was a good guess. After he removed the wire, they told him to get back in the car and keep driving west. He got another call close to the 1A exit. They told him to take it, then continue until he heard from them.

"One of the detectives followed my dad after they made him ditch the wire. But when he saw my dad's car turn onto Highway 1A, he knew they would spot him. So, he decided to keep heading west, cross the median further ahead, and double back.

"My dad got another call telling him to stop at the first bridge and throw the money and his phone down into the ravine, then get back into the car and circle back to Calgary on Highway 1A."

"These guys knew what they were doing."

"Yeah. By the time the detective caught up to my dad's car, all of maybe five or six minutes later, he had no way of knowing that my dad had already made the drop."

"So, they got away with the five million."

Sebastian nodded.

"What about your sister?"

"That was another whole ordeal that took us years to recover from."

FORTY

Kate wasn't returned to her parents once her father threw the ransom money off the bridge into the ravine below. Sebastian told me his father returned home after the drop but there was no phone call from the kidnappers. With his cell phone now in the bottom of the ravine, he knew if there was to be any communication it would be through the landline.

"My mother had a panic attack and had to be sedated. The detective returned to the house shortly after my father. By then he knew the ransom money must have been dropped off. The RCMP were dispatched to the location where my father was instructed to drop the money, but by then it was nightfall. The area was searched the next day, and my father's cell phone was found, smashed, of course, but the money was gone."

"Did they try to get the data off the phone?"

"They were able to extract the number of the phone the kidnappers were using but it came from one of those throw-away kinds."

"What about footprints or anything like that?"

"The ravine was rocky, with lots of low shrubs. They found a few broken branches, but those could have been made by deer. The

RCMP figured the kidnappers had waited under the bridge in a Zodiac or some other boat and that's how they made their getaway."

"And no word on your sister. She must have been gone for over two weeks by now."

"The ransom was dropped nineteen days after my sister was taken. After the ransom was paid, I flew home again. It was one of the worst weeks of my life. The detective in charge of the case kept the phone wired for five more days. After that they told my parents that the chances she would be returned alive had dropped to almost zero. They packed up all their equipment and left."

"Oh my gosh." My hand flew to my mouth, even though I knew Kate had been alive at the time, otherwise she wouldn't have been murdered two weeks ago.

"My brother Michael was calling daily from Malaysia. He made plans to return to Calgary."

"What about Rupert?"

Sebastian pressed his lips together and gave his head a slow disbelieving shake. "Ah yes, my brother. He dropped by the house almost every day up until the ransom was paid. Then about a week later he showed up...stoned. I figured it was his immature way of dealing with the situation but the more that I thought about it over the years..." He shook his head.

I sat up. "Are you saying what I think you're saying?"

Sebastian contemplated my question for the longest time. Finally, he brought himself back from wherever the memory had dragged him. "I told myself he couldn't have anything to do with it. The kidnappers had it all worked out. My dear brother can't organize two thoughts let alone plan and carry out something that slick. But someone was feeding them information. The way Rupert always hung around the periphery of the room, listening to but never taking part in conversations.”

“You were bothered by more than this behaviour, weren’t you?”

“You know, the day he showed up at the house, five or six days after the ransom was paid, he went upstairs to see our mother. I went up a few minutes after him. Rupert had a way of making everything about him all the time, and I was worried that instead of comforting our mother, he’d be whining about what he needed. When I got to the bedroom door, Rupert was kneeling beside my mother’s bed. I heard him say ‘she’ll be back, Mom; she’s okay, I promise.’

“At the time I was annoyed with him and chalked it up to his pathetic attempt to comfort my mother without really thinking about what he was saying.”

“Do you still think that?”

“I don’t know. The kidnappers were one step ahead of us all the way. I went back to university to defend my thesis. About a week later, a woman called the police saying that when she came out of the grocery store, she found a little girl, sitting in the back of her car. Her clothes were filthy, she was terrified, but couldn’t say why.”

“Your sister?”

Sebastian let out a huge sigh. “Yeah, it was Katie. We couldn’t believe it. The woman who found her was shopping at a mall in Varsity Acres. Katie was taken to the hospital and came home six days later.

“I flew home and so did Michael. We were ecstatic that Katie was back. Rupert didn’t come to see Katie. Not until much later. By then the doctors had told us that her memory of the event might never come back. I found Rupert's lack of interest in Katie's return odd. Don't you?"

"You said he was smoking a lot of weed back then. Still, it does seem strange."

"He was living in a rental near the university, but later I found out he wasn't attending classes—so not like he was short of time. They tossed him out the following year."

"I heard you mention the lingering trauma that followed Kate for years, in your eulogy."

"Katie wasn't the same little girl she was before she was kidnapped. She needed a lot of emotional support. She didn't speak for almost a year, so the police weren't able to get any more info as to who had taken her. Then my mother's headaches got worse, and she was diagnosed with brain cancer. Rupert was addicted to meth amphetamine by then and living with his druggie friends in a flop house that he paid for with the money our grandmother left him."

"That's a lot to deal with. I can't imagine how hard it must have been on you and your family."

"Michael came home two more times during the next year. At least he had a chance to visit our mom, before she died. Rupert seemed oblivious to what was going on."

"Kate never said anything once she regained her ability to talk?"

"No. She didn't remember much—only that there was wood on the floor where she had been kept, and it was always dark. She remembers finding herself in a huge parking lot with no idea how she got there. She said a cloud told her to get into the car—the car that ended up belonging to the lady who found her."

"A cloud?"

"The doctors figure a hallucination, or perhaps even the voice of one of the kidnappers as she was coming out of sedation. The blood work they did at the hospital showed she had zolpidem in her system."

"Zolpidem. That's a type of sedative, isn't it?"

"It's a hypnotic, similar to the benzodiazepine used in sleep medications but with fewer side effects. The sleeping pills my mother used to take for her insomnia were hypnotics. Of course, later we realized that our mother's insomnia and headaches were caused by a growing tumour in her brain."

"Did the police ever find anything related to the kidnapping?"

"No. Not that they didn't try. Al Walker, the detective in charge of the case, called us from time to time to let us know he was running down some new bit of information, but it always turned out to be a dead end. He's retired now. He came to Katie's funeral last week."

Sebastian took a sip of his coffee and grimaced. "Ice cold." He set the coffee mug back down. "Rupert will always be my little brother, and I hate to admit it, but the idea that Katie's murder might be connected to her kidnapping has gripped me."

"You said you thought he couldn't have masterminded the kidnapping but it's possible he was feeding them information. That was what, over twenty years ago. What's made you wary this time?"

"Rupert's lived a shiftless life. It's not what our grandmother intended when she set up a trust fund for us. A lot of Rupert's inheritance has gone up his nose. The only difference over the years is that his friends changed. They're wealthier, they live a flashier life. Rupert has had a hard time keeping up appearances. Then about a month ago I saw him with one of his old roommates. I've forgotten the fellow's name. He looked rough."

"Could he have been hitting Rupert up for money?"

Sebastian snorted. "Rupert's broke. This guy, though—his family owned a rustic cottage up at Gull Lake. Rupert used to go up there with him. Detective Walker always figured it might be where Katie was held after she was kidnapped, but he could never prove it."

I walked out of Sebastian's office with Detective Walker's contact information and my gut telling me that Sebastian's theory deserved further investigation.

FORTY-ONE

Rebecca Edelman was one of these women who never worried about what she was wearing or eating, or what other people thought of her. She had that fresh-faced glow that came with healthy eating and just the right amount of expensive foundation. She reminded me a bit of the woman whose picture I had pinned to my vision board—confident, smart, sure of herself, and exuding positive energy.

Rebecca had just finished a tennis lesson and was wearing a bright-pink, long-sleeved cardigan over a short, pleated tennis skirt and V-neck top with pink trim. Her tennis shoes were pristine white and her short ankle socks had tiny pink tennis rackets circling the cuff.

The server set down two drinks on the small table separating us, a superfood smoothie for her, a pressed orange juice for me. We had already got the introductions and niceties out of the way.

"How long were you and Kate friends?"

"We met just after she came back from Italy. Gosh, that was eight years ago. We met at a Van Charles art exhibition."

"So, you shared a love of art, and tennis perhaps?"

"Kate was more into art than I am. I'm a better tennis player though." She laughed, her wide smile exposing beautifully aligned, pearly-white teeth. My tongue pressed against the back of my upper teeth, feeling the small gap that existed there.

"Everyone I have talked to so far has nothing but good to say about Kate. It sounds like she was a remarkable person."

"Kate was that rare individual that comes along once in a while. She left an indelible mark on everyone she met. It wasn't just her generosity. She showed genuine concern and empathy for everyone around her."

"Did you notice anything different in her in the days leading up to her death?"

"No. If anything, I thought she seemed even happier than usual."

"Was there anything contributing to this happiness?"

Rebecca took a sip of her murky green smoothie and didn't even flinch. She pressed her lips together and gazed at the other people sitting on the patio. The popping sound of tennis balls cut through the silence. A group of women near the massive patio fireplace burst into laughter. Rebecca drew in a deep breath and turned back to me.

"I think she was in love."

I met her eyes and nodded. "Do you know with whom?"

She nodded. "She swore me to secrecy, so I'll never reveal his name."

"Do you think her husband knew?"

"That reprobate? I'm sure he could tell that Kate had fallen out of love with him, but he was going to make her stand by him anyhow."

"He didn't want another divorce?"

"If Cole wanted a divorce, it would happen in a nanosecond. He left his wife of seventeen years for his second wife and dropped her like a hot potato when he met Kate. I tried to warn Kate, but she had stars in her eyes."

"You referred to him as a reprobate. Is he that wicked? Could he be the one behind Kate's murder?"

"If Kate knew or found out something about him, that could hurt him...I can see it."

"Hurt him how? Financially?"

Rebecca tilted her head and pursed her lips. "Yes, financially, but more so if it threatened his megalomaniac image of himself. The man is a narcissist. He has no empathy for anyone. Men like that are dangerous."

I nodded. We had no shortage of evidence as to her statement. The history books were full of examples. "Was she planning to leave him? Could she have told him of those plans?"

"I don't think there were any such plans. At least not yet. I mean, I don't really know, but she seemed happy to just be living her life and to have found love again. I remember when she felt like that about Cole. But that was before she really got to know him."

"She married him pretty quickly, didn't she?"

"He pressured Kate into marriage. I think if she had been allowed to get to know him better, she never would have agreed to become his wife."

"That's probably why he rushed things. What kind of pressure did he exert?"

"Oh, he promised her the world. Kate was twenty-four when she met him. She told him she wanted to travel, to set up an art foundation, to have a child later, and he agreed to it all. But when she turned thirty and wanted a child of her own, Cole refused. He said he already had two money-grubbing offspring and didn't want more."

"Kate must have felt betrayed."

"It gutted her. And all that travel? She did manage a few trips, but Cole always wanted her home, ready to pop up whenever he needed her on his arm to make himself look good." She grimaced. "Or to play gracious hostess and smooth out the waves his misogynistic, unethical, and socially inappropriate behaviour created."

"Unethical?"

"You won't have to dig very deep to read all those as-of-yet un-substantiated accounts of the unethical ways he's managed to grow his business. Bribes, payoffs, side deals, fraud—he's been accused of them all."

"Has he ever been charged?"

"Of course. But it's never stuck. Why do you think he surrounds himself with the best lawyers he can find?"

"Why didn't Kate just leave him? She had money of her own."

Rebecca pressed her lips together and shook her head. "She did, but it wouldn't support her current lifestyle. I don't mean to make her sound money hungry. Despite Cole's reputation as some sort of business guru, he lost a lot of money over the years. Kate's money had been shoring them up for years."

Ironically, someone had killed Kate, not Cole. "Kate wasn't mur-dered by accident or a random shooting. She was down by the river late that night for a reason. I believe she went there to meet someone,

someone she knew. You probably know more about what was going on in her life than anyone. Who could that have been, Rebecca?"

Rebecca picked up her smoothie and took another sip. Her unfocused stare as she gazed out over the green space surrounding the patio told me her mind was somewhere else. After a few minutes she gave a shudder and put down the glass she was still holding.

"You might want to talk to her brother, Rupert."

I remained silent, hoping she would tell me more. She didn't disappoint me.

"Rupert's in debt. He owes people money, people who aren't forgiving when you miss a loan payment. Kate had given him money several times, but he kept coming back for more. She even leased an apartment for him. Finally, she told him she couldn't help him anymore."

"Do you know when she told him that there would be no more handouts?"

"A couple of months before she was killed. He didn't seem to want to accept no as an answer. He kept badgering her. She felt awful about it but told him that she didn't have the kind of money he needed."

"Do you know how much he wanted?"

"I know she gave him twenty thousand last year, but each request came with a higher amount. The last time he asked for forty thousand. Can you imagine. Even if she could have come up with that kind of money, she knew it wouldn't be the last time he asked."

"Wow. That's a lot."

"You know what he said when she told him that even if she wanted to keep giving him money that getting her hands on that kind of cash wasn't as simple as going to the bank? He told her she should sell some of *her* jewellery or her fancy purses. This from a man who drives an Audi, wears brocade smoking jackets, and has a different Rolex for each day of the week. Well, good luck to him now that his sister isn't here to shore up his depraved lifestyle."

"I can just imagine how that would have sat with Kate." I would have been more than annoyed if I had been in Kate's shoes. Then again, maybe the car was on lease and the Rolexes good fakes. But something about the situation didn't make sense to me. "Kate's brother, Sebastian, told me Kate changed her will last year. Do you know if Rupert would have known about that? My understanding is that Rupert wasn't one of the beneficiaries."

"Thank the good lord." Rebecca raised her eyes heavenward. "The topic of Rupert came up more than a few times in our conversation. Kate was too forgiving, too soft-hearted. I told her repeatedly that giving him money was enabling him. The family had paid for his rehab more than once. I mean, how many chances did he think he'd get."

"Do you think he could have done something to cause Kate's death?"

"Rupert?" Her mouth tightened as she drew her head back. "I seriously doubt it. At least not directly."

"Not directly. But you do think Rupert is somehow to blame."

She grimaced, then glanced around uneasily. "The people he owes money to won't just walk away when he can't pay."

"Do you know who he owes money to?"

Rebecca shook her head. "No. You asked me for a possible reason why Kate would have been by the river the night she was killed. I think she went down there to help someone in trouble. I don't know who, but someone took advantage of her kindness."

Rebecca's theory made sense to me. The reason for Kate being there the night she was killed jelled with what I had learned about the woman. An image of Rupert at his sister's funeral appeared in my mind. He had been drunk, but it was more than that. He looked like a broken man. He was either taking his sister's death exceptionally hard...or he was reeling under the weight of guilt.

FORTY-TWO

The drive out to the Pine Valley Spa and Golf Club to meet with Kate's friend, Rebecca, had given me time to think. I kept circling back to that damn gun over and over again. I refused to believe it was a coincidence that Kate had been killed by a gun stolen from her lover's wife. Could Rupert have known about the affair? Could someone have bribed him to provide information about his sister? Two people who knew him well had just told me that he was in dire financial straits. If Sebastian's suspicions were correct about his involvement in Kate's kidnapping all those years ago, who's to say he wouldn't do a repeat.

Sebastian's theory about Rupert's possible involvement in her kidnapping had etched a small furrow in my mind and I was having a hard time jumping out of the track. But I still had a few other leads that weren't complete dead ends. I told myself that I had to keep chipping away at those as well, until one of them led somewhere or definitively nowhere.

I was at the city limits when my phone buzzed. My Bluetooth announced the call was from Sal.

"Hey doll, got a name for you."

"Sal, where are you? I can barely hear you."

"I'm at the store getting cat food. They're ripping up the asphalt outside. Hang on."

The growling noise faded. "Can you hear me now?"

"That's better."

"Josh's last name was Neeley. I scouted the area around where River said he found the handbag, if we can believe anything that skank told us. There are two CCTV cameras that might be of interest. I'll send you the locations."

"Thanks, Sal. You're worth your weight in gold."

I heard a cackle and something about two hundred grand and then the line went dead. I smiled. The cops should employ a few Sals. People on the street weren't afraid to talk if they didn't perceive you as a threat.

I headed for the nearest Starbucks, got a coffee, and connected to the Wi-Fi. The place was humming with customers. A group of women joggers entered the coffee shop, rosy cheeked from their run around the reservoir. I eyed the banana loaf in its brown-paper envelope next to my coffee and sighed. Maybe if Luis and I continued down our current path, his health-conscious habits would rub off on me. I shuddered and took a bite of the loaf. Let's face it, I was a fair-weather jogger. I didn't like jogging when it was colder than minus five outside, never if the wind gusts exceeded thirty-five kilometres, or if the pathways were covered in snow or ice. I took a sip of coffee, sucked in my gut, and started googling.

There didn't seem to be anything in the news about Josh Neeley's death. Overdose cases were so common they rarely made the news anymore. I searched the funeral homes in the area and found an obituary listed on the Eternal Ridge Cremation website. It took me fewer than thirty seconds to read it.

We are sad to announce that on May 16, 2023, Joshua Samuel Neeley passed away at the age of forty-six. If you would like to pay a last tribute to Josh, or leave his family a message of condolence, please do so on his memorial page. In his honour, donations can be made to the Calgary Nova Recovery Drug Centre.

I clicked on the link at the side of the obituary that led to condolences. There was only one.

Rest in peace, Josh. "God of all grace, who called you to his eternal glory in Christ, after you have suffered, will himself restore you and make you strong, firm, and steadfast." Peter 5:10

Your friends at Nova Recovery.

The Nova Recovery website provided an overview of their drug rehab programs, which were, according to the website, founded on evidence-based therapies. They also provided access to support groups and aftercare programs to help individuals avoid relapse while navigating the challenges of living everyday life without substances.

Despite the attempts to save Josh from the drugs that controlled him, and maybe himself, his time had run out. I jotted down the phone number for the Nova Recovery centre on my napkin and then called it. I talked to a woman named Wanda, who transferred me to a colleague who in turn transferred me to the program director.

The program director wouldn't give me the names of any of the group leaders for their support sessions, but he did tell me that the support groups met each evening at either the Knox United Church on Fourth Street or the Abundant Spirit Church in the far southeast corner of the city. Given River's statement that she had seen Josh at a drug-fuelled party in Hillhurst, I figured his attendance at support group meetings might have fallen off. Still, the downtown location would likely be my best bet.

Since the meetings were held in the evenings, I had some time to kill. I briefly considered going home, changing, and going for a run, but after all the coffee I had just consumed, the idea didn't appeal. I stared out the window at the steady stream of cars making their way in and out of the parking lot.

My mind circled back to the upcoming meeting Mike had set up for us with Willie. I could feel the resistance seeping back into my body. I should just follow my gut and tell Willie that I appreciated hearing about the opportunity, but the timing just wasn't right. *When will it be right?* The two voices in my head continued to banter back and forth. The louder, more aggressive one reminded me that rewards came to those who took risks. The other voice countered that taking a big risk didn't always result in a fuller, richer life. Sometimes it led to disaster.

My phone vibrated on the table next to my coffee, jolting me out of my inner debate. I glanced at the screen and picked up.

"Hey babe, where are you?"

"I'm sitting at a Starbucks, debating whether to go home or go check out some CCTV footage."

"Hmmm. Want a third option?"

"I'm game. What do you have in mind?"

"I have a surprise for you. You'll have to come over to get it."

"Is it the same surprise as last Friday night?"

"Yeah." His voice got huskier. "I cleared off the kitchen island, so no wine glasses take a hit this time."

"Hey. You can't blame me—as I recall, that was a team effort."

FORTY-THREE

Needless to say, I didn't make it to the Nova Recovery support group meeting last night. Despite my lack of sleep, I felt great. Mike's and my meeting wasn't until one o'clock, so I walked the few blocks from Luis' place to the first CCTV camera location Sal had sent me. This one was mounted at a furniture store loading dock just down the alley from the back of the Westin Hotel.

I climbed the steps to the loading dock and examined the camera angle. With any luck, it would offer at least a partial view of the bin behind the hotel. A man came out through a side door and startled. "Can I help you?"

The scowl on his face told me he really wasn't planning on helping me.

"Morning. My name is Jorja Knight. I'm a detective. I'm looking into Kate Barrett's murder, the woman who was found two weeks ago just east of here. I'd like to see the footage from your CCTV camera. We think the culprit ditched some evidence in one of these dumpsters." I nodded at the bins that dotted the alley.

"You'll have to talk to the foreman."

"Where can I find him?"

He scowled at me for another full minute then nodded his head toward the side door. He turned and I followed.

The foreman turned out to be a guy named Arlo, who looked to be about fifteen. He didn't ask for ID when I told him I was a detective. I followed him into a tiny windowless office, and he found the dates I was looking for on his computer. He offered me his desk chair, but I told him I was fine standing. I squinted over his shoulder as the video came to life.

"Feel free to fast forward when there's no activity." He nodded eagerly. I got the impression that this was the most exciting thing that had happened to him all week. Maybe all year.

We watched in silence for the next ten minutes. Arlo stopped the video a few times, but we quickly decided that the image on the video footage wasn't one we were looking for.

"There." Arlo stopped the video and pointed at the screen.

"An image appeared in the alley, already darkened by night. The figure wore a grey jacket with the hood pulled up, jeans, and sneakers. Arlo slowed the video to a crawl as we watched him take something orange from beneath his jacket and throw it into the dumpster.

"Okay, there." I didn't need to speak; Arlo had already stopped the video. He read out the timestamp at the bottom of the screen.

"Got it. That's our guy. Scroll back, let's see it again."

He turned back to the screen, his excitement palpable. The second and third time we watched the video, I paid attention to the image. The person wearing the grey jacket was thin, maybe five-eight or-ten. He moved quickly, his movements jerky. His head, hair, and face remained obscured the whole time, but his hands told me he was

Caucasian. The orange object he threw into the bin appeared to be a handbag. After he threw the handbag away, he scurried out of view.

I took a few photos of the image with my cell phone.

"What now?" Arlo looked up, his eyes bright.

"Keep it rolling." I wanted to see if River was the one who retrieved the bag from the dumpster. We watched as daylight returned. A woman came out of the Westin and threw three trash bags into the dumpster, then later a man came out and tossed in a stack of flattened cardboard boxes. The light in the video faded as the sun set. A figure appeared in the frame. Thin, grey jacket. "Stop."

I peered at the image. It was the same guy who threw the bag into the dumpster. We watched as he shifted a few bags in the dumpster, surveyed the area around him, and climbed in. A minute later, he crawled back out, clutching the orange bag.

"Whaaat?" Arlo squawked. "That's the same guy."

"It is, indeed." River had sort of told us the truth. The bag had been in a dumpster behind the Westin and the same guy who threw it there later picked it up. Could this be Josh Neeley? I took a few more photos of the guy on the screen, this time capturing a partial view of his face as he climbed back out of the dumpster.

"This footage doesn't overwrite, does it?"

Arlo peered at the date on the screen. "Not for another month."

"Okay, great. Listen, I'll have a police officer come over to pick it up. I want to make sure that we execute the proper chain of evidence. Don't let anything happen to that video."

Arlo actually saluted me. It made me realize how dull his workday must be. I shook his hand and promised that someone would come by to pick it up in the next few days. "Best not to mention this to anyone until the evidence has been collected and is safely locked up. I wouldn't want you to put yourself in any danger."

Arlo almost swooned at the word *danger*. He'd be telling his buddies how he helped out on a murder investigation for years. I planned to let Ryker know about the video. It was the least I could do, considering that I refused to tell him why I had been parked down the highway from the Barrett house a week before Kate Barrett was murdered. I didn't think Arlo would be in danger, but there was no use risking the video going missing until Ryker or one of his team could pick it up.

After leaving Arlo I followed the same path the image on the CCTV footage had taken, looking for signs of any other cameras. I saw none as I made my way to the end of the alley, which intersected Second Street. I inspected the buildings lining the road. No cameras—not surprising, as their front entrances faced the avenue side.

Now all I had to do was identify the image on the video. Why had he retrieved the handbag after discarding it? If it was Josh, maybe he realized that the bag could net him some cash. But where did he get the bag in the first place? Could he be Kate's killer?

I would have to compare this image to the one captured by the dash-cam video I retrieved from one of Sherrie's to see if it could possibly be the same person Sherrie let into her house. My excitement grew. Maybe, just maybe, this thread wouldn't disappear when I pulled on it.

FORTY-FOUR

MIKE WAS WAITING FOR me as I pulled into visitor parking next to a low-rise red-brick and metal-sided building, one of a dozen buildings configured in a campus-style arrangement with gardens, grass, and seating areas between them.

Mike had dressed up. Today he wore grey slacks and a dark-charcoal jacket over a black crewneck shirt. His face broke into a grin as I stepped out of the car.

"You're looking sharp." Mike nodded appreciatively at my black pencil skirt, grey-and-black geometric-patterned silk shirt, and black suit jacket. It was pretty much the same outfit I wore to funerals, except today I wore black heels and carried a tan briefcase.

"You're looking pretty sharp yourself."

"I take it you had no trouble finding the place?"

"Just off Deerfoot, first right after the rows of red storage units. Not a bad location, just six or seven minutes east of downtown."

"They just signed a lease for 16,000 square feet of space, but there's a unit next to the one they're leasing that will be coming available in November should they need to expand."

I followed Mike inside. Pale wood floors stretched out from the front door to the back windows. Florescent lights above added to the illumination coming in from a row of windows at the back of the space. The interior office walls were made of frosted glass set into metal frames. My heels echoed on the floor as we made our way past an unoccupied reception desk. Willie came out of one of the offices and strode toward us.

"You found us. Welcome." He stretched out his arm to shake our hands. He hadn't aged much since I last saw him a little over three years ago. His closely cropped salt-and-pepper hair was mostly salt now, but his solid upright frame and piercing blue eyes were exactly as I remembered them.

"After you." He waved us toward a conference room to the right. A young man jumped to his feet as we entered. He pulled nervously at the belt circling his thin waist. "I'd like you to meet Aadesh Kudari."

"Nice to meet you." Aadesh reached out to shake our hands. He was handsome but not in a Bollywood kind of way. His thin face was topped with a mop of unruly brown hair, and when he smiled his whole face lit up, like a kid getting his first bike.

"Aadesh is my partner and our resident cybersecurity expert. He's worked with some of the most complex and secure systems and networks in the world."

How old is this guy? I suddenly felt out of my depth...and ancient. Even my skills as a former forensic lab analyst seemed pedestrian in comparison to his experience. What could I possibly add to this organization? I took a deep breath and told myself to stop the negative self-talk.

Willie pointed us to the coffee and tray of muffins and danishes in the middle of the table. We made small talk as coffees were poured and settled into our chairs.

"I assume you've had a chance to read the dossier I sent over." Willie's English accent had all but faded except when it came to words like *dossier*. I wanted to turn and run. I had skimmed the document, after I returned home this morning from my night with Luis, but my eyes had glazed over and not much had sunk in.

Mike nodded. "Yes, thanks for sending it over. It's a very concise yet thorough overview of the company."

I, on the other hand, avoided Willie's gaze.

"So, you're familiar with our goals and objectives, the management and legal structure for the company, and planned growth projections. If you'll bear with me, I'd like to spend a few minutes reviewing the key points before throwing the meeting open for any questions you have."

Thankfully, Willie reiterated some of what was in the dossier he had sent us. CanNet planned to differentiate itself from its competitors by not only providing risk assessments but remediating them as well. Their services would encompass data systems, as well as physical facilities and infrastructure. Their risk assessment tools could be used to conduct environmental scans and even evaluate how an organization was perceived by its customers, the community, and their adversaries.

Willie closed the dossier in front of him. "Well, there you have it. Questions?"

Mike jumped right in. "Are you planning to use commercial risk assessment tools or build your own?"

"Initially we're licencing commercially available tools, starting with Riskonnect. If we find something lacking, it will be an opportunity to partner with them to expand the offering."

I was dying to ask where he thought I would fit in, but Willie beat me to it.

"The one area where these risk assessment tools fall short is on the human side." He turned to me. "That's why I'm glad you're here, Jorja. I was telling Mike the last time we met how hard it is to find people who know how to think these days. I need someone who can use their imagination, knowledge, reasoning, analytical skills, and senses to evaluate, make judgments, problem solve, and make decisions. I need someone with highly developed cognition to evaluate and mitigate human threats and risks."

I swallowed. The jargon was bringing back memories of working at Global Analytix. After a while you stop realizing you're using words no one outside the company understands. I cleared my throat. "So, if I understand correctly, the services your company will provide includes the identification of potential threats or risk to others, directly by people, not just through their use of technology."

"Yes. It's one of our toughest challenges. As I'm sure you're aware, constantly changing factors combined with an individual's personal experiences and perceptions can make these threats difficult to detect and respond to."

"So, the goal is to identify behaviours or circumstances that might indicate someone's intent to cause harm, before it happens."

"Ideally, yes."

"What are we talking about? Fraud, theft, sabotage?"

"All of that yes, as well as espionage. Stealing and selling trade secrets or sensitive information has skyrocketed lately. And as you know from personal experience, violence. It doesn't have to be a mass shooting like the one you survived at Global. Violence also comes in the form of sexual harassment, bullying, and verbal abuse."

Willie's eyes bore into me as if he was trying to read my inner thoughts. "We'll of course be working with the local and national security agencies when the situation is called for."

I nodded. He could read my mind. "You mentioned potential threats being exerted by people outside of the organization. Wouldn't most of the threat posed from the outside come as a cyberthreat?"

"Of course. There's no end to the viruses, malware, worms, botnets, and so on. It's hard to keep up. Besides the hackers and lone wolves out there, we're now up against social engineers."

"Social engineers?" I glanced at Aadesh, and he squirmed in his chair.

"It's a broad term that includes attacks that are the outcome of psychologically manipulating people into performing actions desirable to an attacker."

"You mean like sending an email to someone with a link to a malicious website, or one that infects the computer when the user clicks on it?"

"We've all gotten used to those. Today, there's a growing sophistication to the threats people receive that's exploding by leaps and bounds. Dating sites don't have a monopoly on deceiving people. Voice phishing attacks use social engineering techniques to get targets to divulge financial or personal information over the phone.

And they're not just targeting someone's grandma anymore. They are going after high-profile employees like the CEO or the Chief Financial Officer. The threat actor's job is to get the target to disclose confidential information."

"Threat actor. I've never heard that term."

Mike chimed in. "They have their own version of a honey trap. The threat actor sets up a fake identity as an attractive person working in the target individual's general area of interest and strikes up an online relationship, which eventually leads to that person extracting sensitive information from the target."

"Ah." I nodded. "Same principles, different targets."

"Now you get it." Willie's eyes met mine, and he smiled for the first time since we arrived. "There's no end of what these people will do to get what they want. Threat actors can trick a courier into going to the wrong drop-off location and then intercept a package that was intended for someone else or start an online relationship with a high-ranking official to groom them to become their source for information later. We're starting to use AI as a way to help us identify these potential risks and prioritize how we and our clients can best use our limited resources to eradicate those activities that can create the most damage. Of course, the criminals are also using AI." Willie sat back. "So, Jorja, any of this interest you?"

Willie held my gaze while I scrambled for something to say that wouldn't commit me and yet would leave the door open for a while.

"Mike mentioned that you're looking to staff up pretty quickly. What kind of timeline are you talking about?"

"We'd like to be fully operational by September. Ideally, you'd come on in July, or early August at the latest, so that we could get you up to speed and give you a chance to meet the rest of the team."

"How big is the team?"

In the area you would be in, we have two offers out. Ideally, we'll grow that number to six by fall. After that, we'll grow at the rate the market demands."

I sat, my mind whirling.

Mike's foot nudged mine under the table, reminding me that I needed to say something. "July or August might be hard to swing. I'd appreciate some time to think about it."

"That's fine. I know there's lots to consider. I can give you until June fifteenth. In the meantime, I'll send you the job description and other details. I'm sure you'll have more questions for me as you consider the opportunity. Give me a shout when you do. Anytime."

I left the meeting horrified. Now I had exactly eleven days to decide what my next move would be. The sickening feeling in my gut was telling me to stay in my current lane. Yet my last few conversations with both Mike and Luis made me realize that if I didn't keep up with the times, I was going to find my services as popular as that of the elevator operator.

FORTY-FIVE

AFTER MY MEETING WITH Mike and Willie, I headed back to the Pine Valley Spa and Golf Club. I had no specific reason to drive back out there, but I had a sudden urge to get out of town. Soon I was on Highway 8, the rolling tree-dotted landscape and occasional acreage community flashing by me. I wasn't far out of the city but, with the sight of the mountains in the far distance and baby-blue skies above, I could breathe again.

I turned into the Pine Valley Spa and Golf Club parking lot and parked a short distance from the clubhouse. A stone path led me to the patio where Kate's friend Rebecca and I had sat talking, just two days ago. Today the patio was packed. I meandered past the tables arranged below the massive timbers framing the steepled roof of the clubhouse and into the cool air of the clubhouse itself. Another stone fireplace, situated on a wall of windows to my left, added to the luxurious, modern-lodge appearance.

The inside was brighter than the outside predicted, largely due to floor-to-ceiling windows and half a dozen chandeliers suspended below the wood-beamed ceiling. Leather club chairs and sofa seating areas were casually arranged in the space. An informal dining area framed by a wall of windows was tucked into the corner to my right. I turned toward it and was soon seated at a table near the windows. A woman wearing a Pine Valley uniform brought me a glass of water and a menu.

"What a marvellous day. You've decided not to enjoy our patio? We just opened it last week."

"It is a beautiful day." I smiled back at her, noting her name tag—*Rose*. "All the tables outside are full, and I didn't want to have to wait."

"Well, my dear, whether you're inside or out, the food here is fabulous. Give me a shout when you're ready to order."

The sunshine filtering in through the windows of the restaurant put me in better spirits. Now that I was here, I noticed that I was actually hungry. I perused the menu and decided on the crab cakes, a side salad, and a glass of pinot grigio. The minute I laid the menu down, Rose appeared at my table.

I ordered, and once Rose left with my order, studied the surroundings. A long farm-style table bisected the restaurant and banquet-style seating tucked into alcoves framed the far wall. My gaze shifted to the lounge area, and I caught a glimpse of one of the fairways beyond the windows on the far side of the room. My food arrived, and Rose and I exchanged a few more comments. I found out that she had been working at the clubhouse for over sixteen years.

The food was divine. I tried not to think about the forty-two-dollar price tag as I savoured each bite of crab cake. The salad dressing was bright and crisp, and the pale-gold pinot was perfect, leaving a smooth silky taste on my tongue. When my plate was cleared, Rose asked if there was anything else. Now that my stomach was full, I was ready to think again.

"Those were the best crab cakes I've ever had. There is something else, although it's not food related. I'm a private investigator, and I'm working with the defence team on the Barrett murder case. Can you spare a few minutes? I'd like to ask you some questions."

Rose checked over her shoulder. Both couples seated at two other tables in her section had just started their meals. "If it's only a minute."

"Did you know Kate Barrett?"

"Oh yes. Most of the staff, at least the ones who have been here any time, know who she is...was."

"What was she like?"

"She was a lovely woman. Very kind. Beautiful too. She was always very nice to the staff."

"Was she at the club often?"

"Oh yes. I'd say two or three times a week. She played tennis here regularly and she and her friends would come into the dining room afterwards for a bite to eat."

"Then you must have seen her in the weeks before her death. How did she seem?"

"Fine." Rose shrugged.

"She didn't seem worried, or upset?"

Rose bit her lower lip. "I did see her upset one day. She was crying."

"When was this? What happened?"

"She was here having lunch with her brother. The younger one, Rupert." Her face puckered. "He's not as nice as Kate." She leaned in closer. "He likes his drink."

I nodded. "So, they were having lunch and something Rupert said made Kate cry?"

"Yes. I remember Rupert was particularly aggressive that day. I kept my eye on him. It wouldn't be the first time we had to have the security staff escort him out of the building. I could tell by Kate's face and demeanour that she wasn't in favour of whatever they were discussing."

"You didn't happen to hear what it was about?"

"No. Kate got up in the middle of her dinner and headed for the washroom. When she passed me, I could see that she was crying. I went over to their table and asked if everything was all right. Rupert said, 'clearly not.' Then he threw his napkin on the table and told me to put the meal and drinks on Kate's tab and walked out. Well, I certainly wasn't going to put it on Mrs. Barrett's tab without her say so." Rose bristled. "I waited until she returned and asked if she was okay. She said she was fine, but I could see that she wasn't. She looked sad. Anyway, she asked me for the bill, so at least that was settled. That was the last time I spoke with her."

I thanked Rose and settled up the bill. After leaving the restaurant I sat in my car for a while and mulled over what I had just heard. This was the second time in as many days that someone mentioned Rupert's destructive relationship with alcohol and resulting boorish behaviour.

Could Rupert have killed his sister, hoping for a larger chunk of his family's inheritance? I discarded the idea just as quickly as it materialized. If he had loan sharks breathing down his neck, a future inheritance wouldn't help him. Maybe he thought Kate would leave something to him in her will. But most people would have tried to find out the details of the will, instead of blindly killing the person.

I ran through all the possible scenarios I could think of for how Rupert could have managed to get Kate to meet him in such an isolated nighttime location. Based on what Rebecca had told me, the family and Kate had cut Rupert off. Even if Kate had a change of heart, she would hardly have agreed to meet him at that location and time of night. I kept mulling over the possibilities as I drove back into the city.

One possibility is that Rupert had called in a panic, late that night. Maybe the people he owed money to were threatening to harm him unless he made a payment. The idea grew on me as I drove. Cash would have been difficult to come up with on short notice, but maybe Kate had brought jewellery or something of value to bargain with. Another thought appeared. An authentic Hermes purse was worth upwards of fifty thousand. Then why had the killer thrown the bag into a dumpster? I was assuming the figure on the CCTV footage was the killer, but it was a dangerous assumption to make. I sighed. Would we ever know what actually happened to Kate Barrett, or was Sherrie Langcaster destined to be etched into history as her killer?

FORTY-SIX

After a quick change, I headed to my office. I still had a few hours to kill before tonight's support group meeting for recovering addicts, where I hoped to find someone who had known Josh Neeley. I swore I wouldn't let anything derail my plans tonight, although Luis was one distraction that I couldn't seem to resist. Although we had spoken several times over the last week, I hadn't mentioned that my office lease was being terminated or that I was entertaining the idea of mothballing Knight Investigations to work at CanNet.

I tilted my office chair back and stared at the ceiling tiles. Was I really entertaining the idea or was I doing mental gymnastics as a way of procrastinating? Was I ready to decide or would I delay until Willie's deadline for an answer passed. That would be one way for me to solve the dilemma. A sudden compulsion to get drunk made me sit up. *Yeah, that'll solve things.* Waiting until the offer deadline passed was a chicken-assed way to deal with this. So was getting drunk.

"Chicken-ass," I muttered as I turned to my computer. I logged into my inbox and my heart jumped. An email from Willie was already waiting for me. I took a deep breath and clicked on the attachment. The attached job description was five pages long. The first two pages described the responsibilities, tasks, and goals that came with the role of Senior Investigator–Homefront Investigations. That was followed by a page and a half of desired skills. A short list of required qualifications which included job experience and education followed. I scanned the list. I could meet most of CanNet's requirements.

The next section outlined the physical demands and working conditions associated with the job. The overall role of the senior investigator was rated as high demand, moderate risk. The job would involve some travel, and acceptance of the offer was conditional upon my ability to meet certain legal requirements such as obtaining police clearance, not having a criminal record, and being bondable. I would also need to pass a fitness test—the same one currently administered to RCMP recruits.

My stomach churned as I turned to the offer page itself. My eye ran down a list of benefits that included health and pension contributions, subsidized membership to a fitness gym, long-term and short-term disability, and landed on salary. A hundred and thirty-two thousand a year plus a sliding scale bonus based on performance. Double what I had made last year.

My phone rang just as I got to the end of the material Willie sent. Mike's name came up on the screen. For the first time ever, I let Mike's call go through to voice mail instead of picking up.

· · •·•·•·•· ·

THE KNOX UNITED CHURCH described itself as an affirming congregation, which meant they were committed to the full inclusivity of all people in the work of the church, regardless of race, sexual orientation, or gender identity.

I parked on the side street and walked around to the front. A cabinet-style acrylic sign stood off to one side of the main doors. The plastic letters adhered to the tracks in the sign gave the time for tonight's choir practice and the location of the Nova Recovery support group meeting.

I entered the church through the large double wood doors and stopped to admire the stained-glass windows and polished wooden pews in the nave, then followed the sign pointing me downstairs. My boot heels clicked on the tiled staircase as I descended into the lower level.

A confusing array of doors and a series of small halls met me. I didn't see anything that offered a hint as to where I should go next. I wandered down a hall, then turned a corner. The sound of voices drew me further into the dark recesses of the church basement. I rounded another corner and came across a flip chart with the words Nova Recovery and a large hand-drawn arrow pointing to the doorway next to it, as if directions were needed at this point.

I peeked through the open doorway. Several people sat talking amongst themselves, in the semi-circle of chairs arranged at the front of the room. Four or five men stood at a long table at the far side, munching on donuts and gesturing as they argued whether last night's penalty called against the Flames hockey team should have been allowed. I stepped aside as a young man brushed past me, muttering under his breath, and stormed down the hallway.

I stepped into the room. Now I could see a man and a woman engaged in conversation at the front of the room. The woman wore jeans and a ski jacket, despite it being early June, and the man next to her wore khakis and a striped shirt. I stepped hesitantly toward them.

"Maria, that's normal," the man was saying. "It's just your body re-adjusting to not having the drug anymore. The symptoms will go way. You're doing great. Hang in there—it'll get easier. I promise."

The woman nodded and gave him a weak smile. She turned and headed to the coffee and snack station on the other side of the room. The man noticed me.

"Hi. Can I help you?"

"I hope so. I'm a private detective. I'm looking for anyone who might have known Josh Neeley. He overdosed a couple weeks ago. I'm hoping to talk to someone who might have known him. I saw his obituary and there was a condolence message left there from members of Nova Recovery."

"Josh. Yeah. I knew him. He came to some of our meetings this winter, but then dropped off. It's like that sometimes. I didn't know him very well. One of our regulars mentioned his death to the group at our last meeting."

He peered past me. "Hey Theo, got a minute?"

Theo was five six or five seven and all of a hundred pounds wet. His spindly arms were covered with tattoos and his jeans were literally falling off his hips. He walked over with a jaunty gait, the kind guys adopt when they want you to know they aren't scared of you.

"What's up, bro?" he called out as he drew nearer.

"This lady is a detective. Sorry, I didn't catch your name," he said, turning back to me.

"Jorja Knight. And I'm a private detective."

Theo reached us. "Cool." He jammed his hands into his jeans and waited.

"She's been trying to find someone who knew Josh. You kept in touch with him, didn't you?"

"I seen him around from time to time. He wasn't a close pal."

I turned to Theo. "Do you know where he was staying right before he died? Do you know who he hung around with?"

Theo shrugged.

"Someone told me they saw him at a party in Hillhurst a few days before he died. Know anything about that?"

"Nope. I stay away from those, now that I'm clean."

I pulled out my phone and found the photo of the man climbing out of the dumpster behind the Westin. "Can you tell me if this is him?"

Theo squinted at the screen for a minute. "Looks like him, yeah."

"Did Josh ever mention a roommate, family, or a place he worked?"

Theo sniffed; he twisted his pursed lips to one side. "Dude said he didn't have family. Last year a friend did him a solid and got him a gig at a golf course. He made paper for a while, but then he got sacked."

"Do you remember the friend's name or which golf course?"

"Aw man." Theo shook his head. "Now, what was it?" He shook his head again and stared at the floor. "Brayden, I think. Or maybe Hayden. Didn't catch a last name."

"What about the golf course? Do you know which one?"

"It was in the boonies. They had to keep chasing deer off the course." He snorted out a high-pitched laugh as if it was the funniest thing he had ever heard of.

"You don't remember the name of the golf course?"

"One of those fancy spa places where a burger costs fifty bucks."

A shiver ran down my spine. "Could it be the Pine Valley Spa and Golf Club, west of here?"

"Booyah. That's it." Theo's face broke into a grin.

I swallowed down my own yelp of glee. After thanking Theo, I rushed upstairs and into the night air. Finally. A thread that didn't dissolve in my hand but was actually connected to another thread. It shouldn't have left me as excited as it did. But discovering that the person who supposedly found Kate Barrett's handbag was a friend of someone who worked at the Barretts' private golf club sent a shot of dopamine straight to my brain.

FORTY-SEVEN

THE SUN WAS BARELY over the horizon when I arrived at the Pine Valley Spa and Golf Club the next morning. I parked in the small lot at the side of the clubhouse and made my way around the building to the front door. The patio was deserted but would be busy once the morning chill wore off.

I stepped through the front doors, past the restaurant I had eaten at yesterday, and made my way across the room. I passed by a curved bar and continued toward a marble-topped reception desk near the back of the room. Just past the reception desk the room split, and a short hall led into each of the two wings of the building. I followed the hall to my right and found the golf shop. A foursome checking in for their tee time were huddled around the front counter.

Once the four men left, the man behind the counter turned his attention to me. I introduced myself and said that I wanted to talk to an employee of theirs, whose name was either Brayden or Hayden. I explained that this person might know where I could find another man I was interested in, one who had information about a murder I was investigating. At the word *murder*, he hustled me off to the side and told me to wait. A few minutes later, he returned with a grey-haired man with broad shoulders and muscular arms.

"I'm Chip Boyd, the director of the Pine Valley Golf Club." I gave him my name and we shook hands. "Why don't we step into my office?"

Chip clearly lived his life outdoors. Skin that dark brown could only be obtained by years of being in the sun. I followed him back to his office, a smallish room at the far end of the hall. It held a desk, two wooden chairs, and four leather armchairs arranged around a coffee table. Dozens of trophies lined a low bookshelf below a window at the back of the room.

He waved me to one of the chairs in front of his desk. "Would you like a coffee, or water?"

"I'm fine, thank you."

"Now, Max said you're investigating a murder. What's this all about?"

I dug out a card for him and slid it across the table. "I'm working with Neil Trent; he's the defence lawyer representing Sherrie Lancaster in the Kate Barrett murder."

The way he tipped his head back and nodded at hearing the name Barrett told me he'd heard about the case.

"How can we help you with that?"

"I believe you employed a man named Josh Neeley for a short while last year. He was apparently let go after a brief time. I was told that another of your employees knew Josh and had helped him get the job by putting in a good word for him. I'd like to talk to that person. All I know is that he and Josh worked on the maintenance side. I don't have his full name. His first name is either Brayden or Hayden."

Chip leaned forward and rested his clasped hands on the desk. The man had serious muscles in those arms and well-developed pecs. Can't blame a gal for noticing. I moved my gaze to his face. A furrow developed between his eyes.

"This employee of ours that you're looking for, are you saying he's involved in Barrett's murder?"

"No, no. But his friend Josh Neeley might have had some information relevant to the case."

"Might have had?"

"Josh died of a drug overdose a couple weeks ago."

Chip leaned back, clearly relieved. "I see. This Brayden or Hayden you're looking for, do you know if he's full time, part time, or a seasonal worker?"

"Sorry, don't know. The person who told me about him said he and Josh would have to chase deer or other wildlife off the course occasionally. Don't know if that's true, or if it helps or not."

Chip slipped on a pair of reading glasses. His fingers pecked away on his computer keyboard. "Does sound like one of our maintenance guys. They refill the water stations on the course and keep the golfcarts and clubs clean and do general housekeeping duties along the course."

I waited while Chip worked away, sometimes leaning forward to stare at the computer screen. "Just filtering here..." His voice dropped off. "Okay, got it. Joshua Neeley worked for us from August first to October fifteenth last year." He picked up the handset on his speaker phone and hit one of the keys. "Teresa, do we keep the original application forms on employees who no longer work here?" He nodded as he listened. "Okay. Thanks." He replaced the handset and shook his head. "Thought I could take a shortcut and that maybe he listed this Brayden or Hayden as a reference on his application, but that didn't pan out. No problem, we'll do it the long way." A minute later, his printer sprang to life and several pages rolled out onto the tray. "Let's see what we've got."

Chip ran through the pages the printer spit out. He couldn't share his employees' personal information with me, so I waited as he checked his lists for employees whose first name might be Brayden or Hayden.

"Let's see here. We have a Brandon Kroger...and a Lin Jaden, whoops, that's a woman." Chip tilted his head back as he peered through his reading glasses. "Found him. Hayden Price." He turned back to his computer and started pecking on keys. Finally, he whipped off his glasses and turned to me. "Looks like he's caught the morning shift this week. Let's get him in here."

A phone call and ten minutes later a man with light-brown hair, wearing a golf shirt with the Pine Valley logo and baggy khakis arrived at the door.

"You wanted to see me, Mr. Boyd?"

"Come in, Hayden. This is Detective Knight. She wants to talk to you about a friend of yours—Joshua Neeley."

Hayden's head swivelled from left to right and, for one brief second, I thought he was going to bolt.

Chip stood and waved Hayden to one of the armchairs by the coffee table. "I'll leave you to it, Ms. Knight. Come find me when you're done here, I'll be out in front."

Hayden whipped off his ball cap and lowered himself tentatively into one of the chairs.

"First of all, Hayden, please accept my condolences. I understand Joshua Neeley was a friend of yours."

"Yeah, thanks. I kinda figured he'd end up OD'ing one of these days."

I sat down across from him and explained that I was looking into Kate Barrett's murder, not his friend's overdose. His eyes widened, as he twisted his ballcap over and over in his hands, crushing the visor.

"How did you first meet Josh?"

"We met at university."

"Was that U of C?"

"Yeah."

"When was that?"

Hayden tilted his head back. "Ninety-six or ninety-seven."

"You must have known him well if you were friends all those years."

"Not really. I mean, sometimes I wouldn't see him for years, you know, between when, well between when we'd see each other."

"I heard you helped him get a job here, at the golf course."

"Who told you that?"

"Someone from Josh's drug recovery support group. Did you know he was trying to get clean?"

Hayden nodded. "It's hard, you know. Hardest thing I've ever done."

"How long have you been clean?"

"Coming up on three years."

"Congratulations." I noticed he was calming down, the rolled-up hat now still in his hands. "When did you last see Josh?"

"I haven't seen him in months." He sounded defensive. His eyes darted to the door and back again.

"But you knew he was trying to quit his drug habit."

"Yeah. After he lost his job here, he went back to rehab."

"Do you know who the Barretts are? Did you hear about Kate Barrett's murder?"

"I know they're members of this club. I never met them, but it's all anyone here talked about. Why are you asking me all these questions?"

His knee was jiggling now. I was just getting started and he was already complaining about all the questions. It was obvious that he'd rather be anywhere else but here.

"You ever meet Kate Barrett?"

"No. Why would I?"

"What about Rupert Gallagher, Kate Barrett's brother? It sounds like you two might have been at U of C at the same time."

"No," he snapped. "I told you. I don't know the Barretts."

"Okay. I'm just asking. Have you stayed in touch with anyone else from your university days?"

He shrugged. "No."

"You sure you didn't talk to Josh recently? He didn't share his latest scheme with you?" I was bluffing, but you never knew what a good bluff might float to the surface.

"There was no scheme. I told you. I haven't seen Josh in months." Hayden stood up. "I gotta get back to work. I don't know anything about whatever Josh was up to."

"Okay then. There's nothing else you want to tell me? You won't be trying to bargain a plea deal later, when it's too late?"

"Plea deal? I don't know what you want, lady, but I had nothing to do with any of it."

Hayden rushed out of the room. I followed him out to the pro shop and found Chip.

"You find what you were looking for?"

"Yes, thank you. Hayden was a big help. Thanks for your assistance and the loan of your office." We chatted for a few minutes. I found out that Hayden had been working at the golf course for almost two years. He liked the work and didn't even mind taking on overtime.

I exited the club house and made my way around the building to where my car was parked. Hayden was already back at work, reparking a golf cart which had just been returned. I took out my camera and under the guise of checking something on my phone, snapped a few shots. Hayden had been a big help. He told me a lot more than he thought he did.

FORTY-EIGHT

Java Junction was located in a wooden, 50s two-storey house on the main drag through Marda Loop. Six small tables stood in what would have once been the front yard. I walked through the open gate and past a chokecherry tree, the fragrant aroma of its white cylinder-like flower clusters filling my nostrils.

The outdoor tables were all occupied, the warmth of the afternoon sun luring customers outside. I headed to a table occupied by an older man. A golden retriever lay at his feet.

"Al Walker?"

The dog sat up; his master stood. "I'm guessing you're Jorja Knight." His green eyes crinkled, and his lips turned up in a smile as he held out his hand.

"Nice to meet you. And who's this handsome guy?" I held out my hand for the dog to sniff, then patted his head when his tail swished vigorously.

"This is Beau."

"He's gorgeous."

Al chortled. "He knows it, too. Here, please sit." He pulled out a chair for me. "What can I grab you to drink?"

"A plain black coffee would be great, thanks."

I waited with Beau while Al went inside. The city was abuzz with energy. After a long cold winter, everyone was anxious to get outside now that daytime temperatures were approaching the high teens. The courtyard was well protected by a fence on one side and a tall hedge on the other. Al returned with our coffees and sat.

"So, you working with the Crown Attorney or defence?"

"Defence. Neil Trent is the lawyer on the case."

"Yeah, yeah." He rubbed a hand over the white stubble on his chin. "I remember Trent. I thought he'd be retired by now."

"He's semi-retired."

"Ah—semi-retired. That means he's got enough to live on but will take on a case if it interests him enough."

"I think you pegged it. How about you? You still dabble in the law?"

"No. I'm fully retired now. Which doesn't mean that I don't have a few cold cases still rattling around in my brain. But I'm not actively pursuing them anymore."

I nodded. "Is Kate Gallagher's kidnapping one of those cases?" I asked, using Kate's maiden name.

He nodded. "I'd like to see the kidnappers caught, but finding Kate's killer is a whole lot more important now."

"I agree. Any chance they could be one and the same?"

Al's eyebrows shot up. "Interesting. You got anything to say they are?"

I shook my head. "Naw. Just one of the half-dozen theories I'm trying to prove or disprove. I met with Kate's brother Sebastian a few days ago. He gave me a rundown of what he remembers about the kidnapping. I was left with the impression that the perps were either one step ahead of the police or were good at predicting their next move."

Al nodded. "I had the house swept for bugs...twice. These guys were really careful. Took their time. Planned out each step."

"Somebody knew the Gallaghers' routines, knew where Kate went to school, the times she was picked up and dropped off."

"I figure they'd either been watching the house for a while or knew the family."

"Were there any suspects at the time?"

"We checked out the housekeeper and a contractor who had been hired to do some repairs on the house, but nothing panned out."

"I get the feeling you have some theories of your own. Would you be willing to share them with me?"

Al took a sip of coffee and leaned back in his chair. His eyes narrowed and took on a distant look as if he was being taken back to 1998. He sat quietly for a few minutes and nodded to himself. "I always thought the younger brother was involved somehow."

The skin on my arms tingled. "Rupert?"

He nodded. "Rupert. I've seen this more times than I care to count. Young man, or woman, grows up not wanting for anything, then a big chunk of inheritance money falls into their lap. At eighteen or nineteen, a million dollars sounds like a lot. But living on a hundred grand a year, if you have no other income, isn't going to get you much these days."

"Is that how much the grandmother left him in the trust she set up?"

"About that. Of course, Rupert's expenses far surpassed a mere hundred grand a year."

"What made you think he was involved in the kidnapping?"

"Just the way he'd hang around, listening in to our conversations. Never taking part in them, just hovering annoyingly across the room. I wondered if that's how the kidnappers managed to predict our every move."

"You figure he was passing on the information. For money?"

"I don't know. He didn't need the money back then, although he's up to his eyeballs in debt now. Might have been misplaced retaliation. I could see that he resented how his parents treated Sebastian and his little sister."

"Did the parents treat him more harshly?"

"Not to my knowledge. The kid was aimless, lazy. He hung around with a bunch of other like-minded dopeheads rather than taking advantage of the privileges he's been granted. His parents weren't happy with the choices he was making. I'm sure they made him aware of how they felt."

"You think his buddies pulled this off? The kidnapping, I mean."

"Hard to say. I went to talk to them after Kate was found. Smug little twerps. Rupert was nervous as all hell. Sweating, fidgeting, wouldn't look me in the eye. But I couldn't find anything that would tie them to the kidnapping. Nothing that would stand up in court, anyway."

"But was there something?"

His head wobbled left to right, and he grimaced. "I dug around, kept my eye on them for a few years. That first summer, the bunch of them spent most weekends at a cabin up at Gull Lake. A family cabin owned by one of the guys. The cabin came with an inflatable Zodiac boat, which I found interesting. We always figured the kidnappers retrieved the money and got away by boat. That fall, Rupert dropped out of university, as did two of his friends—Hunter Redding and Everett Price."

The last name caused me to take a sharp breath.

Al raised his eyebrows. "You know them?"

I shook my head. "No. Sorry. I recently came across a guy named Hayden Price. His buddy Josh Neeley supposedly found Kate Barrett's purse near the murder scene. I don't know if he saw anything the night Kate was murdered or if he came across the bag later. I can't ask him, because he died of an overdose last week."

Al scratched Beau behind his ear, and Beau laid his head on Al's knee. Al nodded slowly. "You going to look into this guy further?"

"You bet I am. Didn't mean to interrupt. What happened to these friends of Rupert's?"

"Kris Holden moved across the country, to attend Concordia University—Film Studies. He died about seven years later, in a car accident. He'd been drinking and rolled his car. Thankfully, no one else was with him at the time."

"And the other two?"

"Rupert and his buddies, Everett and Hunter, lived a party life—out all night, slept all day. Rupert didn't visit his folks very often, even though they lived in the same city. Except when Kate's memory started to come back. It's like he wanted to know how much she knew, what she knew, but was scared to engage with her.

"Kate's therapist urged Kate to draw pictures—of anything, really, not necessarily about the time she was held hostage. One day, she drew a picture of two men; one had a checkmark on his chest. It came up on several pictures. That's when I realized it could be the Nike swoosh logo. I had often seen Hunter wearing a T-shirt with that logo."

"That's interesting. Kate would have been around eight by then, right?"

"That's right. I asked her parents and her brothers if they owned a Nike shirt with a swoosh logo, just in case she was drawing something she had seen one of them wear."

"Let me guess—they didn't."

Al nodded. "Bingo. After she drew those pictures, I never saw Hunter wearing that Nike shirt again. I also noticed another disturbing thing. As everyone was slowly getting used to paying for things using credit or debit cards, Rupert and his buddies paid with cash. Now, that doesn't really mean anything in of itself. Some people just prefer cash. But they would pay cash at the bar, at the nightclub, at the liquor or grocery store, even used cash to buy gas."

"I see what you mean. Seems odd that they all preferred to use cash. Did any of them work, or find a girlfriend, get married?"

"Rupert made a few feeble attempts. Probably under threat from his father. From what I gather, the trust fund his grandmother left him ran out about ten or twelve years ago. By then, his father had sold his diamond mine to Ekati Diamonds. He set up a trust fund for Kate, Michael, Sebastian, and Rupert when he started his new company Northern Energy, but the trust fund pays out dividends only when the company makes money. Exploration is a long game, and although they've found a promising deposit of lithium, it's going to take a lot of money to extract it. In the meantime, Rupert dug himself deeper into debt. The family shored him up for a while. Too long, in my opinion. Last year, his father struck his name from the trust."

"Sounds like Rupert might be out of options. I heard he'd been hitting his sister up for money, but that she cut him off too."

"He's living in an apartment that Kate leased for him. I suspect that might end now that she's gone."

"What about his buddies?"

"They've been bouncing around. Same scenario. Can't or won't hold down jobs. Most evenings are spent partying or in a drug-fuelled stupor. Girlfriends come and go. Hunter has a kid, but he's not taking part in raising him. He lives in Vancouver now or did last I heard. I expect one or the other of them will become a statistic in the country's fentanyl deaths."

"And the other one, Price?"

"Last time I saw him, which was about ten years ago, he was out of a job and couch surfing."

"Who's been lending Rupert money?"

"The banks did at first. Happy I'm sure to lend a Gallagher money. But when he missed his payments, that source dried up. When everyone got tired of him mooching, loan sharks were his next stop."

"Any idea how much he owes?"

"I'd say close to half a mil. If he doesn't find a way to pay it back, he's going to end up face down in the river."

The server at the Pine Valley restaurant said Kate had been upset and crying the last time she saw her. The argument between her and Rupert over lunch that day could very well have been about money.

"Did Kate ever remember anything else, from her time in captivity?"

"She said her pendant broke and she couldn't find it. A little gold necklace with a tiny angel pendant. She was very sad about that. She also said she was kept somewhere dark and that she could hear someone talking once in a while. It could have been a TV. And birds. She said she could hear birds—seagulls."

"Seagulls. We have them in the city, but they mostly stick to the lakes and marshes."

Al set his cup down and leaned forward. "Has anything I've said helped you in any way?"

"The guy I mentioned, Hayden Price, works at the same private golf club the Barretts belong to. He's a recovering drug addict, and although he has a job, I'm wondering if he could be Everett Price.

Al's eyebrows shot up. "Got a photo?"

"Actually, I do." I found the photo of Hayden I had snapped when I was leaving the golf course yesterday. It wasn't a great photo as Hayden's ballcap was covering his forehead and eyes. I held my phone out to Al.

Al studied the photo for a minute. He ran his tongue over his teeth and made a sucking sound. "Guy looks like hell. Older...but it's him."

FORTY-NINE

"Sal, where are you?"

"Just dropping off my recycling at the bottle depot. You need me to do anything?"

"Yeah. I want you to tail a guy for a few days. Name of Hayden Price. He works out at the Pine Valley Spa and Golf Club. He's one of the maintenance staff."

"Sure, doll. You got a car for me?"

"I'm going to JumpIn Jalopies now, to arrange one for you. I'll try to get you something decent, so it won't stand out at the golf club."

Everything Al Walker told me about the lake cabin, inflatable Zodiac, and Kate hearing seagulls when she was being held by her kidnappers was interesting, but I could see that there was nothing concrete. There are thousands of Nike shirts out there with the swoosh logo. What intrigued me the most is that Rupert and his long-time buddies were all in dire straits of one sort or another. And desperate times call for desperate measures.

"Appreciate it. What do we know about this Hayden guy?"

"He was friends with Josh Neeley. They go way back, to university days. I suspect they were drug buddies until Hayden decided to get clean. He claims he hadn't seen Josh in months, but he's lying. Got really twitchy when I asked if Josh had shared his latest scheme with him. Then he pretty much bolted after that.

"There's more. Al Walker, the detective who worked on the Kate Barrett—I mean, Gallagher—kidnapping twenty-some-odd years ago told me that her brother, Rupert Gallagher, used to hang out with a couple of dropouts, one of which went by the name of Everett Price."

"Price, huh? You think it's the same guy?"

"Al Walker says he is. I showed him a photo of Hayden, and even though he hasn't seen him in over a decade, he ID'ed him right away."

"You think he knows something about who killed Barrett?"

"He almost passed out when I asked him if he knew Rupert. Said he didn't, but Al Walker says otherwise. Hayden was more agitated by my questions than he should have been. He knows Rupert and I'm betting he knows something about what was going down the night Kate was killed.

"I'll send you a photo I managed to take of him. It's not great. He has light-brown hair, green eyes, and is about six feet tall. Your best bet will be to park in the far corner of the clubhouse parking lot and pick up his trail when he leaves work."

"Piece of cake. You want the usual stuff, where he lives, where he goes before and after work, who he meets or hangs out with?"

"You got it. I'll give you a call when I have the car arranged. Will you be able to pick it up all right?"

"Don't worry about me. I'll be on my way as soon as you call."

I jumped into my car and headed over to JumpIn Jalopies. It's where I had leased my cars before buying Gab's Mustang. If the mechanic at the shop where I had my car fixed was right, I might soon be leasing from them again. The mechanic who worked on my car told me keeping a car on the road as it approached the two hundred-thousand-mile mark was an expensive proposition. I hadn't asked how expensive, since I literally felt woozy when they handed me the repair bill for what I assumed was a mere fraction of the possible expenses he was warning me about. I shifted lanes and made a mental note to ask Willie if CanNet was going to provide their employees with vehicles or at least a vehicle allowance.

The news came on as I drove into the JumpIn Jalopies parking lot. I turned up the volume.

In a release issued this morning, authorities announced Calgary Police Service and the Federal Policing National Security Team have arrested a fourth man in relation to last week's failed terrorism attack. Local resident, Robert Gagnon, twenty-three, was charged with two counts of facilitating a terrorist activity. Gagnon has been remanded into custody, pending a court appearance. Calgary police have declined further questions about the charges or the man who has been arrested.

And now some breaking news on the business front. After months of speculation, Jackson Equities today announced its acquisition of Avenue 21 Group. The three-billion-dollar deal strengthens Jackson Equities' position in the mid-cap equity market and displaces Encore as top private equity firm in western Canada.

I let out a low whistle. Talk in the business community was that Barrett's company, Encore, had been looking to acquire the crown jewel for their portfolio of assets, prior to taking Encore public. After his company's first three acquisitions, Cole Barrett had bragged in the media that he could get any company he went after. But it hadn't proven out to be true. Last year he failed to acquire a chain of retail stores after the company rejected his two offers and then sold to a rival that swooped in and made an offer they couldn't refuse.

Barrett wouldn't be taking this loss well. I suspected the blow to his image would hurt almost as much as the hit to Encore's bottom line. Then again, narcissists have a way of twisting bad news to make it sound like they came out on top.

Two hours later, I called Sal to let her know that a white 2011 Vitrio was waiting for her at JumpIn Jalopies. They must have gotten a deal on the now defunct Italian car since they had a dozen on hand for me to choose from. The Vitrio had been plagued with issues ever since the first car rolled out of the plant in 2008. The 2011 model was recalled after consumers reported that the steering wheel detached from the steering column while driving. Other problems cropped up including issues with the transmission shift linkage which resulted in cars rolling away after the driver exited and fuel tanks leaking after a crash, which resulted in several explosions. JumpIn Jalopies assured me all these issues had been remediated in their fleet of cars.

On the drive home I noticed that Mike had messaged me to say he was sending over some more information he had received from Willie. I changed lanes, detoured into a small strip mall, and bought more wine.

FIFTY

I PULLED UP IN front of the Little Alley Steakhouse, which wasn't in an alley but a standalone building in a small mall just north of the Grey Eagle Resort and Casino. The restaurant offered valet parking but no detective worth their salt would use valet parking while on the clock. I left my car in front of a pet store and made my way back to the steakhouse.

Rupert Gallagher must have described me to the maître d', because I was greeted by name and taken directly to where he sat. Rupert almost upended the table as he stood to meet me. He was overweight, with soft pudgy hands and face, and reeked of alcohol. The wisp of light-brown hair did nothing to hide the looming bald spot behind it. He had a slight lisp when he talked, and spittle formed in the corner of his plump lips.

"Ms. Knight, a pleasure to meet you."

"Thank you, but please, it's Jorja."

A young server materialized at our table.

Rupert ignored the young man. "They stock a very nice, aged Barolo here, if you're interested. Or perhaps scotch is more to your liking?"

I normally didn't drink with clients, especially during what I would consider to be the lunch hour, but in this case, it could work in my favour. The amber-coloured drink in front of Rupert called my name.

"A scotch would be wonderful. Neat, thank you."

Rupert nodded at the young man, who turned at once and walked away.

"First of all, please accept my deepest sympathy. Your sister's death must have come as such a shock."

"Yes...well, er, thank you." His hand trembled as he lifted the tulip-shaped glass to his lips.

"It was a lovely service. She's going to be missed by so many people."

"Yes. She had a way about her that drew people to her. You could drop her off in the middle the Amazon Rainforest and she'd come out a week later with twenty good friends."

The young server returned with my scotch. Rupert ordered hors d'oeuvres for us. We made small talk until the main meal was served. I noticed that the server brought Rupert another scotch without asking. He raised his eyebrows in my direction, and I shook my head. One of us had to stay sober.

"What can you tell me about your sister that I wouldn't already know?"

Rupert didn't hesitate. "She always got what she wanted. She wasn't manipulative. People just seemed to want to do whatever she asked, give her whatever she wanted."

"Did that include your father, your brothers?"

Rupert cut through a piece of steak and swirled it through the red juice pooling under it. "She was the apple of our father's eye. After three boys, my parents were ready for a child that didn't rough house and break things. She was our little angel." Rupert's eyes were glossy as he brought the steak up to his mouth.

"It sounds like she went through some tough times growing up."

"Our mother died when she was eight. It was hard on all of us, but hardest on Katie."

I nodded. "It's hard to lose a mother at any age. I was nineteen when I lost mine. If I understand correctly, she had been kidnapped the year before?"

Rupert set his knife and fork down and drained his whisky. His upper lip was beaded with sweat and his forehead glistened with moisture. "That was a dark time. At one point, I thought she was dead. My father never gave up, though." He laughed somewhat bitterly.

"I can't imagine what your family went through. The kidnappers were never caught, were they?"

"No."

"Were you living at home at the time?"

"No. I was at uni, so I wasn't around much."

"Your sister recovered though. Your brother mentioned during the eulogy that art was instrumental in her recovery."

"Yes, my dear brother. Always been good with words."

"It was inspiring to hear what she managed to overcome. Maybe that's what drew people to her." I took a bite of my pan-roasted trout and decided to get right into the reason for my meeting.

"Was your sister planning to leave her husband? Do you know if the rumours are true, that your sister was having an affair with Ben Langcaster?"

Rupert almost choked. "I never understood her infatuation with Cole Barrett."

"He's wealthy, for one."

Rupert gaffed. "On paper. All these brilliant business acquisitions he's made. That was with our money. Kate's money. My mother's family was quite well off. Our grandmother left each of us a sizable trust after our mother died."

"Were there any signs that their marriage was in trouble? Did Cole mistreat your sister?"

"Cole can be a real bastard," he spit out. "He's exactly the kind of guy I grew up hating. I'm sure he was a bully back in school. Still is."

"Did he bully Kate?"

"Cole used Kate to get what he wanted."

"Used her how?"

He waved his fork expansively. "Pulling in family favours. Introducing him to influential people my father knew. When he met someone new, he always managed to mention that he was married to a Gallagher. Kate knew how to smooth over the jabs he took at people. Make him look civilized. He was always sending her off to soft talk someone's wife into getting her husband to invest in his schemes."

"Kate went along with that?"

"She didn't have much choice if she wanted to stay married. He would badger her until she gave in. He could get nasty just like that."

Rupert snapped his fingers. "That good ol' boy demeanour, that big smile of his...it's just a front."

"Did she want to stay married to him?"

"Kate was a smart woman. She had her reasons for staying with him."

"What reasons?"

"She should have gotten Cole to sign a prenup to protect her interests, but Cole convinced her that their assets were equal in value so no need for one. The guy's a liar. I think a prenup would have shown Cole for what he was—you know, the Emperor's New Clothes and all that."

"What about the Avenue 21 Group acquisition I just heard about? If the rumours were true, Kate and Cole's fortunes would have doubled if he had managed to get it."

"Convenient for Cole that Kate's dead, isn't it?"

"What do you mean?"

"Kate's share of the company stays in the company. Without her shares, Encore is worthless."

"Are you saying Cole might have known he wasn't going to be successful in his bid for Avenue 21 and killed your sister to protect Encore and his interests?"

Rupert patted his mouth with his napkin and laid it on the table. "You tell me. I'd love to see him hang, for my sister's murder. He's too smart to get caught if he did it."

"If it wasn't Cole, who else would have wanted your sister dead? Was there anything going on in the family, or anything from her past that might have come back to haunt her?"

Rupert drained his second scotch, or maybe it was his third, and signalled to the young man who was hovering nearby for another. "It's best to leave the past in the past."

"Can't argue with that. Unfortunately, the past sometimes refuses to stay in the past and comes back to bite us."

Rupert's eyes swung in the direction the server had gone and back to me. His hands fumbled as he adjusted the knot in his tie.

"One of the theories I'm working on, and it's just one of several, is that maybe Kate recognized one of her kidnappers. I talked to Al Walker, the detective on the case. Remember him? He thinks the theory warrants a look. What do you think, Rupert?"

Rupert choked and brought his napkin up to his mouth. His face grew red. He stood, held up a finger, and rushed off, coughing. All that rich food and alcohol must be doing a number on his GI track.

I played with my empty scotch glass while I waited for Rupert to return. Things were not as rosy in the Barrett household as Cole would like the world to think. Rupert made no attempt to hide his feelings about his brother-in-law. Yet it was his kind and loving sister who had been murdered, not her despicable husband. The timing of Rupert's choking episode with my reference to Kate's kidnapping all those years ago hadn't gone unnoticed.

I glanced at my watch. Rupert had been gone for over ten minutes. The prudent thing to do would be to send someone to check on him. I looked around for the server and spotted Rupert across the room. He paused then continued his unsteady gait across the restaurant toward me.

He reached the table without incident but didn't sit. "Sorry about that," he slurred. "You'd think I'd know how to swallow properly by now. I have a meeting, so I have to run. I've taken care of the bill."

I stood up. "Oh, I would have gotten it, but thank you."

He waved a floppy hand over himself. "Next time."

I thanked him for meeting with me and headed to the entrance. Instead of exiting, Rupert turned and strode back across the restaurant, stopping once to regain his balance.

I paused at the door and watched Rupert's unsteady gait as he made his way into the restaurant's lounge. If I were to guess, I'd say Rupert was an unhappy man. And he couldn't have made it any clearer that he didn't want to talk about his past or Kate's kidnapping. Which made me even more determined to find out why.

FIFTY-ONE

I GLANCED OVER AT the TV and sat up. The news reporter was standing in front of the Helix Tower downtown saying something about Jackson Equities' latest acquisition. I reached for the remote and turned up the volume.

"Encore's private investors were rattled after news that Avenue 21 Group had been snapped up by Jackson Equities, leaving Encore scrambling to readjust its timeline for releasing their preliminary prospectus documents for public review. President Cole Barrett issued a statement yesterday that plans to take the company public have been in part delayed by the tragic death of his wife Kate Barrett, who owned significant interest in Encore.

"Kate Barrett's body was found downtown, on the morning of May ninth, where she had been shot. Police have brought charges against Sherrie Langcaster, wife of Ben Langcaster, a long-time friend of Cole Barrett's, rumoured to have been in a relationship with Kate Barrett at the time of her death."

The reporter recounted most of what I already knew about Kate's death and the acquisition. Now that the terrorist threat was behind us, the news channels needed something to talk about.

Sal called while I was making my third feeble effort to leave.

"Hi Sal. What's up?"

"I got some news on Price."

"That's great. What have you got?"

"Followed him home from the golf course. He lives in an old condo complex near the university. I didn't have much to do last night so I thought I'd keep an eye on the place a bit longer."

"I take it your diligence paid off."

"He went out 'round nine. On foot. I thought he might be going to a bar or out to eat. Followed him to the mall on the north side of Crowchild. He stopped by the TD Bank and just stood there. After 'bout ten minutes a car pulls up. Nice car. An Audi. Our guy gets in."

"Did you get a plate number?"

"You know I did. I'll send it to you."

"Where did they go?"

"Nowhere. Just drove around for maybe half an hour."

"Did you see who was driving?"

"Nope. Tinted windows."

"Okay, sorry, go on."

"After they finished drivin' around, our guy gets dropped off back at the mall."

I held my breath, hoping Sal did what I would have done next.

"So, I follow the Audi to a fancy schmansy townhouse on Riverdale Avenue. Didn't see the driver. Car drove into the underground garage. I'll send you the address."

"Great job, Sal. I mean it." Sal didn't need to send me the address. I knew who lived in a fancy schmansy condo on Riverdale Avenue.

Rupert Gallagher. And now I knew that we were finally onto something.

· · · ● · ● · ● · ● · ● · ·

THE BUILDING FELT QUIETER than usual. I noticed the accountant on my floor had already moved out. A sign on the English Language School door announced their impending move on July first and gave their new address. Guess Florence found a new location.

I unlocked my office and flipped the light switch. The lights flickered and buzzed as I made my way to the back office. The mind map I had drawn days earlier was still hanging on the wall. The cops call them murder boards but not all of my cases involved murder, so I referred to mine as a mind map.

I sat, put my feet up on the desk, and stared at the map. I had veered away from the theory that Kate Barrett's murder was related to her infidelity and had started down the money trail, although the possibility of both couldn't be ruled out.

Money. Wasn't there a saying about money being the root of all evil? Every corner I had poked into to try to find the motive behind Kate's murder quickly bumped into money. Todd Paquet lost his scholarship. Rupert was in dire financial straits after Kate and the family cut him off, leaving him with loan sharks breathing down his neck. An expensive purse belonging to Kate traded hands a few times and then was sold to an unknown buyer, leaving the original finder of the purse dead from an overdose. And now rumours that Encore might be in financial trouble after failing to acquire Avenue

21 Group. The remaining question, of course, was how did Kate's murder factor into any of this?

After staring at the wall chart for another hour, I got up and added a few more notations. Rupert and Hayden Price knew each other. That was huge. Especially as Hayden had been friends with Josh Neeley, the man who showed up with an expensive bag belonging to Kate Barrett. When I talked to Hayden, he tried to make it sound like he and Josh were mere acquaintances. He lied and said he didn't know Rupert Gallagher, except by name. Yet the day after I talked to him, he and Rupert met. They hadn't driven aimlessly around town simply to get caught up. My conversation with Hayden rattled him, and whatever he was worried that I would find involved Rupert.

Then there was the matter of Rupert's and Hayden's possible involvement in Kate's kidnapping twenty-four or five years earlier. Al Walker mentioned three of Rupert's friends who might have been involved: Kris Holden, Hunter Redding, and Everett Price, whom he confirmed was Hayden Price. Could Kate's brother Sebastian have been right when he speculated that Kate could have been murdered because she saw and recognized one of her kidnappers recently? But then what? Instead of alerting the police, she ends up meeting her kidnapper in the middle of the night and is murdered? How could that have come about?

I kept creating possible scenarios. I favoured the one that had Kate bringing someone money the night she was killed. Could she have had the money in an orange Hermes purse? Had her blackmailer shot her and then ditched the bag? But the bag didn't surface until almost a week after Kate's murder. Convenient that the person who found the bag was no longer alive.

Could Josh have been working with Hayden and Rupert to cook up some way to extract money from Kate? Kate's brother said there had been no large sums of money taken from Kate's account in the weeks leading up to her murder. Could the Hermes bag itself be the object of value that traded hands? I'd have to dig deeper to find out.

As much as I liked the theory so far, it left some loose ends. Big loose ends. For instance, the gun. How would Rupert, his buddy Hayden, or Josh, if he was involved, have known about Sherrie Langcaster's gun? I refused to believe that it was just a coincidence that whoever killed Kate picked Sherrie Langcaster's house to rob and that's how they got the gun.

Someone had to have known about Ben's affair with Kate and planned to frame Sherrie for the murder. Hard to imagine that Hayden or Josh would have known about the affair, but Rupert might have. He had ducked answering my question by attacking his brother-in-law. If Rupert had known about the affair, they could have hired someone to gain access to the Langcaster house.

I grabbed my cell phone off the desk and hit the photo icon. The idea continued to swirl through my mind as I swiped through the last dozen or so photos, I had taken. I stopped at the image of the person entering Sherrie's house. I expanded the image. Could this be Hayden Price? The image and Price both had the same kind of build, and both were about the same height. Except Sherrie was pretty sure the person who entered her home was a woman. Maybe she was wrong.

River first told me and Sal that she found the Hermes bag just lying in a dumpster near the Westin. Then she changed her story to say she bought it off Josh. Why had she lied? Was there some reason she didn't want me to know that Josh threw the bag into the dumpster and later retrieved it? Was Josh Kate Barrett's killer?

I glanced at my watch. I'd have to hustle if I was going to corner River before she reported for work. *That sneaky little skank.*

FIFTY-TWO

I ARRIVED AT THE dry cleaners with plenty of time to spare and headed north, the direction I knew River would be coming from—assuming she was working today.

Five minutes later, I spotted River going into the 7-Eleven up the street from her place of work. River was paying for her Slurpee when I got there, so I waited by the door until she came out.

"Hi River."

She whipped around, her eyes wide, almost dropping the Slurpee in the process. "What the hell. You almost gave me a heart attack."

"Why would someone saying hi almost give you a heart attack?"

"This is harassment."

"So, go to the police."

"I'm not talking to you." She turned and shuffled down the sidewalk.

"What do you know about a guy named Hayden Price?"

"I told you. I'm not talking to you."

"River, listen. This is your last chance. If you won't talk to me, I'm going to the police. They will be very interested in how an Hermes bag belonging to a murdered woman got into your dead buddy's hands. And your hands."

River took a loud slurp of her drink and kept walking.

"The truth, River. You'll be charged with obstructing a murder investigation if you don't tell them everything. The detective in charge of Kate Barrett's murder is Sergeant Ryker Cain. I know him personally. I have his number right here." I held up my phone. "Let me make this easier for you. Josh was on the river path the night Kate Barrett was murdered. Maybe he was just out scoring a bump or maybe he was there to help a pal who cooked up some plan to extract money from Kate Barrett. Regardless, he was there the night she was killed. I'm not saying Josh killed her, but he may have seen something or know who did. Are you sure his overdose was accidental?"

River's eyes swept the area between us. Her face was pinched in fear.

"He saw Kate's purse, grabbed it, and ran. How am I doing?"

"I ain't saying nothing. Go away." She picked up her pace.

"I think there was money in the bag. Maybe a lot of money. He used some of it to buy drugs. When the news came out about Barrett, he decided he needed to get rid of the bag. He ditched it in a dumpster behind the Westin, not far from where she was found. This is him, isn't it?" I held up my phone with the image of the guy throwing the bag into the dumpster. River paused mid-step but didn't turn around. "Maybe he took the money that was in the bag or maybe it was empty when he found it. Or maybe someone came and picked up the money, because he was part of the plan. Maybe he didn't recognize the bag's worth. But you did. Is that why he went back to get it? You told him what it could be worth? Come on, River, you know what happened that night because he told you."

River lifted her middle finger, but I noticed her pace had quickened.

I watched until she entered the drycleaners. Time for me to make good on my threat.

• • • ● • ● • • • •

RYKER CAME DOWN THE hall toward me. "Well, well, if it isn't Private Detective Knight." He didn't look happy to see me. If anything, I'd say he was annoyed.

"Hi Ryker. Thanks for seeing me."

"I'm busy. I gather you won't be taking up a lot of my time."

"No, I'll be quick," I said to his back, as he had turned and was already walking down the hall, waving me to follow.

I trailed Ryker up the stairs and into his office. "Okay, Jorja. What's this hot tip you have for me?"

"I've been poking around to see if I could find anyone who might have been in the vicinity when Kate Barrett was murdered or had heard anything on the street. It struck me as odd that she was out at that time of night but didn't have a wallet or purse with her. Turns out she did."

Ryker sat at his desk and waved me to a chair. At least he was looking at me now.

"We found a girl, named River, who claims she bought an expensive Hermes bag off a friend of hers who found it in a dumpster a few blocks from where the body was found."

"Really? Cause my guys had a pretty good look through all the dumpsters and garbage bins."

"I did say *claimed*. At first, she told me she found the bag near the top of a bin behind the Westin Hotel, six whole days after Barrett's body was found. Later she said her friend found it there."

"Okay. I take it you didn't believe her."

"No. When we pressed her on it again, she said her friend found it near where Barrett was killed, but when he realized it belonged to the dead woman, he wanted nothing to do with it. So, a few days later he threw it in a dumpster behind the Westin. I think he told River and River probably recognized that the bag was an expensive one and that they could get some money for it—so he went back to the dumpster and retrieved it."

Ryker was watching my face. "Interesting. I assume you have this guy's name and something to back up this...this story you're telling me."

"Yes, Josh Neeley. And there's a guy named Arlo who works at a loading dock across the alley from the Westin who has some security footage that supports some of what I'm telling you. I told him you'd be by to have a look at it."

"In case you're confused, I don't work for you. We'll just go pick up this Josh Neeley."

"Unfortunately, he overdosed three days later."

Ryker threw himself against the back of his chair. "Seriously, Jorja?"

"Yeah well, he's definitely dead. You can get more details about that than I can. Like I said, there is CCTV footage that shows him throwing the bag into the dumpster days after Barrett was killed. I'll send you the details."

"So where is this Hermes bag now?"

"River says she gave it to her roommate in lieu of some back rent she owes and that she in turn sold it on Facebook Marketplace. Cash."

"Of course."

"The roommate said the buyer contacted her via the phone number she listed on the ad. I'm sure you guys can trace the number, but that's when I hit a brick wall."

"How long have you known about this bag?"

"A few days." Ryker leaned forward but I hurried on before he could speak. "Long enough to make sure that if I brought you the information, I wouldn't be wasting your time."

Ryker rolled his eyes. "Like that's ever concerned you."

"Look, this girl says she found an Hermes bag. It could have just as easily been a knockoff or not related to Barrett's murder. Would you have immediately jumped to the conclusion that it belonged to the victim? But yesterday I discovered something that told me there is a real good chance it is connected to Kate Barrett's murder."

"What's that?"

I lifted my arm and took note of the time. "I'm not keeping you from something important, am I?"

"Don't be a smartass."

I grinned. "What if I told you that Josh Neeley palled around with a guy named Hayden Price who turns out to be an old acquaintance of Rupert Gallagher, Kate's brother. Hayden claimed he hasn't seen

Rupert in years, yet the night after I talked to him, he meets with Rupert—cloak-and-dagger style."

Ryker rolled his arm, prodding me to hurry up.

"Rupert Gallagher owes some nasty people a lot of money. What's interesting is that the detective who investigated Kate Barrett's kidnapping when she was a girl always thought that her brother Rupert was involved. Not that he snatched his own sister, but he may have been the one who was feeding the kidnappers information before and during the kidnapping event."

"You think the kidnapping has something to do with all of this?"

"Not directly. Al Walker, the detective who investigated the kidnapping, never found anything concrete—it was just a gut hunch. But Rupert hung around with three guys, one of which was named Everett Price. Everett Price and Hayden Price are one and the same. Al Walker confirmed it for me from the photo I showed him of Hayden Price. The other two fellows were Kris Holden and Hunter Redding. Holden passed away about sixteen years ago, in a car accident. Redding is still kicking around. His family owned a cabin at a lake north of here. Walker thought it might have been where Kate was kept for the month she was missing, but he couldn't find anything more concrete to prove it."

"Okay, let me see if I got this. Rupert Gallagher feeds his buddies information so they can orchestrate this kidnapping. They get away with it. Rupert and his buddies stay in touch and because you saw two of them together last night it means they conspired and killed Kate Barrett."

"Not that I saw them. They both lied to me. The day after I talk to Hayden, he meets Rupert in a mall parking lot, gets in his car, drives around for half an hour, and then gets dropped off back in the parking lot. He told me he didn't know Rupert Gallagher. Have you looked into Rupert Gallagher's financial situation or talked to his brother about it? The family cut off all his funding last year. Several people told me he owes some nasty people a lot of money. Like maybe close to a half a million."

"You think they were squeezing Kate for money?"

"I think it's a reasonable premise. Kate Barrett was a soft touch. If she thought her brother was in trouble, she would have done what she could to help him out."

"I don't know, Jorja. Sounds a bit too pie in the sky for me."

"Sure, it's a stretch, but so is the idea that Sherrie Langcaster used her own gun, somehow lured Kate Barrett down to the Bow River in the middle of the night, shot her, then threw the gun that she used into the grass two hundred metres from the body, and then returned home. Come on. Have you even considered another possibility?"

"We know Langcaster's husband was having an affair with Kate Barrett. Yeah, no thanks to you. You could have saved us some shoe leather on that one, but I'm sure your testimony in court will confirm it."

"Someone gained access to the Langcaster house, portraying herself to be a rep from Green Energy. We have door security video from the Langcasters that show this woman, using someone else's ID, entering the house. She could be the person who took Sherrie Langcaster's gun. When I find her, its going to blow the idea that Sherrie killed Kate Barrett right out of the water."

"Well, when you find her, you'll let me know, right?"

"Yeah, sure."

I left Ryker's office peeved. I was pretty certain he'd follow up on some of what I gave him, but if he came up with anything, we probably wouldn't know about it until final disclosure right before Sherrie's trial was to start. In the meantime, her entire world had come apart. If we could circumvent a long-drawn-out pre-trial investigation, it would suit everyone. Especially me, as there was no way I'd be available to start working for CanNet in a month—assuming I even wanted to.

FIFTY-THREE

"Hey babe, ready to go?"

Luis and I were going out to dinner tonight. I took one last look at myself in the bathroom mirror and stepped out into the hallway.

Luis' face broke into a grin. "You have no idea how hot you look right now."

The knee-length, dark-grey leather bodycon dress hugged my curves, and the square neckline showed just the right amount of cleavage.

"You look pretty hot yourself, Inspector."

Luis picked up his suit jacket and slipped it on over his white shirt, which skimmed his broad shoulders and trim waist. His dark blue jeans hugged his behind and followed his muscular thighs without being tight.

Since we were walking to the restaurant, I opted for chunky heeled booties instead of stilettos. I picked up my clutch and slipped my arms into the black, cropped wool jacket Luis held up for me. I shivered as his warm breath caressed the side of my neck, and he kissed me.

The city's trees were in full leaf now, creating a bright-green canopy for us to walk under. Tender leaves shimmered in the breeze and their rustling muted all but the loudest street sounds.

We kicked the night off at a cocktail lounge then crossed the street to our dinner place, a hot new restaurant with rave reviews that was located in the former site of an Indo-African restaurant that didn't make it through Covid. After a fantastic meal of Arctic Char for me, and flat-iron steak for Luis, we had moved from the dining area into the lounge for a nightcap. The curved booth was angled in a way that gave us privacy as well as a good view of the rest of the lounge, which was filling up with the after-theatre crowd. I snuggled up to Luis and wrapped my hands around his arm. Luis bent his head and kissed the side of my neck, sending goosebumps down my arms.

"I'm glad we finally got a chance to have a night out."

"Me too. It's been a crazy few weeks, more so for you than me." My eyes dug into his. We had spent the evening talking and laughing about what we'd do if we had all the money in the world, but now his eyes looked as if he were far away in thought.

"What are you thinking about?"

"So much has happened, babe. I don't even know where to start."

I felt myself tense. We had laughed and joked over dinner, but now his voice had a decidedly serious tone.

"Yeah?" I ran my finger lightly down his cheek. "Start anywhere, darling. You can always circle back."

"Right." He cleared his throat, took a sip of scotch, and set his glass back down on the live-edge coffee table in front of us.

"You know we've been reorganizing things, figuring out how to match up the growing need for our services with budget."

I nodded.

"We were finalizing some pretty big changes when the terrorist threat we had talked about for years became reality. Actually, it couldn't have come at a better time."

"Why is that?"

"We had just gone over the report your friend Mike and his cohort delivered on the state of policing in Canada. Police forces across the country are all saying the same thing. Crime—not just the volume but the type of crime and the complexity added by technology—is outstripping our capability and capacity to deal with it." As Luis continued to talk, his breathing quickened.

"When I had lunch with Mike a few weeks ago, he said the recommendations his team made were far reaching and that a complete overhaul of the policing system was needed. He didn't go into specifics, of course."

Luis nodded and ran a hand over his short, cropped hair and rubbed the back of his neck.

"It's going to take us a while to adopt some of those recommendations. The one thing that got hammered home over the last few weeks is how damn weak our information is on these lone-wolf radicals and home-grown terrorists." A muscle jumped in his cheek. "Time is not on our side."

Luis was good at keeping his emotions hidden, but the tightness in his body told me that the stress and fear he experienced on the ground, minute by minute, was radically different from the worry and fear I and most other Calgarians had experienced over the fifty-six hours it had taken to resolve the threat.

I snuggled in closer and squeezed his hand. "I'm so proud of you, Luis. I don't tell you that often enough, but I am. Every single day."

"Thanks, babe." His chest rose as he took a huge breath and then blew it out. "There's been some developments since."

I waited, not daring to breathe. Something was up and he was nervous to tell me. "I hope one of those developments is a raise," I said, aiming to lighten the mood.

He looked over at me and winked. "That's the easy part of what I'm about to tell you."

My heart stopped for a beat.

"Keep this under your hat but our chief has developed some health issues. Over his time off, he was debating whether to stay on while he worked through them but seems like that's not an option now."

"Oh no. I hope he's going to be okay. What happens now? Does that mean you'll continue on as interim chief?"

"It was considered, but they've come up with another plan for me. They want me to work with some other agents and detectives from across North America to set up the first ever North American Integrated Operations and Intelligence Centre. It'll include a Cybercrime Investigations Unit and use a cross-country counter-terrorism strategy and related protocols, and of course use the latest and greatest technologies available."

"Wow."

"My reaction exactly."

"This is good for your career, isn't it?" I forced some excitement into my voice. Something was wrong. I knew from the way his eyes narrowed that there was more he wasn't saying.

"It's an awesome opportunity, babe. I just don't like what it means for us."

I sat up, my heart hammering against my chest. "Um...are you breaking up with me?" I kept my voice as steady as I could.

Luis jerked around to face me. "Oh god, no. No, babe. It just means I'm not going to be able to see you as much."

I nodded, while my heart rate dropped out of the heart-attack zone. "How not much is it going to be?"

"For starters, I have to be in Virginia for three months. That's where we'll kick things off."

Quantico. I took a deep breath as a hollow opened up inside of me. "Of course." I let my breath out. "And after that?" My stomach muscles tensed.

"I honestly don't know. I imagine I'll be able to get back here for a few days every so often while I'm in Virginia. Not sure where the new organization will operate out of, but it will likely follow a centralized command structure. Maybe it doesn't matter. The agents will work a lot like the FBI does now. The agents can live anywhere and be assigned cases that take them wherever the investigation necessitates."

He was describing a work structure similar to what Willie was setting up at CanNet. It was a lot cheaper and more resource effective to move agents or detectives around than to have them sitting in physical locations in every town and city across the country. I realized Luis was waiting for me to say something. I swallowed hard.

"When do you have to leave?"

"Sunday."

"You mean this Sunday? That's fast." Mike's words echoed in my ears. *You'll want to be prepared; things could move pretty fast.*

"We can do this, babe, right? Three months will fly by." He swallowed a few times. "It's a great career move but I don't want to lose you over this."

I had always envisioned Luis leaving law enforcement and entering politics. I knew he wanted to influence change in policing, and I always thought the political arena might allow him to do that. Foolish of me for thinking so. He now had a chance to influence more than policy. I knew what would happen next. He wasn't talking about an academic exercise. After they set up the new organization, he'd be expected to work in it. My chest tightened.

I reached up and kissed him. "It's going to take a lot more than this to get me to change my mind about you." I looked deeply into his eyes needing him to see the truth in my words.

Luis folded me into his arms and squeezed tight. "God, I love you."

I pressed my face against his shoulder and blinked back the tears threatening to overflow. This wasn't in the plan. Finding new office space or shifting my work situation didn't seem like such a massive thing anymore. I could handle all of it with Luis at my side, but my mind was already spinning negative thoughts. *This is the first step. He'll find someone else. I'm going to lose him.* It wasn't the first time these thoughts had infiltrated my mind. I took a deep breath, and then another. *I can't lose him.* I blew out my breath. *Don't be a baby.* I wanted to believe that we would be alright. I wanted to reassure Luis that I could handle this. "I love...you too." My voice cracked and all the tears I'd been holding inside, spilled out.

FIFTY-FOUR

AFTER THE BOMBSHELL LUIS dropped on me, we had gone back to his place and made love three times that night. Luis managed to drop off to sleep a few times, but I had lain awake until the soft morning light crept into the room. Luis had been relieved to hear me say I was willing and ready to accommodate a hopefully short-lived, long-distance situation in our relationship. I worried that it would be him who would be changing his mind after working on the other side of the country and establishing friendships with the like-minded people with whom he'd be working. It sounded like an exciting and energy-charged assignment, the kind that built friendships for life.

Luis wasn't a player, but I knew that he was seeing other women when we first hooked up. Of course, that had been before he declared his love for me, and before we had established clarity around our expectations of one another. When I told him that I wasn't interested in continuing a non-monogamous relationship, it had led to our first breakup. But truthfully, I had been just as scared of the commitment as he was.

For the first time since we started spending nights together Luis hadn't woken up at five o'clock to work out. Maybe he figured last night's activities had burned off enough energy. We sat in bed drinking coffee and talked until he had to get ready to leave for work.

I headed home, showered, and got dressed for the day but couldn't seem to get myself out the door. My condo was my home, my cozy safety zone, except this morning it didn't feel like that. It felt cold and...empty. I poured myself a bowl of cheerios and turned on the TV.

Edna Moss was being interviewed on the morning news. The news host was brazenly cheerful as she mentioned that it had been two days since Encore failed to acquire the crowning gem in an acquisition strategy that would have pushed them into the top tier of mid-sized private equity firms. Edna sat stone faced. She's ready for the obvious question—what went wrong. The news host asks the question just like I predicted. Edna's answer is banal. "We assessed the assets and financial health of Avenue 21 Group and made a fair and attractive offer."

The news host responds, "So, the other company overpaid?"

"We believe so."

The reporter asked Edna what's next for Encore.

Edna jumped into her prepared answer. She talked about their growth over the last three years and used lots of numbers to convince viewers that they could expect to see year-over-year growth into the foreseeable future.

I put my empty dish into the dishwasher, grabbed my jacket, and headed out.

· · · ● · ● · ● · · ·

BEN CROSSED THE LOBBY floor. His hurried steps echoed off the marble tiles. Lines of exhaustion etched his face. I took a step forward and called out a greeting.

"I can give you ten minutes. That's all."

I followed him out the lobby doors and we ran across the street to a coffee shop. Coffees in hand, we settled at a table in the far corner.

"Must be a bit chaotic at work these days."

"Let's cut the chit chat. What do you want?"

"The truth, for starters."

Ben sucked in a breath through clenched teeth.

"Was Kate being blackmailed?"

"No. Not that I know of."

"Was anyone hitting her up for money?"

"Like who?"

"What about this art scholarship recipient who had his scholarship rescinded? I heard he threatened to sue, but nothing came of it...or did it?"

"Oh that. It happened months ago. Kate's lawyer advised her to pay him off, it's a lot quicker and cheaper than dragging the issue through the courts."

"They settled, then."

"Yes. I don't know the details. Ask her lawyer if you want to know more."

"Okay. What about her brother Rupert?"

Ben huffed. "He was always looking for handouts. Kate did everything for him, but it was never enough. She got him into the most expensive drug rehab program in the country. Twice. I was glad to see Kate's family come to their senses and cut him off."

"I heard he's in a lot of debt."

"That's his problem, isn't it?"

"Could she have been going to meet Rupert the night she was killed?"

Ben pursed his lips and shook his head. "I wouldn't know."

"She never said anything to you about where she was going that night?"

"No."

"But you did talk to her, didn't you? I mean, the day she was killed."

Ben didn't answer.

"I want to know what happened that night. I hate to tell you this, but the police know that you were having an affair. And no, I didn't tell them even though I expect to be subpoenaed any day now. Even if you were careful, they can still find you. All mobile phones go through a cellular carrier, and they can find the location the phone was used at, as well as access the call log and data usage. It's hard to remain completely anonymous." That wasn't totally true. If he used the Burner App he could have already burnt the number and all the data associated with it. But maybe Ben wasn't that tech savvy.

Ben stared out the window, his fingers tapping the tabletop.

"Sherrie refused to tell the police anything about your affair when she was picked up. Maybe she knew how bad it would look for her if she admitted to knowing about your affair. Or maybe it was her way of thinking that she could somehow protect your son from all of this. Has the prosecutor asked you if you'd be willing to take the stand voluntarily?"

Ben turned his head back. His eyes were cold, devoid of emotion.

"You do know that the recent changes to the Canada Evidence Act means spouses can be forced to testify and provide evidence through a subpoena, don't you? Are you willing to let Sherrie go to prison? Do you really think she killed Kate?"

"They found her gun." He paused for a second. His next words came out flat. "Sherrie knew it was Kate I was seeing. She recognized her purse in one of the photos you gave her."

Damn. This wasn't what I wanted to hear. Now that I opened that can of worms, I might as well get all the bad news out on the table. I took a huge breath. "What really happened the day Sherrie confronted you?"

"She wasn't in any state to have a reasonable conversation. The minute I got home, she attacked me. Called me names. I denied the affair, tried to get her to calm down, but she lost it. That's when she shouted that she knew it was Kate. She called her all sorts of names. She just kept screaming at me. There was no talking to her, so I left. She followed me to the door. The last thing she shouted at me was she was going to make me pay."

Ben seemed to think her response was unreasonable. He's lucky she didn't meet him at the door with her gun. But the jury wouldn't treat the shouted threat lightly.

"You think this is the way she's making *you* pay? She's the one facing a murder charge."

"She killed Kate." His eyes filled with tears. As unfair and downright shitty as he was being to Sherrie, it made me realize he was no longer in love with her. And maybe hadn't been for a long time.

"You left the house. Then what?"

"I didn't know what to do. I drove around for a few hours then I went to the office. We were working on this acquisition and…anyway, I decided I'd have to go back and be upfront with Sherrie. I had been planning to leave her after Matt went to university, but once it all came out, I knew I couldn't wait any longer. In a way, I felt relieved that Sherrie finally knew the truth."

"Did you talk to Kate?"

Ben swallowed a few times and nodded. "I called her. Told her what happened. She wanted to tell Cole, that she was going to leave him, but I told her to wait a while."

"Why?"

"Like I said, we were working on this acquisition, and I thought it would be best if Kate waited until the deal was done."

"Was that because you thought if this mega deal went through, Cole wouldn't mind losing his wife as much, or because Kate's divorce settlement would be so much larger?"

"That wasn't it at all. It was all just happening so fast. We just needed time to…to work out a plan."

"Go on. You tell Kate. Then what?"

"Like I said, I went to the office. Cole was in a mood. The downtown was cordoned off and the police were urging everyone to stay home. Cole had Edna send out an email to tell everyone who wasn't working on the acquisition to stay home. I didn't go home that night. I caught a few hours of sleep at the office."

"You didn't see Kate that night?"

"No. We had plans to meet the next day."

"The day she was killed?"

Ben shook his head as if in disbelief and his eyes drifted away for a few seconds. "I know what you're thinking, but I didn't kill her."

"But you met up with her that evening, right?"

"No. She had to cancel."

"Did she say why?"

"No. I didn't talk to her. She left a message. I called her later, but she didn't answer."

"That didn't worry you?"

"Of course it worried me. I told myself that Cole probably kiboshed her plans. He was always springing last-minute demands on her."

"Had you planned to meet on the river path?"

"No. A motel, by the airport."

"What did you do?"

"I went back to work. We had a deadline coming up and I needed the time. I thought maybe if I got in a good twelve or fourteen hours that I'd be able to get away the next night with Kate." His voice broke on her name.

"So, you spent that night at the office, as well?"

"Yes. Well, no, not the night—the whole evening. Everyone was working late."

"Including Cole and Edna?"

"Edna was working from home. Cole left around dinner time. I worked until about eleven, then left. I didn't go home though. I hadn't slept much the previous two nights, and I didn't want to get

into another screaming match with Sherrie, so I stayed at the motel
I had booked. The motel where Kate and I were to have met. I told
the police all of this."

"Did you try reaching Kate?"

"Not then, but I tried her in the morning. I was worried that
maybe she had gone ahead and told Cole she was leaving him. When
I couldn't reach her on her cell, I broke one of our cardinal rules and
called her at home, but I hung up when the call went to voice mail.
I told myself that if I didn't hear from her in the morning, I would
make some excuse and drive out to her place to make sure she was
okay." Ben's tortured eyes met mine "Except she wasn't, was she?"

FIFTY-FIVE

Neil and I were meeting with Sherrie today. Neil brought coffee and a box of muffins. Sherrie's sister-in-law was out at a yoga class, so we had the house to ourselves. We grabbed coffee and muffins and settled at the round maple dining table. Neil pulled open his briefcase, took out a file folder, and slid it over to me. "Brought you a present."

I opened it and found six pages of licence plate numbers for the partial plate I had found for the Escalade that had been seen in the Langcaster neighbourhood leading up to the time Sherrie noticed her gun missing. The list came with names and phone numbers, no addresses, but it was a good start.

"Thanks, Neil."

"Let's hope it pans out." Neil pulled a leather notebook from his briefcase and opened it. "Pre-trial disclosure meeting has been set for two weeks from now."

"What happens then?" Sherrie asked in a small voice.

"It will be a meeting between us and the Crown, to exchange evidence."

"What evidence?"

"The Crown is obliged to disclose all relevant information to the defendant, both inculpatory evidence—that which supports the Crown's case—and exculpatory evidence—which is information that favours you, the defendant."

"Will I have to be there?"

"It's not mandatory, but I think you should be there. That way you'll know what they have on you. Once we hear what they have, you might be able to provide further information to dispute what they have gathered, or at least make some informed decisions going forward."

"Informed decisions about what?"

"After we hear what evidence they'll be bringing forward, we'll have to come up with a strategy on how to respond. I'll be frank. If the evidence is solid and there isn't much for us to go on by then, we might want to discuss a plea bargain."

"No." Sherrie's arms crossed her stomach, as she rocked slowly. "I didn't kill Kate Barrett. I won't have my son and family thinking I did. I'm innocent. We have to make them see that." Sherrie turned to me, her eyes pleading. I offered her a weak smile.

"We're trying, Sherrie. No need to panic." Neil gave her arm a pat. "You make any headway, Jorja?"

"Some. Not as much as I'd like."

I updated him on what I had found out about Josh Neeley and filled him in on the inroads I had made on the angle that someone might have been threatening or blackmailing Kate and how the handbag and Josh Neeley might fit in. I shared the dumpster photo with him and told them about Josh's connection with Hayden Price and Hayden's connection to Kate's brother, Rupert.

"Rupert owes loan sharks a lot of money. His brother told me the family cut him off a few months ago, after supporting him for years. His father removed him from the family trust fund he had set up a decade earlier and said the next step was to cut him out of his will."

"That gives some credence to our story. If Rupert was desperate enough, he may well have been blackmailing or otherwise extorting money from his sister." Neil raised his head. "The police know about this?"

"Off the record, yes. I shared the extortion theory with Detective Ryker Cain, gave him River's name, the dumpster photo, and Josh Neeley's and Hayden Price's names as well. Maybe one of them owns a pair of ten and a half shoes that will match the prints found at the scene. Ryker's still peeved with me so I'm not a hundred percent sure that he'll jump on it right away."

Neil rubbed the back of his neck. "Well, investigative decisions lie in his domain, we don't have any authority to dictate who or what he's to investigate."

"I've known Ryker for years. If anything I said raises questions in his mind, it'll push him to run it down."

Neil tapped his pen lightly against his notebook. "Is there anyway to find out if Rupert made a payment around that time, to his loan shark or bookie?"

"That's next on my to-do list."

"Good. Maybe we can string enough of these pieces together to convince the jury that Barrett went down to the river path that night to deliver money either because she was being blackmailed or threatened, rather than to meet her lover's wife."

Sherrie made a mewing noise, maybe in protest or just to remind us that she was still there.

"I'll have a talk with Rupert. Suggest that he might come out better from this if he's the first one to talk."

"Let me know if he does."

"Will do."

"Lots here to think about. So how does the woman who used the stolen ID to access Sherrie's house fit in?"

"I don't know...yet."

"Anything else?"

I proceeded to relay my last conversation with Ben. Neil listened and jotted notes while I talked. Sherrie picked at one of her finger-nails the whole time.

When I finished, Neil sighed and rubbed his forehead. Then he turned to Sherrie. "You knew your husband was seeing Kate Barrett all along. You lied to me. Now, I'm hearing that you told your husband you knew it was her. You recognized her from the photo Jorja gave you?"

Sherrie shrunk into herself and wouldn't meet Neil's eye."

"Unbelievable." Neil looked sad, more disappointed than an-noyed. He turned back to me. "So, neither Ben nor Cole has a solid alibi for the night Barrett was murdered."

"I haven't looked into Cole's movements that night, but I fol-lowed up on Ben's story and it checks out. A security camera picked up his car driving into a motel parking lot, the one where he was to meet Kate Barrett the night she couldn't meet him. I checked the security desk at Helix Tower. There weren't many people coming in and out that night as most people working in the tower had been sent home because of the terrorist threat. It shows him checking in and out at the times he said."

Neil grunted. His eyes met mine. Neither of us had to say the obvious. Sherrie caught our silent exchange and twisted in her seat to face Neil. "What...what about the blood...the sports bag?"

"We know you saw a sports bag, Sherrie. But it's gone now." I pulled out my phone and showed her the snippet of dash-cam video showing a young man stuffing the bag into the neighbour's trash bin.

Sherrie's hand flew to her mouth, her eyes widened. "Matt. Oh, my god. Why...how did he...I can't...does Ben know?"

Neil turned to her. "Sherrie, even if your son testifies that he saw the bag, maybe even a bloody T-shirt of Ben's inside, we don't know whose blood it is. The bag is long gone. If the blood on the T-shirt did belong to Kate, it doesn't exonerate you. The prosecutor will argue that you tried to set your husband up to take the fall."

Sherrie's shoulders sagged as she stared down at her hands resting on her lap.

"There's also a witness out there who claims to have seen you try to run your husband down at the Britannia Club in April. If the prosecutors call this witness, it's not going to do our case any good."

"But that's not true." Sherrie looked up but there was no energy in her denial. She turned to Neil. "Who would say something like that?"

"It doesn't matter Sherrie, unless this witness has proof to corroborate their story. I'm just trying to let you see what we might be up against." Neil picked up his pen and tapped the notes in front of him. "Our best chance is to follow up on this theory that someone was extorting money from Kate Barrett, and she was killed in the process."

I left the meeting encouraged by Neil's response. We didn't have to prove any of this. We didn't need to prove that Sherrie was sane or that she entertained thoughts about killing her husband or not. Neil just had to build a credible story, supported by a few facts and some supporting evidence, that there was a reasonable chance someone other than Sherrie killed Kate Barrett.

FIFTY-SIX

After my meeting with Neil and Sherrie, I called Al Walker. I was hoping he could give me the names of some local loan sharks who could let someone like Rupert run up a tab as big as the one he was rumoured to owing. I wasn't about to ask Luis, and Ryker still had his nose out of joint about me not rolling over on Sherrie when he asked me why I had been watching Kate Barrett's house in the days leading up to her murder. Since coffee and a muffin can hold a person only for so long, I offered to buy him lunch.

Giovanni's Deli was packed when we got there. Gina was behind the counter taking orders and running the till, Aria was running orders out to the customers and clearing tables. Gina waved as I walked in with Al.

Gina was part owner of the place. She and Aria were Gab's cousins. The Giovannis had run the shop since the 1920s when Gab's great-great-grandfather, newly arrived from Italy, started selling sausages he made himself out of the small clapboard house that once stood on this spot. As the business and family grew, he moved the family to a bigger house in Bridgeland, converting the original home into a café, which was later torn gown by his son and replaced with the current brick structure.

Al sniffed the air. "Smells good in here."

"Have you never been here?" At the shake of his head, I listed my three favourite dishes. "I'm always torn as to which one to get. They have several daily specials as well, listed on the board behind the counter, but today I'm going to have the toasted Caprese chicken sandwich. It's loaded with chicken, tomatoes, basil, and fresh mozzarella."

"I'll try that as well."

I placed our order with Gina and, by the time I was finished, Aria had found Al and me a spot near the window. We made small talk until our food came. Al took one bite of his sandwich and threw his head back in ecstasy.

"Good, right?"

"Why have I never heard of this place?"

"If you had a drop of Italian blood in you, you would have. I think they put the name of this place on the back of Italian children's birth certificates."

Al laughed. In many ways, he reminded me of Mike, which reminded me in turn that I owed Mike a phone call. *Tonight. I'll call tonight.*

"I had a little chat with Hayden Price the other day."

"You found him, eh?"

"He's got a general maintenance job out at the Pine Valley Spa and Golf Club. The Barretts are members there."

"I remember you telling me that's the club the Barretts belong to." Al lifted his eyes skyward and shook his head. "What are the chances?"

"Thought you'd find that interesting. What's even more interesting is that after our little chat, Hayden had a meeting with Rupert Gallagher. The very next night. They met in a mall parking lot, drove around for a while, and then Rupert dropped him back at the mall."

"Suppliers usually don't like spending that much time with their customers."

"Hayden is clean now; or so he says. He told me he knew who Rupert was but otherwise denied knowing him."

Al winked. "Guess your conversation made him want to rush out and make a friend."

"I don't know why he bothered to lie. He must have known I'd follow up. Since we last talked, I found out Rupert's in a lot of debt. Like to the tune of several hundred thousand dollars."

Al set his sandwich down on the plate and wiped his chin and fingers with his napkin. "Why doesn't that surprise me. He always lived the lavish lifestyle, the hell with the expenses." Al picked up his sandwich again and took another bite.

"Any idea whom he might be borrowing from? The brother says not the family, they cut him off months ago."

Al popped the last bite of sandwich in his mouth. "Man, that's good." He wiped his fingers on his napkin. "Are you asking me if I know any local loan sharks?"

"Yeah. I mean, I might as well start with the locals, then move up if I have to."

"The kind of money you're talking about... Gotta be either Jimmie the Knife or Marco Polo."

"Seriously?"

"It's been a while since I've seen either, so not sure they're still around."

"What can you tell me about them?"

Al leaned back in his chair and smiled. He was back on home turf. "Now, Marco Polo—he's what I'd call a professional gambler. Goes to Vegas five or six times a year and Macau, China, at least once a year. They've given him a permanent free suite at the Bellagio in Vegas. Gravitates to blackjack and poker. Never plays the slots. If he's in town, you'll likely find him at the Grey Eagle Casino. You can't miss him. He wears about eighty pounds of gold jewellery and drives a silver Rolls-Royce. He had the interior headliner customized to resemble the night sky. The stars are made with 1200 fibre optic nodes and 600 crystals. Rumour has it that he even hired an astronomer to plot out the constellations, so he'd have an accurate representation of the sky on the night he won twenty million dollars on a 649 lottery ticket."

"What? With that kind of win, why would he be in the loan shark business?"

"It's how he funded his gambling back in the day. He doesn't need the business now, but he's got a couple of guys who run it for him. Head honcho's a Swede by the name of Svensson. The dude is big. And I mean big. The Hulk could be his little brother."

"Great. And Jimmie the Blade...or Knife?"

"He's what we called a dirty gambler. He lies, kills, and cheats to win. He used to be an MMF fighter, but an injury sidelined him.

He did some time for manslaughter. He runs book on anything that moves—even high school football. He owns a bowling alley in Forest Lawn. He'll pretty much loan money to anyone, because he *will* get it back one way or another."

"Who is Rupert's most likely source?"

"I'd say Jimmie the Knife."

"I was afraid you'd say that."

FIFTY-SEVEN

The LuckyRoll Lanes bowling alley was located in a small strip mall on International Avenue. I left the Mustang parked out front and went inside. A set of wide stairs took me below ground to where the bowling lanes were found.

Two lanes were occupied—then again, it was the middle of the day. A young kid with acne was working behind the counter.

"Ah...hello there. I'm looking for Jimmie."

The kid snickered. "Who?"

"Jimmie. The owner?"

A sly smile creased his face. "What was that name, again?"

"Jimmie...the Knife?"

"I'll get him for you." He hit a button on the counter. "Want something while you wait?"

"No, I'm fine, thank you." I moseyed over to a long wooden bench where customers sat to put on their bowling shoes. The kid behind the counter continued to spray something into the inside of the garish orange bowling shoes before returning them to the shelves behind him.

A man walked out from a set of swinging doors at the far end of the counter. He was wiry and grizzled and wore a black patch over his right eye. He rounded the counter and made a beeline for me, grabbing his crotch and giving it a quick hitch.

"Hey sweetheart. What can I do you for?" As he got closer, I could see a scar that started above his eye and ran behind the black patch and ended near his chin. The patch was probably more for his customers' benefit than his. He stopped in front of me and hooked his thumbs into the top of his jeans, splaying his fingers, so they were pointing downward. Was this guy seriously trying to get me to look at his junk?

"I'm a private detective and I'm working on the Kate Barrett murder case." His cocky smile dimmed ever so slightly.

"A lady PI. Now that's what I'm talking about. What's your name, sweetheart?"

I took out a business card and handed it to him.

"Jorja. I like it. Goes with Jimmie. And I sure would like to explore the night part."

It took concerted effort to not to rear back with disgust. "I'd like to ask you some questions."

"Let's go back to my office."

I glanced around. The place was mostly empty. "Let me think about that...yeah, no."

He took a few steps back. "Okay, sweetheart, have it your way. But Jimmie doesn't talk shop out here."

The kid was eyeing us under the pretense of cleaning shoes. He had sprayed the inside of one shoe at least five times. Jimmie kept walking backwards.

I rolled my eyes and followed him into his office. Surprisingly, it was a lot nicer than the bowling alley. It was decked out with leather chairs surrounding a round card table, a juke box that glowed with neon-green lights, and a pool table. The far side of the room held a couch, a mini fridge, and a bar stocked with dozens of bottles of liquor.

Jimmie led me over to the bar area. "Sit, sweetheart. Can I get you a drink?"

I remained standing. "No, thank you."

Jimmie poured himself a half tumbler of amber liquid. "Jimmie doesn't do business with folks who won't drink with him." He waved the bottle of Knob Creek he held in his hand toward me.

The whole 'Jimmie' thing was already irritating beyond belief and now he wanted me to drink rye, which I really disliked. I watched as he poured out a half glass.

"You know there's a hundred percent chance I'm not drinking that."

Jimmie pressed the glass into my hand and tapped it with his. "Come on sweetheart. Relax a little."

"You know Jimmie, I find the idea of relaxing with you totally repugnant. You do know what repugnant means right?"

He scrunched his lips into a fake pout, sat on the couch and patted the cushion next to him. "Come, sit. Jimmie is just trying to be friendly. Jimmie's a friendly guy." I lowered myself onto the edge of the couch. He shifted toward me and spread his legs wide, his right knee touching mine. I cleared my throat. "I'm looking for a potential witness. The guy is about five ten, two hundred and fifty pounds, white, mid-forties. He drives a blue Audi but rumour on the street is that he's broke. Not only broke, but seriously in debt."

He put his hand on my knee. "We should get to know each other a little better, don't you think?"

I put my drink on the coffee table and stood. "Thanks, but I know all I want to know about you already. You can answer my questions on the witness stand, in front of a jury. I'll make sure we get that subpoena out to you right away."

Jimmie struggled to sit up from the depths of the couch. "Hey. Whoa. No. Come on. Sit back down." He patted the cushion next to him. "You think Jimmie's been giving this guy a little cheddar, right?"

I sat back down, keeping a good two feet between us. The next time he touched me he'd need a patch for the other eye. "Somebody has been helping him keep the lavish lifestyle he so desperately wants. Your name kept coming up as one of the best lenders in town." I almost choked on the last few words, but a little flattery might help loosen his tongue. The man saw himself as some kind of swashbuckling Casanova, but I had no desire to say anything that would feed his pathetically misguided self-image.

"Jimmie does have a reputation." He took a swig of his rye and winked at me.

"Do you know the man I'm asking about?"

He nodded. "Teddy Bear. He's come to see Jimmie from time to time."

"How much does he owe you?"

He shrugged. "Jimmie would have to check with his accountant."

"A rough guess would be fine."

"Three hundred Gs, maybe." He shot up from the couch. "Hey, you wanna hear some music. How about a little Bohemian Rhapsody?" He sang the lyrics in a high-pitched voice as he swayed his hips on his way to the juke box.

I peeled off the backing and stuck the mini recording device to the underside of the coffee table, then stood.

"Is Teddy Bear making good on his payments to you?" I walked over to where Jimmie was hunched over the juke box, his hips still swaying.

"Got it." He turned and snapped his fingers in the air, as the music filtered into the room.

"When is the last time he made a payment to you?"

Jimmie danced his way over to me. I headed toward the office door. He sidestepped around me, blocking the way. His face was now inches from mine, the smile gone from his face.

"Too many questions sweetheart. I'd hate to see anything happen to this pretty face." He ran a finger down my cheek.

I pushed past him and slammed open the office door. A group of high school kids were standing at the counter, talking to the kid behind it. I rushed past them, took the stairs two at a time, and shoved open the glass front door. I paused for a second to take a deep breath, then hustled back to my car. Relieved to see that Jimmie the *Creep* hadn't followed me, I locked the doors anyway and started the engine. If I were looking for a missing woman, Jimmie would be at the top of my suspect list.

FIFTY-EIGHT

After leaving, I whipped through a Tim Hortons drive thru and was now sitting two doors down from the bowling alley, eating a sandwich.

The voice activated wireless listening device I had left in Jimmie's office would transmit through walls and other barriers up to a distance of six hundred and fifty feet. At least that's what the manufacture's specs said on the package.

Jimmie was talking on the phone to someone. His voice was remarkably clear given the circumstances.

"You want a spread bet or over under?"

I shuddered. I still felt in need of a shower after my brief encounter with Jimmie. The one-sided conversation I could hear came to an end. I was glad that he had turned off the juke box or it would have really messed things up for me.

Jimmie took a few more calls over the next hour. He also talked out loud to himself and occasionally broke into song. I'd be willing to bet that school had been a real challenge for Jimmie when he was a kid. Some of his behaviour appeared to be consistent with symptoms of ADHD. A lot of his behaviour was consistent with him being a creepy thug.

Jimmie's voice came through the receiver. "Debts don't vanish, pal. Time to pay up."

I sat up. I would have loved to hear both sides of the conversation, but this was as good as it was going to get.

"Forty grand didn't make a dent. Jimmie's closing out your account."

I waited. Sounded like Jimmie was walking around while he made the call.

"What do you mean Jimmie can't." He laughed unpleasantly. "You got two choices. Pay up or face the consequences. Why?" His voice rose. "Listen up. Jimmie don't like people coming around asking questions about your murdered sister is why." Something crashed and I jumped back.

He had to be talking to Rupert. My ears strained to hear every word.

Jimmie's voice was now a low growl. "That's not how this works. You've got two choices. Pay up or lose something valuable."

I held my breath while the person on the other end spoke. Jimmie responded to whatever was said. "All of it."

Jimmie was losing his cool; anger tinged his voice. Another ten seconds passed. "Jimmie's done talking. Pay up or things are going to get a lot worse." Jimmie went silent for a minute, then his voice got louder. "Your niece. Your nephews. You don't think Jimmie knows where they go to school?" He shouted. "Where they are this very minute?" His voice lowered and grew deadly calm. "You've got five days."

Jimmie must have disconnected, because the next thing I heard was some creative cursing and things being thrown around. It had to have been Rupert he'd been speaking to. I mean, how many of his clients had a recently murdered sister. The threat about harming a nephew made me realize how deadly serious he was. He could have easily killed or hired someone to kill Kate Barrett. He could just as easily kill Rupert. Or anyone else he wanted.

FIFTY-NINE

I OFFERED TO MEET Rupert at a coffee shop or a bar or anywhere he wanted. In the end he reluctantly gave me the address to his townhouse which, unbeknownst to him, I already had. Maybe he didn't want to be seen talking to a private eye. He suggested that I come by at seven o'clock. I guess he needed the intervening hours to calm himself and figure out what, if anything, he'd be willing to share with me.

I rang the doorbell at seven on the nose. A light came on and a minute later I heard a lock being slid back behind the massive wood door. The door swung open. Rupert was wearing a black-and-burgundy brocade smoking jacket over a white T-shirt and black pants. He stood back to let me enter. I was clearly underdressed in jeans and a slouchy tan V-necked sweater.

"Thanks for seeing me on such short notice. Hope your day is going well."

Rupert mumbled something I didn't catch, and I followed him into the den. Or maybe it was his living room. A floor-to-ceiling stone fireplace stood against one wall and a massive oil painting of the Tuscan landscape hung over the mantel. He left me standing while he headed to a bar cart standing off to one side. He poured himself a drink and turned to me. "Cognac, Ms. Knight?"

"Yes, thank you, but please, it's Jorja." He sounded sober, but his hand shook as he handed me one of the two tulip glasses.

"Please." He waved at one of the two burgundy leather couches that sat across from each other. A long coffee table sat in the middle. Now I noticed someone had set out a few small plates and a cheese board with Camembert and some other cheeses, along with some nuts, chocolate, raspberries, and dried apricots. An unexpected wave of sadness passed through me. Didn't he have anyone to entertain except for a private investigator who was here to question him about his sister's murder. Or was the sadness for the private investigator with nothing better to do but investigate?

I sat on one of the couches and Rupert sat on the opposite one. Rupert crossed his leg, the leather slipper dangling from his toes jiggling ever so slightly. Neither of us said a word for a few minutes. I took a sip of cognac, its strong aroma filling my nose. I noted the faint flavour of caramelized pear before the smooth velvety texture slid down my throat. I set the glass down on a coaster, crossed my leg over the other and leaned back.

"I wanted to ask you some questions about your old friend Everett Price. I understand he goes by Hayden these days."

His foot stopped jiggling. Rupert remained silent but he kept his gaze on me.

"Was he involved in the kidnapping of your sister?"

He tugged at his jacket, now stretched over his rather expansive girth. "That's preposterous." Rupert looked away.

"Why do you find the idea preposterous?"

"I know Hayden. We were friends in university. I know what kind of man he is. Sure, he's fallen on some tough times now and then, who of us hasn't? He's worked hard to get sober and back on the right track."

"Why did you meet with him night before last?"

Rupert took a rather long sip of cognac, a faux pas with serious cognac connoisseurs. "Why...what...how do you know that?"

"Let's just say it's my business to know."

"Are you investigating me?" Rupert's face went crimson; a fine sheen broke out on his forehead.

"I'm investigating the murder of your sister. There are several people on the suspect list. You're one of them. I'd like nothing more than to cross your name off that list. But you'll have to convince me first."

Rupert stood, glass still in hand, and began to pace. "You can't be serious. She is...*was* my sister, for god's sake! I don't have to put up with this."

His blustering bravado wasn't fooling me. Rupert was seriously shaken.

"You haven't answered my question, Rupert. Why did you meet with Hayden?"

"I hadn't seen him in a while. He heard about Kate. He wanted to offer me his condolences."

"Seems odd that you would pick him up in a strip mall and then drive around for a bit and then drop him back off at the same place."

"His car was in the shop, getting repairs."

"Must have had a sudden breakdown. It was fine when he drove it home from work."

Rupert tipped back the tulip glass and drained the last of the liquid and stormed back to the bar cart.

"Did Hayden tell you that I had been to see him earlier in the day? Did he tell you I was trying to run down an Hermes handbag that one of his other buddies supposedly found near your sister's body? A bag that I suspect might have held a fair bit of money." I stood and took a few steps toward him.

"You can't lie your way out of this one. Was Kate there to meet you, Rupert? Or did you just set up the meeting and Hayden was the one who was there waiting for her? Did you send your sister to her death?"

Rupert was gripping the edge of the bar cart. He was breathing heavily and sweat rolled down the side of his face.

I moved closer. "Rupert, are you okay?"

Rupert's face was an unnatural purplish colour. His hand clutched a fistful of fabric from his smoking jacket.

"Do you need me to call an ambulance?"

Rupert clutched his chest with both hands and toppled over, knocking the bar cart to the floor in the process. I rushed to him. He was gasping for air but still breathing. I grabbed my phone and called 911.

"I've called an ambulance, Rupert. They're on their way."

Rupert's eyes rolled in his head, and he passed out. My own heart thundered against my chest. I held a finger under Rupert's nose. He was still breathing. After a few minutes, I could hear the faint sound of an ambulance. Rupert stirred.

"Rupert, the ambulance is almost here. Keep breathing, slow and steady." I ran to the door and opened it. Two firefighters came up the walk. I breathed a sigh of relief.

By the time the paramedics arrived, the firefighters had Rupert on oxygen. He was still struggling to breathe, and his colour wasn't any better. I told the paramedics what had happened. They checked his vitals, then brought in a gurney and loaded Rupert onto it. I stood in the doorway and watched them leave.

The firetruck left first and then the ambulance. Maybe I shouldn't have pressed Rupert as hard as I did. I wanted information from him, not to kill him. I picked up my phone and called Sebastian. It went to his voicemail. I left him a brief message to let him know what happened, although I wasn't sure he'd care.

Then, since I was already here, I decided to have a little look around.

SIXTY

Rupert's bedroom was exactly as I expected. Expansive walk-in closet or dressing room the size of my living room, a massive four-poster bed, mahogany furniture, a thick Persian carpet over the hardwood floors and burnt-orange velvet curtains that released a whiff of dust as I brushed past.

I had already checked the main area where Rupert had collapsed, the kitchen and another sitting area downstairs. I glanced at my watch. An hour had passed since the ambulance left. I brushed aside a worry that he'd return and find me combing through his personal effects—wait times in emergency far exceeded the gold standard goal of four hours.

I finished riffling through the nightstand and headed over to the dressing room. It would help if I knew what I was looking for. I started with the drawers. The top one held a tray for watches, cufflinks, tie pins, and other assorted jewellery. Three quarters of the tray was empty. I picked up a watch—a Bulova. Nice watch, but he'd probably get no more than a few hundred for it. No sign of any Rolexes or even a Hublot.

The next drawer held several wallets, all empty, his passport, and a cell phone, which had run out of power. I went through all the drawers holding pocket squares, ties, and scarves. Nothing.

I ran my hand past the dozens of jackets, shirts, coats, and pants hanging from the closet rails. If there was anything in the pockets that would incriminate Rupert, I wasn't going to find it. I pulled a metal box standing on one of the shelves and opened it. It held photos and old letters. I took it over to a small built-in table set in front of a mirror and sat on the round brocade-covered stool standing next to it. Opening the box, I pulled out a handful of photos and whipped through them, then grabbed another handful. Most were photos from weddings and Christmas gatherings, a few from travel destinations.

Near the bottom, I found a photo of Rupert and a couple of guys at a lake. Rupert was recognizable even with a full head of curly hair. Despite being thinner in the photo, he still had that soft doughy look. I couldn't identify the two guys with him. They were sitting in a Zodiac boat and holding up cans of beer. Detective Walker mentioned that one of the men Rupert was hanging out with back in his youth had a boat and cabin, or his family did. He could never tie that cabin or the Zodiac to Kate Barrett's kidnapping. The chances of me being able to were almost nil.

Something at the bottom of the box caught my eye. My fingers scraped along the bottom, and I pulled out a necklace. The fine chain was broken. I peered closer at what I first thought was a cross. The tiny pendant was that of an angel, a ruby stone embedded between the outstretched wings. I peered at the clasp and found a 24-carat-gold stamp.

I laid the necklace out on the table and took several photos of it. The necklace was delicate, small, obviously belonging to a child. Had it belonged to Kate? Al Walker mentioned that Kate had lost a necklace similar to this one when she was kidnapped. Why did Rupert have it?

I put everything back, closed up the box, and headed back downstairs. I took one last glance around the den. I had righted the cart after the ambulance left, setting several bottles of liquor and the unbroken glasses back on it. The larger pieces of broken glass were in the kitchen trash. Rupert would have to deal with the rest when he got back. If he got back.

I let myself out and stood at the bottom of the steps, Rupert's keys in my hand. There still was a chance that he'd be checked out and sent home later tonight. Maybe he'd had a panic attack. I hefted the keys in my hand and searched for somewhere to hide them. After a minute, I walked across the narrow lawn to the left of the driveway and stuck the keys into the end of the drainpipe. Rupert had his cell phone on him when he was rolled out, so I left a message telling him where he could find his keys, and said I hoped he was all right.

It was going on ten o'clock by the time I got home. Luis was leaving in two days, but tonight he was at the office, dealing with the last few things he needed to hand off to the new temporary police chief. I was looking forward to seeing him tomorrow night but already feeling the melancholy creeping in. Who knows when I'd see him next.

I told myself to snap out of it. We had phones and video chat, and airplanes, and besides, it's not like he was going off to do a tour of military duty or go to war. Feeling slightly better, I poured a scotch, turned on the TV, and plunked myself on the couch. I should be thinking about what my response was going to be to Willie's job offer, but I felt drained. I had hoped to run it by Luis to get his opinion the night we went out to dinner, but his news trumped mine and I hadn't wanted to turn the conversation around to me, given the enormity of his news. Not sure talking about it on our last night together would be such a great idea, either.

I glanced up. The split screen showed the newswoman on the left, a photo of Cole Barrett on the right. I turned up the volume.

"Cole Barrett, president of Encore, waisted no time to address investors' concerns about the company's future."

The screen flipped to an earlier video clip of Cole Barrett on the steps of the Helix Tower. In that video, he said he'd be strengthening the company's finances in the short term and would then take the company public. He planned to grow Encore into the top equity firm in North America within five years. Audio returned to the newswoman.

"Today, Mr. Barrett announced the company would be streamlining its operations and that one hundred and eighty positions would be eliminated in the coming weeks." A photo of Ben Langcaster appeared on the screen. "One of the first to be let go was Ben Langcaster, head of the legal team who some are saying is responsible for the failed acquisition of Avenue 21 Group. Ben Langcaster has recently been on the news in relation to his wife's upcoming trial in the murder of Cole Barrett's wife. Cole Barrett's wife, Kate Barrett, was found dead in the downtown area in the early-morning hours of May ninth. Speculation has been rampant that the motive behind the killing was Ben Langcaster's affair with Kate Barrett."

Another video clip came on, this one of Ben Langcaster leaving the Helix Tower carrying a box. A dozen or so reporters shoved microphones in his face as he wove through the throng. Some shouted questions about the failed acquisition of Avenue 21 Group, others demanded to know if he had been having an affair with Cole Barrett's wife. Ben ploughed through the crowd, the tension in his neck and shoulders visible, and got into a waiting taxi.

Well, the shit has finally hit the fan.

SIXTY-ONE

I woke up almost as tired as I had been when I went to bed. Strange dreams plagued me all night, waking me, then resumed as soon as my eyes closed. I tried to remember what they had been about, but all but the faintest snippets eluded me. Jimmie the Knife made an appearance in one of them and there had been a chase where I was trying to get away from someone or something in a Zodiac, but it kept deflating as I desperately tried to get away.

I called Rupert's cell phone, and it went straight to voice mail. I didn't bother leaving him another message. I couldn't tell if my questions about Hayden Price or the stress of Jimmie's threats earlier in the day set off his attack. Or perhaps, the combination of the two got to him.

I couldn't see Rupert going down to the river to meet his sister. But I could see Rupert coercing Hayden into making a call to Kate with a threat that he would be harmed or killed unless she made good on the money he owed.

The idea grew on me as I drove to the office. After a while I tried poking holes in my own theory. What didn't make sense in that scenario was Sherrie's gun. How did Sherrie's gun end up being the murder weapon? If Rupert had convinced or coerced Hayden into helping him, he wouldn't have wanted him to *kill* his sister. Could Josh have been involved? Had he killed Kate in a panic when the plan started going south for some reason? But that would mean that he would have had Sherrie's gun and that didn't make sense either.

I drove into a parking lot and realized I had no memory of the drive down here. One of these days this driving around on autopilot was going to get me killed. The two-block walk to the office helped to clear my mind. It was fine to speculate, but Neil needed facts and evidence in order to present a believable story to the jury. I grabbed a coffee in the lobby café and ran up the stairs. I squeezed right as two men came down the hall carrying a desk.

The door to the English Language School stood open. I poked my head in. Florence and two other women were boxing up files from a cabinet.

"Florence, looks like you're moving today."

Her face broke into a grin. "Did you see our news!" She pointed at the sign on the door. "Our school is moving to the Currie Barracks. We have the top floor of the old administration building. A three-year lease. The rent is even cheaper than it is here."

"That's wonderful. I'm so glad you found a place. That's a great location."

"The MAX Yellow Line goes right past there. Good connection to downtown and to Mount Royal University. How about you. Have you found a place?"

"Not yet. I might try out one of those shared office spaces downtown. Just for a month. See how it goes."

"You have to come see us at our new place, Jorja. When you find time."

"I will. Hey, could you use that meeting table I have in my office, the round one with the four chairs? It's free if you want it."

"We could use it. You sure, Jorja?" At my nod she ran over and gave me a quick hug.

"Let your movers know they can come get it anytime this morning."

I stepped back across the hall and unlocked my office. Five more weeks and I'd have to be out of here. Maybe I should just pack up today. My mind ran over all the accompanying changes I would have to make. At minimum, I would need to alter the address on my website, but I didn't yet have an alternate. I wasn't about to let potential clients come to my home. I sighed. Maybe I should sign up for a virtual office space, one that would provide me a corporate address and front office support to answer my phone and store mail until I could pick it up. Or take Willie up on his offer.

I opened the file Neil had given me. The officers investigating Kate's murder hadn't provided Neil with these licence plate numbers. They would be following protocol—which meant Neil had pulled in a favour somewhere.

I took a sip of coffee and called the first number on the list. I had worked up a spiel to tell whoever answered that I was looking for a black Escalade with tinted windows, with a licence plate containing the digits in question because I had damaged the back fender when I was backing out of a parking stall in the mall. I pulled a burner phone from my desk, which I kept for just this sort of reason, and began working through the numbers.

Two people hung up on me. One woman asked why I didn't leave a note on her car and then demanded to know how I got her number. I managed to strike a few plates off the list, but this process was going to take a while. Half the numbers I called didn't answer or my call was directed to voice mail, either because they were busy or because my number came up as an unknown caller.

After an hour or so I found myself staring at the mind map still taped to the wall. My thoughts went back to my latest theory that Rupert had been extorting money from his sister so he could avoid having his legs broken by Jimmie the Knife. I could even convince myself that Rupert had managed to talk his old buddy Hayden into helping him. So how could this plan have ended up with Kate dead? And if Kate had been dropping money off near the river path, what happened to it? Jimmie made it sound like Rupert was behind on payments. Could someone else have shot Kate and taken the money?

I got up and walked over to the mind map. What the hell was I missing?

What were the odds of a random passerby stumbling upon Kate, shooting her, and stealing her purse? Zero to nil. Could Rupert have been aware of Kate's affair with Ben? He hadn't denied it when I asked. I suppose he could have hired someone to obtain the gun, but the notion seemed far-fetched. Why go to such lengths to enter the Langcasters' home, hoping to find a suitable weapon? Even if possible, using an ID card that had been lost from the same energy company the Langcasters used would be too coincidental. Yet, if the plan was to frame Sherrie, discarding the gun near Kate's body would be strategic.

As I paced my office, doubts crept in. Rupert orchestrating this intricate plot to implicate Sherrie seemed illogical. How could he be certain Sherrie knew about the affair, let alone that I had recently confirmed her suspicions? Framing Sherrie was a risky gamble; what if she were able to come up with a solid alibi for the night of Kate's murder?

A knock on the door interrupted my thoughts. Two burly guys stood there. "You got a table for us?"

"Oh right. It's this one here." I pointed at the table. "And you can take those four chairs too."

It took them less than a minute to take the table and chairs out of my office. I felt an odd sensation in my throat. The table meant nothing to me, but it was one more change piled on top of all the other changes I was dealing with. With all that was going on with the office, and an offer from CanNet, Luis' news couldn't have come at a worse time. People were disappearing from my life. Everything that once felt safe and comfortable was changing, leaving me adrift in a sea of uncertainty.

SIXTY-TWO

I was sitting on Hayden's doorstep when he arrived back home carrying a grocery bag in one hand. He stopped when he saw me and weighed up the situation. "What are you doing here?"

"I just have a few more questions."

"I told you everything I know."

"Come on. You and I both know that's not true."

Hayden pushed past me and unlocked his front door.

I got up and brushed the dust off the back of my jeans. "I had a nice long chat with Rupert yesterday."

Hayden opened the door, stepped inside, and turned to close it. I stuck my foot in the doorway. It was time to try out my theory. "I know about the plan to extort money from Kate. Rupert's loan shark has been threatening him and he's afraid they'll kill him next. Poor man collapsed when I confronted him about the scheme. He's in the hospital."

The pressure on my foot eased. Hayden remained silent but his face told me he was weighing what he had just heard. *Maybe I am onto something here.*

"If Rupert survives whatever happened to him last night, he's not going to just get back to his old life. His loan shark gave him five days to pay back what he owes. I met the guy. He's not messing around. And Rupert? He's a total disaster. He's coming apart at the seams. I don't think he's going to be able to keep it together much longer."

"That's not really my problem, is it."

"It kind of is. I don't know what he paid you or what he's holding over your head, but he got you to call Kate, threaten her unless she paid up. You arranged to meet her the night she was killed. Then you took the money she brought in an orange handbag and shot her."

"I didn't shoot her."

"Then who did?"

Hayden turned and walked into his house. I followed him. He wasn't denying everything. I just had to keep pushing harder until he gave me something that I could use.

"Hayden, you know Rupert is smarter than he looks. He set this up so you'd be the fall guy. Just like last time."

"What last time?"

"The kidnapping case. You, Kris Holden, and Hunter Redding were prime suspects. Now that Kate is dead, the detective in the kidnapping case is poking around again to see if there's a connection since the kidnappers were never caught. Think about it. When the cops start looking at your phone logs, the phone GPS locator, what do you think they're going to find."

Hayden set the bag of groceries he had been carrying on the kitchen counter and turned. "I didn't kill her."

There it was. The second time he denied killing Kate but not any of the other things I just said. "Hayden, come on. You were there that night. The police can check your phone, and even if you ditched it, the data still lives on the servers. They'll crosscheck the phone calls made to Kate's number and your number is going to pop up. Your best bet is to come clean."

Hayden's hands jerked toward the bag. He unloaded a carton of milk, almost dropping it, and jammed a couple of frozen dinners into the freezer. There's a fine line between pressing someone for answers and pressing them too far. I waited. After a minute, he turned.

"I didn't kill her. I don't even own a gun."

"But you were there that night, weren't you?"

Hayden walked over to the sink, bashing his hip on the corner of the counter. He dragged his hands through his hair. "Look. I worked hard to get clean. I...it's the hardest thing I've ever done. I still struggle. I um...I didn't do all this so I could spend the rest of my life in prison." He turned away and stared at the sink.

I took a slow breath and reminded myself to exude calm confidence. "I get that. So maybe instead of becoming the prime suspect in Kate Barrett's murder case, you become an informant. A key witness."

Hayden slowly turned. He chewed on the inside of his cheek. "How do I do that? No way I'm walking into the cop shop with any of this."

"Probably best to get a lawyer. They might be able to work out a plea bargain for you. I'll talk to Neil Trent. He's Sherrie Langcaster's defence lawyer. I can set up a meeting for you with him."

The sound of the tap dripping filled the room. I waited.

He ran his hand through his hair again and swallowed hard. "Yeah, okay."

I expelled the breath I had been holding. Our first real break. I believed Hayden when he said he didn't kill Kate, but he knew something.

I dialled Neil's number as soon as I got back to my car. I was expecting his voice mail, and it threw me when he answered on the fifth ring.

"Neil. Hi. It's Jorja. Sorry, I was getting ready to leave you a message, I wasn't expecting you to answer."

"Now that I'm semi-retired, I try to take the weekends off."

"Oh gosh, it's Saturday. Sorry, I've lost all track of time."

Neil laughed. "Just pulling your chain, Jorja. You got something?"

"Yeah. Hayden Price. Just left his place. He's ready to talk, but he wants a lawyer." I filled Neil in on my bluff and Hayden's reaction. "He didn't deny being there when Kate was shot but claims he didn't do it."

"Let's hear what he has to say. If he was there as part of an extortion scheme, I'm not going to be able to represent him, but I can certainly help him to understand his rights and the legal consequences of his involvement in whatever happened that night."

"If he was involved in an extortion scheme, will you still be able to call him as a witness?"

"Of course. His role in a potential extortion scheme remains separate from his role as a witness to Barrett's murder, and his testimony can still be crucial in the murder trial. Assuming he didn't kill her. The court will have to determine admissibility of his testimony. The judge will have to weigh the relevance of his testimony against his criminal conduct."

Neil said he could meet with Hayden and me on Sunday afternoon, but Hayden worked weekends, so we settled on Monday morning. The time worked for me as well. It would help to take my mind off the fact that Luis would already be on the other side of the continent.

SIXTY-THREE

I DASHED ACROSS THE street, entered Luis' condo building, and pressed the intercom button to his unit.

"Hi babe, I'll be right down." I heard the door buzz and I stepped into the lobby.

Luis and I were going out to dinner this evening, our last night in who knows how long. I blew out a deep breath and told myself to focus on the moment. There would be time enough to feel sad later, after he was gone.

I glanced at my reflection in the mirrored elevator doors and adjusted the black lace camisole under my open camel-coloured suede jacket. I tucked a strand of hair behind my right ear and my earing caught the light and sparkled against my dark hair. Tonight, I was wearing open-toed booties with a stacked heel. I turned halfway and checked the dark-wash jeans skimming my own bootie.

The elevator doors opened, and Luis stepped out. I felt the familiar stirring in my solar plexus. He wore a navy crewneck sweater with the sleeves pushed up and a pair of jeans. His eyes met mine, and he smiled.

"Casual yet sexy. How am I going to keep my hands off you through dinner?" He wrapped his arms around me and kissed my neck.

"I was hoping you wouldn't," I murmured against his ear.

He kissed me again, this time on my lips. I felt his warmth and breathed in the complex woodsy scent of his cologne, tinged with a hint of sweetness like apricot or lemon.

He took my hand, and we exited the building. I dug out my car keys as we waited for the light to change.

"How about letting me drive the Mustang tonight?"

I tossed him the keys. "All yours."

Luis opened the passenger door, and after I climbed in, ran around to the driver's side and slid in. The engine rumbled as it came to life. "Just think, if you keep it another thirty years, it'll be a classic."

I laughed. "Are you mocking my taste in cars?"

• • • • • • • • • •

LUIS AND I LINGERED over dinner at our favourite restaurant in Inglewood and then stopped in for a nightcap at a rooftop bar overlooking the Bow River. The evening turned out to be one of those anomalous spring days where the temperature soared to a record-breaking thirty degrees Celsius. The warmth of the day was still evident as we settled ourselves under an already darkening sky on the rooftop patio. The air was still, and faint music wafted upstairs from the bar below.

"I can't believe you're leaving tomorrow."

"I know. I wish we had more time together before I have to go."

"You and me both."

"You still working with that lawyer on the Barrett murder?'

"Yeah. It's a tough one but I think we may have caught a break. We might have a witness who was there that night. We'll know more on Monday."

"Whatever happened to that opportunity you mentioned a few weeks back? You know, the one you stood me up for with Mike?"

"Hey, I didn't stand you up. As I recall, you were late to the party. I made plans to meet Mike, *then* you asked me to dinner."

Luis raised an eyebrow and winked at me. "As I recall, the real party started later."

I bit my lower lip and nodded, smiling at the memory.

"Seriously though, anything come out of it?"

"Nothing earth shattering. Mike has a job offer from a company called CanNet. It's a new company, although the partners, William Carlton Smith and a fellow named Aadesh Kudari, who is a cyber-security expert, have both run former companies."

"Good for him. Full time?"

"I believe so. They're setting up a unit that will offer services to police forces who want to outsource some of their tasks and activities to the private sector."

Luis sat up. "Interesting. I assume they'll have trained personnel."

"Yes. Former police and RCMP officers as well as highly trained new personnel that can meet the same requirements and exams that are needed in order to join regular police agencies."

"Now that's really interesting. Has he talked to Depot about certification?"

Depot was the name of the RCMP's training academy. "Details, sweetheart. Details I'm not familiar with."

"Right, sorry. How does this affect you?"

"Well, I also have an offer from CanNet, to join their Homefront Investigations Unit. He's planning to start with three or four investigators and then grow the unit to match the demand."

Luis' eyes widened, as did his smile. "Jorja, that's fantastic."

"I suppose." I shrugged.

"What? You're not excited? Why not?"

"I don't know. The money will be better, that's for sure. I just like being my own boss."

"But you'd be getting in on the ground floor. There will be more opportunities for you there. Plus, support staff."

"Well, there is that."

Luis reached over and squeezed my hand. "You know I worry about you, right? Out there on your own. It's not a case of me thinking you're not competent, you've more than proven yourself. But it's dangerous out there, babe, working alone. I don't want you to get hurt."

My eyes pierced his. They were serious now. I had known all along that Luis would be pleased when he heard about the offer. And not just because of the safety aspect. I think deep down he liked the credibility that came with being part of a well-organized, structured company like CanNet was aiming to be. Let's face it, would a high-profile CEO being harassed by a cyber stalker take their problem to CanNet or a private eye? A private eye with no office.

"It's your decision, of course. Is there anything else about the offer that you don't like?"

"I put together a list of pros and cons, but they kind of cancel each other out. Lately, I'd been toying with the idea of expanding Knight Investigations. Taking on a few more investigators...well, maybe one to start with. I don't know. Maybe it's just the suddenness of it all. I mean, this job opportunity came out of the blue."

"Sometimes the out-of-the-blue opportunities can lead to something even better than we planned for ourselves."

"Yeah, like you wouldn't know what that's like." I raised an eyebrow and laughed.

Luis sat back and took a sip of his drink. "How long's the offer open?"

I looked at my watch. "Oh, like seventy-two more hours."

"Babe. Well, if you need more time, negotiate."

"Willie was pretty adamant about the timeline. I don't blame him, though. He wants to be fully operational by fall."

"Willie? William Carlton Smith? Why does that name ring a bell?"

"He used to head up the security and threat management division at Global. I did some work for him two years ago. Remember? I was on security detail outside Kulluk Energy's building during a protest when a man was shot. And you were such an asshole to me that day."

"*That* William Carlton Smith." Luis laughed in an embarrassed sort of way. "I did act like a dick. It was a defence mechanism."

"A defence mechanism?"

"I've never told you but in case you haven't figured it out, I had a mad crush on you back then."

"Oh my god." I sat up. "I had a mad crush on you! We're such idiots. It took us, what? Another four months before we even had our first date."

"I remember the night I knew I had to do something about it. Adan's charity event. Remember? You were wearing that silky backless blouse." Luis laid his hand over his heart, blew out a breath, and shook his head. "Seems I recall you turned me down that night, too."

"Okay, my turn to confess. I didn't have plans that evening, but when you asked me if I was free later, I said no."

"What? You lied? Why?"

"It was a defence mechanism."

"Oh yeah? Explain yourself." Luis laughed. He leaned back in his chair, his arms open. I couldn't help but notice the muscles in his forearms.

"I pegged you for a player. I didn't want to be your next one-night stand. I figured if you were really interested, you'd ask again."

"Well, Jorja Knight, you're not only gorgeous, you're also smart. You'll make the right decision about the offer at CanNet. I know you will. Since we're being honest, there's something else I need to tell you. Two things, actually. One of them not so great news."

A gnawing worry materialized behind my smile. "O...kay. Lay it on me."

"First, the bad news. Your Mustang's not only running rough, babe, it has no power. I suspect you're driving on five cylinders not six."

I let out my breath. A costly repair but not the bad news it could have been. "Great. My mechanic warned me it might need more work. Guess you're paying for drinks tonight. What's the other news?"

He reached across the table and took my hand in both of his. "I love you. My feelings for you aren't going to go away just because there's a couple thousand kilometres between us. We can make this work Jorja. I know we can."

I blinked back the tears that suddenly sprang up. People say these kinds of things, but they didn't always turn out to be true. I shook off the thought and wiped back a tear. I stared at his face, as if I needed to memorize every curve and line, then gave a small laugh. "I'm going to hold you to that, Inspector Azagora."

SIXTY-FOUR

I WAS GLAD ONCE Monday rolled around. Yesterday, I drove Luis to the airport and then cried most of the way home. I went for a long run along the reservoir, but the sight of so many couples enjoying the summer-like weather in the park did nothing to cheer me up.

I called Gab when I got home and listened to her excited voice as she shared her plans for her and Andrew's wedding next year. It was something to look forward to. After my call with Gab, I called a company that provided private and virtual office space. It had been dead simple to set up an account for office space in the downtown core. I had signed up for one month. Two hundred and seventy-nine dollars got me five days of office space, four hours of meeting room time, and an address to use for my website and mail. This didn't mean I had yet come to any decision about my office, or CanNet's offer, but this was a good way to try things out.

I spent the rest of the afternoon cleaning my apartment and doing laundry. Evening found me sitting out on my deck surrounded by pots of dead plants from last summer, nursing a scotch and thinking about what I wanted from the next ten years of my life.

Luis texted me in the evening to say the trip went smoothly and he was already missing me. I felt better after, then chastised myself for being such a baby.

On the trip down to my office this morning, I noticed a plume of blue smoke spewing from my car every time I sped up from a stop. Between my bouts of self-pity yesterday I had googled 'engine cylinder repair costs.' Google came back with the news that a typical car cylinder head replacement could range between $1,250 and $4,250, depending of course on the type of car and the labour costs of the mechanic.

I had just spent five hundred dollars getting the Mustang fixed. Now I had another decision to make—pay even more to keep it running or get rid of it. I could always go back to leasing from JumpIn Jalopies. I had no one to blame but myself. Gab had warned me the car was on its last legs.

I parked near my office and walked into the downtown core. Parking rates in the city core were triple what they were near my office, so I didn't mind using a little shoe leather to get there. I had sent Neil and Hayden a quick email yesterday to tell them I was moving offices and sent them the address for the space I was trying out. I had also sent Cole Barrett an email asking him once again to check if any of Kate's handbags or jewellery was missing.

I got down to Bankers Hall with oodles of time to spare, so I settled myself in a nearby coffee shop and made some phone calls while I waited.

My first call was to Rupert. I was surprised when he answered his cell phone. He was still in the hospital. He told me he had a heart attack the night I had searched his house. He was waiting for double by-pass surgery, which was planned for the next day or the one after that. I asked him if he needed me to contact anyone and he said no. I wondered if Jimmie the Knife would grant him a week or two reprieve given the circumstances.

My next call went to Sal. I had scanned the list of Escalade plate numbers and owners Neil had provided, along with my notations beside the ones I'd eliminated, and handed the rest of the task off to Sal. After killing what remained of my time setting up other appointments, I walked over to my newly rented space in Bankers Hall. Neil had already arrived and was waiting for me in the meeting room I had booked for us.

"Nice digs," Neil commented as I walked in, followed by a young man who brought in a carafe of coffee, cups, and a pitcher of water.

"The lease on my old office is up, so I'm trying out this space."

"If I didn't have access to the courthouse, I'd probably try something like this out as well. By the way, I talked to Maria Rios, and she said she's got some time to take on our guy's case if need be."

The young man who brought in the coffee returned with Hayden in tow. "Will you be needing anything else?" he asked before leaving. I was liking the service that came with the space. Maybe I wouldn't miss my old office after all.

I introduced Hayden to Neil and the two men shook hands. Neil poured himself a coffee and took his laptop out of his briefcase, put it on the table, but didn't open it.

"Hayden, Jorja tells me you might have been in the vicinity of the intersection of Third Avenue and a lane connecting it to the Bow River pathway on the night of May ninth."

Hayden glanced at me and then back at Neil. "Are you going to be my lawyer?"

"No, son. It would be a conflict of interest, since I represent the accused. Today, we want to hear what you saw and heard on the night in question, the night Kate Barrett was killed. Depending on what you tell us today, you might need a criminal lawyer. I have arranged a lawyer for you by the name of Maria Rios. She should be here shortly."

Hayden scratched his cheek. "Why would I need a criminal lawyer?"

"Well, if you were involved in a criminal activity at the time you witnessed the murder, and if that activity comes to light during your witness statement, then you would need a lawyer to represent you with respect to whatever crime might have been committed."

"And if I was—I mean, if there was another crime happening, could I give evidence against that crime and get a plea deal?" Hayden looked from Neil to me and back again.

"Yes. Should you be charged in relation to that concurrent crime, your lawyer can negotiate a plea deal with the prosecution for that case, if you're willing to disclose information on that crime and the individuals involved."

Hayden scraped a hand through his hair and nodded.

"Okay, if you're ready, let's get started. You're here today as a witness to what you saw and heard the night of May ninth. I'll be asking questions that I would ask of any witness. If you don't care to answer one of my questions, that's okay too, you can just say 'no comment.' For example, I usually ask witnesses what they were doing at the time they saw the crime in question. If you think your answer would put you in danger or expose another criminal activity other than that of Mrs. Barrett's murder, then you simply tell me that you would prefer to speak to your lawyer about it. She should be here any minute."

Right on cue, Maria Rios arrived. Another round of introductions were made. I poured a glass of water for everyone while Maria pulled out a one-page document and had Hayden sign it, making her role as his lawyer official. Once Hayden had a few minutes to chat with his lawyer privately, we got started.

SIXTY-FIVE

Neil looked over the top of his reading glasses, his laptop open in front of him. "Now, Hayden, just tell us in your own words what you saw and heard the night of May ninth. The night Mrs. Barrett was killed."

Hayden was sitting upright on the edge of his chair. He glanced over at his lawyer, and she gave him a small nod. "I saw Mrs. Barrett walking down the path. The one that connects Third Avenue to the pathway running along the river. She was alone. She was walking toward the river."

"Good, Hayden. Do you remember what she was wearing?"

"She had on a coat with a white sweater underneath. And pants—light colored, maybe tan. She was carrying a purse. An orange purse."

I kept my eyes on Hayden's face, although I wanted to see Neil's reaction at his mention of an orange purse.

"And where were you relative to the vic—I mean, Mrs. Barrett?"

"I was standing by the pathway, the river pathway. At the side of a little playground that's there."

"Okay, go on. What did Mrs. Barrett do?"

"She kept walking until she got to the bench. There's one by the playground at the opposite end of where I was, near the little path that she was on. She waited a minute and then sat on the bench and put her purse down next to her."

"Was there anyone else there, that you could see?"

"No. Not then."

"What happened next?"

"She waited for a minute, then she got up and turned to start going back down the path the same way she came."

"What about the purse?"

"She left it on the bench."

I glanced at Neil and met his eyes. The significance of what we just heard wasn't lost on him.

"Okay, go on."

Hayden shifted in his seat. "I waited. Then I heard two shots. Gunshots. Mrs. Barrett fell down." Hayden alternately intertwined the fingers on one hand with the fingers on the other. "At first, I didn't know what happened. Then this dark figure came out of the bushes on the other side of the path. I ran and hid behind this big metal tube or tunnel in the playground...I thought I was going to be shot too."

"How far would you say Mrs. Barrett was from the bench when she was shot?"

"I don't know." Hayden blinked a few times. "She was maybe ten feet from the bench when I heard the shots."

"Okay, this figure you saw. Can you describe it?"

"It was like a shadow."

"Like what?"

"It was just this dark shape. All black. The face was blank."

"A blank face. Was something covering the face?"

"It was just a black hole."

Maria Rios pulled her hands back from where they had been resting on the table, interlaced her fingers and rested them against her stomach, then leaned back.

Neil continued. "So just black where the face *should* be."

"Right."

"How big was this shape?"

Hayden thought for a moment. "Big. Tall, I mean. But not giant like. More like maybe my height."

"Did you see a gun?"

"No. But I heard one. I know what a gun sounds like."

"What happened next?"

"This shadow moved toward Kate—I mean, Mrs. Barrett. It bent over and did something, but I couldn't see what because the bench and part of a utility box was blocking my view."

"Go on."

"When it stood up, it looked straight through me. Then it turned and took off."

"Which way did it go?"

"Down toward the river. It turned left and disappeared."

"Disappeared."

"Yeah, just vanished."

"So, it must have run right past you, before it turned left and disappeared."

"I guess that's right."

"Did you notice anything else about this figure as it went past?"

"Well, it could have been wearing some kind of cloak or shroud, because I couldn't see its legs or feet."

"Okay, good. This figure you saw might have been wearing a long cloak. Anything else you can tell us about this figure?"

"It must have had a hood, because I never saw hair or anything like that. But it moved really weird."

"Weird how?"

Hayden swallowed. "Like it was floating. Like it didn't weigh anything at all."

Hayden kept referring to what he had seen as a shadow. I remembered another witness had claimed to have seen a shadowy otherworldly creature. His statement to police had been discounted because he was high. But this meant something. Two separate witnesses who claimed the figure or creature they saw was from another world.

"What did you do next?"

"I waited a few minutes and then I went over to where Mrs. Barrett was lying. I got pretty close. I called her name, but she didn't answer." He swallowed hard a few times. "That's when I saw all the blood."

"How was Mrs. Barrett lying?"

"She was face down."

"And was she shot in the chest or the back?"

"I think the chest. I didn't see any bullet holes or blood on the back of her coat. She was lying in a pool of blood. It was running in a stream toward me. I figured she had to be dead."

"Did you touch her or check if she was breathing?"

"No. I'm pretty sure she was dead."

"What did you do next?"

"I got the hell out of there."

"Which way did you go?"

"Back to the river path, but I went the opposite way from the shadow."

"Okay, what about after this shadow creature disappeared. Did you see or hear anything else?"

"No."

"What about the purse Mrs. Barrett had with her?"

His eyes darted to Maria and back again. He shrugged. "Last I saw, it was sitting on the bench."

"Okay, Hayden. Great job. Just a few more questions. Do you remember what time it was when you first saw Mrs. Barrett?"

"It was six minutes after two."

I felt the tension leave my clasped hands. His answer told me he hadn't just been passing by. He had been watching the time and waiting for Kate Barrett to show up.

"And how long would you say it took for all this to happen? From the moment you saw Mrs. Barrett to when you ran off."

"Maybe three or four minutes."

"And had you taken any drugs, legal or otherwise, that night?"

"No." Hayden sounded insulted.

"Okay. Last question. Can you tell us what brought you down to the river path that night?"

Hayden looked at Maria. She sat up. "You might not want to answer that, Hayden."

He nodded and turned back to Neil. "No comment."

SIXTY-SIX

"Well, what do you think?" Neil and I were sitting in the meeting room, debriefing. Hayden had written out his witness statement reiterating what he had told us, and he and his lawyer, Maria Rios, had already left.

"He was there, all right. He knew details that haven't been released to the public. It seems like the orange purse River found"—I air-quoted the word 'found'—"was Kate's."

"I agree. My guess is that Hayden was there to pick up the purse but then panicked and ran off when Barrett was shot."

"Maybe he did pick up the purse and lied to us. At least we have a witness who'll testify they saw someone shoot Barrett."

"It may not be enough to convince a jury. He did mention the figure he saw was tall. That might help. No one would describe Sherrie as tall. What did you make of that whole floating, weightless, faceless description of the shooter?"

"He's the second witness to mention that the person they saw that night was faceless. The other witness described it as otherworldly, although police didn't take him seriously because he was high. They both can't have imagined this strange spirit or ghostly creature."

Neil shook his head. "I almost wished he hadn't mentioned it. We can explain the faceless part. I've seen Halloween costumes like that. The floating thing makes his story seem less credible."

"Anything you want me to focus on next? I haven't heard anything back from Ryker about the Hermes handbag that River or Josh Neeley had in their possession. Not that I expect he'd report back to me if he did find it. Was there any mention of it in the discovery?"

"If they found it, the data hasn't made its way into the prosecutor's file." Neil had received the second tranche of discovery data from the prosecutor's office on the weekend. "There is, however, a list of phone calls made by Sherrie and Ben Langcaster as well as Kate Barrett in the days leading up to the murder, along with data from the cell phone towers in the downtown area for the nights of May eighth and ninth. All five thousand pages of it."

"Great." I grimaced. "I'll comb through them and see if any of those calls were placed by Rupert Gallagher or our friend Hayden."

"I love how you can read my mind, Jorja. Anything on the mystery woman who showed up at the Langcaster house posing as an energy company rep?"

"Still working on it. I also sent Cole Barrett an email asking him to check and see if any of his wife's jewellery or handbags were missing, but he still hasn't got back to me. If she wasn't carrying cash in her Hermes bag the night she was killed, maybe she was carrying items from her jewellery collection. I'm still waiting for his reply."

After Neil left, I jotted some notes down for myself and then headed back to my old office. The walk back gave me plenty of time to think. Neil and I had talked about how the prosecutor's side appeared to have tunnel vision. Once they found Sherrie's gun, they figured they had it all sewn up, otherwise they wouldn't have charged her so quickly with Kate's murder. The fact they had asked for landline and cell phone data for Kate, Sherrie, and Ben, told me they would be presenting evidence from that data to show Ben and Kate had been in a relationship, further lending credibility to the story that Sherrie killed her husband's mistress in a jealous rage.

I believed Hayden. At least the part where he admitted he had seen Kate get shot. His 'no comment' when Neil asked him why he had been in the area that night solidified my belief that he was part of whatever scheme had been set up to lure Kate downtown that night. A scheme that might have been initiated by Rupert to help him avoid getting his legs broken. But I didn't want to fall so in love with the idea that I ignored other bits and bites that didn't make sense. And there were still pieces that didn't fit.

I suddenly realized that I had walked right past my office building. I checked for traffic and started across the street. I heard the car before I saw it.

I felt the impact, then everything slowed as the pavement came up to meet me. I hit the road hard and rolled twice. I lay for a second, stunned, not breathing. A pair of sneakers appeared in my field of view and then a set of women's boots.

"Oh god, is she still alive?"

I felt a hand touch my shoulder. I struggled to sit. Hands helped me.

"Did you see that guy?" a woman's voice sounded. "He came out of nowhere."

"Hang in there, miss, an ambulance is on the way." The man holding me up had spoken. I tried to bring his blurred face into focus but couldn't. I reached out and grabbed his coat sleeve as my world tilted.

The police arrived first, the ambulance a minute later. By then I could see that I had ended up lying against the curb of the sidewalk. I remembered the seconds right before it happened. *My fault.* I had jaywalked.

The paramedics checked my vitals and after a few more minutes of evaluating me, asked if I could stand. I could, with help.

The man and woman who stopped to help me were talking to the police. I heard the man say, "It was black, a newer model, tinted windows."

The woman broke in, "It was a black Escalade. I saw it come out of the alley." She turned and pointed. "He almost hit me too. I recognized the make of car because my friend's husband drives one just like it."

I wanted to stay and ask them questions, but I was feeling light-headed again. The paramedics helped me over to the ambulance. The gurney felt like heaven. The woman paramedic was asking me if I remembered hitting my head. Funnily enough, it was the one thought I did remember having as I hit the ground—my internal voice telling me to keep my head up.

"I don't think so," I replied.

"Good. At first glance, it doesn't look like you've broken any-thing. We'll take you to the Rockyview so you can get checked out."

It felt good to have someone else decide. I lay back and closed my eyes.

SIXTY-SEVEN

It was mid-afternoon by the time I walked out of the emergency unit. A police officer had stopped by to get my side of the story. Unfortunately, I couldn't give him any information about the car that hit me, as I was too busy rolling around on the pavement in agony. I did confirm I had been jaywalking. The fine for jaywalking, I was told, was sixty dollars. He didn't issue me a ticket because, in his words, 'You probably learned your lesson.'

I headed to the main section of the hospital and found a washroom. I rinsed the dirt off my face as best I could with one hand. My left one was wrapped in white gauze. Nothing serious, I was told, just some bruising and road rash. My right shoulder and hip hurt like hell. The hip, from where it was struck by the car, and my shoulder, from being the first point of contact with the pavement.

I had been planning to contact Sal to see if she had made any headway with the list of Escalade owners and then spend the rest of the day searching through five thousand pages of cell phone data, but someone had other plans for me. Someone who drove a black Escalade with tinted windows.

Now that I was here, I decided to take advantage of the situation. I gave my face one last rub with a damp paper towel and headed to the main desk just off the lobby. Once there, I asked for Rupert Gallagher's room number.

The elevator took me up to the fourth floor. I wandered around the Cardiology and Vascular Surgery Unit until I found room 417. An older man slept in the first bed. I tiptoed past the curtain that divided the room and found Rupert. He was propped up against pillows with his eyes closed. They snapped open as I entered.

"Rupert. How are you doing?"

His forehead furrowed. "What are you doing here?"

"I just came from emergency." I held up my gauze-wrapped hand. "Someone tried to run me over this morning. Since I was here, I thought I'd stop in and see if you're up to finishing the conversation we were having before you had your own emergency."

"I have nothing more to say to you." He lay back and closed his eyes.

"We had a little chat with your buddy Hayden this morning. He admitted he was there the night Kate Barrett was killed."

Rupert's head came off the pillow and his eyes opened. "What Hayden does is his business. It has nothing to do with me."

"Ah, yes." I nodded. "Hayden figured that's what you'd say. You set things up so he'd take the fall if anything went wrong. That's why he's got himself a lawyer. A very sharp lawyer by the name of Maria Rios. She's arranging a plea deal for Hayden, in return for his testimony on the Kate Barrett murder."

The machine Rupert was hooked up to beeped faster. I looked at the monitor and saw that all the squiggly lines had spiked.

"You're lying." The beeps ramped up.

"Calm down, Rupert. You'll want to live long enough to tell your side of the story. If you don't believe me, call Hayden."

Rupert struggled to sit up. "I told you I had nothing to do with her death."

"That's not really true, is it. Maybe you didn't pull the trigger, but you're the reason she was down there that night."

Rupert was breathing rapidly. "I didn't do anything wrong. Okay, I asked her for the money. That's not a crime. I didn't threaten her."

"So, tell me what did happen."

Rupert reached for his water and brought the straw to his lips. His hand shook as he put the cup back down on the table.

"Kate knew I was in debt. I had asked her for money before and she helped me out a few times. Then my father cuts me off and tells Kate and my brothers not to lend me a dime."

"Lend you?"

"I was going to pay them back."

Well, that tracked. Said just like any other addict, desperate for money.

"How did you convince your sister to lend you money after she agreed with the family that you were to be cut off?"

"I told her the truth."

"Which is?"

"That the guys I owe money to were coming after me if I didn't pay up. They threatened to hurt me, hurt my family. They even threatened to kidnap my niece or nephews and get their money back that way." Rupert wiped the sweat trickling down his face.

Given Kate's own kidnapping experience, I could see that hearing her niece or nephews might be victimized like she had been would have hit home hard.

"I needed forty Gs for my next payment, which was past due. Kate said she didn't have that kind of cash lying around." Rupert's shoulders started to shake. "I told her to go sell some of her damn purses." Tears intermixed with the sweat as he could no longer hold them back.

"That was the argument you had with your sister at the Pine Valley Spa and Golf Club, in the restaurant, wasn't it?"

"Yes." Rupert wiped the tears from his eyes. "I was... I'm so selfish. I can't believe..." Rupert took a long, shaky breath. "Now Kate's dead. I didn't kill her, but you're right when you said I sent her to her death."

I waited while Rupert tried to compose himself. A nurse walked in. "Rupert, I see you have a visitor," she called out. Then she noticed Rupert's face. She shifted her gaze to me and then back to Rupert. "Everything okay in here?"

"Yes, thank you." Rupert nodded and then blew his nose. The nurse turned and rushed away.

"I had wondered how she got the money together. Kate's bank records didn't show any major withdrawals. What I don't understand is why she just didn't give you the money. How is it that she ended up down by the Bow River in the middle of the night?"

Rupert's hands clenched into fists, and he turned away. "I told her my loan shark would send someone there to pick up the money. That he didn't trust that I wouldn't just spend it if she did come through with the cash."

"Let me guess. You talked Hayden into pretending to be that guy."

"He owed me a favour."

I was tempted to ask if the favour had anything to do with his sister's kidnapping but decided to stick with the current crime. "I still don't get it. Why did it have to go down like that?"

"I wanted Kate to see how serious these guys were." Rupert's body shuddered as he swallowed back a sob. "Hayden was just supposed to scare her...let her know there'd be serious consequences if my loan wasn't paid back. Not just to me, but the whole family."

Now I got it. Rupert had more money to repay. The forty grand was only one such payment. He was grooming his sister so she would be willing to do a repeat when the time came.

"He wasn't supposed to kill her." Rupert's voice cracked.

"He says he didn't. That someone else was there. They killed her."

"Jimmie." Rupert's chest heaved. "That bastard," he hissed between clenched teeth as he clutched his chest. The monitor beside Rupert's bed went crazy. A nurse ran into the room. I was sliding out the door when two more medical personnel arrived.

My head pounded as I got into my Uber ride. Rupert would survive. The universe would make sure of it. Even if he didn't end up in jail, he was going to have to do his time by living with what he had done to his little sister.

SIXTY-EIGHT

THE NEXT DAY FOUND me back in my office staring at the mind map on my wall. Hayden and Rupert cleared up a lot of questions in the last couple of days. Unfortunately, we still had an unknown assailant, whom the prosecutor would insist was Sherrie Langcaster.

Although Rupert spit out Jimmie's name before another medical event felled him yesterday, I knew it couldn't have been him or one of his guys.

The stolen gun, the fake Green Energy rep, the bloody T-shirt...it all smacked of a setup. A guy like Jimmie the Knife wouldn't have bothered with all that nonsense. When Sherrie first called me, all those weeks ago, to say her gun was missing, I thought she might be guilty and was trying to set up Ben to take the fall. Then I thought Ben might have killed his mistress, for some as-yet-unknown reason, and tried to set Sherrie up. Both of those scenarios no longer made sense.

There were two different things playing out here. There had to be. Kate Barrett had gone down to the Bow River to drop off money to her brother's supposed loan shark the night she was killed. Rupert wouldn't have wanted his sister killed. He was counting on her for future payments. Someone else was there and killed Kate for another reason.

What if this wasn't about framing Sherrie? I sat up and gasped as a pain shot through my shoulder. A clear reminder that I'd have to go slow for a few days. What if the person who took the gun from the Langcasters' bedroom thought it belonged to Ben? Could someone have been trying to frame *him* for Kate's murder? Is that why the sports bag and bloody T-shirt were placed at his house?

Could someone be systematically destroying Ben's life? First his lover was shot. Then the mother of his child was charged with her murder. The mega project he was working on for his client failed, and he was taking the heat. Now he was out of a job.

I didn't bother to call Ben Langcaster. He probably wouldn't take my call anyway. On the chance that I would find the recently unemployed lawyer at home, I locked up and made my way back to my car.

When I reached Ben's house, I was happy to see there were no reporters hanging around outside. It had been two days since Ben was fired, and already he was old news.

I cupped a hand around my eyes and peered into the garage's side window. Ben's car was there. I rang the doorbell. After a minute, I rang it again. I let three more minutes go by and then I pushed the doorbell repeatedly.

The door opened. Ben stood there in a rumpled dress shirt, his light-brown hair sticking out in all directions. "Fuck. What do you want?"

"I want to know who hates you enough to want to destroy your life?"

"What?" He rubbed his tangled hair. It looked like he'd been asleep.

"I think that someone is trying to ruin you. That all of this, Kate's murder, the stolen gun, the bloody T-shirt, was aimed at framing you."

Ben stepped back and let me enter. He turned and I followed him down the hall and into his kitchen.

Ben stuck a coffee cup under the spigot of his cappuccino machine. "What happened to your hand?"

"A black Escalade with tinted windows tried to run me down. Sound familiar?"

He looked over his shoulder at me. "Really. You want a coffee?"

"That would be nice."

Ben brought two cups of coffee over to the kitchen table and set them down. "I think there's some..." His words trailed off as his eyes drifted across the kitchen.

"That's okay, I take mine black."

Ben sat and took a sip of coffee. "Hope this caffeine kicks in soon. I haven't been sleeping well."

"It's been a rough couple of weeks."

"It's been a rough year." He ran a hand through his hair, rumpling it further. "What you said, just now, about someone destroying my life. That's exactly what it feels like."

"Maybe, because it could actually be true. So tell me, Ben, who hates you this much?"

"I don't know. No one?"

"You're a corporate lawyer, right?"

He laughed bitterly. "Was." He stared morosely into his coffee cup.

"Oh, come on. You'll bounce back. It always feels colder before dawn."

He gave me a weak smile. "Why do you do this?"

"It's my job."

"Sure. But why did you choose this job?"

It had been something I had been asking myself repeatedly these last few weeks. Spurred no doubt by the new job offer. I took a deep breath.

"I could give you my standard answer, Mr. Langcaster. I like being my own boss. I get to set my own schedule. The job is dynamic, and the cases change from week to week. I'm not stuck in a stuffy office all day, and the pay is reasonable. I'll even throw in the satisfaction of helping others and making a difference in someone's life." I paused. "But the real reason? I have an obsessive need to understand why people do what they do, especially when it results in criminal activity. It's been the underlying passion behind all the work I have chosen to do, even though I may not have understood it myself at the time. Maybe it stems from my failure in preventing my mother's murder. Maybe I erroneously believe that by understanding how humans think I can somehow use that to predict and maybe prevent further crimes from occurring."

I stopped, shocked at the sudden outpouring and the clarity my own words gave me. I didn't often share my inner thoughts and feelings with strangers. Or anyone, for that matter.

"It's Ben."

"What?" I refocused my attention on the man sitting across from me.

"Call me Ben. Sherrie is damn lucky to have you working on her case."

I took a sip of my coffee, then cleared my throat softly. "Now your turn, Mr. Langca—I mean, Ben. Who is destroying your life?"

SIXTY-NINE

BEN AND I WENT over every detail I could think of and now we were getting around to details that I didn't know.

"You've been working exclusively for Cole Barrett for how long?"

"It'll be three years come August."

"But you worked for him before that, right? Through the company that employed you, Finchman Law."

"Correct. I worked on the Capital Equity merger and the Arcadia Industries acquisition. Then in the fall of 2020, Cole asked me to come work for him. I told him I couldn't. There was a non-solicitation clause in my employment agreement, which stipulated that if I left Finchman Law, I couldn't work for any of their clients for a period of three years."

"Got it. Is that when Cole asked your employer to assign you exclusively to his company?"

"Actually, it was my idea." Ben grimaced. "I told him it was the only way he could be guaranteed that I'd be the one assigned to work on his various projects, without waiting three years for me to be unencumbered by my commitments to Finchman."

"Did you work on all of his merger and acquisition deals?"

"I was part of a team with three other lawyers. We assessed a lot of possible opportunities that in the end were rejected for either financial or legal reasons. Cole made me the lead on his last three acquisitions."

"Okay. How many of these targets that you went after worked out in Cole's favour?"

"All of them." He shook his head. "Except for Avenue 21 Group."

"What do you think happened? Was it just luck of the draw? I heard Edna being interviewed and she said Jackson Equities' bid for them was overinflated. That they overpaid."

"That's not true. Yes, the monetary considerations were slightly, just slightly, better than ours. It was all the other stuff that killed us."

"Like what?"

"Clauses in the bid that guaranteed jobs for Avenue 21 Group employees for a minimum period of three years. Carrying over all the employee pensions and benefits. Removing liability from the current management team of Avenue 21 Group from any lawsuits that might be raised with respect to their operations in the past ten years."

"That sounds like a big one."

"There were other sweeteners that the team put forward, but Cole nixed them all. He said we could get Avenue 21 on the strength of our financial offer. Looks like their management didn't agree."

"What about the management team at Encore? Cole can't be the one who gets to call all the shots."

"He pretty much does."

"Didn't Kate have shares in the company?"

"Sure, non-voting shares. If you haven't figured it out yet, Cole's a narcissist. His inner circle knows it and those who want to remain in that circle know what price they have to pay. Cole doesn't need or want the people closest to him to help him make decisions. They're there to stoke his ego. To tell him he's right even when he's not. They work behind the scenes to iron out the issues his ego creates for himself and the company. Our legal team was constantly fighting off potential lawsuits or filing ones against his competitors. Or just people he didn't like."

"He sounds like a nightmare."

"He is. My suggestion that I work for him full time was the worst recommendation I've ever made. Cole can be very gracious and generous when he wants to be. He got my family into one of the most prestigious private sport and social clubs in the prairies. He's made generous donations to Matt's sports club. He gave me bonuses and monetary awards, separate from what he paid Finchman to cover my salary and benefits. But I know now why he does it. He grooms his inner circle. And even though it's unwritten, we all knew that if we crossed him, we'd lose it all."

"Is it fair to say you know where the bodies are buried?"

Ben hesitated for a second. "Some of them."

"What does the loss of Avenue 21 Group mean to Encore, to Cole?"

"The main reason for going after them was to consolidate Encore's position in the marketplace. It's a key goal behind most acquisitions. Cole wants to be number one in the mid-cap equity market. But there were other agendas. He needed Avenue 21's supply and distribution channels. The key suppliers for the assets Encore holds are located in Ukraine. When Russia invaded Ukraine, that supply was severely disrupted."

"So, Cole needed Avenue 21 Group to not only fuel the company's future growth, but he needed their supply and distribution channels to keep the company solvent."

"Correct."

"Now I understand why he had to let so many of his employees go."

"Temporarily strengthening the company's bottom line by shedding employees or non-core portions of the business is just smoke and mirrors. It might appease his investors in the short term, but it won't be long before the financial statements show the real story." Ben lifted his chin and his eyes locked with mine. "By the way, I'll be sued if any of this gets out. So, if you believe that someone is trying to destroy me, leaking any of this to the press will ensure my complete and utter demise."

"Don't worry, Ben. I'm not going after Barrett. I'm only interested in finding the person who methodically planned and carried out Kate's murder."

Ben leaned back in his chair, a thoughtful expression on his face. "Kate was murdered before the Avenue 21 deal came apart. How could it be payback for my involvement in the failed deal, when the deal hadn't happened yet?"

I had been thinking about this all the way over to Ben's house. It was a great question.

"If someone has been working to plan and execute their revenge against you, the timing of which came first, Kate's death or the failed acquisition of Avenue 21, didn't matter to them."

Ben's head tilted as he weighed what I said. "Are you saying it was corporate espionage? That someone had prior information on our acquisition bid package? That would mean someone on our team passed along information. Or they used top-notch technology to bug our offices."

"All valid possibilities. But it had to be someone who also knew you and Kate were...seeing each other." I almost said cheating, but didn't think it was wise, now that Ben and I were on good footing.

"Who knew about your affair with Kate?"

"Cole did."

"He did?"

"When he fired me, he said he could no longer trust a man who was screwing his wife, or words to that effect."

"Whoa. Do you think he really knew or was just parroting the rumours that are out there."

Ben shrugged. "I don't know. Kate and I were pretty careful. We both used Burner App phone numbers to communicate with each other. We met when we knew Cole would be tied up in meetings or out of town."

"When I asked him about the rumours floating around that Kate might have been having an affair, he claimed he and Kate had an open marriage."

Ben gave a disgusted snort. "No way. Kate told me he was extraordinarily possessive. He could stray, but Kate belonged to him and no one else. He was the one who would decide if and when the marriage was over."

I watched Ben's face. It was clear he was still thinking.

"I suppose he could have hired someone to kill Kate when he found out about our affair. And when we lost Avenue 21, he finished the job by firing me in the most humiliating way possible."

Could it be that simple? That Cole had Kate killed because she was sleeping with Ben. Not that orchestrating a murder is ever simple. But it fit certain of the evidence. Whomever he hired could have accessed the Langcaster house, stolen the gun, and later planted the bloodied T-shirt next to his garage the day after killing her. He wouldn't have expected Ben or his son Matt to dispose of the T-shirt or predicted that Sherrie would be charged with the murder, but some of it fit. But what didn't fit was his loss of Avenue 21 Group. Maybe I was wrong about that.

Ben was still talking, rolling the idea around out loud. "I just don't get it. I've known Cole for a long time. He's not exactly a nice guy, but murder? I don't know."

"Maybe he thought you knew too much. I've heard his business dealings weren't always on the up and up."

"If anyone tests the limits of corporate law, it's Cole. But if that were the case, why didn't he have me killed instead of his wife?"

"Could anyone else at Encore have known about you and Kate?"

"Maybe Edna. I've never trusted her. I think Cole pays her to keep tabs on the people working closest to him."

Something tweaked in my mind. "Do you know what kind of car Edna drives?"

"Uh…yeah, a gold-coloured Cadillac Blackwing. She gave me a lift to one of our offsite meetings a few months back. Why?"

"Oh, nothing really." So much for that. But it brought up another loose end I was trying to pin down. "Remember the security video you showed me from before Kate was murdered? A woman carrying a Green Energy ID card came to your house. The ID card belongs to a woman named Elaine Gray. She apparently lost her card, and we know it wasn't her. Can you take another look at this woman?" I found the image and pushed my phone across the counter to him." Ben stared at the photo. "Does she look familiar at all? Could she be from your office—I mean, Encore's office?"

Ben stared at the image and shrugged. "Hard to tell. It could be just about anyone." He handed my phone back.

That was the problem indeed. The image could be just about anyone.

I walked out of Ben's house with a lot still churning through my mind. Like why someone had tried to run me down yesterday. The fact that the car was the same make and colour of the car parked outside of Ben and Sherrie's house before the murder couldn't be a coincidence. Or if it was, it would be a pretty big one. Was the killer worried I was closing in on them?

Then another thought hit me. Hayden had seen the killer. He didn't have a good description, other than that the killer was tall, thin, and...shadowy. But the killer didn't know that. And if they had been following him or me, they knew he had met with a lawyer. I reached for my phone. I had to let Hayden know he might be in danger.

SEVENTY

I rang Hayden's doorbell again. No answer. He wasn't answering his phone, either. I leaned over and peered into the front window, almost losing my balance on the top step. The blinds were half drawn. All I could see was parquet flooring and the base of a mustard-coloured couch.

"Hello. Can I help you?"

I turned. A woman with a Rottweiler stood on the sidewalk leading up to the neighbour's house.

"Oh, hi. I'm looking for Hayden. You haven't seen him around today, have you?"

"I'm pretty sure he's working the late shift this week."

"I tried his cell, but he's not answering."

"His boss doesn't like them taking personal calls at work."

"Okay, thanks."

I walked back to my car and climbed in. The Mustang rumbled to life, the acrid smell of burning oil filling the car. I really had to do something about it, before it up and died one day at the most inconvenient moment.

I was debating what to do next when Sal called.

"Hey Sal. What's up?"

"Got something on an Escalade that might be of interest."

"Yeah? What've you got?"

"One of the plate numbers belongs to a leasing company, Star Limo and Luxury Auto Rentals. You know, like JumpIn Jalopies but for rich folks."

I turned off the car and the rumbling subsided. She had my full attention now. "And?"

"They wouldn't tell me who leased the Escalade. Privacy of information bullcrap. But the guy working the return bay evenings is a bit short on cash. He looks after his son during the day, since his wife has cancer. I gave him a hundred bucks. Star Limo has four Escalades, and two of them are leased to Encore."

"Holy shit."

"Thought you'd like that."

"Great work, Sal."

"There's ten more Escalades on the list that I haven't been able to track down. Want me to keep going or do you think we've found our car?"

"I'm pretty sure this is it. Thanks again, Sal."

"Anytime, doll. You know where to find me if you need anything else."

As soon as Sal and I disconnected, I called Ben. "Come on, Ben, pick up," I muttered. It was almost at the point when it would switch over to voice mail when he answered.

"Ben, it's Jorja Knight."

"Jorja. How's you doing?" he slurred.

"Ben, listen. I think I found something. Does Encore have a couple of Escalades on lease?"

"Ess...salades? Yeah."

It was obvious that he'd been drinking. "Listen, Ben, this is important. Who has access to those cars?"

"Access. Sss...ure. Lemme think."

I waited a full minute. I was about to repeat myself when he answered. "Cole drives Ess'alade...and Edna. Good ol' Edna."

"Thanks... Are you okay? Do you need me to come over?"

I heard a clatter as the phone hit the floor. "Ben? Are you okay?"

I strained my ears and could hear him swearing. His voice came back. "You know...I loved Sherrie. She's a good woman." After a few seconds of static and some mumbling, the line went dead.

A chill ran through me. Maybe I was wrong. Maybe it wasn't Ben's life the killer had been trying to destroy, although he caught some of the backdraft. Maybe it was Cole's. Cole's wife was dead. His company was teetering on the brink of bankruptcy and the only real friend he had had just been fired from his firm. Ben wasn't the only one who knew Cole's business secrets, Edna was part of his inner circle too. She was tall and thin. Why didn't I see it before? She could be the mystery woman who came to the Langcasters' house. Maybe even the shadowy figure who killed Kate.

I had to get a hold of Hayden to warn him. It wasn't a coincidence that an Escalade had tried to run me over. And if Edna had been following me, she would have also seen me talking to Hayden. If she killed Kate, then she might have seen Hayden there that night and knew that he was the one person who could foil her nearly perfect plan.

SEVENTY-ONE

I pushed the Mustang to its limit on the way to the Pine Valley Spa and Golf Club. Had Edna killed Kate out of jealousy? Had her unrequited love for Cole finally turned to hatred? Cole's ex had told me that Cole always went back to Edna when his relationships failed. Was she fed up with being used? As careful as Ben and Kate had been, she could have found out they were having an affair. Was she afraid Cole would again toy with her heart until the next Mrs. Barrett came along? Maybe she didn't care whether it was Ben or Sherrie who would be charged with the murder as long as Kate was out of the picture. Maybe she was done suffering silently.

It was still light when I reached the golf club, but the light was fading fast. I parked and hurried over to the rows of golf carts, all shiny and clean, waiting for the next occupants. A man wearing a Pine Valley Spa and Golf Club shirt and khakis came around the corner.

"Excuse me. I'm looking for Hayden Price. It's urgent. His neighbour told me he was working here tonight."

"Price. Yeah. Saw him about fifteen minutes ago. He was replacing some bulbs in the sport shop." He pointed a thumb over his shoulder in the direction of the clubhouse.

I called out my thanks as I rushed toward the side door of the clubhouse. It was locked. I ran around to the front entrance and pulled open the heavy wood door. There were still a few people sitting in the lounge area. The restaurant was empty.

I booked it across the lobby and turned down the small hall to the pro shop. The door was closed, the lights inside already dimmed. I peered through the glass, but there was no sign of Hayden. I rounded the corner of the pro shop and hurried down the hallway to Chip's office. His door was open, and he was at his desk working on his computer.

I knocked and he looked up, his reading glasses perched near the end of his nose.

"Hi Chip. I'm not sure if you remember me. Jorja Knight. I was here the other day."

"Right." He took off his reading glasses. "I do remember. You wanted to talk to me about Hayden Price."

"Good memory. Something's come up and it's rather urgent that I talk with him. Is he around tonight?"

"Yeah. He was here a few minutes ago. I sent him outside to look at a lady's car. She was having trouble getting it started. Hayden's a pretty handy guy, so I figured if it was something simple, like a loose battery cable, he'd be able to fix it."

"A lady? A club member?"

"I don't think so. She said she had met a friend here for dinner."

My spidey senses were tingling. "I didn't see anyone when I parked back there." I pointed in the direction of the small parking lot next to where they stored the golf carts.

"She's probably parked in the big lot, around to the right of the main entrance. Or even around the corner near the spa entrance."

I thanked Chip and rushed back through the club house and out the main doors. I ran along the side of the building until I reached the main parking lot. There were a dozen vehicles still there. None of them had a hood up or showed any sign that they might be having engine trouble. I wove my way through the parking lot, but there was no sign of Hayden.

I looked back at the club house. The spa parking lot wasn't visible, but I remembered seeing a sign on the west wing of the building the last time I was here. I rushed back to the building. The last of the evening light faded as I ran around the corner. The spa doors were locked.

I gazed across the asphalt. A lone vehicle stood in the far corner of a small lot, similar in size to the one I was parked in on the other side of the building. I stayed in the shadow of the wall and moved toward it. Two people appeared from around the back of the vehicle. I ducked back into the shadows.

The passenger door of the vehicle opened, lighting up the interior and casting a small rectangle of light onto the pavement. A figure stepped forward and climbed awkwardly into the vehicle. It was Hayden. The other figure motioned him to slide over and then climbed in after him. For a second, I thought I saw a gun in their hand. The door closed, but not before I saw that the second person was a woman. A woman with blonde hair.

I ran back around the corner and toward the main entrance. The vehicle would have to come this way to exit. I slid behind one of the massive beams holding up the peaked roof overhanging the front patio just as a set of headlights rounded the corner.

A black Escalade rolled by, its tinted windows preventing me from confirming that the woman in the front seat with Hayden was Edna. I snapped several quick shots of the vehicle plate before the car turned and headed down the small lane out to the main road.

I sprinted to my car, my brain racing. Hayden was being taken somewhere and he wasn't going voluntarily. I said a silent prayer as I turned the key in the ignition and the Mustang coughed once then grumbled as the engine revved. I backed out and headed after the Escalade.

The Escalade had already turned onto the secondary highway by the time I reached the stop sign. My eyes flitted from left to right. Pinpricks of red were visible in both directions. Right went back toward the main highway and town, left to Bragg Creek and further into Kananaskis Country.

I took a left hoping I was making the right move. Hayden's life depended on it.

SEVENTY-TWO

IT WASN'T UNTIL WE reached Bragg Creek that I could confirm I was following the right car. The last four digits of the plate I had snapped matched the digits of the Escalade seen lurking in the Langcasters' neighbourhood. I was ninety percent sure the woman in the passenger seat was Edna. The blonde hair had to be a wig.

Traffic was sparse this time of night, so I held way back. Sometimes the taillights would disappear from view as the Escalade rounded a corner or drove over a rise in the road. I was so far back now that I could use my high beams. Where the hell was she taking him?

The car gave several jerks as I made my way past the Bragg Creek turnoff. I glanced at the gas gauge, noting I had just over a quarter of a tank. I checked my phone. The battery icon showed I had maybe an hour of battery left. Keeping one eye on the road, I scrolled through my contacts and found Ryker's number. On the chance that he was working the night shift, I called. It went to voicemail.

Something moved in front of me, and I swerved as something scuttled across the road. My pulse shot up way past a healthy rate. *Porcupine. Or skunk.* I took a few deep breaths. I was alone and unarmed. I glanced at my phone, held securely to the dash. Mike wouldn't be able to help me out here. Luis was three thousand kilometres away. I called Neil Trent. He answered just as his phone was about to switch to voicemail. He mumbled a hello.

"Neil, it's Jorja. Sorry to call so late. Look, I'm on Highway 66 heading west. I'm following Edna Moss' Escalade. Hayden is driving, but I think Edna has a gun on him. I think she's planning to kill him."

"Say that again." I could hear Neil's voice, clearer, stronger now.

I repeated what I had just said. "I don't have time to explain. I don't know where she's taking him but we're getting further and further out into the forest. I am going to call 911 but I wanted to let you know what was going on in case I get out of cell range."

"Jorja, just pull over. Call the police. Don't put yourself in danger."

"I'm going to send you a photo I took of the car I'm following...you know, in case something happens. The licence plate is readable. Here's the problem. I'm no longer in the city limits, and I just passed Bragg Creek, so I'm sure the RCMP will have to be alerted. I don't know how long this is all going to take or if the gas in my car will last long enough to get to their intended destination. Things might get a bit muddled if different policing units have to coordinate."

"Jesus, Jorja. Turn around. Whatever is going on isn't worth risking your life for."

Of course he'd be the voice of reason. Mike would have told me the same thing. So would Luis, if he were here. But I felt responsible. I was the one who had led her to Hayden.

"I'm staying well back, Neil. I'm going to call 911. I'm hoping I can guide them to where they are heading. Sending the photo now."

I disconnected and sent the photo of the Escalade to Neil's phone. Then I called 911.

I knew the 911 call would be complicated. It took me a full three or four minutes to give my name and contact information and explain the situation in a way that wouldn't make me sound like a crack pot.

"Where are you now, ma'am?"

"Wait a second, please. The Escalade is turning." I slowed and watched as the taillights veered left and disappeared. I slowed even further.

"Ma'am? Are you still there?"

"Yes. The Escalade has turned off on a side road. Looks like, wait...I see a sign. Left onto Range Road 55. I just turned left, off Highway 66, onto Range Road 55."

"Okay, ma'am. I've relayed that information. I'm advising you to pull over and wait for our officers to get to you."

"How long will that be?"

"They're dispatching a unit now."

I slowed but kept going. I felt the Mustang jerk. The earlier thought about the car dying at the most inconvenient time came back to me. *No.* "Come on, car," I muttered. I crested a hill and could see a faint light off to my right. Someone's acreage, perhaps.

"Ma'am, please pull over when it's safe to do so and stay on the line."

"I don't see them anymore. They must be way ahead. Wait. I see a sign. This one says Township Road 220A. I haven't turned off or anything."

"Ma'am. The RC—" Static cut off whatever she said. I glanced at my phone. No bars. Then one bar appeared and disappeared again. More troubling, the battery life on my phone was dwindling fast.

"Sorry, you're breaking up. I didn't catch what you said."

"Have you pulled over, ma'am?"

"I don't see the Escalade anymore. There's a sign up ahead. Just a second. Okay, there's a campground. I'm going to pull in there."

"Please repeat. Did you say you're at a campsite?"

I slowed and turned down a small gravel lane. "Yes. The Fisher Creek Campground."

The screen on my phone went black. I prayed she caught the last part of my message. I glanced at my fuel gauge. I still had an eighth of a tank left—enough to get me back to Bragg Creek.

Tree branches scraped against my Mustang as I manoeuvred around a huge pothole in front of me. I slowed at a wooden sign which depicted where the campsites where located. The map showed that the small lane I was on looped through the campsites and would take me back to the road I had just come off of. With no place to turn around, I kept to the road. A minute later, I reached the large curve, which told me I would now be looping back around to the road.

As I rounded the curve, a figure with a gun stepped out in front of me. I hit the brakes.

"Get out of the car," the figure yelled, pointing the gun at my windshield. "Now."

SEVENTY-THREE

I MADE A SPLIT-SECOND decision, threw the car into reverse, and gunned it. The Mustang leaped back ten feet and died.

A sharp crack sounded, and I ducked. Two more shots hit the windshield, and bits of glass fell on top of me.

"Out of the car. Now."

I sat up slowly, holding my hands up to show that I was unarmed. The woman standing in front of my car gestured with the gun she clasped in both hands. "Get out. Step away from the vehicle."

I opened the door and slid out. The woman was Edna...it had to be. But something about her seemed different. Her hand jerked as she waved her gun at me and repeated her command.

Edna reached back and pulled off the blonde wig, which had half slid over her face. Her mouth was outlined in a garish red colour and her eyes rimmed with dark eyeliner. It wasn't much of a disguise as disguises went, but the change in hair shape and colour had thrown me for a minute.

I could see the Escalade now, parked in one of the camping spots. The headlights were off, but the back of the SUV was open.

"Where's Hayden?"

"Somewhere he won't be causing me any trouble."

My heart pounded. I tried to swallow, but I was breathing too fast. My tongue felt like a wad of cotton. I pushed out the words. "I phoned this location to the police. They're on their way."

"Well then, we'd better hurry." She waved the gun at me and nodded toward the Escalade. I stumbled in that direction. My foot hit a low spot in the road, and I almost fell. A shovel stood upright. Planted in the dirt at the edge of the campsite. She had already been digging. We reached the edge of her excavation efforts. The depression was about three feet long and a few inches deep.

"Start digging."

I picked up the shovel and gasped. A body lay near the front tire of the SUV. I whipped my head around. "You fuckin' killed Hayden. Why?"

"Oh, come on. Really?" Her voice dripped with sarcasm, but she answered me anyway. "I couldn't risk that he could identify me. A face mask only disguises so much, although I'm sure my Russian floating-step dance technique puzzled him for a while. Who knew all those ballet lessons would pay off one day," she snickered. "Start digging. Now. The hole has to be twice as big."

I picked up the shovel, stuck it into the ground and applied my weight to the kickplate. I scooped out a shovel full of pebbly dirt and repeated.

"Why kill Kate? Cole had other wives, since you two were an item. And lots of lovers too."

"Stop yakking and keep digging."

I dug for several minutes. The ground was dry, and full of small rocks and roots. I used the shovel edge to cut through some of the roots. Sweat trickled into my eye. Exhausted, I stopped and wiped at my eyes.

"This is going to take all night. The cops will be here soon."

"Well then you shouldn't be so worried. Keep digging."

"I can't even see what I'm doing."

Edna moved past me and opened the back door of the Escalade. The interior light came on, shedding faint illumination onto the ground near the vehicle.

"Better?" Edna leaned against the open door and thrust the gun toward me. "Now, keep digging."

The hole was now maybe a foot deep and five feet long. The sign at the campground entry said the campground was closed due to the dry spring conditions we had been having and the high risk of fire. If the 911 operator hadn't heard my mention of the campsite before we got cut off, it could be months before anyone came out here.

I tried again. "If you're going to kill me, at least tell me why you did it. Did you really think you'd get another chance with Cole with Kate out of the way?"

"What?" Edna leaned forward, then threw her head back, laughing. "You think I killed that little bitch for love?"

"I don't get it." I groaned as I lifted another shovel of dirt. The repetitive motion had reignited the pain in my hand and shoulder. *Where are the damn cops?*

"I despise Cole," she spit out through clenched teeth. "All those years of kowtowing to him, bringing him coffee, picking up his drycleaning. I was the brains behind Encore. I was the one who helped him get Capital Equity. I paid off two VPs in the Arcadia acquisition to get them to approve the deal. And how did he reward me? He divorced his first wife and married some dried-up shrew just because she had some money. Her money did help us buy Citysafe. He promised me that as soon as we took the company public, he'd divorce her and be with me. That didn't happen either. Then little miss Kate came along."

"So you killed Kate to get back at Cole. Why wait seven years?"

"Cole wanted me to think that Kate was just another cash cow for him. She was richer than wifey number two. Then he started keeping me at arm's length. The company was growing. I could see he was trying to push me out. But he underestimated me." She snickered bitterly. "He's finally getting what was coming to him. I should have taken the bastard down years ago."

"I'm still confused. You killed Kate to get back at Cole? Won't he just get himself another rich wife?"

"Kate was only part of the plan. A bonus really. Imagine my delight when I discovered she was sleeping with Ben, Cole's best buddy. I got two birds with one stone. But the coupe de grâce? I made sure he'd lose the Avenue 21 deal. That's the blow that really kicked him in the balls. Number one, my ass. I turned in my resignation yesterday. Let's see how he gets himself out of this mess."

I grunted as I lifted another shovelful of dirt. A movement caught my eye. Keeping my head down, I looked up from beneath lowered lashes and stifled a gasp. *Hayden's alive.* My heart leapt. I had to keep Edna talking.

"You scuttled the Avenue 21 deal? That must have taken a bit of finagling."

"That idiot thought that whenever I walked into a room to bring him coffee that's all I was doing. I have so much dirt on him and his crooked deals. He thought I'd be happy with the little crumbs he was throwing my way. A Christmas bonus, a VP title, a company car to drive or a ride along on some company trip. He didn't realize I controlled him. I was just waiting for the right moment to take the fucker down. And the bid for Avenue 21 and a chance to leap to top mid-sized equity firm in North America was that moment."

Hayden was standing now, half hidden by the opened back door Edna was leaning on.

The hole was a foot and a half or so deep now. Soon it would be deep enough. I emptied another shovelful and swiped my arm across my forehead to try and stanch the steady drip of sweat that rolled down my face. The nerve endings in my injured shoulder were on fire. I took a deep breath to steady myself. Then another. Hayden was still standing but not moving. *How badly is he hurt?* I resumed digging.

Her voice was louder now, full of bluster. "The look on his face when Avenue 21 announced that they had accepted an offer from Jackson Equities was priceless. I'll never forget it. Best day of my life."

"You fed confidential bid data to his competitor. Didn't Cole figure it out?"

"He actually blamed Ben and fired him. He still didn't know when I handed in my resignation yesterday. He tried to cajole me into staying. He almost had a heart attack when I told him what I did."

I swallowed hard, my mouth suddenly devoid of saliva. "Did you...kill Cole...after you told him?"

"No need. I've sent some data to the auditors and the Alberta Se-curity Exchange Commission." She nodded toward the hole. "That looks deep enough."

Hayden came into full view, stepping to the side of the door where Edna stood. I scrambled out of the hole, groaning and making as much noise as I could to cover any sound that might be coming from his direction.

"Aren't you afraid he'll go to the police?" I panted, leaning on the shovel.

"He can't prove anything, and I've got a whole dossier on him. Tons of emails and other evidence. Threats and bribes and fraud. Proof of insider trading."

A branch cracked. Edna's eyes darted to one side. Her mouth opened as she jerked back. Before she could bring her gun up, Hayden swung the branch he was holding across her face. I sprang forward and hit her with the shovel. Edna fell to her knees, and I swung at her with every drop of strength I had left.

SEVENTY-FOUR

THE POLICE ARRIVED SHORTLY after we put Edna down. Ambulances were called. Hayden left in the first one, Edna in the second. Hayden collapsed again after we managed to subdue Edna. She had shot him twice, the first bullet grazing his side, the second hitting him in the stomach. He had the wherewithal to hit the ground and remain still after being shot, apparently leading Edna to assume he was dead. Edna remained unconscious until the police arrived. I was relieved to learn that I hadn't killed her.

Since the first officers to arrive were from the RCMP Cochrane Division, that's where I was taken first. On the way into town, I thought about how much I should reveal and how it might affect Neil's defence strategy. I decided that telling them everything I knew would probably be the right way to go, since I figured that the murder charge against Sherrie Langcaster had just been torpedoed. I called Neil from the RCMP office before giving my statement just to make sure. He advised me to stick with the facts because in the end, that's all that mattered.

A nice RCMP officer drove me home after I finished giving my statement, which had taken over five hours. I told the police that

Edna admitted to killing Kate Barrett, because she wanted to hurt Cole, as she felt wronged by him. But I didn't reveal her ramblings about espionage or bragging about a file that the security exchange commission might be very interested in since I had nothing to back it up, and Edna could deny everything. If the information didn't come out in the next few weeks, an anonymous call might have to be made.

Other than her confession, I didn't have any concrete evidence that Edna killed Kate, but I was hoping Hayden heard her admission and could back me up on it. I did tell the RCMP about the dash cam video I had found showing an Escalade, leased to Encore, parked outside the Langcaster house around the time Sherrie's gun went missing. I wouldn't be surprised if Edna was the one who entered the Langcaster's house using a former Green Energy rep's ID card to gain access. Maybe she thought she was taking Ben's gun and hadn't known the gun belonged to Sherrie. The RCMP were also aware that an Escalade had tried running me down. Witnesses were able to provide police with a partial plate and said a blonde-haired woman had been behind the wheel. I was certain that I would be called back by the police to answer more questions once the RCMP had a chance to confer with Detective Ryker.

If Hayden survived, he'd be able to back up my story that Edna had confessed to Kate Barrett's murder. He also had his own testimony as to what he witnessed the night Kate was murdered. Based on his description of the killer, it seemed unlikely that it was Sherrie. Edna said discovering Ben's affair with Kate, had been a bonus, that it allowed her to get two birds with one stone. But I still didn't know how she could have known Kate was going to be down by the river the night she was killed.

Edna had put in a lot of time over many months, plotting Cole's demise. If the police couldn't definitely prove that she was the one who killed Kate Barrett, she'd still be facing a prison sentence. She shot Hayden, intending to kill him, and had also been planning to kill me. There was plenty of evidence to support those charges.

After I got home, I showered and changed. As much as I just wanted to collapse on the bed and sleep for several hours, I still had to deal with my out of commission vehicle. Today was also the deadline Willie Carlton Smith had given me on his job offer. As crazy as it sounded, I still didn't know what I was going to do.

Once my phone was partially recharged, I called Neil and arranged a time to meet with him. Then I left Luis a text message, apologizing for missing our evening call last night. I told him I had been out on a surveillance job that took me out of the city, and then my phone and the car had died, in that order, but that I was back now and would explain more tonight.

I called for an Uber, and my mind continued to whirl as we drove to Neil's office. A message arrived on my phone from Cole Barrett. Seems two expensive handbags and three pieces of jewellery from the insured items in Kate's collection were gone. I nodded to myself. Perhaps the police would be able to figure out where they had gone. There had to be a trail.

A few more pieces slid into the puzzle now that I knew what Edna had done. No wonder this case had me running in circles. There had been two crimes being committed on the night Kate was killed. Hayden picking up money Rupert was extracting from his sister under threat, and Edna Moss executing her revenge against Cole Barrett.

By the time I got dropped off at Neil's place I had a text message back from Luis. "Ditch the Mustang, babe." I smiled. The Mustang had a good run. It might even live on through other Mustangs by giving up its parts to refurbish one of its own kind. I guess I'd have to go back to leasing cars from JumpIn Jalopies. I put my phone away and made my way up Neil's sidewalk.

Neil opened the door and stepped aside. "Come on in, Jorja. How are you feeling?"

"I'm fine. Tired. I think I'll sleep well tonight though. Didn't catch any winks last night."

Neil led me into his office. "Just made fresh coffee, if you'd like."

"That would be great."

Neil spoke over his shoulder as he poured two mugs. "I got a call from Maria Rios this morning. Hayden told them that he wasn't going to talk to anyone without his lawyer present."

"Do you know how he's doing?"

"When Maria called, they were wheeling him into surgery. She said he was stable and although the surgery could be a bit messy, they figure he'll come out of it fine."

Then I sat down with my coffee and told Neil everything that had happened since we last met with Hayden and Maria in my new trial digs at Bankers Hall, and Edna's attempt to murder Hayden and me last night.

SEVENTY-FIVE

I HAD BEEN IN countless meetings over the last two weeks, but things were finally settling down. Today I was meeting Neil after work for a celebratory drink at The Pub Stop. I parked my lime green Ford Fiesta on the side street and made my way around to the front door. The car was on a three-month lease from JumpIn Jalopies. So far, all that I could find wrong with it was a finicky temperature control fan and the glove box didn't open. Last year I would have rejected the car because of its bright neon green colour, believing that private investigators should drive something pedestrian, something that didn't stand out or attract attention. Now I was operating on the belief that no one would expect the dark-haired, fortyish woman in the bright green hatchback to be a private eye.

Neil already had a table inside. I slid in across from him. After ordering drinks we spent a few minutes chatting about the summer heat, made worse by smoke-filled air from the hundreds of wildfires burning across the western provinces. The conversation inevitably turned to the Sherrie Langcaster case. The charges against her had been dropped at the preliminary hearing once information about Edna Moss had been made known. Edna was now the one sitting in prison and facing a murder charge for Kate Barrett, two attempted murder charges with respect to Hayden and me, and a half dozen lessor charges related to her attempts to cover up her involvement in Kate's murder.

I took a sip of my pinot grigio and set the glass back down. "Do you think the charges against Edna are going to stick?"

Neil tilted his head. "No doubt. With Hayden's and your testimony, and everything that they found in her apartment it will be hard for her lawyer to refute her not guilty plea."

"I heard they found the floor length cloak she was wearing the night she shot Kate Barrett."

"Better still, there were traces of Kate's blood on it. Hayden says he saw her bend down over Kate's body before gliding off. The hem must have dragged through Kate's blood, unnoticed by her."

"Why did she stoop down by the body? Do you think she was checking to make sure Kate was dead?"

Neil pursed his lips. "Maybe she wiped up some of Barrett's blood with Ben Langcaster's T-shirt."

"Ah, the one Sherrie swears she saw in Ben's sports bag. Makes sense if she was trying to frame him. Has she said anything about that?"

"Not to my knowledge. Then again, the sports bag never made it into evidence, so no one has questioned her about that. You can bet this dance cloak of hers will make it into the evidence locker though."

"She mentioned a Russian floating-step technique to me when I asked her why she killed Kate. I looked it up. It's a special Russian dance form used by trained ballet dancers and choreographed to make them appear as if they are floating or gliding. Apparently, Edna's grandmother learned the technique as a young woman when she danced with a Russian ballet troupe. She must have taught Edna the technique."

"Amazing. Edna went to a lot of trouble to frame Ben Langcaster for Kate's murder. With the dance technique, the long robe and a mask hiding her face, it's no wonder the two witnesses there that night thought they had seen something from another world." Neil took a sip of his wine and sighed in appreciation.

"She told me she wanted to hurt Cole in everyway possible. When she discovered Kate was cheating on him with his best friend, she called it a bonus. She could hurt him emotionally as well as crater his financers and ruin his business reputation."

Neil raised his glass. "Congreve said it the best in his play, The Mourning Bride. 'Heaven has no rage like love to hatred turned, nor hell a fury like woman scorned.'" He took another sip and set his glass down.

"I'll say. But how did Edna get Elaine Gray's Green Energy ID card to gain access to the Langcasters' house? That one had me tearing my hair out."

Neil slid back in his chair and stretched his legs out under our small table. "Too bad she didn't destroy the card, and her gray contact lenses. Police found both in her house. Turns out she was the one at Encore who organized access cards and workspace for summer students or temporary contractors. Elaine Gray's boyfriend did a summer internship at Encore last year. He and Elaine were in the midst of a move and Elaine's former Green Energy card got into his briefcase by accident. When he discovered it, he ended up just sticking it in his desk. Elaine didn't need it, as she was no longer working for Green Energy. Then when he finished his assignment at Encore, he left the card there or simply forgot to take it."

"Wow. Do you think Edna had plans for that card, all the way back to last year?"

"Maybe not. But it turned out to be useful to her, when she wanted access to Ben Langcaster's house and obtain the gun. It will definitely prove Kate Barrett's murder was premeditated."

"Yeah, about that. How did she know that there was a gun in the house?"

"She overheard Ben talking about it with some of the other lawyers on the floor. Just a general discussion I guess on guns and whether they should be controlled more, and someone in the group asked if anyone of them had a gun in their house."

"I shook my head. "Unbelievable. Although Ben did tell me that he didn't trust Edna and he felt like she was spying on him and the others in the office and reporting anything of interest to Cole."

"Well looks like she kept some things to herself."

I emptied the last bit of wine in my glass but waved the server off as he approached to see if I wanted another. "When you told me that the Police discovered that Edna had been using a luggage tracker to keep tabs on Kate Barrett's movements I just about fell over. My friend Mike Saunders is right. For every case where technology has been developed with good in mind, someone manages to find a malicious use for it."

Neil had called me last week to tell me that the Police had figured out how Edna knew that Kate Barrett would be by the Bow River the night she was killed. Edna discovered that Kate and Ben were seeing each other when she saw them embracing in the office underground parking lot. That's when she started to listen in to calls Kate made to Cole through the office line. But it wasn't enough. She purchased a set of luggage trackers and slid one under the seat in Kate's car when she came by the office one day to speak to Cole. After that it was easy. The tracking app on her phone could track the location of Kate's car and she could follow her to wherever she and Ben were meeting.

Somewhere along the way Edna started looking for a way to kill Kate and frame Ben for her murder. She entered the Langcasters' house using the Green Energy ID card and took the gun she found in one of the nightstands in Ben and Sherrie's bedroom. Then she just had to wait until she knew when they were to meetup next.

Edna must have overheard a conversation between Ben and Kate about their intended meeting on May ninth and decided it would be the night she would kill Kate, but she didn't realize there had been a change of plans. When she saw the tracker she had planted in Kate's car start to move, she figured their rendezvous was still on. She followed Kate downtown and watched from the shadows as Kate made her way on foot toward the River. She may have thought Hayden was Ben when she saw him standing off in the shadows. She shot Kate and then did her disappearing act, not realizing that she had inadvertently inserted herself into Rupert's plan to obtain money from his sister by telling her the whole family was under threat from his loan shark. Once the police arrested Edna and took her phone, iPad and computer they found the tracking app and were able to link it to a luggage tracking device they found in Kate's car.

Neil sat up and shook his head. "Makes one wonder how anyone can stay safe these days. I mean what kind of person figures out that they can use a key or luggage tracking device to stalk and track a person. And then kill them." He shook his head again. "Maybe I'm getting too old for all of this."

"It's going to be a challenge to stay up to speed on all the technology out there. Too bad there wasn't a tracker in the handbag Kate had with her that night."

"Far as I know, Hayden is still claiming that the last time he saw it was on the bench next to where Kate Barrett's body was found."

I thought for a minute. "You know, I kind of believe Hayden. But there's a lot he's not saying. Too bad his buddy Josh Neeley OD'ed. I think Josh was there that night. Maybe Hayden brought him along as backup in case anything went wrong."

"Which it did," Neil added.

"Yeah. But I'm betting he saw what happened and after everyone took off, ran over and grabbed the handbag."

"Too bad the police weren't able to find any of Neeley's belongings to check if the footprints they found at the scene were his."

"That's a shame but since the guy was living out of a backpack and sleeping wherever he could find a couch, I'm not surprised. You know, his friend River said he threw a big party a few days after Kate was murdered. Drugs were spreading through the crowd like it was Christmas morning. But everyone we talked to said Neeley was broke, he was homeless, he was couch surfing. Then suddenly he's handing out pills like they're penny candy."

Neil nodded. "You think he kept the money Kate was carrying in her handbag that night."

"Well, someone ended up with the money. He may not have taken all the money, but maybe he got a cut. Where the rest went is anyone's guess. Maybe Josh or Hayden squirreled it away somewhere. Didn't sound like it made it's way into Rupert's loan shark's hands. River's lifestyle hasn't changed, although if she has it, she'd be smart to wait a year or two before using any of it. There's no way Edna ended up with it as she thought Kate was there that night to meet Ben, not to deliver a bag of money to a loan shark."

I didn't think Rupert knew where the money was either. But he had bigger things to worry about. I heard he had another heart attack while in hospital waiting for bypass surgery. Maybe facing death would offer him an opportunity to reevaluate how he wanted to spend the rest of his life. Then again, maybe Jimmie the Knife would take the matter out of his hands. Which brought me back to my own dilemma. Was I simply going to let CanNet's job offer expire or was it time to step up and steer my life in the direction that had the best chance of leaving me with no regrets?

SEVENTY-SIX

I threw my makeup kit into my carry-on bag, zipped it shut, and took one last look around the room. My newly purchased fiddle leaf fig was watered and standing in its preferred spot—near enough to the patio window to get plenty of light, but out of reach of direct sunlight. The girl at the garden centre said it was critical that I let it settle into its new home. Fiddles apparently love consistency and moving homes is a big change, so I needed to be careful not to introduce more change than necessary. It was a plant I could relate to. After giving it more hours than I cared to admit, I finally named it Miss Figgy.

"Sorry Miss Figgy, but I gotta go. Okay, not sorry, but still, I gotta go." I slung my purse over my shoulder, picked up my carry-on bag and locked up after myself. I was only going to be away for four nights. A wave of excitement tinged with trepidation rolled through me. Four nights with Luis. This is how drug users must feel before they take their first bump of the night.

It had been a whole month since I last saw Luis—in person that is. His new assignment in Quantico, Virginia was turning out to be much more intensive than either of us expected. We facetimed a few times a week but lately when the calls ended. I was left with a sick hollow ache inside. I told myself it was normal. I had never been in love before...not like this. Sure, I had been infatuated with other men, even told myself that I was starting to fall in love, but I really didn't understand what love felt like, or what it felt like to be away from someone I loved, until now. And now I was sick with worry that I was going to lose it all.

Mike was waiting for me outside my condo building, parked in the drop off zone. He jumped out of his truck and ran around to the passenger side, opened the door for me, and threw my carry-on onto the jump seat in back.

"Is that all you're taking?" He nodded at my small carry-on.

"It's only for four nights." I felt myself blushing. I was counting on spending most of those nights in Luis' hotel room, not out on the town. "Thanks for giving me a ride to the airport. I could have taken an Uber."

"It'll give us a chance to get caught up. Besides, if Mrs. Niedswiki doesn't spot me leaving the house, she'll be bringing me yet another casserole. I don't have the heart to tell her that I'm not particularly fond of casseroles."

I laughed as I climbed into the passenger seat. Mrs. Niedswiki was Mike's Polish neighbour, and self-appointed babushka. Mike told me she and her late husband never had children, and after her husband passed, Mrs. Niedswiki poured all of her pent-up grand-motherly care and attention onto Mike, bringing him soup, jams and preserves she made herself, and her speciality...casserole. Her austere upbringing made her a whiz at combining leftovers, not always in ways that Mike found appetizing. She had also taken a distinct dislike to me. Even though Mike's and my relationship was strictly platonic I always felt she was evaluating me as future wife and baby mama potential. Clearly, I wasn't making the cut.

"How's the new job working out?" I glanced over at Mike. The new job at CanNet must be going well. Mike always exuded a calm confidence, but these days he seemed happier, more invigorated than I'd seen him in a while.

"Best decision I've made in a long time. I'm having the time of my life. You're going to love it, Jojo."

"Am I? I realize I'm not exactly the poster girl for positivity, but you sound a lot more confident than I feel."

"I am confident, because I know you. You love a challenge and are willing to take risks...smart risks. Remember your old job as forensic lab analyst? Didn't the everyday repetitive tasks wear you down?"

I thought about it for all of five seconds. "They did, but that's why I like what I'm doing now." I detested the whiny sound I heard in my own voice.

"Well, you'll keep doing what you're doing, just in a bigger way. Think about the new cases working for CanNet will present. What creative and intellectual avenues it could open up. Hell, I'm excited for you."

"Yeah, you're right. I don't know why I am still worried about it. I gave Willie my answer. It's already done."

It had taken me longer to accept CanNet's job offer than William Carlton Smith, my new boss, wanted. After Edna had been arrested for Kate Barrett's murder, I had called William asking for more time. I made it sound like Neil Trent still had me chasing down information on Kate Barrett's murder and I threw in the bit about me still recovering physically from Edna's failed attempt to kill me. He had been super kind and told me to get back to him when I felt ready. It had taken me three more weeks. I finally accepted the job offer, telling myself that if it didn't work, I could always resign and re-hang my shingle as sole proprietor of Knight Investigations.

Truthfully, it hadn't taken me very much time to wrap up my work on the Kate Barrett case. I had visited Hayden in the hospital to reassure myself that he was going to be alright. Then I went to see Al Walker, the detective who had investigated Kate Barrett's childhood kidnapping. I told Al that Kate Barrett's insurance files showed that several handbags and pieces of jewellery were discovered missing after her death. The police had managed to locate an exclusive second-hand boutique for top-tier fashion items and confirmed that Kate had sold the items through their boutique. It was impossible to say if the money from the sale of these items was in the Hermes bag Kate Barrett had with her the night she was killed, but the money hadn't been deposited in any of her known bank accounts.

I shared my suspicion that Rupert had threatened to expose Hayden as one of Kate's childhood kidnappers if he didn't help him lean on his sister for money now. That, and that I had found a small child's necklace, with Kate Barrett's birthstone nestled between the wings of the small angel pendant, hidden away in Rupert Gallagher's bedroom. Al had told me that when Kate was found after her kidnapper's released her, she was missing the angel pendant her mother said she always wore. Even if newer trace DNA forensic analysis could prove the necklace belonged to Kate, it wouldn't prove Rupert's connection to the kidnapping, if indeed one existed, as the necklace would be considered circumstantial evidence. I'm sure Rupert would find some semi-plausible explanation as to how he came to have it in his possession. The only way the truth would come out was if Hayden admitted his and Rupert's involvement in Kate Barrett's kidnapping all those years ago, in his current witness statement. But there was no need for him to do so and I assumed his lawyer would have advised against it, unless some crisis of conscience led him to do so.

Mike's voice brought me back to the present. I had been listening with half an ear as he described some of the data mining tools that CanNet was bringing in to help with investigations, but I had zoned out once his description veered into clustering and regression analysis. I liked the idea of what such tools could provide in an investigation but wasn't at all keen on learning how to use them.

"Here we are, gorgeous. How's that for door-to-door service? And under thirty minutes no less."

"You're the best Mike." I climbed out of the truck while Mike retrieved my carry-on. I gave him a huge hug before taking my carry-on from his hand. "I mean it Mike. I don't know what I'd do without you."

"Aw shucks. You're making me blush." Mike mimed, ducking his head.

My friend Gab had always hoped Mike and I would evolve our friendship into something more, but it hadn't happened. Mike was a standup guy and the kind of friend most would give a body part for. He knew me—everything from how I liked my eggs in the morning to my thoughts, feeling and beliefs on a dizzying array of topics, from free will to second chances, corporal punishment and organized religion. I shared my thoughts and feelings with Mike without fear of being judged. He was someone I could count on, no matter what, and he knew that I would always have his back.

The only other person in my life who truly accepted me for who I was, flaws and all, was Gab. I loved Gab, and I didn't mind admitting that I loved Mike, just not in that heart pounding, blood rushing, stomach fluttering way that I felt around Luis. There had been times, when I worried that Mike's feelings for me were dipping into that dangerous 'in love' phase. I say dangerous, only because I couldn't love him back in that way.

I gave Mike a final hug and with the handle extended on my carry-on, walked through the terminal doors. Maybe I was being foolish. I knew my obsession with Luis would likely be short-lived. The obsession would either eventually fizzle and we'd part ways or turn into a different kind of relationship. Not that a long-term relationship can't be romantic and sexy, but it needed to be built on more than adventure, fascination with someone new, and sex, sex and more sex. All the relationship experts out there, at least the ones Google brought up, advised that I could expect our infatuated lovers phase to last three years, max. If it didn't evolve beyond our current fiery, hot desire and lust stage, it was doomed. Even discounting the breaks in our relationship, we were well into year two.

Maybe that was what was driving my trepidation. Being away from Luis had raised questions in my mind. The serotonin and dopamine my brain produced in the early stages of our relationship were no longer doing the heavy lifting they once did. I was longing for something more. I wasn't looking for marriage, although if it became an option I'd give it due consideration. What I was looking for was a sense of calmness and comfort that came from trusting, caring for, and relying on someone other than myself. A comfort formed through a physical and emotional union with another human being. A space where I could take a breather from the ugliness that existed out there. I was longing for something that felt like home.

Pulling the carry-on behind me, I headed for my gate. I was coming to the realization that I wanted to be with Luis for the long haul, but had no idea if lust was the only thing keeping Luis interested in me. Maybe I was feeling this way because almost everything in my life, except for Mike, had been up ended in the last few weeks. I had created my life by slowly, carefully and precisely evaluating and choosing each and every move in response to what the universe sent me. Was I making the right choice this time?

I squared my shoulders and took a deep breath. I didn't know how things would turn out but whatever the future held...I was ready.

•••••••••••

YOUR FREE BOOK IS WAITING!

Want to find out what drove Jorja Knight to leave her career as a forensic lab analyst and become a private investigator? Find out in *Knight Shift,* the prequel to the Jorja Knight mystery series. This exclusive book offer is only available here.

CLICK HERE and claim your free copy of *Knight Shift* now! Or type https://bookhip.com/PMSDZ into your browser.

She wants to prove her worth as a new PI...but first she has to survive!

. . . . ● . ● . . . .

Thank you for reading *Knight On Edge*. I hope you enjoyed it! Reviews help other readers to discover new books and decide if the story is right for them. If you want to share your love for Jorja Knight, please leave a review on your favourite book retailer's site. Readers will appreciate it— and I will too!

ALSO BY ALICE BIENIA

Knight Blind
Knight Trials
Three Dog Knight
Knight Vision
Knight In The Museum
Knight In Peril
Knight Shift (prequel)
Anthologies
Last Shot
Crime Wave
The Dame Was Trouble
For an up-to-date list visit www.alicebienia.com .

ACKNOWLEDGEMENTS

I can hardly believe that *Knight On Edge* is the seventh novel in my Jorja Knight mystery series. This milestone wouldn't have been possible without the support of some very special people.

First, I'd like to send out a huge thank you to you, my readers—thank you! I'm forever grateful for your encouragement and support! Some of you have been with me since the beginning, watching Jorja grow from her early forays into private investigation to the skilled professional she is today. Your enthusiasm fuels my creativity and keeps me motivated to bring Jorja's story to life. With each book, I've aimed to craft more complex cases, pushing Jorja to her limits and beyond. I hope you enjoy reading *Knight On Edge* as much as I loved writing it.

Alongside your support, there are a few key people who have been instrumental in this journey. I would like to thank my brilliant editor, Taija Morgan, for her insights, encouragement, and dedication. I'm thankful to have you in my corner! A huge shout-out to my ARC team for their invaluable feedback and help in getting the word out there. Your voice really does make a difference. And to my amazing family and friends, thank you for cheering me on and for your unwavering support. You mean the world to me!

I'd be remiss if I didn't send out thanks to the writing community, including all the bloggers, reviewers, podcasters, and my fellow crime authors. You are instrumental in helping readers find my books, and in providing me with that all-important sense of belonging, which makes the solitary life of an author like me so much more enjoyable.

The title, *Knight On Edge*, reflects the uncertainty Jorja faces, both professionally and personally, as she navigates yet another pivotal change in her life. This sense of being on edge paralleled the global unease of 2024, a year marked by significant challenges. Writing *Knight On Edge* provided me both an escape and a way to process what was happening in the world, and although my books are fiction, I couldn't help but notice how the weight of these world events influenced the themes in the book.

If you're new to Jorja's world, I invite you to explore the earlier books in the series. While they can be read as standalones, following Jorja's entire journey offers a richer experience. Please consider leaving a review of my book at your favorite bookstore or sharing your thoughts on social media. I love hearing from you.

I'm thrilled about what's next for Jorja but brace yourself—Jorja's next steps will push her even further out of her comfort zone. I'm also venturing into new territory with a psychological thriller. It's an exciting challenge, and I look forward to sharing this new creative journey with you. For updates on these projects, please consider joining my reader list. As a thank you, I'll send you a free copy of

Knight Shift, the prequel that reveals how it all began. You can **join here** or through my website: www.alicebienia.com.

Thank you for being part of Jorja's journey and mine. Your support makes every word worthwhile. Until next time, stay well and keep on reading!

ABOUT THE AUTHOR

ALICE BIENIA IS THE best-selling author of the Jorja Knight mystery series. A three-time Crime Writers of Canada Awards of Excellence Finalist and 2022 Indie Author Project regional winner, her page-turning mysteries combine tight plots, realistic characters and surprising twists to create edge-of-your-seat whodunits.

Taking an unconventional route to becoming an author, Alice earned a Bachelor of Science degree in Geology and spent her early career conducting field exploration programs in remote regions of Canada, where she honed her passion for reading, storytelling, coffee, and adventure.

After riding the energy industry rollercoaster for thirty years, Alice has found a way to put her inherent introversion to use and now writes full time. When not plotting a murder, Alice amuses herself watching foreign flicks, reading, and exploring Calgary's urban parks and pathways.

· · · • · ● · • · ·

JOIN ALICE'S READER LIST at www.alicebienia.com and be the first to hear about her new books, contests, and exciting giveaways, and receive a free copy of *Knight Shift*, the prequel novella to the Jorja Knight Mystery series.